State of Grace

Justine O'Keefe

ONION RIVER PRESS

Burlington Vermont

Onion River Press
191 Bank Street
Burlington, VT 05401

ISBN: 978-1-949066-42-5 paperback; 978-1-949066-55-5 eBook

Library of Congress Control Number: 2020912784

DEDICATION

To my father

PART 1

1919-1920

1

THE SICKROOM

The door was ajar. Through the narrow opening, Grace stared at the still form under the thin sheet, then stepped into her mother's room. Curtained against the bright July afternoon, the room was dim, the air warm and slightly stale. Grace wrinkled her nose. The cloying odors of the tinctures and potions cluttering the bedside table made her queasy. She stood, barely breathing, watching for the rise and fall of her mother's breast.

Ill as she was, Mama was still lovely. Her dark hair tumbled across the pillow and the smooth skin of her face was pale as milk. On the counterpane, one hand lay open, her fingers curling upward like the petals of a flower. Grace ached to touch that hand, to trace the creases crossing the palm, to feel the cool fingers interlaced with hers. But she wasn't even supposed to be in here. Dr. Halvorson had told her to stay away, to not bother her mother, as if Grace was a pesky toddler who didn't know how to behave.

Mama shifted on the bed. Turning toward Grace, she blinked, her eyes dark pools in her pallid face.

"Gracie," she said, her voice low.

"Yes, Mama. I didn't mean to wake you. Doctor Halvorson said to stay away, to let you rest, but the door was open and I ..."

Her mother smiled and patted the bed beside her. "Never mind what that old ogre tells you, sweetheart. You can come and see me anytime you want." She reached a hand toward Grace. "Come sit down and tell me what you've been up to."

Grace eased herself onto the bed, careful not to cause her mother added discomfort. Mama stroked her cheek with the back of her hand and pushed the stray hair off her forehead. Her touch, smooth and dry as paper, made Grace's chest tighten.

"So, what have you been doing with yourself this afternoon?" Mama tilted her head on the pillow and the corners of her mouth turned up in a small smile.

"Oh, not much. Reading, mostly, up in the tree house. It's cool up there."

"I thought you'd abandoned that tree house long ago. You must be getting a little tall for it now." Mama arched an eyebrow and looked critically at Grace's too-tight cotton dress. "Didn't we buy that dress for you last summer, sweetie? It's two sizes too small already." She ran her hand under the elastic of the puffed sleeve and frowned. "Way too tight. I'll ask Mrs. Blanchard to take you shopping for a few things."

Grace didn't want to go shopping with Mrs. B. That was Mama's job, something they'd always done together. Browsing the dress shops on Main Street, with lunch at the hotel or cafe. Mama was good at finding things Grace liked, simple frocks with polka dots or tiny flowers, and she never insisted on plaid.

Grace smoothed the front of her dress. "Don't you think I'm old enough to shop on my own, Mama? I know all the shopkeepers and I know what I like," she grinned, "and I know what I don't like, too. If Mrs. B had her way, I'd be outfitted in plaid everyday of the week ... even to my hair ribbons." She gave a mock shudder. Mama chuckled softly and clutched Grace's hand.

Feeling her mother's grip loosen, Grace raised the slack hand to her lips. She should go and let Mama sleep, but several minutes passed before she could bring herself to leave the comfort of her mother's side. Finally, slipping off the bed, she made her way to the door.

Leaving it slightly ajar, Grace walked down the carpeted hallway to the broad staircase with its carved newel posts and wide banister. From the landing, she could see the open front door. Through the screen, the green of the wide lawn was lit by the afternoon sun, the street hidden behind the darker green of the privet hedge. Anxious to escape the gloom of the sickroom, Grace ran lightly down the stairs and pushed open the screen door, catching it before it slammed behind her. Leaping, she cleared the porch steps and ran around the house to the back garden.

The tree house, nestled in the branches of an old sugar maple, had been built by Grandpa Seymour when Mama was a girl. Then Daddy had put in a new floor and fixed the roof and replaced some rungs on the old ladder and it had become Grace's place. Her thinking, reading, drawing, dreaming place. She hadn't used it much the last two summers, but this year she'd found herself drawn back to its leafy seclusion.

Grace climbed the ladder, crouched through the opening, and crossed the planked floor. Mama was right. She was a bit tall for the house now, but there was still plenty of room to stretch out on her pile of old cushions and blankets against the far wall. Clasping her hands behind her head, she watched the sky through the window opening. The air was heavy with moisture and great clouds, like dark dollops of whipped cream, massed overhead. Some July afternoons these clouds brought rain, quick downpours that cleared the air. Other times, the wind came up, turning the leaves inside out, whistling through the pines, pushing the clouds before it and leaving blue sky in its wake.

Today, though, the brooding pile sat sullenly in place. The still air, thick and suffocating, bore down with the weight of water. Grace could hardly breathe. No one had told her what was wrong with Mama, not her father or Mrs. Blanchard or even Grandma. Sometimes she listened at the closed door of her father's study, listened to the rumble of Doctor Halvorson's deep voice, but could make no sense of the few words she could make out. Once she'd heard Mrs. Murphy, their charlady, tell Mrs. Blanchard that "cousin Betty had suffered from the same kind of woman troubles as plagued the missus," but Grace wasn't sure what that meant.

Mama had seen specialists, had even gone into the hospital for several days of treatments. But when Grace had asked her father about it, he said they'd just have to wait and see. She'd wanted ask if they were waiting to see if Mama was going to die, but the look on Daddy's face had kept her quiet. Besides, if she knew her mother was going to die, surely he did, too.

She had no idea how long she lay thinking on her dusty pallet, but long enough to be startled by the sound of her father's voice calling her from the back door.

"Gracie," he called again. "Are you up there? Grace?"

Sitting up, she scrambled on all fours across to the ladder and poked her head out of the doorway. "I'll be right there, Daddy. I must have dozed off. I'm coming right down."

As Grace entered the kitchen, Mrs. Blanchard turned from the stove pushing a strand of damp hair off her forehead. The room was hot and poor Mrs. B looked as wilted as an old lettuce leaf. Her face was shiny with sweat and her lace collar, usually starched to crispness, drooped around her thin neck.

Grace crossed to the sink to wash her hands. "Can I help with anything, Mrs. Blanchard?"

"No, thank you, Grace. Your father's waiting for you in the parlor. I'm about to drain the potatoes and then we'll be all set."

Daddy was at the sideboard when Grace came through from the dining room. He'd removed his jacket and loosened his tie and looked only a little less done-in than the housekeeper. His face was flushed, but whether from the heat or the contents of his empty glass, Grace didn't know. She crossed the room, planted a kiss on his cheek, and perched on the wide arm of the sofa. As her father refilled his glass, Mrs. B came in to say dinner was ready.

Weeks before, the leaf had been removed from the dining room table, transforming it from a rectangle into a square. Grace thought the table looked too small for the room now, but she also knew better than to ask her father about the change. He'd say something silly or put her off by turning her attention elsewhere. This evening, as usual, he made a great show of pulling out her chair and, once dinner was underway, filling up the silence with funny stories about the customers who'd come into his shop for straw boaters or new collars or ladies looking to outfit their squirmy little boys for special occasions.

While they ate, her father filled and refilled his wine glass. As the level of wine in the decanter dropped, the color rose in his cheeks and his voice got louder. Grace watched him warily. Would the funny stories see them through dinner or would some imagined slight or annoyance at work kindle his anger, causing him to push his plate away and leave the room?

Tonight, though, her father maintained his good humor and Grace relaxed. He was a good storyteller, painting a picture of the large woman who favored the blue serge and her small son who insisted on the tweed. The boy would roast in that suit this time of year, her father said. He hoped it was a hundred degrees the day of the wedding. It would serve the little twerp right.

After dinner Grace's father closed himself in the room her mother teasingly called his study. Grace suspected he did little studying in the small, dark paneled room, the air rich with the smell of tobacco and leather. She knew he read the paper and napped in the club chair and drank whisky. His good-night kisses were always flavored with the smoky taste of liquor.

For the rest of the evening, Grace sat with Mrs. Blanchard in the parlor, working on a jigsaw puzzle of a covered bridge in winter. A sleigh drawn by a Dapple Gray approached the bridge. Its passengers, a group of young people muffled in furs and lap robes, laughed and waved. Sparkling mounds of fresh snow blanketed the scene. The edge of the puzzle was complete, the sleigh and bridge suspended in the empty space described by it. The bare trees, grey sky, and endless whiteness remained to be fitted together.

Working on one of the trees, Grace tried first one piece and then another. When her third attempt failed, she tossed the piece onto the table with an exasperated sigh.

"We'll never finish this thing, Mrs. B. Every piece looks the same to me. I'm ready to give up the whole thing." Resisting the impulse to sweep all five hundred pieces onto the floor, Grace crossed her arms tightly over her chest and kicked the chair leg with the heel of her shoe.

Studying the pieces spread out on the table, Mrs. Blanchard selected one and fitted it easily into the section of sky she was working on. Grace gave the chair leg another kick. The housekeeper looked at her and Grace looked back, frowning at the woman's fussy lace collar and dull, wispy hair. If her mother were here, doing the puzzle with her, they'd be laughing at the futility of puzzle making, giggling at the stupidity of struggling to fit five hundred pieces together only to take them all apart again.

Mrs. Blanchard said, "I expect you're tired, dear. It's always easier to find what you're looking for with fresh eyes." She smiled and checked the watch pinned to her dress. "Anyway, it's time you got ready for bed. It's past 9:00." She tilted her head, studying Grace.

"Go ahead upstairs and put on your night dress. I've got to give your mother her evening dose of tonic and when you're ready you can come in and say good-night."

Pushing back her chair, Grace said, "I'll just say goodnight to Daddy and I'll go right up." Hurrying out, she turned and added, "Thanks, Mrs. B. I'm sorry I was cross."

At the door of her father's study, Grace paused, listening. She hesitated, then quietly turned the knob. Her father was lying back in his chair, eyes closed, his legs stretched out before him. The newspaper lay open on the floor. The glass on the end table was empty.

"Good night, Daddy," she whispered and closed the door.

Upstairs, she changed into her nightie and hurried to her mother's room. Mrs. Blanchard had left the door open and, as Grace entered, was measuring tonic into a spoon. Though the room was close with the accumulated heat of the summer day, her mother lay with the covers pulled tight to her chin. Her eyes were closed and for a breathless moment, Grace wondered if she were still alive.

As Mrs. Blanchard approached the bed, her mother opened her eyes and pushed herself up to receive the proffered spoon. Swallowing the dose, she settled back against the pillows and, catching sight of Grace, smiled and held out her hand.

Mrs. Blanchard said, "Can I get you anything else Mrs. Montel?" When her mother said no, the housekeeper turned to Grace. "Don't stay too long, dear. Your mother needs to sleep and so do you."

Studying her mother's face, Grace thought how tired she looked, exhausted really, though she rarely left her bed. And she'd gotten so thin. Curled on her side under the covers, Mama seemed hardly bigger than Grace herself.

"How are you feeling, Mama?"

"Not too bad," her mother said, "now that you're here." She shifted to make room and patted the space next to her. "Lie down next to me for a while, sweetheart."

Grace snuggled against her mother's warmth, remembering the many evenings they had lain together on Grace's bed after the story and before lights out. These were the times Mama told stories of when she was a little girl growing up in this very house or helped Grace understand the mysterious ways people behaved. She longed for that familiar ritual and the longing made her feel hollowed out.

Her mother said, "How's Daddy?"

Grace considered the question. Daddy loved Mama as much as Grace did, so how could he be anything but miserable, seeing her sick like this?

Shifting her gaze to the open door, she said, "Oh, you know Daddy. Always talking about the shop and telling stories about the customers. He's in his study now—"

"Yes, I expect he is."

Her mother sighed and wrapped an arm around Grace. For a long moment, neither of them spoke. Grace lay listening to the quiet rising and falling of her mother's breath. Just when she thought Mama had slipped off to sleep, she heard her voice, dreamy and low.

"He'll need looking after, Grace. He'll be no good on his own."

———————◆◆◆———————

The day of the funeral, Grace woke to the muted light of a sunless morning. Rain thrummed on the roof and sloshed in sheets over the gutters. She rolled onto her side, staring at the grey translucence of the window, watching raindrops make their somber way down the pane. It seemed right that the sky should shed tears today. Grace was in no mood for blue skies and sunshine.

Later as she stood at the graveside in her stiff black dress, the last of the rain clouds dispersed and the sun appeared. Grace's skin prickled and sweat gathered on her forehead and upper lip. The heat bore into the dark fabric and she wiped her brow. Irritated and uncomfortable, she wished herself in some dark place, cool and solitary. A place where she could be alone with her grief, far removed from the sight of the gleaming casket and the mournful sound of the minister's voice,.

After the funeral, Grace went to stay with Grandma and Grandpa Montel. Their house, the one her father grew up in, was on Pleasant Street a few blocks from her own. The street was tree-lined, tall elms spreading their canopies over the road and front yards of the spacious, well-kept houses. Many of her grandparents' neighbors owned businesses in town, but others, like Doctor Halvorson and Attorney Peterson, were what Grandpa called professional men.   Like Grace's grandmother, the wives on the street volunteered at the hospital, ran church bazaars, and organized community suppers. Some attended afternoon card parties or belonged to the local choral society. When Daddy and Aunt Louise were growing up here, they'd played jacks and hopscotch and stick ball with the neighborhood children, but they and their friends were all grown up now and the street was quiet.

Grace didn't mind the quiet. She didn't feel much like talking these days. Mostly, she stayed in her room, the room that had been her aunt's before she'd married and moved to Vermont. There was a window seat overlooking the back yard and Auntie's collection of books: *The Bobbsey Twins, The Wizard of Oz, Little Women, Aunt Jane's Nieces*. It was easier to travel the yellow brick road with Dorothy or bask in the always sunny lives of the twins than it was to be Grace with her grief and loneliness and worry about the future.

One afternoon about two weeks after the funeral, her friend, Mary Devlin, dropped by. She lived on the next block up from Grace's house with her parents and several brothers and sisters. Mrs. Devlin was a pale woman with faded red hair and a lilt in her speech. Grace enjoyed her endless stories, usually delivered with a baby on her hip and a toddler hanging on the hem of her dress. Mr. Devlin worked at the mill, came home for supper and headed out to the pubs most evenings.

It was unusual for Mary to have an afternoon away from home. In the summer, she spent most of her time looking after her younger brothers and sisters. But today Mary had brought along her skipping rope and asked Grace if she'd come out and jump with her. Grace was tempted to refuse; all she really wanted was to be left alone. But something in Mary's voice made her relent.

"Come on in," she said. "Gram's in the parlor. We'll go in and say hello and I'll go up and look for my rope. I'm pretty sure Mrs. Blanchard packed it for me."

Grace knew exactly where the rope was. She retrieved it from the closet floor, then sat down on the edge of her bed. Grandma was pleased that Mary had come by and Grace knew she was expected to be pleased, too, but these days she felt so tired. She wondered where she'd find the energy to make conversation with her friend, let alone skip rope. She took a deep breath, picked up the rope, and headed downstairs.

Out on the sidewalk, the girls found a smooth section of pavement under the shade of the elms. They took it in turns to pick the skipping songs and it wasn't long before the exhilaration of pumping her arms and legs to the familiar rhymes replaced the lethargy that had dragged at her limbs for days. They sang about Miss Mary Mack and Ladybug, Ladybug and then began to chant A my name is Alice. By the time they got to X and Mary said, "X my name is Exhausted," Grace was surprised to hear herself laugh.

Flushed with heat and exertion, she suggested they find something cool to drink. They rounded the house and while

Mary rested on a bench in the shade, Grace entered the kitchen where Mrs. Henderson was polishing silver.

"Bless us and save us, Miss Grace," she said, wiping her hands on her apron. "You're red as a lobster. What have you been up to?"

"Mary and I have been skipping rope, Mrs. Henderson. We're awfully thirsty. May we have something cold to drink?"

"Why sure, and don't I have some nice fresh lemonade just waitin' for thirsty young ladies? You fetch the glasses from the cupboard. I don't suppose you'd mind a bit of shortbread to go with that, now would ya?"

Grace carried the snack tray into the back yard and the girls settled onto the grass under the maple her grandfather had planted as a young man. Now it soared into the summer sky, its foliage blotting out the afternoon sun and rustling in the faint breeze. For a while the girls were quiet, savoring the competing flavors of tart lemonade and buttery sweet cookies. From high above, a squirrel scolded. Then a grasshopper landed in Mary's lap making them both jump.

Mary put down her glass and said, "I'm awfully sorry about your mother, Gracie. Ma says I shouldn't talk about it, but I can't help thinking how sad you must be."

"It's almost worse when people don't talk about it. I end up feeling like I've done something bad, like Mama's dying was shameful, somehow." She frowned. "I can't explain it, really, but sometimes I miss her so much I can hardly breathe."

Mary reached over and patted Grace's hand, her eyes moist with sympathy. She asked, "Where's your father? Is he staying here, too?"

Grace shook her head and pulled a hanky out of her pocket. "No, after the funeral he went to Vermont with my Aunt Louise. Gramp's taking his place at the shop for a few weeks. When he comes back, I guess we'll both go home, but I'm not sure when that will be."

That evening after Gram had come in to say good-night, Grace lay awake for a long time. She hadn't wanted to jump rope or have company, but she'd enjoyed the afternoon with Mary just the same. Talking about Mama had made her feel like crying, but it had been a relief, too, like telling a secret you just couldn't hold in. It seemed no one wanted to talk about Mama anymore. Even Grandma and Grandpa hardly mentioned her. Maybe they thought if they didn't say anything about her, Grace wouldn't miss her. But Grace would always miss her mother.

She wondered how it would feel to be back in the house Mama had lived in her whole life. To walk past her mother's empty room, to see her brushes and comb and mirror laid out on the dresser, her clothes hanging in the wardrobe. Grace drew a ragged breath and turned onto her side. She wouldn't think about that now. It would be weeks before Daddy came home.

Grace came awake with a start. Some noise, like the bump of a heavy object or the slamming of a door. She didn't know how long she'd been asleep or what time it was, but she thought it must be late, too late for anyone to be up. Certainly too late for visitors. Then footsteps in the hall and her grandfather's voice, querulous and scratchy with sleep.

"Francis, what in blazes are you doing here? You're supposed to be in Vermont with your sister."

"I've come to get Grace," her father said. "I'm taking her home."

Grandpa's tread was heavy on the stairs."Not at this time of night, you're not. Besides, you're in no condition to look after yourself right now, let alone your daughter."

"She's my child and I'll do what I want. Now, get your hands off me." Loud and angry, her father's words were thick with drink.

Grace lay rigid, her heart pounding in her ears.

"That's enough you two. You'll frighten the child."

Hearing Grandma's sure, steady voice, Grace exhaled.

"Now, calm down and come into the parlor, both of you."

The parlor door clicked shut. Grace could hear the distant sound of voices, but the words they spoke remained maddeningly indistinct. She pulled the covers up to her chin and lay still, praying that Grandma would make everything all right. She didn't know why her father had come for her, but she knew she didn't want to go.

2

FATHER AND DAUGHTER

Grace woke with the familiar sense of sorrow, of missing Mama. Then a new worry surfaced as she remembered Daddy's sudden appearance in the night. She was just getting used to being with Grandma and Grandpa, just beginning to feel more comfortable around them, and now Daddy was back. She wondered if he'd gone home, wondered why he'd come for her. Grace loved her father. He was kind and funny and clever, but he was as changeable as the weather. Showing up in the middle of the night and causing a ruckus was just like him. You never knew what he'd do next. Grace couldn't imagine how she and her father would manage now that Mama was gone.

Sighing, she tossed back the blankets and swung her legs over the side of the bed. She could hear Mrs. Henderson banging about in the kitchen and thought about the blueberry muffins she'd been promised. In the bathroom, she splashed cold water on her face and worked her hair into a single braid. It wasn't tight and straight the way Mama used to braid Grace's hair. It was loose and wispy and would soon unravel, but it would have to do.

Entering the dining room, she found Grandma and Grandpa already seated at either end of the long, polished table. Her father, across from her own empty place, was spreading butter on a muffin. Grace paused, watching the three grown-ups, trying to gauge the atmosphere in the room.

"Ah, there she is," her father said, opening his arms. "Come over here and give your old dad a hug."

Grace slipped into his arms, comforted by his embrace and the clean smells of soap and bay rum.

Leaning against him, his arm around her waist, she said, "What are you doing here, Daddy? I thought you were going to stay with Aunt Louise and Uncle Arthur for another couple of weeks."

"Aren't you glad to see me?" he teased, giving her an affectionate squeeze. "Anyway, there's nothing for me to do there. It's time I got back to work, and besides, I missed my girl."

"I missed you, too, Daddy," she said, not really sure she meant it.

"Sit down and eat your breakfast, Gracie," her grandmother said. "Mrs. Henderson made those muffins especially for you. She'll be disappointed if you don't have at least two of them."

Grace did as she was told, listening to the careful conversation of the grown-ups as they passed dishes around the table. Her father asked Grandpa about business at the shop, Grandma wanted to know how Aunt Louise's husband, Arthur, liked his new position as Headmaster at the Normal School. No one mentioned the commotion in the foyer in the middle of the night. No one told her if she was to remain with her grandparents a while longer or go home with her father today. She itched to know, but the question stuck in her throat along with a mouthful of Mrs. Henderson's muffin.

Before long, her father set his napkin next to his plate and pushed his chair back from the table. "Well, Dad," he said, "isn't it time we got down to the shop? I want to inventory the summer items and figure out what we should put on sale next week. We don't want to get stuck with too many of those awful seersucker suits."

Grace saw her grandparents exchange glances. Then Grandma said, "That's right. You fellows get along to work now. Gracie and I are going to get out in the garden before it gets too hot." Turning to Grace she added, "Go on up and put on your pinafore and straw hat, dear. Oh, and tidy up your room a bit before you come down. You could start by getting some of those books back on the shelves where they belong."

The adults were quiet as Grace left the room and climbed the stairs. At the top, she stopped, listening for the sound of their conversation, hoping for a hint of what would happen next. When she saw her father and grandfather enter the foyer, she ducked out of sight and hurried along the passage to her room. She wished Daddy had stayed in Vermont the way he was supposed to, but that was the thing about her father. Just because he said he was going to do something, didn't mean he would.

Gaining her room, Grace sat on the window seat and began stacking the scattered books into a pile. She could hear the rhythmic clatter of Mr. Landry's lawn mower through the open window. The smell of cut grass made her nose itch. She reached into her pocket, pulling out a wadded up handkerchief, one her mother had edged with crocheted lace. Absently, she ran the lace through her fingers and gazed out at the blurred mass of the maple's foliage.

Mama. She whispered the word again. Mama. Grace's chest ached, like some dark presence held her heart in its fist. How was it possible that she would never see her mother again? How was she to live without her smile, the sound of her voice? More than anything, who would answer her questions, explain the things that seemed unexplainable? Who would help her untangle her own feelings, help her figure out why she was angry or confused or sad?

Daddy never talked to Grace the way her mother had. When she asked him a question or voiced a concern, he turned it into a joke, pinched her cheek, and tried to make her smile. And as kind as Grandma and Grandpa were, they didn't ask her how she felt or what she wanted. Out of all the grown-ups in Grace's life, only Mama ever asked for her opinion or took her worries seriously. She sniffed and picked up the pile of books, stumbling slightly under its weight.

In the yard, Grandma set Grace to work deadheading the hydrangea while she cut back the late blooming phlox from the perennial beds along the south side of the house. They worked without speaking, the mumble of bees and the distant sound of traffic on Main Street filling the space between them. Grace had never paid much attention to the hydrangea before. Growing in nearly every yard in the neighborhood and covered with the big, white blossoms everyone called snowballs, they were as ordinary as grass. Now that Grace looked at them up close, she saw they were really clusters of hundreds of tiny flowers, their petals tinged with faint blushes of color. Up close they were beautiful.

Interrupting her thoughts, her grandmother said, "School starts in a few weeks, Grace. Are you looking forward to seventh grade?"

Grace tossed a rusted blossom onto the pile. "I don't know, Gram. Mrs. Thurston will be my teacher and everyone says she's really nice, but ... " She didn't know how to tell her grandmother that she dreaded facing the sympathy of her teachers and the curious looks of her classmates.

She remembered in third grade when Becky White's little brother had died of pneumonia. It had been hard to even look at Becky. Grace had felt sorry for her, but didn't know what to say to her. Nothing seemed right, so she'd avoided Becky and that had made her feel guilty.

Her grandmother took off her gloves and got slowly to her feet. "Time for a little break," she said. "Why don't you go in and see what Mrs. Henderson has to drink. We'll sit on the porch and rest for a few minutes."

When Grace came back carrying two tall glasses of switchel, Gram was seated in one of the rockers, staring out at the tree-lined street. Sitting next to her, Grace watched the neighbor's dog lope down the porch steps and begin his lazy circuit of the yard. He dug briefly under the hedge, snuffling in the newly turned dirt, then sat abruptly, scratching his ear vigorously with a hind foot. Satisfied, he gave his head a good shake, crawled under the porch steps, and disappeared.

Gram said, "That old dog's been sniffing that same spot and scratching that same ear ever since he was a pup. I wonder he doesn't look for something else to do."

Grace smiled. It wasn't like Grandma to make jokes, but she was beginning to see that she didn't know her grandmother as well as she'd thought. She'd always been a little in awe of her grandmother's composure and quiet confidence, but since Mama died, Grandma had changed. She seemed softer, some-how, more approachable.

"Your grandfather and I would like you to stay with us un-til school starts in September, Grace. That was our original plan, but your father seems to have changed his mind." She paused and added, "What would you like to do?"

The question surprised Grace. She hadn't thought it mat-tered what she wanted to do. She figured she'd do what the grownups told her to do. She turned toward her grandmother whose gaze was fixed on the street.

"I think I'd like to stay here with you for a while longer, Grandma," she said, feeling her eyes burn. "It's going to be aw-fully lonely at home without Mama there."

"My thoughts exactly," her grandmother said. "Best to give yourself a bit more time, eh dear?" Patting Grace's hand, she stood. "Now, if you think you can manage that old wheelbarrow, we'll dump these clippings out back of the shed."

The shop closed at 6:00 on weeknights and Grace's father and grandfather arrived home that evening just before 7:00. Her dad seemed in fine spirits, telling Gram how he had ordered sale signs and a newspaper advertisement to kick off the end-of-sea-son sale and how he'd measured Mr. Avery, the undertaker, for a new black suit.

"The Widow Hilson must be a dab hand in the kitchen," her father said. "Since Avery and the Widow have been keeping company, old Dan's put on quite a bit of weight. I told him if we went with the same measurements as his last suit, the jacket would gap and the trousers would be too tight. He was none too pleased with the news. Kept insisting it was this muggy weather we're having, didn't he Dad?"

Gramp grinned and shook his head. "Said he was all swole up with the heat and that as soon as the weather turned, he'd be back down to fightin' weight."

Grace laughed, relieved that her father and grandfather were back on good terms. Lying in bed last night, listening to their angry voices, she'd been afraid, just as she had always been when her parents argued. There was something awful about grownups fighting.

After dinner they all sat together in the parlor, where the big windows overlooking the side yard were open. The evening air was cool and moist and filled with the late summer sound of busy crickets. Her father sipped his whiskey and patted the sofa next to him. Grace sat down and he wrapped an arm around her shoulder. Her grandparents sat in their customary chairs; Grandpa with his brandy and newspaper and Grandma working her cross-stitch, a tiny glass of sherry on the table beside her.

No one talked much until Grandma set down her handwork and said, "Francis, Grace and I had a little talk this morning and we both think it would be a good idea for her to stay here until school opens." She folded her hands in her lap. "That was our original plan and we think we should stick to it."

Pulling his arm away, Grace's father looked at her. "Is that right, Gracie? You'd rather stay here than go home with your old dad?" He was smiling, but he didn't sound happy.

"It's not that, Daddy, it's just that ... " Grace glanced at her grandmother.

"Of course that's not it. Don't put words in her mouth, Francis." Grandma looked at the mantel clock and turned to Grace. "It's getting late, dear. Time you went up and got ready for bed. One of us will be up soon to say good-night."

They were going to talk about her. They would decide whether she would stay with her grandparents or go home with her father and then they'd tell her how it was going to be. Grandma had asked her what she wanted to do, but it wasn't really up to her after all. Grace kissed her father and grandparents and left the room, lingering at the closed parlor door for a minute before making her way upstairs.

She was propped up in bed reading when her father appeared in the doorway.

"Hi sweetie," he said, sitting on the edge of her bed, "what're you reading?"

"Oh, it's one of Auntie's old books," she said tossing it onto the counterpane. "I've already read it once."

"So, you'd like to stay here for a couple more weeks? I thought maybe you'd be missing home by now, but your grandmother seems to think you're not ready for that yet." Before she could think of what to say, he went on, "When it comes to that, I'm not sure I'm ready to go home either. Mrs. Blanchard's still away at her sister's and we'd be all at sixes and sevens without her. Best just stay put until she gets back, right?"

Grace and her father settled in to life on Pleasant Street. Her father and grandfather went off to the shop each day, though Grandpa was threatening to go back into retirement now that Daddy was back. Grandma took Grace school shopping, buying her three new frocks and a pair of lace-up shoes. She'd wanted the shiny ones with the pointed toes she'd seen in the window, but both the shoe salesman and her grandmother had agreed they weren't sturdy enough for everyday.

While she didn't get the shoes she most wanted, Grandma did let her pick out a sketch book and set of colored pencils at the stationery store. Grace told her grandmother that she wanted her first drawing to be of a hydrangea blossom.

"Is it all right if I cut a snowball to bring inside, Grandma?" she asked. "I'm going to make the drawing up close, like it was magnified. I want to show all the little flowers and how they bunch together."

Her grandmother said she could cut as many of the blossoms as she wanted, but she guessed it would take some doing to draw all the individual flowers.

"That's why I'm only going to pick one, Grandma," Grace told her, "but I'm going to make it big and fill up the whole page." She frowned. "Do you think Grandpa will let me use his magnifying glass? I'll be ever so careful with it."

"You'll have to ask your grandfather, Grace. I wouldn't presume to say. You know how he is about his precious coin collection."

Grace did know. Grandpa had been collecting coins since he'd found his first Flying Eagle penny. He was fourteen, working at the shop with his father, sorting the cash box at the end of the day when he'd come upon it. He substituted a penny of his own for the unusual coin; the coin that was to be the beginning of his Early American collection. Time and again Grace had seen her grandfather peering through his glass at a coin or studying his books to find out what metals it was made of or where it was minted. Her father joked that you didn't ask Grandpa a coin question unless you had an hour to spare.

When Grace asked her grandfather about using his magnifying glass, he said yes, but set certain conditions. She could use it during the day when he didn't need it and must never take it outside. Mrs. Henderson found a small table for Grace that she could pull up to the window seat in her Aunt's room and use for a desk. She set out her sketch book and pencils, an India rubber, and a bud vase with the giant hydrangea blossom she'd cut. With Grandpa's magnifier, she could easily make out the individual petals and stamen of each flower and study the delicate washes of color that existed within the overall white. The work absorbed Grace's attention and blunted the pain of missing Mama.

Most evenings, the family played cards or sat on the front porch enjoying the last of the warm evenings. The first few days after his return from Vermont, Grace watched her father warily, wondering how long this calm interval would last. But Daddy was different around Grandma. He didn't argue with his father even when Grandpa became surly or cross. And he didn't drink too much.

Often during dinner, Daddy and Grandpa talked about the store. The topic this evening was the dressing of the big display window that took up two-thirds of the front of the shop. Summer was coming to an end and the new window would feature garments for the fall season. There would be a fellow in a business suit, another in golfing attire, and a third dressed for an evening at the opera house. Most shop talk didn't interest Grace, but she'd always loved the window displays. Daddy created a tableau in the way he dressed the manikins and set up the props, telling a different story every time.

She heard her grandfather say, "Maybe you could get Gracie to help with the window while I mind the shop tomorrow."

"That's a great idea," her father said. "What do you say, sweetie? Want to help your old dad with the display?"

It was a short walk from Grandma and Grandpa's house to the shop. Main and Pleasant Streets ran parallel to each other and Elm Street connected the two. The following morning Grace walked between her father and grandfather, down Elm and onto Main where shopkeepers were pulling up shades, sweeping their small patches of sidewalk, watering the flowers in their window boxes.

Mr. Scapellini was unrolling the red and white striped awning that shaded the outside vegetable bins of his deli and greengrocer. Next door, the bank's heavy revolving doors were still closed, but Grace could see that the ceiling lights were lit and that the banker, Mr. Evans, was already seated at his big, shiny desk. Across the street, the front door of Mr. Vincent's pharmacy was propped open. In the window, the huge apothecary bottles of colored liquid glowed like jewels in the sun.

As they walked along Daddy and Grandpa greeted the other merchants, stopping to tip their hats and say good morning to Miss Andrews who had the millinery shop next to the tobacconist's. Miss Andrews was a tiny woman, not much taller than Grace. She wore her hair tightly waved and Grace greatly admired the milliner's lovely clothes. Today she wore a dropped waist dress of pale rose and a gauzy scarf wrapped around her slender throat.

Unlocking the door of her shop, Miss Andrews said, "What brings you to Main Street so early, Grace?"

"I'm going to help Daddy dress the big window," Grace said. "Grandpa says it'll be a good way for me to get started in the business."

"Well then," Miss Andrew's said. "I'd better leave you to it. I'll be interested to see what you and your father come up with."

The display window was covered in brown paper which Daddy said kept nosy folks from watching them work. When the window was done, they'd tear down the paper to reveal their handiwork. Grace's first job was to sweep out the display space where there was plenty of dust and a surprising number of dead flies. When she finished that task, Daddy handed her three tissue wrapped packages, each containing a different shirt. The opera house mannequin would wear a stiff white shirt with French cuffs and rows of tiny pleats running down the front. The business-man's shirt was white, too, but it had buttons on the cuffs and no pleats. For the golfer, there was a striped shirt with a detachable collar.

Tackling the dress shirt first, Grace found that it was tight-ly folded and each fold was secured with a straight pin. One by one, she worked the pins out, sticking them in the pincushion Daddy had given her. There seemed no end of folds and pins, and as she worked, she discovered thin strips of cardboard in-side the body and under the collar of the shirt. After sustaining several good pokes from hidden pins, she finally managed to free the shirt from its wrapping. She hung it on a wooden hanger and took a deep breath. Two more to go.

Just then her father said, "I've got these fellows into their trousers and I'm about to wrestle them into their shoes and stockings. How're you coming along with those shirts, Gracie?"

Quickly Grace took up the golfer's shirt and set to work. "I'll be done in a minute, Daddy," she said, resolved to keep up her end of the job. The unwrapping was easier now that she knew where the pins and cardboard would be and before long she carried three neatly hung shirts to her father.

"Nice work, my girl," he said. "They truss these things up pretty good, don't they?"

She buttoned the mannequins into their respective shirts and then watched as her father completed each outfit with a matching jacket. The golfer's jacket had wide pleats in the front and back and, instead of trousers, he wore knickerbockers and long stockings. It seemed an outlandish costume to Grace, but she didn't say so.

Instead, she took a step back and said, "They look very fine, Daddy. I like the opera house fellow best, though. I think he's quite the elegant gentleman."

Her dad smiled. "Next step is to make these gents look like they're doing something. Let's see, this should do it for the opera house fellow," he said, moving a small table next to the mannequin and setting a potted fern on top of it. "I've got a nine iron here for the sporting man. We'll just prop this against his leg and rest his hand on top. There now, how's that?"

"It's perfect, Daddy," said Grace. "What about the fellow in the business suit?"

"Haven't quite figured that one out yet, sweetie. Why don't you look around and come up with something while I clean up here?"

With an idea already taking shape in her mind, Grace headed for the counter. Behind the glass display case with its array of watches and cuff links, billfolds and key chains, Grace found what she was looking for. She pulled a blank invoice sheet out of a box and studied it. The store's name ran across the top in fancy script. Under that there were spaces for the date, a description of the item purchased, its cost and a total. In her best handwriting she carefully entered the details of an imaginary purchase complete with prices and total.

Satisfied with her work, she brought the invoice to the window and fitted it into the mannequin's outstretched hand. She was appraising her work when her father returned from the back room.

"Well now, Grace, that's pretty clever. You made that fellow look busy and managed to show off the name of the store to boot." He put his arm around her and Grace leaned against him, pleased that he was pleased. "From now on, I'll consider you my Assistant Window Dresser." Then he offered her his arm. "Is mademoiselle ready for lunch?"

Over lunch, Daddy praised Grace's work on the window and talked to her about his plans to expand the store. He said the tobacconist's shop next door was closing soon and that he'd already talked to the landlord about taking over the space. He asked Grace not to mention this to Grandma and Grandpa just yet. He would tell them himself when everything was arranged. She was flattered that her father was confiding in her, telling her about his plans. She hadn't seen him look so animated, or so handsome, in a long time. With his wavy hair and shining eyes, she thought him every bit as good looking as the actor, Douglas Fairbanks. And she thought Mr. Fairbanks was very good looking indeed.

After lunch, Daddy went back to the shop to spell Grandpa, and Grace headed to Pleasant Street. On the way, she talked to her mother as she often did when she was alone. She told her about helping dress the shop window and about having lunch in the hotel dining room. She reminded Mama that she'd said Daddy would need looking after, but Grace said he was doing a fine job taking care of both of them.

She didn't tell Mama that she was afraid to move back home. Afraid that once he was not living with Grandma, Daddy would begin drinking again in earnest. These were things she couldn't say, even to herself.

3

HOME AND SCHOOL

Grace followed Mrs. Blanchard up the porch steps, paus-ing while the housekeeper unlocked the front door. It swung open and Mrs. B stepped aside. Grace peered into the dim foyer. From the threshold, she could make out the cleaning smells of ammonia and lemon wax. Everything was scrubbed and shiny and strangely unfamiliar, as if her mother's death had changed the house as much as the people in it.

Two nights before, Daddy had told her they'd be going home before the start of school and, now, here she was. Placing a hand on Grace's back, Mrs. Blanchard steered her into the foyer and shut the door. Mrs. B removed her hat and set it on the hall table, all the while cataloging the work she and Mrs. Murphy had done to "spruce the place up."

Only half listening, Grace stood dumbly with her back to the door, and didn't move even when Mrs. B picked up her valise and made for the stairs. Halfway up, the housekeeper stopped. She turned and, tipping her head, smiled that gentle, sad smile Grace had come to recognize as the grown-up way of showing sympathy. Slowly, the housekeeper descended the stairs and, sitting on the second step, motioned for Grace to join her. The big house was silent except for the ticking of the hall clock and the soft rustle of Mrs. Blanchard's dress. Grace pulled her knees into her chest and rested her forearms across them. The sun shining through the stained glass on the front door scattered patches of color on the polished floor. Through her tears, she watched the colors blur and shimmer.

"It's going to be very hard for a while, Gracie," Mrs. Blanchard said, her voice low, "probably for a long while. We never quite get used to being without our mothers. I still miss mine and she's been gone more than twenty years." She passed Grace a handkerchief. "We have to find a way to go on, though, just as our mothers would want us to do."

Grace blew her nose and wiped her streaming eyes. She took a deep breath and straightened. "I'm afraid to go up there, Mrs. B. I don't think I can bear to walk past Mama's room."

"You've nothing to fear, dear. The room's been redecorated with new curtains and counterpane, and the furniture rearranged. Your father and grandmother have sorted through your mother's belongings and put aside a few special things they knew she'd want you to have." Mrs. Blanchard smoothed back Grace's hair. "Let's go up, now, and get you settled."

At the top of the stairs, Grace paused at the open door to what, for her, would always be her mother's room. Through the window, the afternoon sun shone on the glossy woodwork. The bedside table, empty of its medicinal clutter, held a vase of lavender and lemongrass. Grace took a deep breath and stepped inside. She paused, her senses alert to some sign of Mama: the scent of her perfume, the sound of her bedside clock, the cut-glass dish in which she kept her hairpins, but there was nothing. Sighing, Grace turned and continued down the hall.

In her own room, she lay on her bed curled onto her side and listened as Mrs. Blanchard made her way downstairs. Mrs. B had closed the curtains and covered Grace with an afghan, saying she should rest before dinner. Grace wasn't tired, but it felt good to be alone. She stared into the dim room, everything tidy and neat, her books lined up on their shelves, the embroidered scarf on the dresser starched and ironed. And on the chair by the door, the carton of Mama's things, the ones Grandma and Daddy had picked out for her.

Tossing off the afghan, she got up and opened the box. Mama's silk shawl lay folded on top. Grace ran her hand over the smooth fabric, taking in the subtle shades of blue, grey, violet, and green. As she wrapped the shawl around her shoulders, she caught the faint aroma of rosewater and her heart contracted. Next, she came upon the jewelry box that had always held pride of place on Mama's dressing table, and a pair of crocheted gloves, yellowed with age, each with a single pearl button at the wrist. Mama had showed her these gloves once. They had belonged to her mother, Grandmother Seymour, who died before Grace was born. The gloves were tiny, but when Grace slid her fingers into their lacy weave, she found they fit perfectly.

Sitting on the edge of her bed, Grace studied her gloved hands. She pictured her mother after that terrible accident, a young woman missing her mother and wondering, as Grace did now, how she was going to live without her.

Hearing a knock on the bedroom door, Grace struggled up through sleep. She was still wrapped in the silk shawl, her gloved hands tucked under her chin, her head stuffed and aching. The door opened and Daddy peeked into the room.

"Hey sweetie," he whispered. "Mrs. B said you might be sleeping." He smoothed her hair back and kissed her forehead. "What are you all dressed up for?" he said, grinning. "Stepping out with that elegant gentleman from the store, perhaps?"

Grace felt silly to be caught wearing Mama's shawl and gloves, but she couldn't help smiling. "Hi, Daddy. I guess I fell asleep."

"Sure looks that way."

Sitting up she asked, "How did things go at the shop today?"

"Come on down to dinner and I'll tell you all about it."

❧

The following Tuesday, Grace lay in bed dreading the day to come, her insides slithery with nerves. She'd never much liked the first day of school anyway, even though she knew everybody in her class, practically in the whole school for that matter. But today would be worse than any other first day; today she'd have to face the awkward looks of her classmates and the sympathy of the teachers. Today she'd have to face the world of school as the girl whose mother had died.

She could tell it was early. The light behind the curtains was a dull grey and she could hear the clink of bottles as the milkman delivered up and down the street. She tried closing her eyes, but her lids fluttered with the effort so she gave up and got out of bed. Padding across the room, she opened her wardrobe and took out the new navy gabardine skirt and white middy blouse Grandma had bought for her. The saleslady had called it the latest style and told her she looked very smart when she'd tried it on. She laid the skirt and blouse on the bed and headed to the bathroom to wash up.

Confronting her image in the mirror a few minutes later, Grace turned first one way and then the other, admiring the fit of her new clothes. She had gotten taller over the summer, but hadn't filled out much. If anything, she was longer and straighter than ever. Reaching into the jewelry box, she pulled out the gold locket that had been her mother's. She fastened the clasp and settled the pendant in the V of her blouse. She was fumbling with the tie when Daddy knocked on the door.

"Well now," he said, appraising her new outfit. "My little girl doesn't look so little anymore. I think you must have grown a foot this summer, Gracie."

"Oh, Daddy, I did no such thing and you know it." She frowned at her reflection. "I don't know what to do with this tie. It won't lie flat."

"What you need is a good old Windsor. Here, let me show you." He moved behind her and took hold of the ends of the tie. A few deft moves and it was done. A perfect knot, neat and flat. "How's that?" he asked.

"It's just right." She smiled at him in the mirror and he smiled back.

Mary was waiting for Grace at their usual meeting place on the corner of Pleasant and Elm Streets. They'd been walking to school together almost from first grade and here they were about to start seventh, their next to last year at Marston. Mary was wearing a dress Grace recognized as one her older sister, Agnes, had worn the year before. One of her stockings was darned at the knee. Grace waved and called hello, suddenly ill-at-ease in her new clothes.

As soon as they were together, Mary took Grace's hand. She looked happy, her smile wide and her blue eyes flashing. "Oh Gracie," she said, "I'm so glad to be going back to school. I've spent most of my summer looking after Billy and Sean." She shook her head. "Those two little twerps are lucky they made it out alive. I swear if I had to spend one more day playing hide-and-go-seek and Duck, Duck, Goose, I'd go crazy."

Grace laughed. She couldn't help it. "I know it's not funny, Mary. I sure wouldn't want to take care of two little boys all summer. Your mother must be happy to have you all back in school."

"Well, we're not all back in school," Mary said. "Fiona is only three and Jake's just a baby." She frowned. "Poor Ma. There'll probably be another one by the time Fiona's old enough for first grade."

They were near the top of Willard Street where the school stood surrounded on three sides by playing fields. Kids ran around or gathered in groups talking; some were already standing in line. Grace's stomach tightened. She stopped.

Mary stopped, too, and looked at her. "It won't be so bad, Gracie," she said. "Once you get through the first day, you'll see. Come on. It'll be all right."

They headed for the side entrance and got into the girls' line. They'd entered this door last year, too, when they were in sixth grade with Mr. Morris who was also the school principal. Grace and Mary watched the boys chase each other on the playground or toss balls back and forth. Some girls jumped rope, but most stood in line talking. The bell rang and everyone scurried into line as Mr. Morris stepped out onto the portico. A second later, Mrs. Thurston joined him.

Grace studied her new teacher. She was tall and slim and wore her dark hair in a tight coil at the back of her head. Mrs. Thurston had come to the school last year and was said to be strict, but fair. She'd also heard that Mrs. Thurston had moved from Maine where her husband had been a teacher, too. That was before he'd gone to France to fight in the Great War and not come back.

Mr. Morris gave his usual lecture on what he called deportment — no running, no talking, do not push or shove, stay in line — before leading his class into the building. Then Mrs. Thurston stepped forward. Her lecture was more of a welcome than a talking-to. They would have a good year, she told them. They had much to do to prepare for eighth grade and they would begin that very day.

As the class filed into the building, Grace knew that any curiosity or questions her classmates had about Mama's passing would at least have to wait until recess. She took her assigned seat, her textbooks already piled neatly on the desk. Obviously, Mrs. Thurston was ready to get to work, and that suited Grace just fine.

Late that afternoon, Grace was in her room struggling with her arithmetic homework, when Daddy got home from the shop. She heard Mrs. Blanchard meet him at the door and followed the sound of his footsteps up the stairs and down the hall to her room. He opened the door and stepped in.

"Well, Gracie," he said. "How'd it go today?"

"Better than I thought it would," she said. "I think I'm going to like Mrs. Thurston. She knows how to handle the boys and she's definitely going to keep us busy. I've never had homework on the first day of school before, and these percentages are giving me a headache."

"You've never been in seventh grade before, either." Daddy came in and looked over her shoulder. "And don't worry about those percentages. After dinner I'll show you a few tricks of the trade. Once you get those down, you'll be able to do the figuring in your head."

The next day, as the kids filed out to recess, Mrs. Thurston told Grace she had a little job she'd like her to do before she went out. The teacher closed the classroom door and called Grace up to her desk. She told her how sorry she was to hear of her mother's passing and asked her how she was coping with the loss.

Grace didn't know what to say. She wasn't sure she was coping with the loss. She wasn't even sure she knew what that meant. She shrugged and looked out the window at the pale gray sky.

"I know from my own experience how hard it is when a loved one dies," the teacher said. "For a long time I felt as though a part of myself was missing. Sometimes I still feel that way." She picked a pencil up off her desk and slid it through her fingers. "And people don't know what to say, do they? They're afraid to talk about death."

The word made Grace catch her breath. She supposed it was true. Death was not something anyone wanted to talk about, including Grace. The teacher was watching her, absentmindedly toying with the pencil. The wall clock lurched ahead another minute.

"I miss my mother very much, Mrs. Thurston. It hurts to talk about her ... and it hurts just as much not to."

Slipping the pencil into the holder, the teacher smiled. "Well said, Grace. That's exactly the problem, isn't it? And your classmates share that problem. They don't know what to say to you, but they want to say something. Accept their condolences. Be grateful and try to keep from turning away from your friends. Grieving is a lonely business, but people can help us through it ... if we let them."

She stood then, and Grace knew their talk was over. "Thank you, Mrs. Thurston. I'll try to do as you say." At the door, she stopped and turned to the teacher. "I think what you said yesterday is true. This is going to be a good year."

In the following days, it became clear to Grace that Mrs. Thurston had talked to the rest of her classmates, as well as to her. Several of them told her how sorry they were to hear of her mother's passing. At first, Grace felt uncomfortable with their awkward sympathies, but Mrs. Thurston had been right. Once they said they were sorry and Grace thanked them, everyone relaxed. Since Mama died, Grace had spent most of her time alone, but now she began to reacquaint herself with her long-time classmates. She even made a new and unexpected friend.

Jerome Davison was new to Marston School, having moved with his parents from Massachusetts over the summer. From the first day of school, it was obvious to Grace that Jerome was going to have trouble fitting in with the other boys. He didn't play chasing games before the morning bell, and appeared to have no interest in having a place on the teams the boys set up every day at recess. Often during the morning break, he sat on the wide stone steps of the portico reading or working crossword puzzles.

It didn't take long for the other boys to label Jerome a sissy and tease him when the playground teacher was out of earshot. He'd look at them and shrug, then go right back to his book. He didn't get mad or tattle on them, he just didn't seem to care. Grace was impressed, especially when she realized that his strategy was working. They couldn't get a rise out of him and pretty soon they stopped trying.

The less Jerome interested the other boys, the more he intrigued Grace. He wasn't like any boy she'd ever known. He was quiet, but not stuck-up. He was smart, but he didn't wave his hand in the air every time the teacher asked a question. And he was the handsomest boy Grace had ever seen.

Jerome sat across the aisle from her and one seat up, so she could watch him undetected. His nose was long and thin and his thick brown hair fell over his forehead and curled at the nape of his neck. His fingers were long and tapered and his nails were clean. There was something noble and dignified about him, like the profile of Augustus Caesar in their history book. He seemed to Grace as different from the other boys in the class as a sleek racehorse is from a mule. Much as she admired Jerome, she couldn't bring herself to talk to him. Sometimes she caught his eye and he smiled and once or twice she thought he was watching her, but she was too flustered to meet his gaze.

All that changed one Saturday morning at the public library. Mrs. Thurston had given them a research assignment as part of their nature study. They had to choose a plant common to the region and write a report about it. They also had to draw a picture of their plant and give a short presentation to the class. Grace knew right away what she would choose for her topic. She had always loved the great arching elms on her grandparents' street, loved the way their canopies made a shady tunnel over the pavement. She liked the shape of the trees, too, like giant open umbrellas. She'd use her new colored pencils for the drawing.

In the card catalog, she found the book she was looking for, *Trees of North America,* but when she looked for it in the stacks, it wasn't there.

"Blast!" The word echoed in the quiet space and Grace held her breath, expecting to be shushed by Mrs. Proudie, the sour librarian.

"Is this what you're looking for?"

Grace peered through an empty space on the shelves. Jerome was sitting at a nearby library table holding up a large book and grinning like the cat that ate the canary.

"As a matter of fact, that's exactly what I'm looking for." She was grinning, too. Surprised at her own boldness, she sat down beside him and pulled the book in front of her. Sure enough it was the very book she needed.

"It's the only copy," Jerome said, "but I'll be happy to share it with you."

The book was open to a page on white birches. Grace kept the place with her finger and flipped through until she found the page on elms. She slid the book back to Jerome and said, "It's nice of you to offer, but we can't both use it at the same time."

"We could set up a schedule to use it," he said. Grace caught a glint of mischief in his eyes. "Or better yet, we could work together. You know, help each other get information. That way, you'd learn about birches and I'd learn about elms."

Intrigued, Grace said, "How would that work?"

"Oh, you know, I'll read to you while you take notes, and you read to me while I take notes, that sort of thing. It might be fun. What do you think?"

Grace thought it would be fun, and even better, a good way to get to know this very interesting boy.

In the days after meeting in the library, Grace and Jerome spent several afternoons working together on their nature study assignment. At first, she half expected him to be bossy or smart-alecky, but he wasn't. He was smart, but in a helpful way and he made her laugh. Grace had always been shy around boys, even the ones she'd known all through grammar school. She was put off by their loud voices and the insults and punches that passed for friendly give and take among them. And she certainly didn't understand their compulsion to toss, chase, catch, and kick balls around a playing field.

Grace was mystified by most boys, but her friendship with Jerome was the biggest mystery of all. Once they'd completed their nature study assignment, they continued to spend afternoons together during that long, mild fall. They explored the woods behind Grace's house and one day followed the dry stream bed part way up Jasper Mountain. Jerome told her about growing up in Massachusetts and spending his summers on Cape Cod. She told him about her great-grandfather Montel whose general store had become Montel's Haberdashery. Most afternoons they climbed the ladder to the tree house where they read or drew pictures until the light faded.

One chilly day in October, Grace and Jerome sat in the tree house among the bare branches of the maple, listening to the wind rustle the fallen leaves below. Jerome sat cross-legged with his back against the wall, his hands jammed in the pockets of his wool jacket. Across the narrow space, Grace huddled in her nest of cushions and old blankets, wondering what they'd do when it got too cold for the tree house.

"Tell me about your mother, Grace. What was she like?"

Startled, Grace looked at Jerome. His brows were drawn together and his dark eyes searched her face. For a moment, she was quiet, considering. "Well, she was quite lovely and very kind. She was funny, too, and even a little ... I guess you could say, mischievous." Jerome raised an eyebrow and smiled. "That is, sometimes she'd scold me for something I said or did, but I could tell she didn't really mind. Her face would be serious, but her eyes would be laughing."

"Was she sick a long time?" Jerome's voice was quiet.

"Pretty much from the time the baby boy died."

The smell of burning leaves drifted through the tree house. Somewhere a dog barked. Grace swallowed. She'd never talked to anyone except Daddy about the baby. And then only that one time the day after it happened.

"I'd spent the night at my grandparents," Grace said. "My father came over in the morning. He told me my mother was all right, but she'd lost the baby."

Grace gazed past Jerome out the tree house window to where the maple's bare branches were etched darkly against the pale sky. Exhaling, she looked down at the white knuckles of her clasped hands.

4

THE UNRAVELING

Alone in her room that night, Grace sat propped up in bed, *Anne of Green Gables* unopened on her lap. Her conversation with Jerome had brought back a lot of unwelcome memories, dark thoughts she couldn't reconcile with the carefree adventures of Anne Shirley. Anne was an orphan, a girl alone in the world; how could she be so relentlessly cheerful? Because she wasn't real, that's why. Tossing the book aside, Grace slipped under the covers.

Squeezing her eyes shut, she pulled the blankets up to her chin and tried to banish the images and feelings Jerome's question had awakened. He'd meant to be kind, she knew that, but now her mind was full of pictures she didn't want to see and sounds she didn't want to hear.

On the January day she'd turned twelve, her parents woke her with birthday wishes and the news that Mama was expecting a baby. They had waited to tell her until Doctor Halvorson felt sure that this baby would be carried to term.

"We didn't want to disappoint you again, darling," Mama said, kissing her cheek, "but everything has gone much more smoothly this time." Daddy took Mama's hand and they smiled at each other. "We expect you'll have a new brother or sister by early summer."

That evening Grandma and Grandpa came for dinner. After the dishes were cleared away, Daddy dimmed the lights and Mrs. Blanchard came in with the cake, her face alight with the glow of thirteen candles, one for each year and another to grow on. She joined everyone else in singing the birthday song and watched as Grace blew out the candles.

"Take a deep breath, sweetie," Daddy said. "You've got to get them all at once if you want your wish to come true."

Eyeing the wrapped packages on the sideboard, Grace felt a rush of excitement. All this and a new baby, too. Surely this was the best day of her life. She closed her eyes, made a wish, filled her lungs, and blew with all her might. The tiny flames went out; all, that is, but the one to grow on.

Throughout the winter months that followed, Grace watched her mother, anxious for signs of trouble. By the time sugaring season came, though, she'd stopped worrying. Mama had slowed down with the expansion of her belly, but she was as cheerful and bright-eyed as Grace had ever seen her. Daddy was different, too. Instead of hiding in his study after dinner, he sat with Grace and Mama in the parlor. While a fire burned in the hearth, he read aloud, poetry by Robert Frost, Shakespeare's sonnets, and Grace's favorites, *The Pickwick Papers* and *David Copperfield*.

In late April, Grace and her classmates were released from school for their spring vacation. For the first time in months, she and Mary shed their heavy winter coats and clumsy boots. During the long, mild afternoons, they played hopscotch or jumped rope or visited the shops on Main Street.

On Friday, she and Mary had gone to the movie house and afterward had chocolate sundaes at the drugstore soda fountain. When Grace returned home late that afternoon, she found Mama in the parlor, lying on the sofa wrapped in an afghan. Her eyes were closed, but she did not seem to be sleeping. Her face was ashen, all the color washed away, but whether this was a sign of sickness or a trick of the light, Grace wasn't sure.

As she stood wondering, Mama's eyes fluttered open and she smiled. "Hello, darling. How was the movie?" She struggled to sit up, rearranging the pillows against the arm of the sofa, and leaning back. "Was it 'Huckleberry Finn' you saw?"

Cheered by Mama's smile, she said, "That's right, 'Huckleberry Finn', and it was quite good. The high school band played the music. Mary's brother, Paddy, plays in the band and she was so proud. Then we went to Vincent's for ice cream sundaes. It was great fun." She sat on the edge of the sofa next to her mother. "Can I get you anything, Mama? A cup of tea or something?"

"A cup of tea would be lovely, sweetie. Ask Mrs. B to put the kettle on and tell her not to bother with a tray."

"Okay, Mama, I'll be right back."

Grace was about to push open the kitchen door when she heard Mrs. Murphy's voice. She'd forgotten it was the charlady's day, the day she came to clean and often stayed for what she called tea and a gossip with Mrs. Blanchard.

"That's a very bad sign, that is, Mrs. B. The missus had better take to her bed and stay there if she don't want to lose this one, too."

Listening, Grace held her breath and felt her stomach tighten.

"I'm sure if the doctor thought that was necessary he would have said so," she heard Mrs. B say. "As it is, he's prescribed a tonic to build her strength. I suppose if Dr. Halvorson is not worried, there's no call for us to be either."

The door swung open, startling Grace. She stepped back, ashamed to be caught eavesdropping.

"Is everything all right, Grace?"

"Oh, yes. I was just coming in to ask you to put water on for tea."

As she passed through into the kitchen, Grace saw the two women exchange glances.

That evening at dinner, Grace watched her parents warily. The atmosphere in the room was heavy, like a summer afternoon before a storm. Mama pushed her food around on the plate, eating little, and saying less. Daddy talked and talked, filling his fork and his wine glass like a man dying of starvation and thirst. Mama pulled a hanky from her pocket and wiped the beads of sweat that had gathered on her forehead. Earlier, Mama's skin had been almost white, but now her cheeks were flushed and her eyes burned like blue flames.

Pushing her plate away she said she couldn't stomach another mouthful of beef stew. She'd always hated beef stew, the very thought of it made her sick. Daddy offered to get her something lighter, broth or toast maybe, but Mama gestured impatiently and told him not to fuss. Grace was surprised. It wasn't like Mama to be short-tempered, especially with Daddy. Just then, Mrs. Blanchard came in to clear the plates and made the mistake of commenting on Mama's uneaten portion.

"How many times have I told you that I can't abide beef stew? Yet you persist in making it and then wonder why I leave it on my plate?"

She threw her napkin on the table, Daddy stood up, and poor Mrs. B, wide-eyed, backed out the door, her arms full of dirty dishes. There was a long silence. Then Daddy came around the table and put his hand on Mama's elbow saying he thought it would be a good idea if she turned in early.

Mama pulled away and said, "For God's sake, Francis. Stop pestering me. Can't you just leave me alone?"

Grace winced. Daddy's face crumpled and for a terrible moment she thought he might cry. Instead, he held both hands up in front of him, turned, and left the room. A moment later, she heard the door of his study close. Mama slid her chair into the table and stood looking at Grace, her hands resting on the chair back.

She smiled weakly and said, "I think Daddy's right. I should turn in early. Would you tell Mrs. Blanchard I'm sorry I was short with her, and ask her to come upstairs?"

Dumbly, Grace nodded, still stunned by Mama's outburst. She wanted to ask if Mama was all right. She wanted to know what Mrs. Murphy had meant by "bad sign." But she didn't ask. Instead, she went in search of the housekeeper.

A while later, Grace was sitting at the window when Mrs. B came into the parlor. The sun was setting and the still bare trees stood in lacy, black silhouettes against the low-lying pink clouds. On the lawn, she watched a robin pause in his busy hopping and cock his head, his tail bobbing up and down. Before the housekeeper crossed the room, he'd flown away.

Mrs. Blanchard laid a warm hand on Grace's shoulder. "Your mother's resting now, Gracie. I've given her a dose of tonic that will help her sleep."

"Is something wrong, Mrs. B ... with the baby, I mean?"

"No need to fret, dear. Your mother's tired is all. She'll be right as rain in the morning."

Grace turned her gaze back to the window. That was exactly the kind of answer she had expected, and she didn't believe it for a minute. Something was wrong with Mama, she was sure, and she was just as sure no one was going to tell her what it was.

Not for the first time, Grace wished she had a brother or sister to talk to, someone close to her own age to help her figure out what was going on, another pair of eyes and ears to help her unravel the mysterious, secret world of adults. Mary's parents, she knew, couldn't keep much from their children. The house was so small and the family so big, that everything was out in the open. If Mary didn't understand what her parents were talking about, all she had to do was ask Agnes or Paddy and they'd explain. No one told Grace anything.

Through the window she watched the shadows darken and the light fade. The house was quiet. Mrs. Blanchard, after telling Grace it was time for bed, had retreated to her third-floor apartment. Daddy was still in his study. A terrible emptiness settled on Grace, a hollowed-out feeling like something had been gnawing at her insides. The mantel clock struck nine and she sighed. Reluctantly she left the parlor, stopping at Daddy's door to whisper good-night.

In her room, Grace switched on the bedside lamp and began to undress. As she slipped her nightgown over her head, she caught sight of Sally, her old doll, sitting in her usual place in the rocking chair. Impulsively, she picked the doll up and held her close, but Sally's stiff, cold limbs offered no comfort. She put the doll back and climbed into bed.

When Grace woke some time later, wind howled through the trees and icy rain pinged against the windows. The gust of wind that had woken her was followed by a sharp crack and an unearthly scream. Grace sat up in bed trying to make sense of what she was hearing. Crossing to the window, she peered out at the storm. Wind-driven sleet splattered against the window, rattling the panes. Then she heard the scream again, louder this time, a sound that made her spine tingle.

"Mrs. Blanchard, Mrs. Blanchard come quick!" Daddy's voice rose above the storm, sending Grace to her door.

Mrs. Blanchard was hurrying down the last few steps from the third floor, her dressing gown billowing out behind her. Grace followed her to Mama's room and stopped, stunned by what she saw.

Daddy was leaning over the bed, holding Mama's hand. The blankets were tossed aside and Mama lay on her side, her legs drawn into her chest, a dark stain soaking the sheet under her. She was crying, making sounds that Grace had never heard before, waves of strangled sobs and piercing howls of pain. Terrified, Grace clamped her hands over her ears, but she couldn't tear her eyes away from the scene on the bed.

"Call the doctor, Mrs. Blanchard, quick. Tell him it's an emergency. I think Mrs. Montel's gone into labor. Go on! Hurry!"

Rooted to her spot just inside the door, Grace was hardly aware of Mrs. Blanchard's rush from the room. She stared at Mama's contorted features, at Daddy leaning over the blood-soaked bed, at the rain-lashed windows. Surely, Mama couldn't be having the baby tonight. It was way too early, weeks and weeks before the baby was due.

Another violent gust of wind shook the house. Again, Mama cried out, a long anguished keening more of heartbreak than of fear.

Grace moved quickly toward the bed.

"Gracie," Daddy yelled. "Gracie, get out. Get out, I tell you." But Grace just stood staring at her parents, unable to move, hardly able to breathe.

"The doctor is on his way, Mr. Montel," Mrs. Blanchard called from the doorway. "Gracie, what are you doing here?"

"For God's sake, woman, get that child out of here!"

Throwing off the covers, Grace sat on the side of her bed and turned on the lamp. The windows were shut tight against the October chill, the curtains drawn to keep out the dark, but the image of Mama in the blood-soaked bed was impossible to shut out. Grace had told Jerome about her dead baby brother, but there was more she had not told him.

Jerome didn't know that when Daddy came home from the baby's burial, Mama had refused to see him. He'd wanted to tell her about the graveside service, but she told him to please go away. All she wanted was to be left alone. For days after, Mama had lain in bed, staring at the ceiling, refusing food and company. Grace swallowed, remembering the loneliness of those weeks following the death of her baby brother. Like a ghost haunting the hallways, she'd wandered through the silent house from Mama's bedroom to Daddy's study, listening at closed doors.

Her father took to sleeping in his study. Grace pictured him slumped in his easy chair, the fire burning low, the empty decanter on the end table. In the mornings, Mrs. Blanchard woke him with a brisk knock on the door and Grace, dressing for school, would hear him make his way upstairs. As she finished the last of her breakfast, Daddy would appear freshly bathed and shaved, an unconvincing smile fixed on his ravaged face.

In those first weeks after the baby's death, Grace saw little of Mama. Her bedroom door remained closed to all but Mrs. Blanchard and Doctor Halvorson. Some days after school if Mama was awake and felt up to it, Grace was allowed to visit, but these visits left her feeling sad and afraid. Mama didn't complain, but the life was gone from her voice. Her eyes had lost their shine, her hands felt limp and cold.

Grace learned to dread the long, quiet evenings of the lengthening days. She did homework in her room or read snuggled into a corner of the sofa, filled with the desolation of the big house. Sometimes she could persuade Mrs. B to play a card game or work a puzzle, but Grace knew the housekeeper's time was her own once Mama had been settled for the night, and she didn't like to impose.

One evening in early June, she sat at the open parlor window breathing in the sweet scent of lilacs blooming on the old bush at the side of the house. The setting sun painted broad strokes of light across the lawn and Grace could hear the shouts and laughter of kids who had yet to be called inside. She decided to go out to the street and see what they were up to. There was no one to stop her and she was tired of sitting here by herself.

She crossed the parlor and was entering the foyer when she saw Daddy on the stairs. He was moving slowly, gripping the hand rail, taking one careful step at a time. Standing in the shadows, she watched him gain the landing and turn toward Mama's room. She moved closer to the bottom of the stairs and listened.

Accustomed to Daddy's gentle knock and quiet request for entry, Grace heard, instead, loud, insistent pounding on the bedroom door and harsh demands to be admitted.

"Evelyn, Evelyn, wake up. I want to talk to you. I'm coming in."

Grace hurried up the carpeted stairs and, crouching on the top step, pressed herself against the newel post. Peeking down the hall, she saw Mama's door ajar and heard Daddy's voice from within the room.

"Evelyn, you can't shut me out anymore," his voice was pleading, his speech slightly slurred. "I need you. Gracie needs you. We can't go on like this." Grace heard the floor creak as Daddy moved further into the room. "It's time you got out of that bed." To Grace, he sounded angry, but more than that, he sounded desperate. She couldn't make out Mama's murmured response, but her father continued in the same tones.

"I talked to Doctor Halvorson today. He said you need to get up out of that bed or else you're just going to keep getting weaker and weaker. If you won't get up on your own, then by God, I'll get you up!"

Mama let out a cry. Jumping up, Grace ran to the doorway. The blankets were thrown back and Daddy was gripping Mama's arm, pulling her toward the edge of the bed. Mama was holding tight to the bedpost and begging him to stop.

Without thinking, Grace rushed into the room. She grabbed her father's arm, shouting, "Daddy stop! You'll hurt Mama! Stop!"

Roughly, he shook her off, his face knotted and dark. Grace stumbled and fell back against the bureau. Her head slammed into the corner of the dresser and she screamed, as much from shock as from pain, and crumpled onto the floor.

Daddy dropped Mama's arm and looked down at Grace. For an instant, he didn't move, just looked at her as if he didn't know how she got there. Then he was kneeling by her side, lifting her away from the bureau, cradling her in his arms. "Gracie, Gracie, are you all right? I'm sorry, sweetie, I ... I didn't mean to hurt you. Are you all right?"

From the bed, Mama struggled to sit up. "Gracie are you hurt? Oh, Francis, what have you done?"

"I'm okay," she said, sitting up and gingerly touching the back of her head. Her fingers came away clean, but the spot was tender.

Daddy helped her stand and led her to the bed. Mama held out her arms and Grace, snuggling against her, began to sob. She wasn't hurt, not really, but she couldn't stop crying. Mama held her, murmuring, "There, there, sweetie." Daddy sat on the edge of the bed, rubbing her back, saying he was sorry again and again. It was a long time before the tears stopped and when they finally did, Grace was exhausted.

She lay between her mother and father, trying to untangle her jumbled feelings. She was angry at Daddy for what he'd done to Mama and for the way he'd shaken her off and made her fall. She was sorry for Mama, sorry that she'd lost the baby, but it had been a long time since Mama had held her, a long time since she'd even noticed her. And Daddy was right, Grace needed Mama.

Tenderly, her mother explored the bruised spot on Grace's head. She frowned and said, "Francis, we need to get some ice on this, it's already beginning to swell. Would you go down to the kitchen and fix a compress?" Her voice was kind and she smiled. "Otherwise Gracie's going to sprout a great big goose egg back there."

Daddy touched Grace's cheek and looked at Mama for a long moment. "I'll be right back. You girls just lie there and rest." He walked to the door and stopped. Without looking at them he said, "I'm sorry. I don't know what got into me. I just — "

"It's going to be all right, Francis." Mama said. "Hurry back."

Late the next morning, Mama got out of bed for the first time in weeks. She sat in the easy chair by the window and Grace read to her from the newspaper. In the afternoon, she got up again and Mrs. Blanchard steadied her while she walked the length of the upstairs hallway. That evening Daddy didn't go into his study. Instead, he invited Grace to take a walk with him.

The dusky air was mild and alive with birdsong. Turning onto Pleasant Street, her father suggested they stop in and say hello to Grandma and Grandpa. As they passed under the elms lining the street, Grace paused. Looking up, she felt her spirit rise and mingle with their leafy canopies, vivid green against the indigo sky.

In the days that followed, Grace felt her tattered family begin to mend. Mama returned to the dining room for the evening meal after which the three of them listened to the gramophone or took turns reading aloud until Mama went to bed. Grace and her father often went for walks if the weather was nice, stopping off at the recreation field to watch a softball game or the soda fountain for a cone.

Daddy's awful outburst that night in Mama's bedroom had changed things for Grace. Her parents had come out of their separate rooms and the three of them had come together as a family again. It was as though Mama and Daddy had finally stopped brooding about the child they'd lost and remembered the one they still had.

Doctor Halvorson had said that Mama would get better if she got out of bed, but he'd been wrong. In spite of her daily exercise with Mrs. Blanchard and her visits to the dinner table, in spite of trying to take a more active role in the household, Mama did not get better. Finally, Daddy spoke to another physician who arranged an appointment for Mama with a specialist at Dartmouth Medical Hospital. Mrs. Blanchard accompanied Grace's mother and father to Hanover for a consultation. The news was not good.

Daddy and Mrs. B returned the next day, but Mama was admitted to the hospital where she began radiation therapy to treat a cancerous tumor. She came home a week later, and the following month returned to the hospital for what turned out to be the final treatment. The specialist told Daddy that the radiation failed to shrink the tumor and the disease had spread. There was nothing more he could do.

Mama came home and Dr. Halvorson resumed his regular visits, prescribing medication to ease the pain and help her sleep. Of course, Grace knew about the specialist and the hospital stays, but it was her mother who told her about the cancer. She didn't tell Grace she was going to die, but she didn't have to. Grace knew.

The doorknob turned and Grace found herself sitting on the edge of her bed. Her feet were freezing and her muscles tight with cold. Turning toward the door she saw Daddy, his brow creased with worry.

"Gracie," he said, crossing the room, "Gracie, honey, are you all right? He sat down beside her and wrapped his arm around her shoulder, pulling her close. "What are you doing up at this hour? Did you have a bad dream?"

She shivered. "Not exactly."

5

FALL INTO WINTER

Towards the end of October, the weather turned sharply colder and Grace and Jerome had to abandon the tree house. Some days they headed to the town library after school, where they did homework or hunkered down with their favorite books in the Reading Room. Mrs. Proudie discouraged conversation, so if Grace and Jerome wanted to talk over their work or discuss books, they settled for one or the other's kitchen table.

One afternoon just before Halloween, Jerome invited Grace to his house where he promised her a surprise. They walked with their hands jammed in their pockets. The wind off the river swirled the fallen leaves into little tornados and snaked icily down their necks. Heading around to the back door, they found Jerome's mother in the kitchen, her apron covered with flour and the smell of something delicious baking in the oven.

"Now, if you two don't look chilled to the bone," she said. "I've got some hot chocolate here that will warm you right up."

Grace didn't have to be asked twice. She took a seat at the table and wrapped her frozen fingers around the warm mug, taking a tentative sip. "Mmm, thank you, Mrs. Davison. This is delicious. It's gotten so cold all of a sudden."

"It's not so sudden," Jerome teased. "It's practically November."

Grace screwed up her mouth and rolled her eyes. "So, what's this surprise you told me about?"

She watched Jerome cast a sidelong glance at his mother, who winked at him. Reaching into an overhead cupboard, Mrs. Davison pulled out a metal tray, set a plate of cookies on it and added two luncheon napkins.

"Here you go, Jerome," she said. "Set your mugs on this and take it with you. No need to keep Grace in suspense any longer."

Jerome took up the tray and Grace followed him out of the kitchen and into the hallway that ran the length of the house and led to a flight of stairs. They took the stairs to the second floor and then climbed another, steeper flight to a short landing on the third floor. Stopping in front of a door, Jerome grinned at Grace. There was a sign on the door that said, "Headquarters."

Grace wondered what Jerome was up to now. "Go ahead in," he said. "This tray is getting heavy."

The room was small, lit by a dormer and a circular window of stained glass. Jerome set the tray on a table in the center of the room and turned on a lamp on the nearby bookshelf. In the far corner of the room, two shabby upholstered chairs sat catty-corner to each other, a small table between them. A radiator hissed against the opposite wall.

"Well, what do you think?" Jerome asked. "It was a maid's room, but my parents said I could use it for a study. My dad helped me with the painting. Most of the furniture was left in the barn by the people we bought the place from. It was some job getting it down from the loft and up two flights of stairs, I can tell you."

Grace spun around, taking everything in. "Oh Jerome, it's wonderful! And so cozy and warm." Taking up her mug of cocoa, she settled in one of the easy chairs. "Sure beats the tree house this time of year."

Taking his place in the opposite chair, Jerome grinned. "And no Mrs. Proudie to tell us to be quiet, either."

In the following weeks, Grace spent more and more time at the Davisons'. The house was so much more welcoming than her own. For one thing, there was a mother stationed in the kitchen, ready with a cup of something hot and a taste of something delicious. Mrs. Davison loved hearing about their school day and Jerome did not disappoint; he always had a story to tell. If nothing interesting had happened, he made something up. It didn't matter if the story was true, it only mattered that his mother enjoyed it.

After their snack they went up to Headquarters to do homework. When their assignments were finished, they played checkers or drew pictures or just talked. Their teacher, Mrs. Thurston, encouraged her class to memorize poems or passages from literature and held recitations in class and at school assemblies. Grace and Jerome spent the dark winter afternoons poring over poetry collections and the works of Shakespeare, looking for pieces to learn. They had contests to see who could memorize the most lines in the shortest time and made each other laugh using silly accents and dialects.

Once in a while, Grace was invited to have dinner with the Davisons. She was fond of Mrs. Davison, whose warmth and kindness helped to fill the empty space left by Mama's passing. Mr. Davison was easygoing and quiet. He liked to engage Jerome in conversations on all kinds of topics from school, to politics, to the latest dance craze. They talked about Mr. Coolidge and even discussed the possibility that a law prohibiting the sale of alcohol might pass.

Most evenings, though, Grace had dinner alone with Daddy. Sometimes they talked about school, but mostly they talked about the shop. Daddy was deep into plans to expand the store and Grace couldn't remember ever seeing him so excited about Montel's. She'd often suspected that he was bored with the work, tired of fitting suits and trying to please customers, but now the shop took all his attention. A work crew was already busy in the old tobacconist's space and once the wall between the two rooms was down, the Haberdashery would be almost twice as big as it was now.

Grandpa had made it known to anyone who'd listen that he was opposed to the expansion. They'd taken out a big loan with Mr. Evans at the bank and he was sure they wouldn't increase their profits enough to pay it off. They'd wind up in the hole, running in the red, something that Great-grandfather Montel had always warned him against. Daddy saw things differently. A bigger store meant a bigger inventory and a bigger inventory meant bigger sales. Grace hoped he was right, but she put a lot of trust in Grandpa's judgment. Her father could get carried away sometimes.

In late February, Daddy went alone to Boston on a buying trip. He and Grandpa had argued about the new departments he was adding to the shop. Her grandfather said no one in town was going to buy fancy cigarette cases or high-priced shaving kits. Daddy said there were plenty of up-and-coming fellows in Chester who were ready to look the part of the prosperous businessman or municipal official. Grandpa shook his head and said he'd stay home.

Grace went to the train station with her father the morning he left. It was a frigid February day and they stood in the station until the train pulled in. Daddy kissed her good-bye and said he'd be home by dinnertime on Monday. On the way home, Grace stopped in to see Grandma. She knew Grandpa would be at the shop and she wanted to talk to her grandmother alone.

Letting herself in, Grace took off her coat and boots and climbed the stairs. She stopped in the doorway of Grandma's sitting room and knocked gently on the door casing.

"Why, good morning, Grace. What brings you out so early and on such a cold day, too?"

"I went to the station with Daddy to see him off. He's left for his buying trip." She crossed to the hearth and stood with her back to the fire, watching Grandma finish her letter. When she'd slipped the folded sheet into the envelope, Grace said, "I don't like that he's gone to Boston alone, Grandma. I wish Grandpa would have gone with him. Surely, Raymond could have minded the store."

Grandma fixed the cap on her fountain pen and moved to the settee. She sat down and patted the spot next to her.

"You heard that discussion your father and grandfather had last Sunday when you came for dinner. Grandpa made it clear he wouldn't go."

"But if he's worried about what Daddy will buy, wouldn't it be better for him to go and, I don't know, keep an eye on things?"

Her grandmother chuckled softly, but Grace wasn't trying to be funny, she was trying to understand.

Grandma shifted in her seat and took Grace's hand. "That's a sensible suggestion, Grace, but I'm afraid at times your father and grandfather are anything but sensible." She shook her head. "If Grandpa had gone, they probably wouldn't have agreed on anything. This way, at least the orders will be made and there'll be inventory to fill the new space." She sighed. "Your grandfather has been against this expansion right from the start. His father started the business as a general store nearly sixty years ago. Grandpa turned it into the Haberdashery and made a success of it. He doesn't see why it needs to change."

"But Daddy says it's time for the store to enter the 20th century. He says the business has to expand in order to keep growing. Is he wrong about that?"

"I really couldn't say, Grace. I don't pretend to know much about business, but I do know your father. He's impulsive and sometimes his enthusiasms get away from him. He's not always as cautious as he could be."

Grace nodded. She'd lived with Daddy long enough to know that what Grandma said was true.

"Your grandfather worries that your father will get in over his head and won't be able to meet his loan obligations. He thinks he's taking on too much and should bring new inventory in slowly." She frowned. "Grandpa is as careful as your father is hasty. And they're both equally stubborn."

On the morning her father was due home from Boston, Grace walked to school under an unbroken mass of clouds, heavy with the threat of snow. She hoped the storm would hold off until Daddy got home, but by late morning, snow was falling in earnest, melting against the classroom windows and piling up on the outside sills. Grace walked home that afternoon through deserted streets, veiled and muffled by the mounting snow.

Grace's worries mounted, too. Would the train be able to move over the snow-covered tracks? What if it got stuck somewhere, or worse, derailed? Visions of broken bodies scattered across a wilderness of drifting snow filled her head. She pushed them away and scolded herself for being a ninny.

As soon as she got home, she went in search of Mrs. Blanchard. The housekeeper was in the sewing room taking down the hem on a wool plaid skirt Grace had hoped never to wear again.

"Why Grace, I didn't even hear you come in. How is it out there?"

"It's coming down hard, Mrs. B. I'm kind of worried about Daddy. Do you think the train will be able to make it through this storm all right?"

"Oh, I'm sure everything will be fine, dear. After all, it's not a blizzard so there won't be a lot of drifting, but I imagine the going will be slow. I expect the train will be delayed, but I doubt that your father's in any danger." She smiled. "There's a snack on the table for you and you may as well join me in the kitchen for supper. Your father's unlikely to make it back by dinnertime. We'll make up a plate for him just in case, but I expect he'll take his meal in the dining car."

Mrs. Blanchard was probably right. Probably the train would be late, but Daddy would be fine. Grace thanked the housekeeper and headed downstairs. In the kitchen, she bit into a molasses cookie and made a face. Tough and dry, just like everything else poor Mrs. B baked. When she lifted the lid of the big Dutch oven though, the savory aroma of chicken stew filled the warm kitchen. She replaced the lid, finished her cookie and went up to start on her homework.

When Grace joined Mrs. Blanchard in the kitchen, the housekeeper was dropping dumplings onto the top of the bubbling stew. The room was cozy and she sat at the scrubbed table picturing the lighted train snaking its way through the dark and snowy evening. She hoped Daddy would be home soon. After dinner, she made up a plate for her father and helped Mrs. Blanchard with the dishes before heading into the parlor to wait for him.

At the front window, Grace peered out into the winter dark where the streetlights illuminated the fast-falling snow. There was no sign of Daddy or anyone else on the empty street, so she settled onto the sofa with her book, an afghan pulled over her against the chill of the dying fire.

She woke sometime later to the sound of Daddy stomping snow off his boots in the front hall. Tossing off the afghan, she hurried to meet him.

"Daddy, I'm so glad you're home." She reached up to kiss his cheek.

"It's a wild one out there, Gracie. Snow's piling up fast," he said, brushing snow off his hat.

"I was getting worried, Daddy. You're so late." Helping him off with his overcoat, she caught the mingled smell of tobacco and wet wool.

"Sorry to worry you, sweetie. It was slow going, but we made the best of it." He grinned. "Ate in the dining car and then played poker with a few fellows to pass the time. It wasn't so bad."

His face was flushed, his eyes heavy-lidded and bloodshot. He wrapped a heavy arm around her shoulders and they went into the parlor. Squatting in front of the fire, he stirred the embers back to life before adding more wood. Grace took her place on the sofa.

"How did the buying go, Daddy?"

Her father straightened and returned the poker to its stand. "Wait till you see what I bought, Gracie. Montel's Haberdashery's going to have the finest inventory of luxury men's furnishings between here and Boston." He stood, one hand on the mantel and the other in his trouser pocket, watching the fire until the coals ignited the fresh logs. Then he turned and grinned at her. "Can't say your grandfather will be too pleased, but I'm running the place now." His tone was defiant. "He'll just have to get used to my way of doing things."

Grace watched him cross to the sideboard. She hated to hear Daddy talk about Grandpa that way, but then, she didn't understand why her grandfather was so against the expansion. They both cared about the business, but they were always at odds. Why couldn't they just get along? Stubborn, that's what Grandma said and Grace supposed it was true. And if Grandma couldn't make them see reason, then no one could. She sighed and watched her father fill his glass.

During the rest of February and into March, Grace saw little of her father. He left for work just as she was coming down to breakfast and returned from the shop long after closing time. In the evenings, he pored over catalogs choosing fixtures and shelving and puzzled over paint colors. He met with the builder before and after store hours and wrangled with wholesalers about pricing and deliveries. Daddy had always talked about the shop a lot, but now he talked of nothing else.

One blustery March evening, Grace was reading in the parlor when she heard the front door slam. As soon as her father entered the room, she could tell something was wrong. There were deep lines between his brows and along the sides of his mouth. With barely a greeting, he crossed to the sideboard, sloshed whiskey into a glass and downed half of it. She watched him warily, afraid to speak. Draining his glass, he set it back on the tray with such force he nearly upset the decanter.

"Well, Gracie," he said, turning to her, "we're in a fine pickle now. This afternoon the builder told me they'd uncovered some major structural problems in the new space. The landlord won't touch it. Says if I want the wall removed that's my business, and I'll have to pay for it." He crossed the room and threw himself into an arm chair. "Looks like we'll have to take out an additional loan."

"Will the bank give you another loan, Daddy?"

"Oh, Evans is dying to lend me the money. That's not the problem." He ran his hands through his hair, making it stand on end. Grace waited. "Your grandfather's the problem. Evans wants him to co-sign the loan and I don't think he'll do it."

Grace didn't think Grandpa would either, but she wasn't about to say so. Her mind raced back to Grandma saying Grandpa was worried about meeting their loan obligations. It seemed unlikely that he'd be willing to sign on for more debt.

"Blast!" The sound broke the silence, startling Grace. "This is all I need." He slapped the arms of his chair and got to his feet. "Might as well get this over with. See what the old man has to say."

"Daddy," Grace said, getting up from the sofa, "I'm sure Mrs. B has dinner ready. Why not eat something first and then telephone Grandpa? He and Grandma are probably in the middle of dinner by now and you know how Grandma is about interruptions at meal time."

To her relief, her father laughed. "You got a point there, sweetie. No reason to ruffle the old girl's feathers and make a bad situation worse."

During dinner, Grace tried to soften her father's mood. She told him about the auditions Mrs. Thurston had held for the class play that was scheduled for the end of May.

"We're doing *Oliver Twist*, Daddy, and Jerome tried out for the Artful Dodger. You should have heard his cockney accent! No one else can do it nearly as well. I'm sure he'll get the part."

Her father pushed his food around on the plate, but didn't eat much. He wasn't really listening either, because he asked her twice what part she wanted even though she'd already told him she tried out for one of Fagin's pickpockets. Daddy was thinking about the telephone call to Grandpa and so was she.

As soon as Mrs. Blanchard cleared the dishes, Daddy went straight to the telephone. From her place on the sofa, Grace couldn't see into the foyer, but she could easily hear his end of the conversation. At first, she thought things were going well. She could tell her father was trying to be reasonable, saying that the wall between the two spaces was load-bearing and would need to be replaced with a heavy beam. This would require more extensive work on the ceiling as well.

Neither the builder nor the landlord had anticipated these changes, so the expenses had not figured into the original budget. No, there was no way to complete the renovations without this step and yes, the wall had to be removed. No, he couldn't cut out other expenses to make up the difference, he'd already tried that. And what would be the point of canceling the orders for new inventory? He needed the inventory, for God's sake.

Every time Grandpa asked a question, Daddy's voice got louder until he was practically shouting into the mouthpiece.

"Don't you understand, Dad? We need this loan to finish the expansion and that means borrowing more money. And the only way we can borrow more money is if you co-sign the loan. It has to be done and you have to do it."

Grace's heart sank. Telling Grandpa what he had to do was the worst thing Daddy could have done. He'd never agree to sign for the loan now.

"Forget it, then," she heard her father shout. "I'll raise the money without your help." He slammed the earpiece onto its hook so hard he made the telephone bell ring. Then his study door banged shut and Grace let out her breath.

Daddy didn't come down to breakfast the next morning and Grace left for school without seeing him. That evening, he returned even later than usual, but seemed in better spirits. He'd met with Mr. Evans at the bank and had taken out a loan to cover the balance of the renovations.

Grace had no idea how her father had managed to get Mr. Evans to agree to the loan. It would be years before she found out.

On Thursday afternoon, just before the final bell, Mrs. Thurston told the class that she had nearly completed the casting for *Oliver Twist* and that the results would be posted on the bulletin board the following morning. In the cloakroom at dismissal, kids were talking about who would get what part, though most everyone thought Jerome would be the Dodger and that Roland Devereau, the tallest, skinniest boy in the class, would be Fagin. The big questions were who would play Oliver and who would be the arch villain, Bill Sykes. Grace and Jerome were still talking about the play when they reached Headquarters.

"I'm betting on Bobby Thorne for Sykes," Jerome said.

"Are you kidding? Mrs. Thurston would never pick him. I mean, he's big and scary, all right, but he can hardly read and he mumbles so you can barely understand him."

"True, but getting the part might make him work harder." Jerome dropped his books on the table. "You know Mrs. Thurston, she doesn't do anything just for the fun of it. This whole play idea is just another way to get us to buckle down and learn more." He grinned. "She's not getting us ready for Broadway, you know."

Grace laughed. "I guess you're right. All I have to say is if Mrs. Thurston manages to get Bobby Thorne to memorize lines and speak so people can understand him, she'll really have accomplished something." She shrugged. "Well, I guess if anyone can get Bobby to shape up, it'll be Mrs. T."

They were sitting in the corner easy chairs finishing their snacks when Jerome asked how things were coming along at the shop. Right from the start, he'd taken an interest in the renovations and he and Grace often stopped into Montel's to follow the progress of the work.

Grace frowned into her cup and sighed. "They're just about ready to take down the wall between the two shops, but now the builder's run into trouble." She kicked off her shoes and pulled her feet under her. "That means my father needs to borrow more money. Mr. Evans said he'd lend Daddy the money if my grandfather would co-sign the loan, but he refused. The two of them had an awful row on the telephone." She shrugged. "Then I guess Mr. Evans changed his mind about the co-signing because the next day Daddy got the loan." She looked at Jerome.

"Or maybe your dad found someone else to sign for it," Jerome said. He set his empty cup on the tray, sat down at the table, and opened his geography book.

Grace stayed huddled in her chair, wondering who that someone might be and what Grandpa would think when he found out.

6

TWISTS AND TURNS

It was still dark when Grace woke the following morning. The Baby Ben on her bedside table read just short of six. In a few hours, she and her classmates would know who had been cast in the play. It was too early to get up, so she lay thinking, aware of a fluttery feeling in her stomach. There were only a few female parts in *Oliver Twist*, but there were lots of orphans in Fagin's band of thieves, so she and several other girls had tried out for those parts, too. Grace knew just which orphan she wanted to play.

She was already at the table when Daddy came down to breakfast. He looked very handsome this morning in his blue serge with the blue and silver tie she liked. Surprised to see her up so early, he planted a noisy kiss on her forehead and said, "Well, to what do I owe this honor, Gracie? I haven't seen you up this early in ages. No, wait, don't tell me." He held up a hand giving her a devilish grin. "This is the day you finally find out which of Mr. Dickens' lowlife characters you'll be playing." He shook out his napkin and tucked it into his stiff collar. "Now, let's see, it was Nancy right? I think you'd be perfect for the part."

Grace rolled her eyes and made a face. It had been a long time since Daddy had been in such a good mood. "Oh, don't be silly, Daddy. You know I don't want to be Nancy. I tried out to be one of the orphans."

Pouring himself a cup of coffee, her father frowned. "Still seems like an odd choice of play for a bunch of seventh graders. Why, in my day, we stuck to Greek myths, *Icarus* and *Jason and the Golden Fleece*, stories of heroes and gods. Now it's pickpockets and thieves and ladies of the night." He tut-tutted and shook his head in mock horror.

Grace stirred maple syrup into her oatmeal and in her best snooty voice said, "I'll have you know that according to Mrs. Thurston, Charles Dickens is one of the most important authors in the English language and that educated people should know his work. Furthermore, she says *Oliver Twist* is the perfect introduction for young people. She told us that Dickens wrote about real people in real situations and there's a lot to be learned about life from his stories."

"Sounds like your Mrs. Thurston has a lot to say. I'm sure she's right about Dickens, but there's plenty of time for you to learn about the seamy side of life. I just think she's rushing it, that's all." He smiled at her over the rim of his cup, his blue eyes bright. "Anyway, I hope you get the part you want, sweetie. Just don't practice your pick-pocketing skills on me, all right?"

Grace was already in line when she saw Jerome approach the schoolyard. He took his place opposite her in the boys' line and made a great show of reaching into his trouser pocket. He pulled out a thin, gold coin and held it up for her to see.

"It's too late for good-luck charms, Jerome," she said. "I'm sure Mrs. Thurston's list is already posted and your special coin isn't going to magically change what's on it."

Mary, standing behind Grace, added, "We're the ones needing good-luck charms, Gracie. Jerome's a shoo-in for Jack Dawkins. You just watch, he's going to steal the show."

Jerome swept off his cap and bowed low. "Much obliged to you, Mary, but it won't do to try to second-guess the honorable Mrs. Thurston. She's got her own way of thinking that we mere mortals can't hope to understand."

Before Jerome had completed this speech, Mrs. Thurston stepped out of the door and took her place in front of her seventh graders. She silenced the class with a raised hand and glowered at Jerome.

"That's correct, Mr. Davison. You may trust that my choices have been made with the utmost pedagogical consideration and are not subject to discussion." She gave him a playful smile and said, "Now class, the parts for *Oliver Twist* are listed on the back bulletin board. Try not to injure yourself or anyone else in your haste to locate your name on the list."

Everyone followed Mrs. Thurston into the building. Once inside, the teacher stepped aside, wisely Grace thought, and the class surged up the stairs treading on one another's heels along the way. By the time Grace reached the classroom, many of her classmates were already jostling for position in front of the bulletin board, so many, in fact, that all she could see was a score of bobbing heads. Loud whispering told her Jerome had gotten the part of the Dodger. And he'd been right; Bobby Thorne would play Sykes. Straining to see which of the orphans she'd been cast as, Grace stood on tiptoes, scanning Mrs. Thurston's list until she found her name.

Charley Bates, the Artful Dodger's sidekick. Perfect.

Though they were busy with the play, Grace and Jerome stopped by the shop every couple of days to check on the renovations. Daddy had told her that the wall between the two spaces was scheduled to be torn down on the last Saturday in April. That morning, Grace and Jerome worked with Raymond, Grandpa, and Daddy to empty out the shop. They boxed up merchandise, covered display cases, and carried as many of the movable furnishings to the storage room as they could manage. When they broke for lunch Daddy sent them home, saying the demolition of the wall was dangerous and he couldn't take a chance on one of them getting hurt. Jerome was disappointed, but Grace knew better than to argue.

Once the new beam was up, though, Daddy asked them to come over and help with the cleanup. "The place is a mess," he said. "So put on your work clothes and get there as early as you can. It's going to be a long day."

When Jerome and Grace stepped into the shop, plaster dust hung thick in the air and coated every surface. In the new section, sawdust drifted into corners, bits of wood and bent nails lay scattered over the floor, and unused materials were stacked against the walls. A tarpaulin hung between the two spaces, and while the carpenters cleared away their mess on one side, Daddy and his crew tried to put the other side to rights.

Grace and Jerome were assigned to work with Mrs. Murphy, the charwoman who regularly cleaned the building as well as their house. Surveying the space, Mrs. Murphy outlined what had to be done. "Well, first off," she said, resting her hands on her hips, "someone of you has to sweep up all this truck and litter off the floor. Then, one of youse will need to get them dust covers off and clean and polish the furnishings. I'll take care of the washing and polishing of the floor, but we won't get to that for a while." She looked from Grace to Jerome and frowned. "And take care to wrap them covers up good, so's you don't spread any extra dirt around ... and then take 'em out back and give 'em a good shake before you fold 'em up."

Jerome gave Mrs. Murphy a smart salute and with exaggerated care, began carrying out her directions. Grace stifled a smile and grabbed the broom as the charwoman bustled off to fetch her bucket and mop. The floor was thick with dirt. Grace attacked the mess vigorously and found herself in the midst of a small, but choking, dust storm. Jerome coughed loudly and fanned his hand in front of his face.

Waiting for the dust to settle, Grace considered a change in technique. She found that short, slow strokes of the broom kept the dust from billowing into the air and allowed her to push the dirt into a pile. It was tedious and she had to stop often to toss larger debris into the waste bin. The broom handle was too thick for her small hands and she soon had a blister forming on her palm.

Meanwhile, Jerome seemed to have his task well in hand. In no time, the dust covers were stacked in a neatly folded pile and he was carefully applying lemon oil to the newly cleaned furniture. Grace had finished sweeping and was helping Mrs. Murphy wash windows when disaster struck.

One of the workmen pushed aside a section of the tarpaulin divider looking for Grace's father. Spying him on the sidewalk, he crossed the freshly swept floor and opened the front door. As he did so, a huge cloud of dust from the construction side of the space was sucked into the nearly clean shop, spreading a layer of dirt onto the freshly oiled surfaces.

Jerome groaned and threw down his rag. He was still staring open-mouthed at the mess when the workman sauntered back through the shop, pulled the tarpaulin closed and disappeared into the other side. Grace looked at Jerome. He stared at the tarpaulin, his chest heaving, his face a dangerous shade of red. In all the months they'd known each other Grace had never seen Jerome so agitated. She'd marveled at the way he ignored the teasing of his classmates or fearlessly debated a point with Mrs. Thurston, and here he was mad as a hornet over a little dust. She couldn't help but laugh.

"You think this is funny?" he yelled. "I've spent an hour cleaning and oiling these shelves and now look at them." He ran his hand across the wood and held up a sticky palm. "Just look at this. How am I supposed to get this stuff off?"

Grace turned away, trying to compose herself, but it was no good. Now that the laughter had started, she couldn't stop it. Her eyes filled with tears and her sides ached. She knew Jerome was watching her, knew how angry and hurt he must be, but the laughter kept coming.

She heard him move toward the door and looked up to see him standing outside. As she watched, he headed up Main Street, hands shoved in his pockets, his shoulders hunched. Without thinking, Grace took off after him.

"Wait, Jerome," she called, but he kept walking. "Jerome, please wait. I'm sorry, really, I'm so sorry." Catching up with him, she grabbed his arm. He stopped, but didn't look at her.

Grace stepped in front of him. He didn't shake her off or walk away, but he still wouldn't look at her. He just stood there. "Jerome," she pleaded. "I didn't mean to laugh. Really I didn't. It was just that, I don't know, the way it happened and the look on your face. I — "

He looked at her then and she took a step back. His mouth was set in a hard line and his eyes were stony under his dark brows. She was a poor excuse for a friend. Here he was, all his hard work ruined, and all she could do was laugh.

"Jerome, please, listen to me. I am sorry. I know that doesn't change what happened. I should have stuck up for you, I wish I had, but ... . Please, Jerome, come back to the shop. We'll get that mess cleaned up in no time, you'll see." She stepped closer and raised her eyes to his.

Jerome let out a long breath. After a moment he said, "Okay, Monty, okay. What happened back there wasn't your fault, I know. But I was so mad at that fellow and when you laughed, I felt like you were taking his side."

Grace tipped her head and smiled. "It's me, Charley Bates, remember? I'll always be on your side."

She watched Jerome's face soften, saw the light come back into his eyes. He grinned. "Come on, let's go back to the shop. What do you say I call that fellow out and give him a good thrashing?"

"Great idea. Let's go."

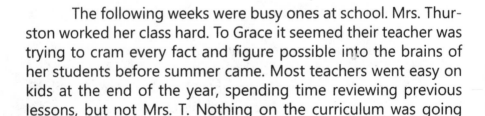

The following weeks were busy ones at school. Mrs. Thurston worked her class hard. To Grace it seemed their teacher was trying to cram every fact and figure possible into the brains of her students before summer came. Most teachers went easy on kids at the end of the year, spending time reviewing previous lessons, but not Mrs. T. Nothing on the curriculum was going to escape her notice; her students were going to be ready for eighth grade. But for the class, the play was the thing.

Rehearsals were scheduled to begin the second week of May and Mrs. Thurston expected everyone to have learned their lines by then. Grace and Jerome spent hours in Headquarters studying their parts and prompting each other through their recitations. Grace easily memorized Charley Bates's few lines, but acting the part of a London guttersnipe was a lot harder. Jerome, on the other hand, took to the role of the Artful Dodger like it had been written for him.

When he ran through his lines, Jerome became Jack Dawkins. It wasn't just the swagger and the accent, it was everything: the squinty eyes, the bow legs, even his long nose seemed to turn stubby. Grace thought him the very picture of Dickens' description of the Dodger. And there was more.

One warm afternoon she and Jerome left High Street, passing through a vacant lot and along a path leading to the Davisons' house. The shortcut was impassable in winter, but this time of year it was covered with fresh grass and sprinkled with tiny, white strawberry blossoms. The trees were bright with new foliage and filled with the chatter of birds and squirrels. Everywhere there was new growth and all of it made Grace's nose itch. At the back of his property, they helped each other over a section of sagging barbed-wire fence and into the Davisons' yard.

Up in Headquarters, Grace sat at the table working on an illustration for the program cover for *Oliver Twist*. Jerome was in one of the easy chairs reading passages of Dickens' novel, looking for ways to perfect his performance. He let out an exasperated breath and said, "You sure are doing a lot of sniffling over there, Monty. Do us a favor and blow, why don't you?"

Grace rubbed her nose and looked over at him. "Sorry. My hay fever is awful this year." She reached into the sleeve of her cardigan, but couldn't find the handkerchief she'd stuffed there earlier.

"Darn," she said fumbling in the other sleeve, "I must have lost my hanky. I know I had one when we left school. Mrs. B sends me out with two or three every morning. She hates sniffling." She shrugged and smiled apologetically.

"Here, I've got a clean one you can use." He pulled a small, lace-edged square from his pocket and shook it open.

"Hey, where did you get that? That's my hanky. How — ?"

"Hullo, my covey," he said grinning. "What's the row? If I didn't know better, I'd say you 'ad yer pocket picked."

------------◆◆◆------------

While Grace struggled to take on the persona of the Dodger's sidekick, her father was deep in preparations for the Grand Opening of the newly renovated and expanded Montel's Haberdashery. He spent hours hunched over his desk sketching floor plans and designing displays for the new merchandise. At dinner, he talked constantly about advertisements, inventory and displays, and railed against late shipments and unreliable suppliers. Even if he bothered to ask her a question about school or the play, he was too preoccupied to listen to her answer.

One evening on her way upstairs, Grace paused at the open door of her father's study and watched him work. His brow furrowed, he scribbled and scratched out and scribbled some more. The desk top was piled with stacks of catalogs and invoices and the waste bin overflowed with crumpled paper.

Lately, he'd been so tense that the air round him seemed to vibrate. Grace didn't know from one minute to the next what to expect from him. In an instant his confidence and high spirits could dissolve, his anger flare like a struck match. The mantel clock chimed the hour, and her father looked up from his work.

Grace took a step forward. "I just wanted to say good-night, Daddy. I'm heading up to bed."

"Come give your dad a kiss, honey," he said, holding out an arm.

Grace crossed the room and stood by his chair. He wrapped his arm around her waist and she leaned against him. His desk really was a mess. "Don't you think it's time to take a break, Daddy? You should get some sleep; you look awfully tired."

He rubbed his eyes and yawned. "You're right, Gracie. I am

tired and I've got an early meeting with Evans tomorrow at the bank." He shook his head. "This Grand Opening is already over budget, but you've got to spend money to make money. At least that's what they always say."

Grace didn't know who 'they' were, but she was pretty sure Grandpa was not one of them.

Ever since her grandfather had refused to co-sign the loan for the renovation's added expenses, Grace had seen less of Grandma and Grandpa. Grandpa had gone back to being retired, and she and Daddy no longer ate Sunday dinner with them. Grace missed those family gatherings and was anxious to see her father and grandfather reconciled. She didn't know how to mend the rift between the two men, but she knew who to ask.

On Saturday morning Grace headed to Pleasant Street for a chat with her grandmother. She wasn't surprised to see Gram wearing her gardening smock and gloves, working in the perennial bed bordering the front porch. It was unusual to see her grandfather there, too, standing over Grandma with his hands in his trouser pockets. He wasn't dressed for outdoor work, but wore his usual dark suit, a watch chain looped across his tightly buttoned vest.

As she came up to them, she heard her grandmother say, "For goodness sake, Henry, stop hovering. I've been tending this bed without your help for the past forty years. I'm not likely to need your advice now." Driving the trowel into the soil, she turned to look up at him and noticed Grace coming through the gate.

"Here's our Gracie come to visit, Grandpa," she said. "It's so nice to see you, dear. What brings you out on a Saturday morning?"

Giving her grandfather a peck on the cheek, Grace stooped to kiss her grandmother. "Oh, I just came by to say hello. How are you both?"

Gram got to her feet, brushed the dirt off her gloves, and tossed them into the wheelbarrow. "I'm fine, but it seems your grandfather doesn't know what to do with himself." Raising her eyebrows, she gave Grandpa a teasing look.

"Just a minute there," her grandfather said, tugging on his vest. "I just thought I'd point out that those phlox are taking over and should be thinned, that's all. And now you've gone and got yourself all worked up over a little free advice." He winked at Grace.

"And that's just about what it's worth," Grandma said. "Now, why don't we all go in and visit for a while?"

"Can't do that right now. I'm headed down to Smitty's to get the paper. Got to keep up with the news, you know. You ladies go in and I'll join you when I get back." He tipped his hat and strolled away.

When they were settled in the parlor, Grandma asked Grace how the play was coming along and what her plans were for the summer. Then she said, "Did your father tell you I stopped by the shop the other day? I wanted to see how the place was shaping up."

"No, he didn't mention that you'd been by." Grace frowned. "He's so distracted lately. Seems like the only thing he thinks about is the Grand Opening. I'll be glad when it's over." She sighed and ran her finger along the striped fabric of the sofa. "Daddy isn't himself these days, Grandma."

"What do you mean, Gracie?"

"I don't know exactly. He's just so worked up." She looked at her grandmother. "I can't explain it, but he makes me jumpy."

Gram sighed and patted Grace's hand. "Your father is out to prove something, Grace. He's put everything he has into this expansion. If it goes well, and I hope it does, he'll have proven to himself and to his father that he can successfully run the business on his own." She shook her head. "Francis has spent his life trying to live up to your grandfather's expectations. Trouble is, I'm not sure what it would take for him to do that. I'm not even sure your Grandpa knows."

"What don't I know?" Grace looked up to see her grandfather in the doorway, the newspaper tucked under his arm.

Without thinking, she said, "You don't know what it would mean to Daddy if you went over to the shop, Grandpa. He's got so much to do to get ready for the Grand Opening and well ..."

Seeing her grandfather's face, she paused, but Grandma gestured for her to continue. "Daddy needs your help, Grandpa."

Her grandfather cleared his throat and rocked back on his heels. "Did he send you over here to tell me that? If he needs my help, why doesn't he ask for it?"

"For heaven's sake, Henry, of course Francis didn't send Grace to ask for your help. Can't you see the child is worried about her father? We're both worried about him and you should be, too. This foolishness has gone on long enough." She stood up and fixed Grandpa with a look. "If you won't lend your son a hand, then I suppose I'll have to."

7

OPENINGS

Grandma and Grandpa glared at each other across the room. Looking from one to the other, Grace was sorry she'd blurted out that Daddy needed Grandpa's help. If her father found out what she'd said, he'd be mad, too. She'd come over to ask her grandmother's advice and instead she'd made a mess of things.

"I'm sorry," she stammered, "I didn't mean to — "

"Don't worry about it, dear." Grandma put an arm around Grace's shoulder and led her to the front door. "You were just trying to help. Now it's up to the adults in the family to sort things out." She kissed Grace's cheek. "You go on and enjoy your Saturday."

Once out on the street, Grace paused, wondering where to go next. There was nothing to do at home. Besides, the house was so big and empty, she felt like a marble in a shoebox rattling around in there alone. Jerome was in Massachusetts for the weekend and Mary was always busy looking after her little brothers and sisters. Heading up the street, she stopped at the corner, then turned right in the direction of Montel's.

A shortcut down the alley between Pleasant and Main led to the back of the shop. The door to the service entrance was open. Inside, a maze of cartons filled the hallway next to the new retail space. She found her father crouched on the floor near an open box, checking off items on a packing list. He looked up when she said hello.

"Grace," he said, sliding a pencil behind his ear, "you're a sight for sore eyes. How would you like to give your old dad a hand here? Raymond's wife is sick and he had to stay home to look after his little girl."

"I'd love to help, Daddy. Just tell me what to do."

Her father handed her a sheaf of packing slips. He showed her how to account for shipped, backordered, and missing items, then hurried off to the front of the shop.

Grace opened the largest of the cartons. Inside were stacks of hats, nestled one inside the other in neat piles. There were fedoras in black, brown, and grey, tweed, corduroy and broadcloth caps. Lifting a black derby out of the box, Grace carried it to a mirror and set it on her head. The hat slid down to rest on top of her ears, almost covering her eyes. Pushing it back off her forehead, she made a face at herself, laughing at her reflection. She finished checking off the hats on the packing slip and started on the next box.

This one contained leather and canvas carryalls, briefcases, and shaving kits. There were mother-of-pearl inlaid hair brushes and tortoiseshell combs, silver lighters, and black umbrellas with curved wooden handles. Grace was just wondering what Grandpa would make of all these fancy things when she heard a commotion in the next room and got up to investigate.

Grandma was laying a cloth over one of the display tables and Grandpa was standing near the doorway holding a large picnic hamper. Just then Daddy came in from the back room carrying a stack of wooden hangers. He stopped in his tracks and stared at his mother and father. For a long moment no one spoke. Grace held her breath wondering what would happen next.

Finally, Daddy dropped the hangers into a nearby box and wiped his hands down the sides of his trousers. "Well, this is a pleasant surprise. What brings you two here?"

"We've brought a picnic lunch," Grandma told him, taking the hamper from Grandpa. Grace watched her grandmother set the basket on the table and open the lid. She looked from her father to her grandfather wishing one of them would say something.

Grandpa cleared his throat. "I thought I might be able to make myself useful. Looks like you've got your hands full here."

Grace slipped into the darkened area behind the stage to join her classmates for opening night. Backstage, the cast was making last-minute adjustments to their costumes or going over their lines one more time. Mrs. Thurston was answering questions, giving final directions, and trying to quiet her agitated actors. The teacher peeked into the auditorium and reported that the seats were filling up nicely. Grace swallowed. Her father and grandparents were out there somewhere, a fact that did nothing to calm her nerves.

At a signal from Mrs. Thurston, Joey Fletcher struck a chord on the piano and the audience quieted. Two stagehands raised the painted curtain to reveal a dirty street fronted by a series of dingy, ramshackle buildings. Entering stage left, a rotund, uniformed fellow carrying a tall staff walked officiously down the street, trailed by a waiflike boy of about nine. Mr. Bumble, the beadle, was escorting the orphan, Oliver Twist, to his new situation with Mr. Sowerberry, the undertaker,.

Offstage, dressed in ragged knickers and oversized boots, her hair firmly tucked under a newsboy cap, Grace shifted uneasily, stomach squirming like a nest of snakes. She couldn't do this. She couldn't remember a single line or cue. Everything she'd learned was gone; her mind was blank. She rubbed her sweaty palms on her trousers and looked at Jerome. He gave her an encouraging smile, and whispered, "'Ave no fear, Master Bates, you'll come out all right. The Dodger will look after ye."

He was right. Grace did come out all right and so did the rest of the cast. The audience laughed at the swaggering Jack Dawkins, cheered Oliver's rescue by Mr. Brownlow, and hooted at the greedy Fagin. When the Dodger was apprehended and threatened with deportation, his friend Charley Bates recited the Artful's impressive list of misdeeds without bungling a single line.

The afternoon was sultry, much too warm for the first week in June. Grace ran her fingers through the condensation on her glass, laughing as Jerome tried and failed to catch the fly threatening their plate of snacks. Admitting defeat, Jerome leaned back against the opposite wall and chewed thoughtfully on a cookie.

"I remember the first time I came here," he said. "It was pretty soon after we met in the library that day." He grinned. "It's a good thing there was only one copy of that book or you might never have talked to me."

"I wanted to," Grace said. "I'd watched how the other boys teased you and how you just ignored them. I thought that was a pretty smart way of getting them to stop bothering you."

"Oh, they bothered me, but I wasn't going to let them know it." He shrugged. "Besides, I was curious about you. After Mrs. Thurston told us about your mother's passing, I kept thinking what that would be like. And you were so quiet, I was afraid to talk to you."

"I dreaded starting school. I thought everyone would look at me like I had two heads, but Mrs. Thurston knew just what to do." Grace sighed and gazed out the window opening. "The house still feels empty without her. My mother, I mean."

"I know who you mean, Monty. I can't imagine life without my mother. She does everything for my dad and me."

"Your mother is special, Jerome," she smiled, "and not just because she makes the best pies and cookies in town." Grace took a sip of lemonade and set her glass down. "I like your father, too, of course. He seems so steady and reliable."

Grace was quiet, watching the play of light on the wooden floor boards. "My father's good to me, but he's kind of unpredictable. Sometimes I wish he was a little calmer. My grandmother says he's impulsive. She says he gets carried away and I guess she should know. She raised him."

"Your dad's got a lot of energy, that's for sure," Jerome said. "When we were helping with the renovations at the shop, it seemed like he was everywhere at once." He chuckled. "My dad's the tortoise. Yours is the hare."

In early July, Jerome and his mother left Chester for Cape Cod. Mrs. Davison's parents owned a summer home there, and every summer Jerome's aunts, uncles, cousins, and grandparents gathered for a month at the beach. Mr. Davison and most of the other men in the family spent just a week or so there, but for Jerome and his cousins the days at the beach stretched out before them like the sand at low tide.

Grace had known for months that Jerome would be away during the whole of July, but she hadn't let herself think much about it. Now that he was gone, she realized how much she'd come to rely on his company. She missed their hikes and bike rides, missed visiting with his mother at the Davisons' kitchen table, but mostly she missed their quiet times reading, sketching, or just talking. It was, also, the first summer she'd spent at home since Mama died and the echoing halls and empty rooms made her feel doubly lonely.

Her father was busy all day at the shop, but now that the renovations were finished there was nothing for Grace to do there. Sometimes Mary could get an afternoon off from her duties at home to go to the cinema or have a picnic on Jasper Mountain, but most days Grace was on her own.

Once in a while, she went to an outing or birthday party with some of her classmates, but she didn't really enjoy these events. Somehow, she always felt outside all the chatter and activity, like she was standing behind a thick pane of glass. Usually, she'd leave as soon as she could get away without being impolite or hurting anyone's feelings.

One humid afternoon Grace sat on the front porch reading the latest Betty Gordon novel. Through the open parlor window she heard the telephone ring and listened to Mrs. B's muffled greeting. Soon the housekeeper was at the door to say that Mrs. Montel was on the line. Grace slipped her bookmark into place and went inside.

"Gracie, I've just had a letter from your Aunt Louise and I'd like to talk to you about it. Are you busy?"

"No, Grandma, I'm not busy," Grace said. "What about Auntie's letter?"

"Why don't you come over, dear? Mrs. Henderson's made some lovely ginger snaps and has set a table under the maple. I'll tell you all about it when you get here."

"All right, Grandma. I'll tell Mrs. B and then come right over."

Before Grace had rounded the corner at the end of the block, the heavy clouds let loose and she hurried to open the umbrella Mrs. Blanchard had insisted she bring along. So much for ginger snaps under the maple, she thought, hurrying through the downpour.

Grandma was on the porch when Grace arrived. The rain had let up and already the sun was slipping through the gaps in the spent clouds. Shaking out her umbrella, she sat beside her grandmother on the wicker settee. The bottom of her dress was wet and her shoes were soaked, but otherwise she was dry.

"That umbrella was a good idea, Grace," her grandmother said, pouring iced tea into a tumbler.

"It was Mrs. Blanchard's idea," she said, taking the glass. "If she hadn't reminded me, I'd be drenched."

Grandma shook her head. "It's typical of the weather to rain long enough to get everything wet, but not long enough to cool things off. Look at the way the sidewalk is steaming now that the sun's back out." She wiped her forehead with a hanky. "This humidity takes the starch right out of me."

Grace looked at her grandmother, sitting straight backed, every hair in place. "You look starched to me, Grandma," she said shaking out the hem of her dress. "I'm the one who looks like a drowned rat." They both laughed.

"Help yourself, Gracie," Grandma said, indicating the plate of cookies.

Though she was itching to know why she'd been summoned to hear about her aunt's letter, Grace dutifully finished a ginger snap before asking.

"Well, dear, it seems that Louise and Arthur have rented a lakefront cottage for two weeks at the end of July. I wrote and asked how they'd feel about having a visitor for a week or so and today I received a reply."

"You're going to stay in a cottage, Grandma? I wouldn't have thought you'd like that sort of thing. Aren't cottages kind of rustic?"

Her grandmother shook her head and smiled. "Not me, silly, you. Wouldn't you like to spend a week at the lake with your aunt and uncle, dear?"

Would she like it, Grace wondered? It might be better than moping around the house all day waiting for Daddy to come home, but at least at home things were familiar. She didn't know how it would feel to spend so much time with her aunt and uncle. She'd only ever seen them at family gatherings; she'd never spent any time alone with them. What would they talk about? What would they do?

"Grace? What do you think?"

"I'm not sure, Grandma. Wouldn't I get in the way of their vacation? I mean, this is their holiday. Why would they want me around?"

"Because you're their niece, dear. And because you've lost your mother and it's lonely for you all day with nothing to do." Grandma sighed. "You spend too much time alone. It isn't healthy. At the lake you can swim and hike and there's a rowboat, too. Besides, your aunt and uncle would like to get to know you better." She took Grace's hand. "Why don't you give it a try and see how it goes? After all, it's only a week."

In the end Grace agreed, more to please Grandma than for any real wish to swim or row a boat or spend a week with relatives she hardly knew. Mrs. Blanchard would take her down on the train and her father would drive down on the following Sunday to fetch her. It seemed that it had all been worked out even before she'd been asked. Now all Grace had to do was generate some enthusiasm for the plan.

The following Saturday, Grace and Mrs. Blanchard boarded a train to Concord, Vermont where they'd be met by Grace's aunt and uncle. They traveled through what seemed to Grace to be endless miles of farmland: fields of hay and corn, fields of grazing cows, fields of potatoes, alfalfa and barley, more fields of grazing cows. Most of the stops were little more than the station itself, a general store, a church, and a scattering of houses.

"Vermont is so empty, Mrs. B. Where are all the people? Where are the towns?"

"Well, you can't tell much from a train, Gracie.

Mrs. Blanchard smiled and patted Grace's hand. "Vermont is an agricultural state and most of the towns are small. St. Johnsbury is not too far from Concord, though, and it's a good-sized town with a shopping district, a library, and even an opera house. Don't fret, dear .You'll have a lovely time at the lake, I've no doubt."

Shortly after Grace and Mrs. Blanchard finished their bag lunch, the train pulled into the Concord station. As promised, Aunt Louise and Uncle Arthur were waiting for them on the platform and in no time Grace's bags were stowed in the boot of their automobile. They dropped Mrs. Blanchard off at the hotel and headed out of town to the lake.

The cottage was only a few miles away, but Uncle Arthur said it would take the better part of an hour to get to it. Grace soon saw why. The road was not really a road, more of a muddy track, narrow and bumpy, with trees and bushes crowding along the edge. Finally, Uncle Arthur pulled the Hudson to a stop under a thick stand of conifers and pointed to the sparkle of blue water shimmering through the foliage.

Aunt Louise took Grace's hand and led her through the stand of pines, down a sloping lawn, and out onto the end of a wooden dock. Dense forest circled the lake, but tucked into the woods Grace could see a number of small cottages along the shore. The water reflected the deep blue of the summer sky and across the lake she could hear the shouts of children and the barking of a dog.

"Lovely, isn't it?" her aunt said. "Turn around and look at the house, Gracie."

From where they stood at the end of the dock, the cottage seemed far away. It sat on its little knoll like a dollhouse, all white clapboards and blue gingerbread trim. There was a wraparound porch, too, bordered by a flower bed. Grace smiled and shook her head.

"It's nothing like I imagined it would be, Auntie."

"And what was that?"

"Oh, something like the Arnold's deer camp, I guess. I went there once with Daddy and it was kind of — "

"Primitive?" Her aunt laughed. "That's not my style, Gracie. Come, let me show you. It's just adorable."

When her aunt showed Grace to her room, she found her valise and train case just inside the door. The narrow bed was covered with a flowered counterpane that matched the window curtains. A mirror of wavy glass hung over a white-painted dresser and there was a small easy chair and side table tucked in a corner by the window. The perfect place to snuggle in and read.

"Go ahead and get unpacked, Grace," her aunt said, "and change into a play dress and your tennis shoes. Then we'll go for a walk."

A wooded path covered in pine needles followed the edge of the lake which was half again as long as it was wide. The distant sounds of conversation and the rasp of oars in oarlocks carried over the expanse of water that reflected the tall pines and low-lying scrub along the shore. Breathing in the spicy scent of balsam and sun-warmed earth, Grace relaxed. The forest whispered all around, at once tranquil and bristling with life.

By the time she and Auntie got back to the cottage, Uncle Arthur was busy raking out the fire pit that sat on a sandy patch of level ground a few yards from the house. Propped against one of the large stones around the pit was a heavy iron grate and, close by, a neatly stacked pile of logs.

As they got closer, Grace studied her uncle. She'd only ever seen him at family gatherings dressed in a suit, his pomaded hair parted precisely in the middle and combed back off his high forehead, looking every bit the schoolmaster in his tortoiseshell spectacles. Today, though, his hair blew willy-nilly in the lake breeze, the cuffs of his cotton trousers were rolled up over worn canvas shoes, and his rumpled shirt had come untucked. The few times she'd met her uncle, Grace had not said more than a few words to him. Now she wondered what they'd talk about if they were left alone. She'd didn't have to wonder long.

As soon as they got back to the cottage, Aunt Louise said she was going in to start dinner. Grace offered to help, but Auntie told her she had everything under control and she should stay outside and enjoy the day. Grace watched her walk away, leaving her and her uncle to themselves.

"I'm going to set to work cleaning this grate," he said. "How would you like to collect some kindling for the fire, Grace?"

Getting up off his knees, he brushed his hands together and gestured for Grace to follow him to the back of the cottage. "See all these twigs and broken branches that have fallen from the pines? They're dry as old bones and will burn like a house afire. It would be a big help if you'd gather an armload and pile it up over by the fire pit."

Glad for something to do, Grace collected several armloads of twigs and sticks, piling them where Uncle Arthur had instructed. When he returned from the lake with the grate, he praised her work and explained what he needed her to do next. Aunt Louise came outside some minutes later, carrying a bowl of large baking potatoes. She stopped short when she saw Grace whittling sharp points with a jackknife onto what Uncle Arthur called "toasting sticks." Her uncle held up a warning hand, her aunt shrugged, and Grace went back to peeling the wood away with careful strokes. She was conscious of the trust her uncle had placed in her and pleased to be of use.

The following morning, Grace woke to rain drumming on the roof and running in sheets down the bedroom window. There was a damp chill in the room and, snuggling down into the covers, she wondered what the three of them would do all day cooped up in the tiny house. There was a knock at the bedroom door and her aunt peeked in. She wore a checked apron over her cotton dress and her bobbed hair was held in place with a yellow ribbon. Her smile was as warm as the room was cool.

"Not the best weather today, Gracie," she said, "but there's pancakes and maple syrup for breakfast. Your uncle is manning the griddle at this very moment, so you'd better come along or I might be tempted to eat your stack as well as my own."

Grace tossed back the covers and swung out of bed. "Oh, no, you don't, Auntie. I'll be right out."

In the kitchen, Grace found her uncle flipping pancakes on a cast iron griddle. He turned and waved his spatula at her, gestured for her to take a seat at the table, and told her breakfast was almost ready. While her aunt brought the heated syrup to the table and poured Grace a glass of milk, Uncle Arthur pulled three plates off the warming shelf, adding a fresh pancake to each one.

Grace had never seen her father so much as boil water, so it was a novelty to think of her uncle mixing batter and frying flapjacks. Her aunt and uncle took their seats, smiling at one another across the table. When her aunt got up to pour more coffee, she rested her hand on her husband's shoulder. He murmured his thanks and touched the small of her back. Grace looked away.

The rain did not let up until late afternoon, but Grace didn't have time to be bored. After breakfast, her aunt and uncle taught her to play dominoes, then while a beef bone simmered in the pot, she and her aunt cut up vegetables for soup. Grace liked watching the soup take shape, liked the easy way her aunt went from one part of the preparation to the next. Mostly, though, she liked the comfort and warmth of the kitchen, a warmth that came from more than the cook stove.

Shortly after lunch Uncle Arthur said, "I understand you and your class put on *Oliver Twist* this spring. What do you think of Mr. Dickens?" Grace told him that *David Copperfield* was her favorite so far, but there were lots of his novels she hadn't read yet.

Her uncle grinned and said, "Well, I'm glad to hear you say that. I just happen to have brought along a copy of *The Old Curiosity Shop* that I thought we might read aloud. Would you like that?"

Grace was nervous about reading in front of her aunt and uncle, especially her uncle, who was the Headmaster of the Normal School. He began the reading and Aunt Louise took up where he left off. By the time it was Grace's turn to read, she was too absorbed in the story of poor Nell and the ghastly Mr. Quilp to worry about making mistakes.

In the late afternoon, the rain stopped and a watery sun shone through the leftover clouds. Grace and her uncle bailed water out of the old rowboat, while Aunt Louise packed cookies and a thermos of tea for the voyage. The wind had gone with the rain, leaving the water smooth as glass. They rowed to the eastern end of the lake and watched the sun slip under the clouds, turning them every shade of pink and orange.

Alone in her room that night, Grace thought about her day. She'd been silly to worry about spending time with her aunt and uncle; they were both so kind and easy to be with. It was plain that they were happy together, too. She wondered if her parents had ever been as relaxed and carefree with each other as her aunt and uncle seemed to be. Maybe once they, too, had sung silly songs and stolen kisses behind the kitchen door. Maybe they'd teased and laughed and gazed fondly at each other across the room. Maybe, but those were not the things Grace remembered.

Almost before she knew it, her week at the lake was over. On Sunday morning, Daddy arrived, driving an old Dodge borrowed from Hancock's Livery. Grace showed him around the cottage and took him down to the dock, pointing out where they'd spotted the great blue heron and telling him about their hikes around the lake. After lunch, Grace's father packed her belongings into the automobile while she made her good-byes. Hugging first her aunt and then her uncle, Grace was genuinely sorry to leave.

Turning quickly, she slipped into the seat next to her father. Aunt Louise and Uncle Arthur stood together under the pines, his arm around her shoulder, hers around his waist. Grace leaned out the window waving and calling good-bye.

"We'll expect you here again next year, Grace," her uncle called.

8

CLOSINGS

Curled in her favorite chair at Headquarters, Grace put down the poem she was practicing and looked across the room at Jerome. Eighth grade had been a good year. She and Jerome had spent much of it together working on assignments, talking about books, laughing and teasing each other. Now, he'd been selected valedictorian and was bent over his notebook working on his commencement speech. Next month, he'd be off to the Cape with his mother and she'd visit her aunt and uncle again at the lake.

Tossing his pencil down, Jerome ran his hands through his hair. "There, I'm done. I don't know if it's any good, but I've had enough."

"Do you want to read it to me?" Grace asked.

Jerome left his place at the table and threw himself into the other easy chair. "Later. Right now I want to talk about ninth grade."

Grace caught her breath. She didn't want to think about high school, let alone talk about it. She knew Jerome's parents wanted him to attend a private school in Exeter and clung guiltily to the hope that he wouldn't be accepted. She exhaled. "What about ninth grade?"

"A letter came from the Academy in Exeter a while back, Monty. I ... I've been accepted for the fall term."

Grace had dreaded this moment ever since Jerome told her about applying, but when May ended and she hadn't heard anything, she began to think it wouldn't happen. "How long is a while back?" she said.

Leaning forward in his chair, Jerome rested his elbows on his knees and stared at his clasped hands. "I've known almost a month, but I couldn't tell you. I guess I didn't want to believe it myself."

"You've known all this time and you didn't tell me?" Grace stared at Jerome, but he didn't look at her. "How could you string me along like that? Let me think there was a chance you might not go?"

Jerome straightened and shook his head. "There wasn't much chance I wouldn't go, Monty. I put off telling you because I knew you'd — "

"You knew I'd be upset. And I am. It's no secret that I don't want you to go."

Jerome rubbed his forehead and looked away. "I should have told you sooner, but I kept putting it off. Trying to work up the courage, I guess."

Grace stared at him, but didn't say anything. She'd been worried about high school for months. All those new people to get to know, the unfamiliar teachers and their demanding subjects, and all along she knew, deep down, that she'd have to face it without Jerome.

"Monty, I have to go. You know that. My parents want this for me, my grandparents, too. I can't let them down."

"But you can let me down," she said. "I'm just a friend. You'll make lots of new friends at the Academy. People who are smarter and funnier and more interesting than I am. People who are more like you." She sniffed and rummaged in her sleeve for a hanky.

Jerome pulled his from his pocket and held it out to her, but she shook her head. He tossed it into her lap, and turning, walked to the window.

"Monty, please. Don't make this any harder than it already is. You think I like the idea of leaving home? It'll be like starting over. I won't know anyone. And I'll be leaving everybody I really care about, my mom, my dad," he glanced over at her, "my best friend."

Grace heard a sob catch in his throat and went to stand next to him. She wanted to tell him she was sorry, to say how much she'd miss him, how much his friendship meant to her. Instead, she slipped her hand into his and felt his warm fingers tighten around hers. They stood that way for a long time, unable to let go.

The Davisons left for Cape Cod the first Sunday in July. Trying to stave off the boredom and emptiness of the long summer days to come, Grace thought about asking her father if she could help out at the shop a couple days a week. Knowing Daddy, he'd tell her to relax and enjoy the summer. He'd say she should get out and have fun with her friends before she had to buckle down to high school in the fall. But Grace wanted no part of those picnics on the river or hikes up Jasper organized by the popular girls in her class. And there was just so much reading and sketching a girl could do to fill up the quiet days. Working at the shop was the perfect solution. She'd just have to wait for the right time to ask.

Like all the shops in town, Montel's was closed on Independence Day. As they always did, Grace and her father stood with the crowd on Main Street to watch the parade and then walked to Grandma and Grandpa's house for lunch.

The day was fine, warm and sunny. Rounding the house, Grace and her father found her grandparents sitting in lawn chairs under the big maple. The scene reminded her of a watercolor painting. Dappled sun filtered through the foliage, glinting off the glasses and silverware on the cloth-covered table.

Grandma wore a wide-brimmed straw hat and pale grey frock, Grandpa his seersucker suit and straw boater.

"What a lovely scene," Grace said by way of greeting. "Just like a painting of an English garden."

Grandpa scowled and waved a hand in front of his face. "Blasted deer flies are enough to drive you crazy back here. I told your grandmother we should eat inside like decent people, but she wouldn't hear of it. Said the Fourth of July is a day for picnics."

"And she's right, too," Grace said, giving Grandpa a kiss on the cheek. "It's much too nice a day to be cooped up inside."

"Help yourselves to lemonade or iced tea," Grandma said. "Mrs. Henderson will be out with the food in a few minutes."

Before long, the family took their places around the table laden with platters of sliced ham and turkey and plates of pickled beets, deviled eggs, and pickles. When everyone's plate was full, Grandpa said grace and Daddy lifted his tumbler of iced tea in a toast to the holiday. It was well past her usual lunch time and Grace was famished. The food was delicious and she ate steadily only half listening to her grandfather's story of a bootlegger who'd been caught smuggling a boatload of alcohol out of Canada. She knew the talk would eventually turn to the shop, and when it did she'd be ready.

Grace had decided that this family lunch would be the best time to bring up the idea of her working at the shop. That way, if Daddy dismissed the idea out of hand, as he probably would, Grandma would be there to give Grace a hearing. Finally, her father and grandfather began talking about the sales numbers for June and how the fiscal year was shaping up. Grandma turned to Grace and asked what she planned to do in the weeks before she left for the lake.

"I've about exhausted my reading list, Grandma. With Jerome away and Mary always busy with her little brothers and sisters, the days are feeling awfully long." She folded her napkin, setting it beside her empty plate. "I've been thinking I'd like to spend some time at the shop. You know, filing invoices, helping with the displays ... whatever needs doing."

She was talking to her grandmother, but it was Grandpa who said, "Well, that sounds like just the thing. It's never too early for a Montel to learn the ropes. Why, I had your father putting in time at the shop before he was out of short pants." He leaned back in his chair and clasped his hands across his stomach. "Didn't I, Francis?"

"You sure did, Dad, and I can't say I was too keen on it either. I would much rather have had the summer to lark about with my friends, fishing and playing ball." He shook his head. "I want Grace to relax and have some fun this summer. She'll work plenty hard once she gets to high school."

Grandma glanced at Grace. "Well, I hardly think Gracie will be fishing or playing ball, Francis. I don't see what harm it could do for her to help out at the shop a couple mornings a week. Besides, it would give the two of you a chance to spend more time together."

"Please, Daddy," Grace said, "It'll only be for a few weeks ... just until I leave for the lake. I'm tired of spending so much time alone."

Her father frowned and looked around the table. "Seems I'm outnumbered again," he said. "How can a man win when it's always three against one around here?" He shrugged. "All right, Grace. We'll start you out two mornings a week and see what comes of it."

On Wednesday, Grace and her father walked to the shop together. While Daddy set up the cash drawer, she straightened the goods on the shelves and dusted the display cases. Once they opened her father put her to work in the office. She filed a stack of invoices, put the catalogs in alphabetical order and, at her father's request, telephoned Mrs. Jeffords to say her husband's suit was ready to be picked up. The work satisfied her penchant for organizing and made her feel useful. It also kept her from missing Jerome.

Montel's Haberdashery had been a part of Grace's life for as long as she could remember and she enjoyed being part of life at the shop. Over the ensuing weeks, she helped with the inventory, going through the stacks of neatly folded shirts, counting how many of each size were on hand, while her father filled in the order form. She tidied the files; by the sorry state of the drawers, she could see it was a job that had long been neglected. She replaced or repaired torn folders and put the contents in chronological order.

Grandpa was lavish in his praise of Grace's work. He told her he'd never seen the files so well organized or the office look so shipshape. Mostly though, she thought he was happy to see his granddaughter take an interest in the place that had meant so much to him and where he'd spent his entire working life.

"A business should stay in the family and who would do it if you didn't, Gracie? I can see you've got this work in your blood just like I did when I was your age. Who knows, maybe you'll be running the place someday." He pulled an envelope out of his pocket. "Here's something for your trouble," he added lowering his voice. "Let it be our little secret."

The night before Grace was to leave for the lake, her grandparents had a farewell dinner at their house on Pleasant Street. Aunt Louise had driven up that afternoon to spend some time with her parents and drive Grace back to Concord the next day.

Her grandparents sat at either end of the long table and Grace sat across from her father and aunt. They were talking quietly together and seemed to be sharing some reminiscence from long ago. Aunt Louise leaned over and whispered in Daddy's ear and he chuckled and shook his head. Grace thought of the baby brother who had not lived, the brother she'd never share such moments with, and felt a stab of loneliness.

Grace and her aunt left after breakfast the next morning. The Hudson was roomy, its hood looming large and shiny through the windshield. She admired Aunt Louise's handling of the heavy automobile, the confident way she negotiated the winding roads at a steady speed. Settling into the scratchy upholstery, Grace rested her head against the seat back and watched the countryside slide by.

For the next two weeks, she told herself, she was going to take pleasure in the woods and water and the company of her aunt and uncle. She wasn't going to think about the sheaf of un-paid bills she'd found crammed in the back of the desk drawer at the shop, bills she was sure her father had not meant for her to find. She wasn't going to worry about high school or brood over Jerome's leaving. She was going to enjoy herself at the lake. Or at least try.

"Your uncle has bought a canoe, Gracie," her aunt said, as if reading her mind. "He says it's a great way to explore the shoreline and the shallow end of the lake. He's got in mind to show you how to paddle so the two of you can take in some of what he calls the aquatic bird and plant life." She glanced at Grace, wrinkling her nose. "I'm not much for getting up at dawn to watch the birds, so I'm counting on you to take on that chore while you're here."

Grace laughed. "I'll be happy to, Auntie. It's the least I can do to earn my keep."

When her aunt brought the car to a stop under the pines, Grace spotted Uncle Arthur crouched at the water's edge. He waved and gestured for her to come down.

Aunt Louise laughed and shook her head. "Your uncle can't wait to get you out in that canoe, Grace. We'll get your things inside and get you settled once you've paid proper hom-age to his new boat."

Reaching the lake, Grace saw that the canoe was pulled onto the narrow sandy beach. Inside were two wooden paddles, two bulky orange life jackets, and a canvas bag with a towel thrown over the top.

"What do you think, Grace?" her uncle said. "Are you ready for your first paddling lesson?"

She laughed. "Right now?"

"Well, we can unpack the car and have a little lunch first, I suppose." He grinned. Shielding his eyes with his hand he looked out over the expanse of water. "It's a perfect day for a paddle. Most afternoons the wind comes up, but today there isn't so much as a ripple." He tugged the canoe a few inches higher on the sand and turned toward the cottage. "Come on. Let's get your things inside."

By mid-afternoon, Uncle Arthur had shown Grace how to hold the handle and shaft of the long wooden paddle and pull it steadily through the water."Put your weight behind the stroke and your arms won't tire as quickly, Grace. I'll steer from the stern and as long as neither of us makes any big, sudden moves, we'll be fine."

Grace liked the quiet of the canoe; the way it glided soundlessly through the water. Her uncle plied the paddle with long, sure strokes, steering them along the edge of the lake and avoiding the large rocks that lurked just below the surface. Grace enjoyed the rhythm of the paddling, but it wasn't long before her arms and shoulders were feeling the strain.

"Am I doing something wrong, Uncle?" she asked. "My shoulders are getting sore."

"You're doing fine, Grace, but you've got to build up some muscle. We won't push it today. You sit back and I'll take it from here." He laid his paddle over his lap and said, "But first, open that canvas bag, Grace. There's something in it for you."

Grace removed the towel covering the bag and pulled out a package wrapped in tissue paper. Inside, she found a sketch book with a black cover and two drawing pencils.

"That's a bribe, Grace ... a little incentive to get you up early so we can take in the wildlife." He smiled.

Grace flipped through the blank pages of the sketch book. The paper was heavy and slightly textured, the kind used by real artists. She thanked her uncle for the book and pencils, but couldn't find the words to say the way she really felt. Daddy barely noticed her interest in drawing, but somehow her uncle understood. Returning the gift to its wrapping, she slid it back into the canvas bag.

"It's a beautiful sketchbook, Uncle." She looked over her shoulder at him and grinned. "Well worth getting up at the crack of dawn for."

In the days that followed, Grace and her uncle often stopped to sketch the tall cat tails or velvety petals of the pond lilies floating on their flat rounded leaves. Once, they drifted up to a heron staring fixedly into the water. The great bird stood so still, Grace was able to sketch its outline, the sinuous curve of its neck, the sharp pointed beak, the thin legs and knobby knees.

Later at the cottage, her uncle showed her how to develop her sketches. He taught her about shading and perspective and how to layer on thin coats of watercolor to create depth and volume. Her uncle worked alongside Grace, completing his own sketches. She watched him closely, following the steps he took to achieve a given color or texture. By the end of her stay, her sketchbook was a record of their explorations, filled with drawings and descriptions of things she'd hardly noticed before. She was learning that ordinary plants and birds and trees became extraordinary when you really looked at them.

On the last night of her stay, Grace sat with her aunt and uncle at the supper table. Aunt Louise said, "Will most of your school chums be going on to high school this fall, Gracie?"

"Most of them, I guess," Grace answered, "but now that she's graduated eighth grade, Mary's taken a job with Miss Andrews. She's going to learn the milliner's trade. Her father says she's had enough schooling and it's time she earned her keep." She pushed away her empty plate. "Mary doesn't seem too bothered, though. She's known for a long time this is how it would be. Her older brother and sister went to work after eighth grade, too."

Grace really didn't want to talk about high school. There'd be plenty of time for that once she got back home. Her aunt began clearing the table and Grace stood to help, but Aunt Louise said, "Sit down, Gracie. I'm going to put the coffee on and cut the pie. It'll just take a minute."

Her uncle reached for the pitcher, refilled his water glass, and took a long drink. "I suppose there will be lots of new kids in your classes at the high school, kids from the other grammar schools in town?" He looked thoughtful. "That will be different after being with the same classmates since first grade."

"Sounds like it will be a nice change," Auntie said, setting a plate of blueberry pie in front of Grace. "You'll get a chance to make new friends."

Staring at her plate, Grace said quietly, "I'm afraid I'm not very good at making friends."

Her aunt sat down and looked across the table at her. She tilted her head and pursed her lips. "What do you mean by that?"

"Oh, I don't know exactly. It's just that when I'm around new people I don't know how to get started. Talking, I mean." She shrugged. "I end up standing around feeling foolish." She looked quickly from her aunt to her uncle, then cut the tip off her wedge of pie.

"Well, you're a good student and that will help," her aunt said. "And you'll know some of the kids already. Everyone else probably feels pretty much the same way you do right about now."

"What about your buddy, Jerome?" her uncle asked. "From what I've heard, the Artful Dodger and his sidekick, Charley Bates, make an unbeatable combination. High school should be no match for the two of you." He smiled, but at a look from his wife, the smile faded. "I'm sorry, did I miss something?"

"Jerome's going away to school, Uncle Arthur." Grace managed a rueful smile. "As Charley Bates would say, the Artful's booked for a passage out."

A few days after Grace returned to Chester, she stopped into the shop on her way home from the library. She knew that her father would be at the Rotary meeting at the hotel and that Grandpa would be minding the store. She was no longer officially working at the shop, but wanted to see what needed filing in the inbox. And, more important, to check on those unpaid bills she'd found tucked in the back of the desk drawer.

Her grandfather was waiting on the minister's wife when Grace arrived. She gave him a little wave and pointed to the office and he nodded in answer. As she'd predicted, the inbox had not been sorted through since she left for the lake. She put the catalogs in their proper place on the shelf and filed the invoices and correspondence. Then she reached into the back of the middle drawer. The unpaid bills were right where she'd left them, except that now they were an additional two weeks overdue.

Sliding the drawer closed, Grace glanced into the shop, relieved to find her grandfather still engaged with his chatty customer. She stood wondering what to do. The bills had to be paid, that much she knew. Ignoring them, which her father seemed to be doing, could only mean trouble. If she showed the bills to Grandpa, Daddy would be furious with her. And he'd be just as mad if she asked him about them. Taking a deep breath, she pulled the bundle of papers from the drawer, smoothed them out, and slid them into a clean folder which she placed in the empty inbox.

Grace said good-bye to her grandfather, kissed him lightly on the cheek, and stepped out into the hazy August sunshine. At the door of Scapalini's Delicatessen she caught sight of a familiar figure. He crossed the street and stood before her holding up a white paper bag.

"How about some lunch?" he said.

"Jerome, what are you doing here?"

"I stopped by your house and Mrs. Blanchard said you'd gone to the library, but when I checked there, Mrs. Proudie told me you'd already left." He grinned. "Come on, Monty, we'd better get to the tree house before this bag soaks through."

Jerome turned toward High Street and Grace fell into step beside him. In spite of the heat, something cold sat in her belly, something hard and mean that made her impatient with Jerome's friendly chatter. Here he was acting like everything was fine, when they both knew it wasn't. In a few weeks, he'd leave for the Academy where his friends would not be her friends and his school experiences completely different from her own. They'd have nothing in common anymore and that would be the end of their friendship. Her head was still filled with these dark thoughts when they reached her home.

Grace hadn't used the tree house since Jerome had left for the Cape and the place had a forlorn, deserted look. Twigs and leaves littered the floor and Grace's nest of pillows and blankets was damp and musty. Jerome ran his foot along the floor, clearing away the debris and pulled two long, wrapped sandwiches from the bag. He tore the bag in two and handed a section to Grace along with one of the sandwiches, and settled himself against the wall with the other. They ate in silence for a while, resting their messy sandwiches on the open wrappers and using pieces of the torn bag for napkins.

Jerome talked about his time at the Cape and asked Grace about her vacation, but she didn't have much to say. He might be able to pretend this was just another hot summer afternoon, but she couldn't.

Finally, Jerome said, "What's wrong, Monty?" He inclined his head, searching her face. "Something's the matter, I know. You might as well tell me what's going on."

Grace shook her head. She knew she was being unfair to Jerome. It wasn't his fault he had to go away to school, but she couldn't shake the feeling that she was being abandoned. Lifting her gaze, she saw the hurt in his dark eyes. "I'm sorry, Jerome. I know I'm being ... I mean I'm glad you're home, but, well, you won't be for long. I know it's not your fault, but...," She crumpled the torn bag and hurled it at him. "I'm still mad about it."

Jerome picked up the dripping wrapper from his sandwich, wadded it into a ball, and sent it flying in her direction. It landed in her lap and she flung it back, hitting him squarely on the forehead.

"Now you've done it," he shouted, flinging a slice of tomato at her. It missed its mark, landing just short of her shoe. She reached for it and was ready to heave it back when another slice hit her shoulder and slid into her lap.

"Jerome! Stop it. What do you think you're doing?"

"I'm paying you back. You're not the only one who's mad, Grace. Ever since I told you about Exeter, you've been awful. What are you trying to do, make me glad to leave? Can't you get it through your head? I have to go." His voice cut through the muggy air. He glared at her across the small space, then looked away and stared through the window opening just beyond her left shoulder.

Grace watched him, her eyes filling with hot tears. Slowly, she picked the tomato slice off her lap and wiped the splotch of mayonnaise it left behind.

"You're right," she said. "I have been awful. I haven't wanted to be. I didn't mean to ruin the time we have left, but I couldn't seem to help it." She ran the back of her hand over her wet cheeks and sniffed. "I know you have to go, but you're the best friend I've ever had. And it's so hard."

Jerome didn't say anything, didn't look at her, just kept staring out the window. Finally, he turned his eyes to hers and she saw just how hard it would be.

Hearing the front door close, Grace took a clean frock from her closet and slipped it over her head. She'd gotten it buttoned and was brushing her hair when there was a knock on her bedroom door. Mrs. Blanchard peeked in.

"Gracie, your father's just come home and he wants to talk to you."

Turning from the mirror, Grace said, "What is it, Mrs. B? Is he all right?"

The housekeeper frowned. "Oh, I expect he's all right, but he seems a bit upset. You'd best not keep him waiting."

Picking up Grace's soiled dress, she added, "I'll take this down to the kitchen and see what I can do about that stain. You get your hair tied up and go see what your father wants."

At the parlor door, Grace saw Daddy standing in front of the empty grate. Taking a sip from his glass, he set it on the mantle and waved her in.

"Sit down, Grace," he said. "I want to talk to you."

Grace did as she was told. Her father picked up his glass and stood looking down at her. "You caused quite a little row at the shop this afternoon, Grace." His voice was hard. "I'm not sure what you thought you were doing there."

"I just went in to — ." Grace started to explain, but he cut her off.

"You made your point, Grace. That is, if your point was to give your grandfather an excuse to come down on me for the way I'm running things." He finished off his drink and set the empty glass on the sideboard.

"I don't understand, Daddy. What did I do?"

"What did you do? You left those bills right where your grandfather couldn't miss them. He hit the roof, Grace. Accused me of mismanaging the business. Said that when he was in charge, Montel's was never in arrears to their suppliers. Told me if I kept on like this he'd have no choice but to push me out."

He turned and took up the decanter. Grace watched him refill his glass, her stomach tight, shivering in spite of the late afternoon sun pouring through the parlor windows.

"I'm sorry, Daddy, I just — "

He glared at her, his brows drawn together, his lips a thin, hard line. "You have no right to interfere, Grace. Do you hear me? I don't want you looking over my shoulder. I know what I'm doing and I don't need you or your grandfather telling me how to run my business." He drained his glass and turned away.

Grace stared at his back, her hands clasped tightly in her lap. She was afraid to speak, afraid to say or do anything to provoke him further. Huddling in the corner of the sofa, she fought back tears, trying to think of some way to smooth things over between them.

Her father set his empty glass on the sideboard. His face, reflected back to her in the mirror, was red and blotchy. Grace knew that look. She watched him warily, feeling like an animal caught in a snare. They both turned at the sound of the dining room door opening.

Mrs. Blanchard cleared her throat. "Sorry to interrupt, Mr. Montel, but dinner's ready. Shall I serve it now?"

Without looking at Grace he said, "No, I'll take mine on a tray in the study. Grace will eat with you in the kitchen tonight."

PART 2

LATE 1922-1925

9

BLEAK NOVEMBER

Sitting at her desk in front of the bedroom window, Grace looked out at the fading light of the November afternoon. The wind moaned in the maple, the bare branches scraping against the house as though trying to find a way in. The desk lamp, illuminating a scattering of books and papers, seemed to accentuate the darkness outside and a cold draft snaked its way under the sash. Pushing her chair back, Grace stood and drew the curtains tightly, shutting out the advancing dark.

Turning, she surveyed the room with satisfaction. Cleared of its childish picture books, teddy bears, and dolls, it was now the room of a girl on the cusp of womanhood. On her last birthday, when she'd turned sixteen, her grandparents had given her the small, roll-top desk along with the green-shaded brass lamp. Mrs. Blanchard had helped her arrange the bedroom furniture to create a study in one corner. Next to the desk, a floor lamp shed light on the damask chaise lounge that had once belonged to her mother.

Most weekday afternoons Grace spent at her desk, working on the numerous homework assignments that were the scourge of her life as a high school student. In truth, she didn't really mind the hours spent reading, taking notes, and working algebra problems. The assignments kept her busy and gave her an excuse to hole up in her room away from the well-meaning Mrs. B.

Grace pulled a sepia-toned photograph from one of the pigeon holes that ran across the top of her desk. The photo, taken early in the school year, was of the Class of 1924. In the second row, Grace sat between her friends, Alma and Christine. She smiled at the image. Aunt Louise had been right; she had made new friends in high school and they had all come from different grammar schools.

Hearing the front door close, she replaced the photograph in its pigeonhole and checked her watch. It was just after 6:00. Her father was home. Grace heaved a sigh and moved to the dresser. She pulled the side combs from her hair and brushed out the tangles before working it into a braid and fastening the end with a length of black ribbon. Looking at her reflection, she fixed a smile on her face and headed downstairs.

Grace entered the parlor and crossed to the sideboard. "Hi Daddy," she said, kissing his cheek. "How was your day?"

"Oh, not too bad, I guess," he said, setting down the decanter. "Things are picking up now that we're getting closer to the holidays." Giving her arm a gentle squeeze, he picked up his glass and settled into his chair. "How'd things go at school today?"

Taking her place on the end of the sofa nearest her father's chair, Grace pulled her feet under her and leaned against its padded arm. "Pretty much as usual," she said, staring absently at the glass in her father's hand. Prohibition had been law for more than two years now, but Daddy's glass had not gone dry.

Shifting her position, she said, "In chorus we're practicing for the Christmas concert and Miss Mathews asked Alma and Christine and me to sing a couple of verses of one of the songs as a trio."

Over the rim of his glass, her father raised his brows. "Well, that's nice. Are you going to do it?"

"Mmm, I suppose so." She shrugged. "I can't read music and I can't harmonize, but both the others can. So I'll sing melody and they'll do the rest. It should work out all right." She grinned. "Miss Mathews likes us. This is her first year of teaching and some of the fellows give her a hard time, but we're nice to her, so she kind of favors us."

Her father laughed. "You could do worse than be the teacher's pet, Gracie. Though I wouldn't know myself. I would have been one of the fellows giving your Miss Mathews a hard time."

As they did most evenings after dinner, Grace went to her room and her father withdrew to his study. This was not a new arrangement. Grace had become used to spending her evenings alone while her father made his nightly descent into inebriation. Usually she was in bed by the time he stumbled up to his room. Sometimes he'd pause at her door, mumbling good-night or apologizing for not being a better father. Lying still, every muscle tense, Grace feigned sleep, willing him to go away.

Once, he'd fallen in the hallway and been unable to get up on his own. Hearing him thrashing about and cursing just feet from her door had filled her with both revulsion and fear. Throwing on her dressing gown, she'd helped him up, supporting him to his room where he'd flopped onto his bed barely conscious. As she removed his shoes and covered him with a blanket, Grace had felt her chest contract as though a cold fist had closed around her heart, hardening it against the one parent she had left.

Entering her room, she felt for the light switch to the right of the door and pushed the button. The murky glow cast by the ceiling light always depressed her, and she moved quickly to turn on the bedside and desk lamps, before switching it off. Slipping out of her blouse and skirt, she reached behind the closet door for the flannel wrapper Mrs. B had made for her.

In the next hour, Grace finished an essay for Mr. Trudeau's English class and read a chapter on Greek architecture in her history text. After packing her books and papers into her book bag, she set out her clothes for the following day. Then, settling onto the chaise lounge, she tucked her feet under the hem of her robe and picked up her sketchbook.

The sketches she'd done with Uncle Arthur that second summer at the lake were followed by others she'd completed at home. There were studies of wildflowers and several disastrous attempts to capture the blowsy grandeur of peonies, so beautiful and so impossible to draw and paint. Flipping through studies of tree bark and leaves, pinecones and fir boughs, she paused at a watercolor of a bowl of lilacs. Her uncle had complimented her on this piece, pointing out the various shades of violet she'd achieved and the articulation of each tiny bloom. She frowned, thinking she hadn't done anything as good since, then shook her head. She could almost hear Uncle Arthur chiding her for being too hard on herself.

Closing the sketchbook, she pulled another from her book bag. This one was smaller, with a red leather cover. "Sketch Book" was written across the top in gold lettering and a spray of branches and leaves curled around the bottom left corner. Grace turned to the inscription on the flyleaf. "Christmas, 1919, To Monty, best friend and budding artist. From Jerome."

Smoothing her hand across the inscription, Grace closed her eyes and rested her head against the back of the chaise. She'd dreaded Jerome's leaving and it had been every bit as awful as she'd imagined. Worse, really, because she'd had no idea that his absence, the loss of his day-to-day companionship, would reawaken the pain and loneliness of her mother's passing. And just as when Mama died, she'd been overcome with lassitude, dragging her heavy limbs from class to class during those first days of ninth grade, her mind as fuzzy as an old sweater.

Then on the Saturday after Jerome had left for school, Grace received a letter from him. In typical Jerome style, he detailed his first days at the Academy. He described the sleepless nights in the dormitory, listening to his roommates wheeze and snore and the poor fellow who cried into his pillow three nights running. He talked about the vaulted ceiling of the dining room, the long, cloth-covered tables, the china emblazoned with the school crest, the ghastly chunks of questionable meat entrapped in congealed gravy. He included a sketch of his Housemaster, Mr. Finch, a man whose hearing was as acute as a bird dog's.

Grace smiled to herself. Since they'd started high school she and Jerome had maintained a regular correspondence, the tone of which was set with that first letter. Grace kept a sharp eye and ear out for any anecdote or observation that might spice up the humdrum routine of her school and home life. Stories about poor Miss Mathews' trials as a first-year teacher or Grace's own less than brilliant performance on the parallel bars. Their letters kept them in touch and eased their infrequent reunions. Grace cherished the growing bundle of Jerome's correspondence tied with a ribbon and tucked safely in the back of her desk drawer.

Sliding the sketch book into her book bag, she rose from the chaise and stretched. She'd been wrong about Jerome. He hadn't disappointed her and he hadn't left her behind. Instead, he'd proved that they could be apart and still be together.

The next morning Grace sat alone at the dining room table. She'd finished her oatmeal and was spreading jam on a slice of toast when she heard her father's heavy tread on the stairs. It had been late when he'd paused at her door last night. She always slept lightly until she knew he was in bed, and had come fully awake when he stopped and whispered his good-night. It pained her to think of the shape he'd be in this morning.

Entering the room, he wished her good morning. His voice was husky and Grace studied his face as he took his seat across from her. His freshly shaved cheeks were blotchy and traced with tiny red veins; the skin of his neck hung in folds over his tight white collar. She didn't meet his gaze, but she knew his eyes were puffy and bloodshot.

Her father shook out his napkin and laid it across his lap. He reached for the coffee pot and, filling his cup, took a tentative sip.

"Ah, that's better." Coffee sloshed over the rim as he set the cup in its saucer. "There's nothing like that first sip in the morning."

Grace forced a smile, but didn't say anything.

"What's the matter, Gracie? Aren't you talking to your old dad this morning?" His voice was cajoling, but Grace heard the undertone of anger, too. "You've grown sullen lately, young lady, and it doesn't suit you."

"I'm sorry, Daddy. I didn't sleep too well last night ... worried about that algebra test, I guess."

"Seems we both have a lot on our minds," he said. He smiled at her and picked up his cup. "I've got a shipment of holiday orders coming in this afternoon. How would you like to come by and help me check them in? Then maybe we could head over to the hotel for an early dinner ... give Mrs. B the evening off."

Grace told him she'd be happy to help and thanked him for the dinner invitation. She knew he was trying to make amends, to say he was sorry for his late nights and uneven temper. Sorry for not being the father she needed him to be.

It was close to 5:00 when Grace arrived at the shop. She'd had chorus practice after school and had stayed another half hour to work out the parts she'd sing with Alma and Christine. The store was quiet. Grandpa didn't work on Wednesdays and there were no customers this close to closing time. Grace dropped her book bag in the office and slipped a smock over her school clothes.

Her father was in the hallway off the back entrance surrounded by unopened cartons, a sheaf of packing slips and invoices fastened to a clipboard.

"Hi Daddy," Grace said. "Sorry I'm late. I got held up at school." She knelt beside him. "What can I do to help?"

"I think we'll start with that big carton, sweetie. Once we get that out of the way, we'll have more room to move around." He handed her his pen knife and she slit the brown paper tape and pulled open the flaps.

"You go ahead and pull stuff out and I'll check it off. We'll see how it goes. We may not get to it all." Stifling a yawn, he turned to her. She wondered what his customers made of those dull, empty eyes, what they said to one another about poor, widowed Francis Montel.

Grace and her father had worked this way many times, unpacking boxes or taking inventory, and before long they settled into a familiar rhythm. Opening, unpacking and breaking down the cartons, Grace maintained a brisk pace and, for the most part, Daddy managed to keep up. When he couldn't locate an item on the corresponding sheet, she resisted the impulse to point it out to him.

They'd worked about an hour when her father suggested they call it a day and head over to the hotel. He'd finish the rest tomorrow morning before the shop opened. But Grandpa's maxim echoed in Grace's head: an owner never closes his shop until it's ready to open. If her grandfather came in the next day to find boxes and goods piled in the hallway, he would be sure to repeat this axiom to his son. Grace wanted to spare her father that indignity.

"If it's all right with you, Daddy, I'd like to stay and empty these last two cartons. It won't take long and that way you won't have to bother with them in the morning." She smiled and cocked her head. "I'll enjoy dinner more knowing we're done here."

He ran a hand through his hair and rubbed his temple. "That sounds good to me, Grace. I'm pretty beat." He pulled a key from his pocket. "The front door's all set, so go out the back way and make sure you try the door after you lock it. Sometimes it doesn't close right."

School let out early the day before Thanksgiving. Grace hurried out of the building with Alma and Christine, relieved to have a few days off. As they did most days, the girls walked home together, dropping Alma off first. They stood chatting together at her gate, shivering in the damp November cold, until Alma's little sister called from the door that Mama wanted her to come inside. Alma rolled her eyes, then hugged her friends and hurried away. Two blocks further down the same street, Grace said good-bye to Christine, then walked on alone. One more block and a right turn would take her to High Street and home, but she turned left instead.

Though it was early afternoon, the relentless grey of the November sky made it seem more like twilight. What a melancholy time of year this was. No snow to light up the long nights, just bare branches and frost-burned grass. Walking around to the back entrance of the Davisons' house, Grace was cheered by the bright lights shining from the kitchen window. At her knock, Mrs. Davison opened the door, wiping her hands on her apron and smiling warmly.

"Ah, Grace," she said. "What a nice surprise. I'm so glad you stopped by. Come on in and get warm, you look chilled to the bone."

"Thanks, Mrs. Davison. I've been walking my friends home and decided to come by to wish you a Happy Thanksgiving." Stepping into the warm kitchen, she said, "Oh, it smells wonderful in here. What delicious thing are you making now?"

"I'm up to my elbows in pie baking and you're just in time. I have a little treat almost ready to come out of the oven. Sit down, dear, and tell me what you've been up to."

As she'd done so many times before, Grace hung her coat on a hook behind the kitchen door and sat down at the table. She watched as Mrs. Davison picked up two woven pot holders and opened the oven door. Sliding out a cookie sheet, she set it on top of the stove where a kettle hissed and sputtered on the side oil burner.

"I had a little extra pie crust, so I made some rolled cookies. I must have known you'd stop by, Grace. They were always a favorite of yours."

"My all time favorite," said Grace, inhaling the rich scent of cinnamon and brown sugar. "Mrs. Blanchard buys all sorts of fancy butter cookies for the holidays, but none so good as these."

Jerome's mother smiled and Grace thought how much she must miss her son. The two were so close. Jerome delighted in making his mother laugh and she was forever making him treats. No doubt some of today's goodies would make their way into a package bound for Exeter before the day was out.

Mrs. Davison slid three cookies onto a plate, setting it in front of Grace along with a cup and teabag. She filled the cup with hot water, then returned to the floured board at the far end of the long table and began rolling out another pie crust. Grace took a bite of the hot, tender pastry, uttering a low sound of satisfaction as the sweet cinnamon burst onto her tongue.

"Mmmm, delicious," Grace said. Mrs. Davison smiled, but Grace saw her eyes darken and heard her sigh.

"I miss my boy today, Grace," she said. "I do so wish he was coming home for Thanksgiving."

Grace took a sip of tea. "I do too, Mrs. Davison, but Jerome said they just get the one day off and then it's back to work on Friday." She shrugged. "I know I'm ready for a break, even if it's just for a few days. School's been awfully busy this fall."

"They work you children too hard. I say that to my husband all the time. Poor Jerome's always busy. Classes all day and then prep until eight or nine at night." She set down her rolling pin, and pushed a stray lock of hair off her forehead with the back of her floured hand. She brightened. "But the Christmas holiday is coming right up and he'll be home for almost a month." She tilted her head slightly and looked at Grace. "I know he misses you, dear."

Grace felt the heat rise in her cheeks and looked away. "I miss him too," she said.

For a while the room was quiet. Grace listened to the rhythmic click and glide of the rolling pin, watching as Mrs. Davison fit the perfectly round crust into the pie plate. She folded and crimped the edges, then poured the pumpkin filling into the tin.

Sliding the pie into the oven, she asked, "How are things going at the shop, Grace? Do you still help out there?"

Something in Mrs. Davison's tone made Grace hesitate. "Once in a while I help with the shipments, but ... . She paused. "My father says he doesn't believe in child labor."

Mrs. Davison chuckled. "You're hardly a child, Grace. As a matter of fact, you're looking quite grown up these days. You've got a birthday soon, haven't you?"

"Not till January," Grace said. "I'll be seventeen. I'm just a few months younger than Jerome."

"Yes, but girls mature earlier than boys and I can see that in you. Jerome shot up like a weed around eighth grade, but there's still something in his face that keeps him looking like a little boy, whereas your face has thinned out." She smiled. "You've gotten taller, too, and you're looking altogether more womanly." She gave Grace a sly smile. "I think Jerome will be delighted with the changes."

When Grace did not reply, Mrs. Davison began collecting the pie making dishes, and picked up the thread of their earlier conversation.

"I was in Montel's a week or so ago getting a few things to send to Jerome. I thought the shop was looking very smart. Your father does a wonderful job arranging the clothing and setting up displays." Wiping flour off the board, she continued. "I did think he looked a bit tired though, and I wondered if he'd been ill."

Grace toyed with the tag of her teabag. Mrs. Davison wasn't a nosy gossip probing for answers, but there were plenty of them around. She imagined people talking on the street and over the telephone about how bad Mr. Montel looked. Shaking their heads and speculating about what he'd been up to.

"He's not ill, Mrs. Davison, but he is very tired. He works awfully hard and he ... well, I don't think he gets enough sleep."

Jerome's mother placed a warm hand on Grace's shoulder, but said no more. Grace longed to unburden herself to Mrs. Davison. To tell her about the loneliness and uncertainty of life with her father, and be shown a way out of her difficulties. But to do so would be to admit to the great shame of her life, an admission she had not fully articulated even to herself.

Grace walked home in the near dark, the warmth of the fragrant kitchen and of Mrs. Davison's kindness cooling as she got closer to the looming bulk of the big house. A single lamp in the parlor shone weakly through the bay window, but the rest of the house appeared dark. Letting herself in, she dropped her book bag on the hall chair and slipped out of her coat. She had just started up the stairs when Mrs. B stepped out of the door leading to the dining room.

"Well, there you are Gracie," she said. "I'd begun to think I ought to send the Mounties out looking for you. I expected you long before this." She checked her watch. "It's almost five. Where have you been?"

"I stopped by to visit Mrs. Davison and she fed me fresh cookies and tea." Grace tried to keep the annoyance from her voice. She knew Mrs. Blanchard was looking out for her, but she didn't like being questioned. She was almost seventeen after all. "I was just going up to change. I'll be down when my father gets home."

"Your grandmother called earlier. She'd like your help decorating the table and making place cards and asked if you could go over around ten."

Grace nodded and made her way upstairs. In her room, she changed out of her skirt, pulling an old corduroy jumper over her blouse and buttoning the front of her cardigan. The room was cold and cheerless in the gathering dark. Sighing, she sank onto the chaise, leaning back and crossing her arms tightly over her chest.

Grace dreaded the next day. Even the prospect of seeing Aunt Louise and Uncle Arthur did little to lift her spirits. She knew from experience that family gatherings were fertile ground for Daddy to take, or give, offense. At least at home, she and her father had their routine. They ate dinner together, then went their separate ways. If he became combative or sullen, she was the only one to witness his anger and dark moods. Tomorrow she'd have to watch the family watch her father. Watch them exchange glances every time he refilled his glass. Watch them try to redirect the conversation when he became belligerent, and pretend not to notice his slurred speech and clumsy gestures.

Everyone would watch and everyone would notice, but they'd say nothing. And nothing would change.

10

HOLIDAYS

Thanksgiving dinner began in much the same way as all the others Grace remembered. The table was beautifully set with the Montels' best china and crystal. Mrs. Henderson roasted a turkey that would have fed twice as many people as those gathered around the board. There were mashed potatoes and squash, Brussels sprouts and peas, and a condiment platter, too. By the time they got to the pumpkin and apple pies, they'd be too stuffed to enjoy dessert.

Grace kept a wary eye on her father. He'd been out late the night before and had woken up that morning in a foul humor. On the walk to Grandma and Grandpa's he'd groused about holidays in general and Thanksgiving in particular. He'd complained that it was ridiculous to eat so much food in the middle of the afternoon and then have nothing to do the rest of the day but make small talk with the family. Everyone acted like they were having a great time, when they couldn't wait for the day to be over.

As soon as they arrived, Grace's father made straight for the liquor cabinet. He didn't wait to be invited, just filled his whiskey glass, and asked who'd join him. No one did. When Mrs. Henderson called them to the table, he topped off his drink and carried it with him to the dining room. During dinner he helped himself to wine, filling and refilling his glass while the food sat untouched on his plate. Aunt Louise asked him how things were going at the shop. He roused himself enough to say they were set for the holidays before falling silent. Grace took in his furrowed brow and slack jaw and felt her stomach contract.

Grandma turned to Uncle Arthur and said, "I suppose you're busy with exams and so forth at the school."

He nodded and said the students were out straight writing end-of-term papers and studying for exams. He was busy, too, preparing a course for the spring semester based on the recent discovery of Tutankhamen's tomb.

"To find an untouched tomb, one that has not been molested by thieves, is a significant discovery. And an exciting one. Historians, archeologists, scientists of all stripes will be involved in exploring and cataloging the treasures they uncover there."

Grace's father broke in, "I thought you were training up teachers at that school of yours. What's a dead Egyptian got to do with teaching the 3 R's?" He glared at Arthur, his voice defiant.

Uncle Arthur turned to him. Keeping his voice even, he said, "There's more to being an educated person than knowing how to read, write, and figure. I — "

But he had no time to finish. With an impatient gesture, Grace's father dismissed her uncle's explanation and, as he did so, upended his nearly full wine glass. "Daddy, no," Grace cried, watching the bright red stain spread over the white damask tablecloth.

"Oh, Francis," her grandmother said.

"Leave me alone, all of you!" he shouted.

Tossing his napkin on the table, he staggered to his feet, his chair rocking precariously on two back legs. Stunned, Grace jumped up, but before she could follow him, her aunt caught her hand and held fast.

"No, Gracie, let him go," she said.

"But ... " Grace tried to pull away, but her aunt wrapped an arm firmly around her shoulder and pulled her close.

"Best to let him alone," her aunt said. "There's nothing you can do for him right now."

She led Grace into the small powder room near the stairs and closed the door. Grace lowered herself onto the upholstered bench in front of the vanity and tried to keep from crying. She was angry at Daddy for ruining the day, but mostly she was ashamed. When he acted that way, yelling and upsetting everyone, Grace felt as tainted and soiled as Grandma's tablecloth.

"How can he let everyone see him like that?" Grace said, her eyes burning. "Doesn't he care what anybody thinks?"

At the small sink, her aunt ran a cloth under cold water and wrung it out. Handing it to Grace she said, "Somewhere deep inside, I'm sure he does, Grace. I imagine he's feeling pretty small right now ... or will when he can think straight. But I'm not sure how much control he has over his ... over how much he drinks."

Grace wiped her streaming eyes with the damp cloth and took a deep breath. She turned toward the vanity mirror and groaned at her reflection. Aunt Louise stood behind her, a comforting hand on each shoulder. "What do you say we take a little walk, Gracie? The fresh air will do us good. Your grandmother will have dessert well in hand by the time we get back."

Bundled against the late November chill, Grace followed her aunt down the porch steps and onto the sidewalk. It was twilight and the street lights were coming on as they headed down Pleasant Street and rounded the corner into the park.

"I've been wanting to talk to you about something, Grace, and this seems like the right time. It's something your uncle and I have been thinking about for a while now."

Grace glanced sideways at her aunt, who was hunched into the fur collar of her coat, her eyes fixed on the path ahead.

"What is it, Auntie?"

Pulling her hand out of her pocket, her aunt slipped her arm through Grace's. "Well, the truth is, we're worried about you.

I know what my brother is. Today was awful, but it's not the first time this kind of thing has happened. Seems like every time the family gets together, there's some kind of episode like the one at dinner today."

She tightened her grip on Grace's arm. "We hate to think of you living with that kind of tension and uncertainty day in and day out." She stopped and lifted her gaze to the darkening sky. "I love my brother," she said quietly, "but I don't trust him to do right by you."

They resumed their walk. Coming to a bench along the path, her aunt paused and gestured for Grace to sit down. Huddled in her heavy coat, her hands buried deep in her pockets, Grace stared ahead at the stand of bare maples bordering the far side of the path.

"Your uncle and I want you to know that if you need to get away from the situation at home, you are welcome to come and live with us in Concord. There's a fine secondary school there and, if you wanted to, you could continue at the normal school after graduation. We'd be happy to have you."

Grace's heart lifted at the thought of life with her aunt and uncle. They all got along so well and they were so kind and easy to be with, so steady. Grace managed a watery smile and leaned her head on her aunt's shoulder. The prospect of escaping the twists and turns of life with her father shone like a beacon in the dark, but the idea of abandoning him felt like a betrayal.

Grace sniffed and pulled a hanky from her pocket. "Just before Mama died, she told me Daddy would need looking after. She said he'd be no good on his own." She sighed. "At the time I didn't know what she meant, but I do now. I'd love to come and live with you and Uncle Arthur. You both have been so good to me, but I don't know what would happen to my father if I did."

Louise took Grace's hand. "Being apart would be hard on both of you, but once you graduate you'll have to leave anyway. Besides, you're not your father's keeper. He's the only one who can do anything about his problem and the first thing he'd have to do is admit he has one."

Shivering, she stood and reached out her hand. "We'd better get back or your grandfather will be sending out a search party. But before we go, promise me something. Promise that you'll call us if you need us."

The family was in the parlor when Grace and her aunt returned from their walk. Grandma was pouring tea. Two pies, one pumpkin and the other apple, were sliced and ready on the low table in front of the sofa. Grace was grateful for the hot tea, but had no appetite for pie. She sat in a daze, sipping her tea, barely conscious of the talk going on around her. So much had happened in the past hour and she was unable to reckon with any of it. All she wanted was to be alone.

As soon as she could, she said her good-byes and headed out into the gathering dark. In spite of the cold, she walked slowly, afraid of what awaited her at home. The closer she got to the big house, the more her stomach roiled and pitched, her dinner tossing like loose cargo in a ship's hold.

Grace climbed the porch steps and took a deep breath. Stepping into the foyer, she stopped and listened. The house was quiet. She hung her coat on the rack and peeked into the parlor. It was empty. She dreaded meeting her father. She didn't want to hear him rail against the family or accuse her of siding with them against him. She didn't want to listen to his empty promises or self-pitying excuses. But if he wasn't home, he'd be wherever it was he went in the evenings and that was equally worrying.

Turning from the parlor, she tiptoed down the hall to her father's study. The door was closed and from under it a thin beam of light shone into the dark foyer. Grace exhaled, turned quietly, and made her way upstairs. Gaining the privacy of her room, she sat on the edge of her bed and stared blankly at the darkened window. She was exhausted, wrung out, unable to make sense of the jumble of thoughts and images flashing through her mind. Another ruined holiday dinner. How many had there been? How many more would there be?

Shivering, Grace pulled the afghan from across the bottom of her bed and wrapped it around her shoulders. Her aunt and uncle were offering her a way out, an escape from the endless worry and embarrassment of life with her father. Aunt Louise said that Daddy was the only one who could do anything about his problem and maybe she was right. As much as Grace had tried to help him, to shield him from the judgment of others, to head off the consequences of his absent-minded mistakes and rash tongue, it had never been enough. Yet how many times had he said he didn't know what he'd do without her?

Curling onto her side, she pulled the blanket tighter around her. She was so tired. Tired of being on her guard and worn down by her father's moods. Tired of avoiding the truth of his drunkenness and ashamed to admit that truth.

"I'm sorry, Mama," she whispered. "You said to look after Daddy, and I've tried, but it hasn't done any good."

Mr. Trudeau had a habit of walking distractedly back and forth in front of the chalkboard, an open book in one hand and a nib of chalk in the other. Today he was trying to generate interest in Ishmael's role in *Moby Dick*, but no one was listening. Grace felt a little sorry for him, but neither she nor any of her classmates had much patience for Mr. T's words of wisdom right now. They were too busy watching the minute hand of the clock creep toward twelve. Their books and papers were already packed in their book bags and their minds were already on vacation. All that stood between them and the Christmas holidays, a full, glorious week and a half, was the ring of the last period bell.

At last it sounded. Without waiting to be dismissed, everyone got up, gathered their belongings, and headed for the door. When Grace emerged from the crush in the doorway, she saw Jerome leaning against the far wall. Smiling, he pushed himself upright and stepped towards her. Under his open overcoat, she could see the blue blazer and striped tie that were his Academy uniform. She raised her eyes to his and stood still until jostled by a passing student.

Jerome chuckled and, taking her elbow, steered her through the crowd, down the wide oak stairs, and into the brilliant afternoon. The snow that had fallen the night before lay thick on the ground and, fired by the afternoon sun, sparkled with a million tiny rainbows. Out of the press of students, they stopped and studied each other. Grace had long thought Jerome the handsomest boy she'd ever met, but today she didn't just think it. She felt it deep inside as though the embers of a slow burning fire had shifted and flamed up. The feeling made her blush.

"You're looking grand, Monty," Jerome said, tilting his head and gazing into her face. "And you seem taller, too. How'd you manage all that in three months?"

Grace laughed and looked away. "When did you get in?"

"The train got in about 1:00. I had lunch with the folks and then came on over to find you. I hope you weren't on your way anywhere, because my mother wants you to come by for tea." He grinned. "And so do I."

Grace didn't say there was nowhere else she'd rather go and no one else she'd rather go with, but she was pretty sure Jerome knew. He took her book bag and they headed toward the Davisons' house. On the way they talked about their plans for vacation and what they'd been working on in school. Jerome said he was writing a paper on Renaissance sculpture for his humanities course.

"I thought I'd do a piece called *The Two Davids*," he said. "I'm not sure what my thesis will be, but I'm rather proud of the title."

Grace laughed. "Well, it's a start, I guess, but will the library here have the books you need? I don't imagine there are too many Renaissance scholars in Chester."

"Oh, I raided the Academy library before I left. I should be in good shape as far as the research goes." He shifted the book bag to his other shoulder and grimaced. "If the weight of this bag is any indication, you'll be pretty busy over vacation, too."

"I brought my sketch books home to show you what I've been working on, and I have a couple of books to read for Mr. Trudeau's class. Other than that, it's just the usual history and math assignments." She flashed a smile. "I'm perfectly able to carry that bag if it gets too heavy for you."

Jerome poked her gently in the ribs and said, "How'd the Christmas concert go? I was sorry I didn't get home in time to hear you sing with Alma and Christine."

"It was all right, I guess. We were nervous and didn't sound nearly as good as we had during rehearsals. I felt badly for poor Miss Mathews. She'd worked so hard with us and I felt like we let her down."

"Typical Monty." Jerome shook his head.

"What do you mean by that?"

"I mean you're too hard on yourself. I bet you were more let down by your performance than Miss Mathews was. You're the only one who expects you to be perfect, Grace."

It was close to 5:00 when Grace finally tore herself away from Jerome's company and the comfort of his mother's kitchen. Having eaten too many of Mrs. Davison's butter cookies, she finally headed out into the dark of the frigid afternoon. She refused Jerome's offer to walk her home. She needed a few minutes of solitude to savor their reunion and prepare herself for the evening ahead.

The holidays had been busy at the shop and, in spite of the increased sales, her father often came home bone tired and short-tempered. Grace frowned, thinking of his daily catalog of complaints about finicky customers and what he called his father's interference. She resented having to listen to Daddy's grumblings, especially after the delight of spending the afternoon with Jerome.

As it turned out, she didn't have to. Mrs. Blanchard met Grace in the foyer to say that her father had called to let her know he wouldn't be home for dinner. The shop was open late that evening, and he'd grab a quick sandwich if he had time. He'd be back sometime after closing. Grace ate in the kitchen with Mrs. B and escaped to her room as soon as she'd helped clear the table.

Having changed into her dressing gown and brushed out her hair, Grace settled on the chaise lounge. It was quiet except for the creak and thud of the old house contracting in the deepening cold. In spite of the chill in her room, she felt the heat rise in her cheeks at the memory of her earlier conversation with Jerome.

This was not the first time he'd met her at school upon his return from the Academy, but today had been different. Maybe it was his saying she looked grand or the way he'd studied her face with such frank admiration. Something in his dark eyes had turned her insides liquid and she'd had to look away. Then, as they neared the Davisons' home, Jerome had told her about a talk he'd had with his parents at lunch.

"So, what'd they say?" Grace asked.

"Well, it was all very serious," he said grinning. "My dad said I shouldn't invite you up to Headquarters anymore. My mother said it wasn't proper, let's see how she put it, for young men and women to spend time together unchaperoned."

Grace turned her head in his direction, but Jerome kept his gaze fixed on the snowy sidewalk. "But we've been spending time in Headquarters for years and never needed a chaperone," she said. "Why now?"

"Because things are different now, Monty. We're different. We're not kids anymore." He flashed a smile. "When I saw you coming out of Mr. Trudeau's room this afternoon, I knew my parents were right."

Grace said nothing, thinking of the way her breath caught when she'd seen Jerome earlier, his smile shining in the dim hallway, drawing her to him like a moth to a flame.

"They don't mean we can't be friends anymore, do they?" she said, embarrassed by the pleading in her voice.

"Of course not," he said, stopping to look at her. "We'll always be friends, Monty. Don't worry about that. We'll be friends and then some."

Resting her head against the back of the chair, Grace closed her eyes. She was confused by the changes in her friendship with Jerome. It used to be so easy, but now when they were together, she felt agitated, as though the air around them crackled with static. When he looked at her she felt alternately self-conscious and curiously elated. Sometimes she could hardly bear to look at him and at other times she couldn't look away. How she wished Mama were here. She needed guidance. She wanted answers, reassurance, a mother's understanding and empathy. But it was too late for that.

Grace was unaware of her father's return until he knocked on her bedroom door. Calling to him to come in, she pulled herself upright and secured the tie of her wrapper. He opened the door slowly and peeked in.

"Hi sweetie," he said. "I'm sorry I didn't make it home to dinner, but we were swamped at the shop. Busy all afternoon and evening."

Crossing the room, he pulled out the desk chair and sat down. "I barely had time to get a sandwich from Scapillini before the evening rush. People were coming out of the woodwork. I even sold that silver lighter your grandfather said would never move." He grinned. "How was your day?"

"I never saw the hands of a clock move as slowly as they did in our last period class. Jerome met me after dismissal and invited me to his house for tea." She toyed with the tie of her dressing gown and smiled. "Of course, I ate too many of Mrs. Davison's cookies. I always do."

Her father frowned. "So, you and Jerome are still pretty chummy, I guess. I would have thought you'd have moved on to other friends by now."

Grace was taken aback by the comment and even more by the change in his tone. She looked at him and tried to keep her voice light. "I do have other friends and so does Jerome, but ... well, we still enjoy each other's company." She hesitated, studying her father's face. He looked exhausted. His eyes were dark-rimmed and hooded, but his cheeks were flushed and his left knee jiggled incessantly. She considered saying something more about Jerome, but knew this wasn't the time.

Instead, she said. "It's getting late, Daddy. I expect tomorrow will be crazy at the shop." Shifting her position, she set her feet on the floor, hoping to rouse him. "I could come in tomorrow for a while, if you needed a hand with anything."
"No, no, we'll be all right. Raymond's coming in and, of course, your grandfather will be there minding everybody's business." He stifled a yawn and, clapping his hands on his knees, got to his feet. "I'd best get to bed. Got to get in early tomorrow and pick up the pieces."

He leaned over and planted a whiskey-scented kiss on her cheek. She wished him good night and waited for him to close the door behind him. Then she stood, turned off the floor lamp and slipped into bed. The Baby Ben read just past 11:00. The shop had been closed for three hours.

What had her father been up to all that time? Drinking surely, but where? Not the hotel, which no longer served wine and spirits. Not at Clancy's Saloon on Main Street or Mr. Muller's place across the river. They'd been shut down for a couple years now. And he hadn't been home, where the decanter on the sideboard still held its complement of whiskey and the wine carafe made its nightly appearance at the dinner table.

Grace wondered where her father got off to in the evenings. How did he fill the hours when he wasn't working, yet was absent from home? She'd heard about secret places where people drank and danced, but Daddy had always tucked himself away in his study to drink. He'd never been one for late nights out. Until now.

11

GIVE AND TAKE

On the day before Christmas Eve, Jerome invited Grace to a concert at one of the local churches. By the time he stopped to collect her, the afternoon light was rapidly fading as though blown away by the biting wind. As Grace stepped off the front porch, Jerome offered his arm and looked down at her with a curious gleam in his eyes. He was up to something, she thought, slipping her arm through his, but then it was the season for surprises.

The walk to the church was mercifully short, but long enough on that frigid afternoon to cause Grace to raise the collar of her coat and pull her wool cloche snugly around her ears. Jerome kept her arm tucked closely against his side and set a brisk pace. Even through their thick woolen coats, Grace could feel his warmth where their bodies touched. In the pocket of her free hand, she clasped a narrow rectangular box.

The sanctuary was decorated with garlands of fresh pine and fir boughs. Tall candles, their flames dancing in the drafty space, spilled light onto the plain white altar cloth. Grace and

Jerome slid into a pew to the left of the altar, behind which the choir, wearing deep green robes, clutched their music folders. Studying the bulletin they'd been handed at the door, Grace read that the program included vocal solos and duets, an instrumental interlude with violins and cello, scripture readings, and a carol sing. It also promised a poetry recitation by the Sunday school kindergarten.

People greeted one another with handshakes and best wishes for the season and settled into their seats. Grace glanced sideways at Jerome. She was admiring the pleasing contours of his profile and the way his dark hair curled over his shirt collar when two people approached their pew.

Sliding over to make room for the new arrivals, Grace was pressed against Jerome on her left and the arm that divided the long, curved bench on her right. Unable to squeeze both shoulders into the cramped space, Jerome stretched his arm along the back of the pew, his hand disconcertingly close to her shoulder. He glanced sideways at her, then fixed his gaze on the minister taking his place at the pulpit.

Later, emerging from the church into the December dark, Grace and Jerome headed to the Davisons'. At the back door, they stomped snow off their boots and stepped into the welcome warmth of the kitchen. Fresh scones were cooling on a wire rack and Mrs. Davison was arranging cups and saucers on a tray.

"You go on into the parlor, Grace," she instructed. "There's a fire in the grate and the tea will be ready in a minute." Grace offered to help, but she said, "No no, my dear, go in and warm yourself. Jerome will bring the tray in as soon as it's ready."

Used to being served in the kitchen, Grace was surprised to be directed to the parlor, but as she passed through the dining room she understood the change of venue. A tall fir filled one corner of the room, adding its spicy scent to that of the maple logs crackling in the hearth. Standing with her back to the fire, Grace gazed at the tree lit with strings of colored lights and topped with a blond angel who looked more like a film star than a celestial being.

"The tree is beautiful, Jerome," she said as he came in with the tea tray. "Mrs. Blanchard and I put up a small one, but my father's been too busy at the shop to do much about the holidays at home."

"The lights are a new addition this year," Jerome said. He raised his brows. "Mother's worried they'll get too hot and set the tree on fire, so we only light them when we're sitting in here." He took his place on the sofa and poured Grace a cup of tea. "Here you go, Monty. Come on over and sit down."

Grace set the rectangular box on the table next to a much larger wrapped package. She settled onto the sofa, smiling as she took the proffered cup from Jerome. Maybe it was the glow of the lights or the warmth of the fire or the sweet, buttery taste of the scones that made Grace's chest expand with a giddy sense of well-being. Whatever the reason, she felt a rush of quiet joy and gratitude for this perfect moment.

"It's good to see you smile, Grace," Jerome said, studying her face. "I'm glad to see you looking so happy." Reaching for the large package, he handed it to her. "Here, open this and Merry Christmas." He leaned over and kissed her lightly on the cheek.

Grace could not meet his eyes. Instead she looked down at the package resting on her lap. It was wrapped in silver paper and tied with a wide, green ribbon. Carefully untying the ribbon, she unfolded the ends of the wrapping and the paper fell away to reveal a wooden box. Her name was burned across the top in flowery script. Grace fumbled with the two metal clasps, lifted the lid, and caught her breath. Several metal tubes of paint nestled together in three compartments along the back of the box. There was a small water dish in the middle section along with drawing pencils and two sable paintbrushes. A palette slid out of a frame in the top of the box with a space behind for paper and sketchbook. One by one, Grace read the labels on the tubes: vermillion, cadmium yellow, carmine, cobalt, viridian, sienna. Slowly, she closed the lid, running her fingers over the incised letters of her name.

She smiled at Jerome, but her eyes were moist and she didn't trust herself to speak. She lifted the lid again and gazed at the array of tools and paints, each in its own special place. "Oh, Jerome, it's wonderful. I don't know how I'll ever do it justice."

"I'm not worried," he said. "When I saw it in the window of the art supply store in Exeter, I knew it would be perfect for you." He gave her a crooked smile. "I very nearly ruined it though. After I bought it, I took it to the woodworking shop at the Academy. I had this idea that your name should be on it, but I didn't know how to go about doing it." He chuckled. "The instructor showed me how to use the burning tool and gave me a bunch of scrap wood to practice on. Good thing, too, or that box would have been seriously defaced." He frowned. "As it is, that capital G is pretty awful."

"It's perfect," she said. "Absolutely perfect."

Arriving home in the early evening, Grace was surprised to see a light burning in her father's study. Even though it was Sunday, he'd gone to the shop shortly after breakfast to catch up on inventory and restock the shelves before the last minute shoppers descended on Christmas Eve. She slipped out of her boots and, seeing that his door was open, knocked softly on the doorframe.

Her father looked up from his desk and smiled. "Hello sweetie. How was the concert?"

"It was lovely," she said perching on the arm of his easy chair. "The little Sunday schoolers stole the show reciting *The Night Before Christmas*. They were kindergarteners. Three adorable girls in their best dresses and two squirmy boys whose attention was everywhere but on the poem. Everyone was trying not to laugh, but it was hard to keep a straight face." She pursed her lips. "What are you working on, Daddy?"

"Oh, just cooking the books," he said, giving her a devilish grin. He closed the ledger in which he'd been working and slid it into the top drawer of his desk. "How did Jerome like his fancy pen and pencil set?"

"He liked it fine, but wait till you see what he gave me."

Getting to his feet, her father said, "Bring it into the parlor and we'll have a look." By the time Grace returned from the foyer where she'd left her paint box, he was settled in his chair, a glass of whiskey on the table beside him.

Grace sat on the ottoman, the paint box on her lap. "Look at this Daddy, isn't it wonderful? Jerome put my name on it and everything." She lifted the lid, marveling again at the fat white tubes in their neat compartments each circled with a band of color.

Her father raised his brows and nodded slowly. "Pretty fancy," he said. "Looks like old Jerome really outdid himself." He slid back in his chair and picked up his drink.

Closing the lid, Grace fastened the brass clasps and set the paint box on the table next to the small tree she had decorated with Mrs. Blanchard. She settled into her usual place in the corner of the sofa and watched her father drain his glass. Without another word, he stood, refilled it, and turned to her. His brow was furrowed and his lips were pressed into a thin line. When he spoke his voice had lost its bantering tone.

"What's going on between you and that boy, Grace?"

"Nothing's going on, Daddy. We're friends."

"You go off with him for the whole afternoon and come back with a gift like that and you tell me nothing's going on?" He emptied his glass. "I don't like the idea of you two spending so much time together. You're not kids anymore ... "

Grace felt the heat rise in her cheeks. Why did her father have to ruin everything? She'd been so excited about Jerome's gift. Why couldn't he just be glad for her?

"Jerome and I are friends," she said again, trying to keep her voice level. "And we don't spend a lot of time together; I haven't seen him in months."

She stood and straightened the front of her dress. "I'm going up to change. I'll be down when dinner's ready."

She crossed the room and stopped at the doorway. Turning, she said, "You know, Daddy, I've always tried to do what you and Mama expected of me. I don't think I've ever given you any reason to doubt my judgment and I don't plan to start now."

She passed through into the hall, her knees all but giving way under her. Her father called her name, but she did not stop.

Sleep came late to Grace that night. For a long while she lay awake going over events of the past few days. One thing seemed certain; her friendship with Jerome was changing. They were changing, growing out of childhood and into ... what? She had been furious with her father for suggesting she and Jerome see less of each other, but the Davisons also had concerns about their time together. It wasn't so much Daddy's vigilance that annoyed Grace as the way he practically accused her of wrongdoing. He could stay out to all hours and drink himself silly without having to answer for it, but she couldn't go to a concert with Jerome without getting the third degree. Well, Jerome was going to be home the whole week and she wasn't going to let Daddy spoil another minute of it.

Her father was eating the last of his toast by the time Grace got down to breakfast. As she took her seat, he poured another cup of coffee and wished her good morning.

"Things will be pretty busy at the shop today, Grace," he said. "Your grandfather and I won't make it out of there until late afternoon." His voice was matter-of-fact, friendly even. She understood he had put the evening's unpleasantness behind them and was grateful.

"But don't you always close early on Christmas Eve? We're having dinner with Grandma and Grandpa, aren't we?"

"We are, but it's going to be a late one. First we have to get everyone out of the shop and cash out. Then we've got to set up to open the day after Christmas." He grimaced. "Got to be ready to process all those returns and exchanges." He set his cup down. "I'll get home as soon as I can and try to make myself presentable before we head over to the homestead."

True to his word, Daddy was late getting home Christmas Eve. She was in her room when he knocked on her door to tell her he'd meet her in the parlor after he'd bathed and dressed. Glancing at the bedside clock, she saw it was just after five-thirty. Montel's closed at three on Christmas Eve, so it must have been a busy day. The day after Christmas would be just as hectic. Grandpa had told her that in a good holiday season, the shop would do a quarter to a third of its annual business. If they'd met that goal, Grace thought, the evening might go well.

Grace stood at her dresser and studied the picture again. She'd been leafing through the magazines at Vincent's Pharmacy when she'd come across a two-page spread on holiday hairstyles. The directions made it sound simple, but this would be her third attempt. If she couldn't get it this time, she'd give up. Alma and Christine both wore their hair bobbed, but so far Grace had not been able to part with her long hair. This hairstyle might be the straw that broke the camel's back. Gathering her hair at the side, she twisted it into a tight roll, pinned it along the nape of her neck, and swirled the ends just behind her left ear, fastening the swirl with a decorative hairpin. In the hand mirror, she studied her third and final attempt. Well, she didn't look like the model in the picture, but she liked the soft way it framed her face. The bob could wait.

At the wardrobe, she felt a shiver of anticipation as she pulled her dress off the hanger. She'd seen it in the window of the Mayfair Dress Shop and had immediately gone in to try it on. It fit perfectly and was just right for the holidays. She slipped the deep burgundy velvet over her head, did up the long row of satin-covered buttons, and adjusted the matching collar and cuffs. She stood at the mirror, turning one way and then the other, admiring the drape of the fabric and the way her figure filled out the lines of the dress.

Her father was standing with his back to the fire when Grace entered the parlor a few minutes later. Seeing her, he raised his brows and gave her a brilliant smile. In a dinner jacket, white shirt and black bow tie, freshly shaved, he looked as handsome as Grace had seen him in a long while. All through the busy holiday season, he'd been tired and short-tempered, but this evening he positively glowed with energy and good humor. He was as changeable as the weather and just as unpredictable. Grace crossed the room and planted a kiss on his cheek.

"Merry Christmas, Daddy" she said.

Placing his hands on her shoulders, he studied her at arm's length. "You look lovely, Grace," he said. "And you've done something different with your hair. Turn around and let me have a look." Laughing, she did a quick pirouette. "I wish your mother could see you tonight, sweetie. She'd be so proud."

For a moment they were quiet, then Grace said, "I think you look pretty great yourself, Daddy, and I'm sure Mama would think so, too." She glanced at the mantel clock. "Shall we go?"

They walked to Pleasant Street under gently falling snow. Along the way, porch lights were lit and lamplight shone from house windows. Here and there a house stood dark, its people off celebrating Christmas Eve with family or friends. In the distance, the sound of carols warmed the frigid air. In the bay window of her grandparents' house, the curtains were pulled open, the light from a candelabra bright against the darkness.

Grace's grandparents were in the parlor when she and her father arrived; Grandma in her wingback chair near the fire and Grandpa leaning against the mantel shelf. In a corner, a tall Frasier fir was dressed with silver and gold balls and garlands. Several gifts nestled under its boughs next to the wooden crèche that had once belonged to Grandma's parents.

Grace crossed the room and slipped two wrapped packages under the tree, before kissing her grandparents and wishing them Merry Christmas. Her grandmother squeezed her hand and said, "You look lovely, Grace. So grown up." She shook her head. "Seems like just yesterday you were a little girl. Where does the time go?"

"Seems to go by faster every year," Grandpa said. "Now what can I get everyone to drink?"

He poured whiskey for Grace's father and himself and handed Grandma a glass of sherry. "We're down to the last few bottles of your precious sherry, my dear," he said grinning. "When it's gone, you'll have to switch to Signora Scappilini's homemade wine."

"I'll never stoop that low. There should be a prohibition against Mrs. Scappilini's homemade wine," Grandma said, wrinkling her nose. "Help yourself to some eggnog, Grace, and we'll toast to the holiday."

After they'd raised their glasses in honor of the season, Grandpa cleared his throat. "And a toast to Francis for a very successful year at the shop." Grace saw the wary look on her father's face and wondered what was coming next. "I know we haven't always seen eye to eye on the business, my boy, but you've got us operating in the black again. The bills are getting paid on time and we're back in the good graces of our suppliers. Your grandfather would be proud." He raised his glass. "To Francis!"

Grace's father nodded his acknowledgement, but said nothing.

After dinner the family returned to the parlor to exchange gifts. Grandma gave Grace a leather handbag with a tooled art deco design on the front. Opening the clasp, she found a blue savings passbook nestled in the satin lining. She pulled it out and lifted the stiff cover. The account had a twenty dollar balance.

She looked at her grandmother who shook her head. "Grandpa?"

"It's time you learned to manage money, my girl. There's no better time to begin saving than right now." He rocked back on his heels, hands in his trouser pockets. "We never know what the future will bring."

The following Saturday, her grandfather's words came back to Grace when her father came home in the early afternoon. She'd assumed he was at the shop, so was surprised when he called to her from the bottom of the stairs to come down, he had something to show her. She hurried down to the foyer where Daddy, red-cheeked and breathless, held her coat.

The next minute, she was standing on the porch staring at a sparkling blue automobile with a cream colored convertible top. The tires were rimmed in white and shiny spokes radiated out from the center as though woven by a fantastic species of spider. Two bulbous headlamps sat over the swooping fenders with Chief Pontiac perched atop the grille.

"Isn't she a beauty, Gracie?" her father said. "Wait till you take a ride in her. She's as fast and smooth as a cat." He headed down the porch stairs. "Come see the inside."

Grace followed him onto the sidewalk. He opened the passenger door and gestured for her to get in. She slid onto the smooth upholstery and ran her hand over the gleaming dashboard. The interior smelled of leather and extravagance.

Her father cranked the motor and hurried around to the driver's seat. He pulled away from the curb and turned left onto

Main Street. Soon they were heading north, houses and trees sliding past, the low winter sun glinting off the car's glossy paintwork. Grace had no idea where they were going or where her father's latest folly would take them.

Grace had arranged to meet Jerome at the library the following Monday, New Year's Eve. Pushing open the heavy oak door, she passed the Reading Room where Mrs. Proudie was shelving books. Shouldering her book bag, Grace made her way between the stacks, heading for the same table at which she and Jerome had their first real conversation more than four years before.

Through an opening in one of the shelves, she glimpsed Jerome and stopped. He was bent over a book, his dark hair falling over his forehead, his long fingers toying with the corner of the page. It was a familiar posture, one Grace had seen countless times. It was her reaction that was so singular. For a wild moment, she pictured herself coming up behind his chair and wrapping her arms around his neck. Imagined placing her cheek against his, feeling his warmth, inhaling the scent of his skin. Her cheeks burned. Catching her breath, she exhaled slowly in an effort to compose herself.

Jerome turned then, and through the opening, looked into her flushed face. She did not move, but watched him get to his feet, walk to the end of the row, and turn down the aisle in her direction. Without a word, he placed his hand along the side of her face and bent toward her. His lips were soft and full and Grace leaned into the kiss.

They heard the rattle of the book cart and sprang apart. The librarian pulled the cart behind the circulation desk and, seeing them scanning the titles, asked if she could help them find anything.

Jerome pulled a book off the shelf and held it aloft. "Found it," he whispered. "Thanks, Mrs. Proudie, but we're all set."

Not sure if her legs would support her, Grace walked slowly to the table and fell into the chair opposite Jerome's. He took his seat, placed the book on the table, and folded his hands on top of it. With an exaggerated breath, he widened his eyes and grinned across at her. Grace stifled a giggle, trying to quell the joy and confusion threatening to give her away.

Jerome leaned across the table and whispered, "I think we'd better get out of here, don't you?"

A moment later, they stood on the sidewalk. Grace had the odd sensation of watching herself from above, as though she were outside her body taking in their surroundings from a bird's eye view. Cars cruised down Main Street, people went in and out of shops or hurried by hunched into their heavy coats. The postman sorted a handful of envelopes as he headed up the courthouse steps. The world around them was apparently unchanged, but Grace felt completely transformed.

"Monty," Jerome said, "I ... well, I ... " He paused. Grace looked at him and he shook his head. "I hope ... that is, I ... "

Always quick with a clever comment or apt response, Jerome was, on this occasion, apparently tongue-tied. Touched, Grace smiled and laid a gloved hand on his arm. "I hope you're not going to apologize." She furrowed her brow. "You're not sorry about what just happened, are you?"

He laughed. "Absolutely not, I just wish Mrs. Proudie'd had a few more books to shelve."

Late the next morning, Grace was in the foyer waiting for Jerome. She was dressed for skating in a heavy wool skirt over thick stockings and a bulky sweater. Her jacket, scarf, hat and mittens were piled on the hall chair, but even without them she was perspiring freely under her layers. It wasn't that the hallway was overly warm; anticipation was making her sweat. Peeking again through the sidelight, she saw Jerome coming down the snow-covered sidewalk, skates slung over one shoulder. She slipped on her outerwear, pulled her hat low over her forehead, and stepped onto the porch.

On the sidewalk, they greeted one another awkwardly. Grace and Jerome had been skating together every winter since they'd known each other, but today the experience felt new. They turned onto Pleasant Street, entered the park at its far end, and followed the path to Horn Field, freshly flooded by the fire department pump truck.

Early mornings at the rink were reserved for hockey players. Grace and Jerome waved to a couple of fellows they knew from school. Heated from their game, the boys were red-faced and sweating, jostling one another and bickering about the score. Their skates were hanging from the ends of their sticks which they carried across their shoulders like hobo bindles.

Grace sat on a wooden bench and untied her boots. This was the worst part of skating; getting into and lacing her skates. Stuffing her mittens in her pocket, she pulled on the skates and took hold of the long laces.

"Here, let me do that," Jerome said. "No sense in both of us freezing our fingers off." Kneeling at her feet, he began threading the laces through the rows of eyelets. Grace felt a bit like a lady being paid court by a knight, a sensation that was disconcerting and thrilling at the same time. When he looked into her face and smiled, she could hardly breathe. Something was happening. Something rapturous, and yet exquisitely painful, had erupted between them. Something that could bring them closer or split them apart.

In the hour they spent circling the ice, his arm around her waist, her hand in his, they spoke little. Grace had trouble framing her thoughts; all her attention was focused on the places where their bodies touched. In spite of the cold, the snow and ice, the biting wind, Grace was warm, tingling with nervous energy. Jerome seemed as distracted as she, holding her as close as their heavy clothes allowed.

On the way home, chilled and not quite grounded, they walked past the closed shops along Main Street and took the shortcut down the alley near Montel's. Surprised to see the blue Pontiac parked behind the shop, Grace stopped.

"What is it?" Jerome asked.

"My father's car is parked in the alley. Why would he be at the shop this morning and why would he have bothered driving his car the short distance from home?"

Shifting position, Grace caught sight of an old delivery van, its sign painted out, parked in front of the Pontiac. Then, a man she'd never seen before, dressed in rough work clothes and wearing a flat tweed cap, came out the back door of the shop, followed closely by her father. The fellow pulled a sturdy carton from the van and set it in the trunk of the Pontiac. Grace's father passed something to the man which he stuffed in a trouser pocket, before climbing into his vehicle. As they watched, the Pontiac backed slowly out of the narrow alley and headed up Main Street. A minute later, the delivery van pulled out and turned in the opposite direction.

12

EXAMINATIONS

"What do you think that was about?" Even as she asked the question, Grace knew exactly what had taken place between her father and the man in the cloth cap. Shifting the tied laces of her skates higher on her shoulder, she frowned and pushed her hands deeper into her pockets. Jerome didn't answer and, instead, steered her down the path.

"That man was selling my father whiskey, wasn't he, Jerome?" She exhaled, her breath forming clouds of vapor in the frosty air. "I wondered where he got it and now I guess I know."

Jerome placed his arm around her shoulder and pulled her close. "Don't take it so hard, Monty. I bet half the town gets whiskey from that fellow or someone like him."

"Maybe so, but suppose someone else had seen what we just saw. What would happen to the shop if my father got caught?"

"I care more about what would happen to you, Grace, but if he's careful there's probably not too much to worry about. The police aren't interested in a few bottles of whiskey. The fellows at school from Boston and New York say the bootleggers there pay the cops to look the other way. A lot of people think Prohibition is a mistake." He grinned. "And it's not like your father's a bank robber or a jewel thief. Just because he takes a drink now and then doesn't mean he's a criminal."

Now and then. How different life would be if her father only drank now and then. But Daddy drank every day, drank until he passed out or staggered to bed. Grace sighed. Even if alcohol were legal, that kind of drinking would still be a crime.

Grace woke the next morning to a stuffed head and aching bones. Turning off her alarm, she rolled onto her side and pulled the blankets up to her chin. Her feet were freezing. A rapid volley of sneezes made her eyes water and her nose run. She stumbled out of bed, pulled a handkerchief from a bureau drawer, blew and blew again, then crawled back under the covers. Shivering, she clamped her jaws shut and moaned.

A few minutes later, Mrs. Blanchard knocked on her door. "Grace, it's time to get up." Opening the door a crack she said, "Why, what's the matter, dear. Are you ill?"

"I've caught a cold, Mrs. B. I feel awful." Seized by another bout of sneezing, she fumbled for her hanky. Mrs. Blanchard crossed the room and laid a hand on Grace's forehead.

"You're not feverish, at least. I'll be right back with something hot to drink and an extra blanket."

"Thanks, Mrs. B, and will you tell my father?"

She must have dozed off because it seemed like no time at all before the housekeeper was back carrying a small tray and a hot water bottle, an extra blanket tucked under her arm. Setting the tray on the bedside table, she slipped the hot water bottle under the covers and spread the blanket over the counterpane.

"Here, dear, sit up and I'll get these pillows behind you." She dropped two aspirin into Grace's palm and handed her a glass of water. Grace swallowed the pills and settled back onto the pillows. She was sipping Mrs. B's remedy of hot lemon water laced with honey when her father appeared at the door.

Crossing the room and sitting on the edge of the bed, he said, "Mrs. Blanchard says you're feeling poorly." He was dressed for work and smelled of coffee and bay rum. "You'd better stay put and get some rest, sweetie. Nip this thing in the bud." He checked his watch. "I've got to get going, but Mrs. B will take good care of you, all right?" He bent to kiss her forehead. Then he was gone.

Grace slid further under the covers and woke a couple hours later when Mrs. B came in with a cup of beef broth. The rest of the morning, she sat propped against the headboard reading and working her way through several more hankies. Her head throbbed and her nose felt like it had been rubbed with sandpaper. In mid-afternoon Mrs. Blanchard brought up another of her cold remedies and the current issue of McClure's, delivered that morning.

"I'm going out to pick up a few things for dinner, Grace, but won't be gone for more than an hour or so. Will you be all right by yourself? Can I get you anything before I leave?"

"I'll be fine." Grace smiled. "Thanks to your lemon and honey and the extra sleep, I'm feeling better." She blew her nose and winced. "Except for my poor nose."

When she was alone, Grace pulled the covers up to her chin and closed her eyes. She could hear the housekeeper in the kitchen getting ready to leave, the clang of the woodstove's iron lid and the thump of the back door being pulled shut. For a while she indulged in thoughts of Jerome, replaying the scene in the library stacks and the way she'd felt watching him bent over the laces of her skates. Now he was back in Exeter and it would be months before she saw him again. She sighed and stared at the ceiling.

That fellow with the delivery truck, had he really been selling whiskey to her father? Grace tossed back the covers, put on her robe and slippers, and hurried downstairs. Daddy would be furious if he knew what she was about to do, but he wasn't here and she had to know. Shivering, she entered the parlor and crossed to the sideboard.

She crouched in front of the right hand door and pulled on the brass handle. Inside, standing shoulder to shoulder in the dark were twelve unopened bottles of Canadian whiskey. Straightening, she glanced at the mantel clock. Mrs. B had been gone almost an hour. She should head back upstairs, but there was one more thing she had to do.

Daddy's study door was open. The room was cold and smelled of ashes and aftershave. Her father's desk was tidy, the loose papers piled in a wire tray. Near the inkstand there was a framed photo of her mother and a small ceramic dish of paper clips. Clamping her jaw shut to still her chattering teeth, she tugged at the handle of the middle drawer, the one she'd seen Daddy shove a ledger into the afternoon of the holiday concert. It didn't budge. Locked, but where was the key? She grabbed the ceramic dish, ready to empty its contents onto the blotter, but stopped and held her breath.

Mrs. Blanchard was back. Grace ran from the study and up the stairs. Just as she reached the landing, she heard the tap-tap of Mrs. B's sensible shoes on the foyer tiles. Hurling herself into bed, she smoothed the covers over her lap and picked up the magazine lying nearby. A moment later, the housekeeper knocked lightly and peeked around the door. She asked how the patient was feeling and Grace said she thought she'd be well enough to go to school tomorrow. Mrs. B suggested a light supper on a tray and an early bedtime. Grace agreed.

Alone again, she laid the magazine aside and frowned. Daddy always kept his ledgers in the deep side drawer of his desk, but that day he'd slipped the one he'd been working on into the middle drawer. Had he locked it then? She couldn't remember, but it was certainly locked today. And what about the key? It used to be loose among the pencils and pens in the drawer's tray. She could picture it, a small brass key on a chain. Where was it now?

Grace did go back to school the next day. In every class, teachers were talking about mid-term exams. The results would weigh heavily on the overall grade for the class and Grace was determined to do well. She knew she was lucky to be able to go to high school, even if it wasn't a fancy boarding school like the Academy. Her friend Mary worked long days for Miss Andrews at the milliner's shop and she wasn't the only grammar school friend whose family relied on them for financial help. Grace meant to take advantage of this opportunity, not just for herself or her family, but for Jerome, too.

During the following two weeks, Grace and her friends worked every day after school, preparing for exams and working on end-of-term papers. Mostly, they studied at the Montels' large dining room table where they wouldn't bother Christine's ailing grandfather or be bothered by Alma's pesky little sister. Grace and her friends were a perfect match, each strong in a subject where the others were weak, and all hard-working.

On this first day of the January thaw, Grace was finding it hard to concentrate on the work she, Alma, and Christine had set for themselves. They'd made it through their French review and were slogging through a list of equations Mr. Hughes had given them. Grace slid her work across the table and Alma ran down the list of problems, checking her answers. Most of them were right, but there were three in a row that needed correcting. Grace sighed and tossed her pencil on the table.

"I can't do any more today, girls," she said pushing back her chair. She held up her hand to ward off Alma's objections. "I promise I'll finish them later. Really, cross my heart. But let's get outside before the sun's completely gone. I'll walk you both home."

Christine was on her feet in an instant, gathering up her books and papers. "Good idea, Gracie," she said. "My head feels like it's stuffed with straw."

Alma offered no argument and, hustling into their boots and coats, they were soon out on the sidewalk breathing in the fresh, moist air. They dawdled along High Street, commenting on the snow melt rushing in the gutters and watching a cat follow the drip, drip, drip of icicles from its perch on a porch railing. By the time they reached Alma's house, the sun had set, and when Grace said good-bye to Christine a few blocks later, the street lamps were on.

Grace turned down a side street and onto Main. Walking past the lighted shops, she saw Mr. Scapalini in his white apron behind the meat counter of his deli and glimpsed Miss Andrews chatting with a customer at the milliner's. At Montel's she paused. In the light from the overhead lamps, the wood-paneled walls glowed and a spiral of patterned neckties shone like the jewel-toned shards of a kaleidoscope. Raymond, her father's assistant, looked to be ringing up a sale. Grace recognized the customer as one of Grandma's Pleasant Street neighbors. The woman turned and nodded at Grace as she passed through the door.

Stepping inside, Grace looked around for her father. "Hello, Raymond. I was just passing by on my way home. I thought I'd check with my father to see when he'd be leaving."

"Mr. Montel's not here, Miss. He's been gone since shortly after noon. Set off with a fellow in a black Lincoln, saying he had an errand to run." He shrugged. "Told me I should cash out if he wasn't back by closing time, so looks like that's what I'm going to do."

"Funny, he didn't mention anything about an errand this morning." Grace frowned. "Do you know where he was going?"

Raymond shook his head. "No, just that he'd be a while, that's all."

Back on the street, Grace shivered. It wasn't like Daddy to leave the shop in the middle of the day. She cut through the alley and headed home along the shortcut. There were no streetlights here and the bushes and outbuildings looked slightly menacing in the dark. Grace pulled her collar up and pushed her hands further into her pockets. It was bad enough that Daddy was gone most evenings, but for him to leave the shop in the middle of the day ... and what was this mysterious errand?

Mrs. Blanchard opened the door just as Grace stepped onto the front porch. "I wish you wouldn't go out so late in the afternoon, Gracie. It's not a good idea to be out walking alone after dark."

Sometimes Grace resented the housekeeper's fussing, but not this time. "You're right, Mrs. B. I was dawdling along and didn't realize how late it was. And it got so cold once the sun went down."

Mrs. Blanchard helped her off with her coat and smiled."Well, no harm done. You go on up and change. Your father should be home soon."

In her room, Grace put on her old corduroy jumper and pulled on a heavy sweater. At the dresser, she removed the pins from her hair and shook it out. She worked the brush through the tangles until her hair bristled with static. Making a face at the Medusa in the mirror, she gathered her hair at the back of her neck and fastened it with a barrette.

In the parlor a fire was burning in the hearth and the lamps cast comforting pools of light onto the glossy tabletops. Grace planted herself in front of the fire, holding her hands out to the blaze. Her thawing fingers tingled and she leaned forward blinking into the heat. Then she turned, warming her back, grateful for the cozy room and relieved to be in out of the cold and dark. Where had her father gone in the middle of the workday? What kind of errand was he on and who was he with? She looked at the mantel clock. It was just past 6:00. Would he be back in time for dinner?

Crossing to the sofa, she snuggled into her usual corner, and tucking her legs under her, rubbed her still-cold feet. Her mind was searching for answers, but she had so little to go on. The fellow in the delivery truck. An errand. A black Lincoln. Her father's tread on the porch stairs brought her around and she hurried into the foyer to greet him.

"Hi Daddy, how was your day?" He slipped out of his coat and she took it from him and hung it up.

"Oh, the usual." He flashed a smile, the one he used like a shield, shiny and cool. "Things are kind of slow now that the holidays are over. Won't be a whole lot going on until the spring inventory starts coming in."

They went into the parlor. Daddy poured himself a drink and Grace settled back onto the sofa. He asked her about school and talked about the shop, but she was waiting to see what he'd say about the errand he'd been on. If he didn't mention it, she'd have to in case Raymond told him she'd stopped by.

"Gracie? Honey, did you hear me?"

"What? Oh, sorry Daddy, what were you saying?"

He frowned and took another sip of his drink. "I was saying I have to go out this evening. There's a Chamber of Commerce meeting to plan for the winter carnival over at the Odd Fellows Hall. It'll probably go pretty late. Some of those fellows like to hear themselves talk."

At dinner, they were quiet, busy with their food. Her long walk in the cold had left Grace hungry and Mrs. B's salmon pie was one of her favorites. As usual, Daddy was more interested in the wine than in the food. If Grace was going to say anything, she'd better do it before he downed another glass. She cleared her throat.

"Daddy, I stopped by the shop late this afternoon after walking my friends home." She watched for his reaction, but he didn't look up from his plate. "Raymond said you were off running an errand."

"That's right, sweetie. I had a little business to attend to." He waggled his fork and grinned. "Someone has a birthday next week and that's all I'm going to say."

A convenient excuse, but one Grace wasn't buying.

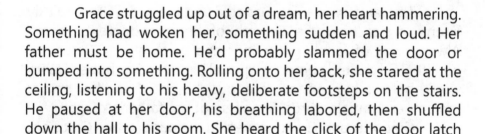

Grace struggled up out of a dream, her heart hammering. Something had woken her, something sudden and loud. Her father must be home. He'd probably slammed the door or bumped into something. Rolling onto her back, she stared at the ceiling, listening to his heavy, deliberate footsteps on the stairs. He paused at her door, his breathing labored, then shuffled down the hall to his room. She heard the click of the door latch and the squeak of springs as he fell onto the bed.

Turning on the bedside light, she checked the clock. Twelve-thirty. Since when did Chamber meetings last until midnight? They might if all the members were as drunk as her father. Grace sat up and folded her arm across her chest. The chill of the room raised goose bumps on her skin, but her cheeks burned with anger. Her father had lied to her again, but she was through lying to herself.

In the ensuing days, Grace applied herself to her studies with a new clarity of purpose. She'd always been diligent about her schoolwork, always taken pride in earning good grades. Now, her future depended on it. The only way she would get clear of the muddle and upheaval of life with her father was to make a life for herself. And to do that, she'd need a job. She'd thought a lot about Aunt Louise's suggestion that she attend normal school where she could work on her art and earn a teaching degree. She didn't have any burning desire to be a teacher, but it would be a way for her to make a living.

When grades were posted at the end of the week, Grace had scored first in English and History and in the top ten in all her other subjects. At this rate, she was almost guaranteed acceptance at Mansfield Normal School with the added benefit of a safe and loving home with her aunt and uncle.

The following Saturday was her birthday. On their way to Pleasant Street for a celebratory dinner, her father was lavish in his praise of her academic successes. She hadn't seen much of him this week; he hadn't been home for dinner the last three evenings. When she had seen him, though, he'd been good-humored and exuberant, the way he'd been during the store renovations: full of nervous energy, almost frenzied. It had worried her then and it worried her now.

The January evening was cold and the two walked quickly, intent on reaching the warmth of her grandparents' home. Always wary of family gatherings and celebrations, Grace was nonetheless excited about this special birthday. She hoped Daddy would behave himself for once, but she was doing her best to remember Auntie's words. She was not her father's keeper.

Grandma and Grandpa were in the parlor when Grace and her father arrived. A fire blazed in the hearth, and on a low table in front of the sofa hors d'oeuvres were arranged on a silver tray. After giving Grandpa a hug, Grace joined her grandmother on the sofa. When she bent to kiss Grandma's papery cheek, she breathed in the familiar aroma of rose water and Pears soap and caught sight of a beautifully wrapped package on the end table.

"Help yourself to the cheese and fruit, Gracie, while your grandfather serves the drinks. We'll go in to dinner once you've opened your gifts." Grandma looked at Daddy. "Is that all right with you, Francis?"

He tapped his jacket pocket. "Fine with me, Mother. No need to keep the birthday girl waiting."

"Your aunt and uncle sent this up for you, Grace. They were sorry they couldn't be here, but the new semester just started at the college and Arthur couldn't get away." She handed Grace the package.

Removing the paper and opening the box, Grace parted the tissue within, uncovering a gorgeous silk blouse. It was the color of the sage Mrs. B grew in the herb garden, shirred across the shoulders with narrow, cuffed sleeves.

"Oh, it's beautiful," she said holding the blouse up in front of her.

"And it matches your eyes perfectly, dear," Grandma said. "Louise has always had excellent taste."

"You'll look a proper lady in that," Grandpa said, shaking his head. "I don't know where the time goes."

Grace's grandparents' gift was twofold: an easel and the promise of art lessons with Mr. Ward Standish. A longtime friend of Grandma's, Mr. Standish was a landscape painter whose work hung in galleries in Boston and New York as well as in local homes. One of his paintings held pride of place over the mantel, a steep waterfall sun-dappled, frothy, and so convincing you could almost hear it sluicing over the rocks.

"What a perfect gift," Grace said, hugging first Grandma, then Grandpa. She raised an eyebrow and pursed her lips. "Though I don't know if I'm quite ready to work with the likes of Mr. Standish. I'm really just a beginner."

"Nonsense," her grandmother said. "You've been drawing and painting for years now, to say nothing of your art classes in school. I think working with Ward is the logical next step, and he seems to agree. He was more than willing to take you on."

Grandpa cleared his throat. "I'll wager there's more to his taking Gracie on than that." He leveled his gaze at Grandma.

Grace glanced from one to another. "What do you mean, Grandpa?"

"Pay him no mind, dear. He's just being cantankerous." She smiled affectionately at Grace's grandfather. "Now, Francis, I believe you have something for your daughter?"

Daddy set down his drink, reached into his pocket, and pulled out a thin velvet box. "Here you go, sweetie. Wear them in good health." He kissed her cheek and, stepping back, picked up his glass.

Lifting the hinged lid, Grace caught her breath. Inside lay a string of perfectly-matched pearls. She looked at the softly glowing orbs on their bed of white satin, then at her father. His smile was wide, crinkling the corners of his eyes and making them seem even bluer than usual. Clearly, he was pleased with his gift and expected her to be, too. She saw Grandpa frown and shake his head, saw Grandma give him a warning glance.

"Here, honey, let's see how they look." He lifted the pearls from the box, and fastened the gold clasp at the back of her neck. Grace turned to face him. He tipped his head, studying her and his smile was quiet, almost sad.

"You look beautiful, sweetie." He blinked. "I wish your mother could see you now."

Grace threw her arms around his neck and he held her tight for a long moment. He missed Mama, too. She mustn't forget that.

13

CHANGING LANDSCAPES

Grace headed down High Street clutching a slip of paper in her gloved hand, studying the house numbers as she moved along. She looked again at the address she'd copied down. 157. Should be right on this block. Then she was there, standing in front of a three-story clapboard apartment house that might once have been white or maybe pale grey. Inside the front door, a poorly lit stairwell led to the floors above. Mr. Standish lived on the top floor. The hallway was a dingy green, the walls lumpy with patches and cracks. Even though Mr. Standish was well regarded as a landscape and still life painter, it appeared money was scarce.

Piles of old newspapers, an empty wood box, and a dozen or so discarded plant pots half filled with dried soil littered the third floor landing. A large, orange cat, perched on the windowsill, peered at her through narrowed yellow eyes. Grace murmured a greeting to the cat and knocked on the door. It was answered by a pale, rawboned woman wearing a dour expression and an apron over a faded house dress. Grace introduced herself. The woman stepped aside, gesturing for her to enter. The cat dropped lightly off the windowsill and followed her in.

Unnerved by the woman's gloomy aspect, Grace stood uncertainly on the rag rug in front of the door. Mrs. Standish, or whoever she was, poked her head into the adjoining room, muttered something Grace couldn't make out, then said, "He's ready for you. Go on in."

On the threshold, Grace stopped. The spacious, high-ceilinged room was flooded with light from the tall windows on its two outside walls. Large canvases leaned against every available surface. The walls were hung with smaller paintings and the table tops and shelving covered with stacks of watercolor studies, bits of bark, piles of stones and minerals, birds' nests and feathers. On an easel set up in front of the west facing window, the afternoon light lit up a medium-sized canvas of a mountain lake surrounded by white birches.

The artist turned from his study of the painting and looked at Grace. He was tall and stoop-shouldered, well past middle age, thin and rangy. His white hair grew in a curly bush and his eyes, icy blue and deep set, were shaded by thick bristling brows. He wore a plaid flannel shirt, baggy corduroy trousers, and paint-spattered tennis shoes. He was everything a painter should be and Grace liked him immediately.

"Ah, Miss Montel, so nice to meet you," he said, covering the distance between them in two long strides. "Please, put your box on that table and sit down." He gestured to a small sitting area in the corner between the two sets of windows where ladder-backed chairs stood catty-cornered on a tattered Persian rug.

Grace smiled and took the chair he indicated. She watched as Mr. Standish folded his long, thin frame onto the other. He was like a great bird, an egret or heron, awkward and graceful at the same time. He crossed one leg over the other, clasped his hands around his knees, and leaned toward her.

"I've known your grandmother for some time, Miss Montel. She tells me you're interested in drawing and painting. I'm usually reluctant to take on new students, but," he smiled and raised his bushy brows, "I never could resist your grandmother."

"Few people can, Mr. Standish. My grandmother is a force."

He threw back his head and laughed. "And you are very much like her if I'm not mistaken. Now, let's have a look at what you've done and we'll go from there."

As the long weeks of winter wore on, Grace's father spent fewer and fewer evenings at home. Some nights, he left shortly after Grace went to her room to study or prepare for her lessons with Mr. Standish. She thought she knew where he went on those occasions. What she couldn't fathom is where he went when he didn't come home for dinner, but was away from the time he closed the shop to well after midnight. Those days she ate with Mrs. B in the kitchen. She'd asked the housekeeper if she knew where her father was or what he was doing, but if Mrs. Blanchard knew, she wasn't saying. Whatever Daddy was getting up to, Grace was pretty sure it wasn't good.

One windy Saturday in February, Grace decided to pay a visit to her old school friend, Mary, whom she knew she'd find at Miss Andrews' Millinery. The bell tinkled as she pushed open the door and stepped into the warmth of the small shop. She approached the counter just as Mary pushed aside the curtain separating the retail space from the workroom behind.

"Well, hello, Gracie," Mary said. "What brings you out on a day like this? It's freezing out there."

"It sure is, but it's nice and warm in here." Grace set a hat box on the counter. "My grandmother's been going through her closet and gave me this hat. She said I should come down and talk to Miss Andrews about getting it trimmed."

"Let's see what you've got there, Gracie. Miss Andrews is running a few errands, but I'm sure I can help you."

Mary was dressed in her navy gabardine uniform with its prim white collar, her hair braided and coiled around her head, looking every inch a working girl. Grace pulled the hat from its box and handed it to her.

"Ah, it's one of ours and in beautiful shape, too. It will go perfectly with your coat, Grace. Try it on, let's see how it looks." She slid an oval mirror across the counter.

Grace picked up the mirror and studied the hat made of wool tapestry in shades of green and brown. The turned up brim was lined in green velvet, bringing out the color of her eyes.

"A new band should spruce it up," Mary said. "Wide gros-grain, I think." From under the counter, she pulled out a tray of ribbon, roll after roll, the colors in hues from light to dark. They agreed on a honey-brown and then Mary said, "Wait here, Gracie. I think I have just the right finishing touch." She stepped behind the curtain, returning from the workroom with two small green feathers, edged in gold.

The business of the hat being decided, Grace and Mary caught up on what each of them had been doing. Mary put in long hours at the shop under the watchful eye of Miss Andrews, but she liked the work well enough.

"It gets me out of the house and brings in a bit of money to help Ma with the bills," she said. She shook her head. "Poor Ma's had another little one since I been here, so she's worked to the bone. Da's as ornery as ever." She shrugged.

"It's a blessing he's not home much. Works all day then heads to Clancy's after supper. Makes a racket coming in some nights, but at least he's not home harping at us all evening."

Grace frowned. Clancy's had been closed for ages, the sign down and the front windows boarded up. "So Mr. Clancy's doing business somewhere else, I guess," Grace said.

"Ever since he had to shut down the saloon, he's been running a speakeasy out of the basement of one of his tene-ments down on Grafton Street." Mary pulled a dust cloth from the shelf behind her and ran it over the glass-topped counter. She glanced at the clock. "Muller closed his saloon, too, but Paddy says there's plenty of traffic in and out of his warehouse after dark. My brother works the late shift at the mill and he says there's no end of cars and trucks going in and out of there." She folded the cloth and put it away.

"They say old man Muller's working for a city fellow who brings in whiskey and beer from Canada."

At the tinkle of the doorbell, Mary straightened and smoothed the front of her uniform. "Hello, Miss Andrews. Grace has brought us a hat to trim. I told her we'd have it ready by Monday afternoon."

Grace thanked Mary, asked after Miss Andrews' mother, and left the shop. Outside, she pulled up the collar of her coat, slid her gloved hands into her pockets, and leaned into the wind. Walking down Main Street past the boarded up remains of Clancy's saloon, she turned onto Grafton. The houses at the top of the street were small single-family dwellings with scruffy front yards and drooping clotheslines out back. Further along these gave way to three-story tenements, their steep stairways covered by shingled overhangs.

The blocks were all pretty much the same, great square buildings fronted by porches on each floor, their weathered clapboards in need of paint. Children played King of the Mountain on the frozen piles of dirty snow left by the plows or chased each other brandishing icicle swords. Grace walked briskly, the cold seeping through her heavy coat and thick stockings, and stopped in front of a faded green block with a wrought iron fence along the front. To the right of the ground-floor entrance, a short set of stairs led to what must be the basement.

Grace followed the fence toward the corner of the building. Midway along, at the bottom of the short flight of stairs, there was a glossy, black door, flanked by a pair of brass lamps. In the center of the door a small opening was covered by a sliding panel.

Stepping back, she looked up and down the street. A boy of about twelve was walking toward her, a large canvas bag slung across his thin frame, a wool cap pulled low over his forehead.

"Not open this time of day, Miss," he said, grinning. "You'll have to come back later if you're lookin' to get served."

Grace didn't answer and, ignoring his cheeky salute, turned her back on him. Once he was out of sight, she rounded the building and walked up the driveway. A delivery van with its sign painted out was parked behind the tenement. Not far from the parked van, there was a kind of lean-to, a makeshift thing with a roof and slatted walls on three sides. Taking a quick look

around to make sure she was alone, Grace crossed the short distance and slid behind it. Several metal garbage cans were lined
up under the roof, their lids askew, and in one corner a couple
of shovels and a rake rested against the wall. Grace wrinkled her
nose. It stank back here of beer and rancid chicken and something like the rubbing alcohol Mrs. B used to relieve her aches
and pains .

As she stood watching the building for signs of life, a car
rolled slowly down the driveway and pulled up just to the right
of the tenement door. It was almost as long as the delivery van,
sleek and black, with gleaming spoked wheels and white-rimmed
tires. Whoever was in the car was not in a hurry to get out. He cut
the engine, but the door didn't open.   What was keeping the
fellow? Was he reading something? Checking accounts or writing up invoices? Loading a gun? Grace shuddered. She was being ridiculous, letting her imagination run away with her. Even
so, she'd better get out of here. The last thing she needed was to
be caught snooping around the back of Clancy's speakeasy. As
soon as the driver went into the building, she'd head home.

Finally, the car door opened. Grace watched the big man
emerge, open overcoat, silk scarf, shiny black brogans. Donning
a grey fedora, he closed the door gently, pulled a key from his
trouser pocket, and locked it. Turning, he looked around, his gaze
moving over the old truck, the lean-to, the back of the building.
He checked his watch, replaced it, and approached the door. He
did not knock.

This was her chance, but Grace continued to peek through
the slats of the lean-to, her mind abuzz with speculation. She
recognized the old delivery van, remembered the fellow in the
flat cap who'd sold Daddy the whiskey stored in the sideboard.
Obviously, Mr. Clancy was in the business of selling alcohol which
he had to buy from someone. Might this fellow in the fancy car
be that someone? One thing seemed clear. At this hour on a
Saturday morning, he wasn't here to patronize the speakeasy.

Grace shivered and looked around for a way to get onto
the street without going back down the driveway. No telling who
might show up here next. She could just imagine Daddy's reaction if they crossed paths in Clancy's dooryard.

On the opposite side of the building, a narrow alley led to the street. Near the entrance, there was a stack of wooden crates and what looked to be broken bits of furniture: a backless chair, a table leg, a shard of mirrored glass reflecting the peeling clapboard siding. She could easily skirt that mess and be on her way home in a matter of seconds.

Inching to the far end of the lean-to, Grace could make out the side of the building facing the alley. There were windows there, three that she could see, five or so feet from the ground. She'd need to be careful passing under those windows, but they were sure to be closed; it was freezing out here. If she didn't get home soon, she'd have chilblains and Mrs. B would want to know why.

Crouching low, she scurried across the dirt yard to the alley, stopping before the first window to gauge its height. Its sill was just above her head, room to pass under and not be seen if she was careful. Grace moved gingerly down the alley, picking her way around broken bottles, rusty cans, and crumpled cartons half buried in ice and blackened snow. Mid-way along, the toe of her boot nudged a stack of crates, sending them tumbling onto the frozen ground. She held her breath and pressed herself against the wall.

Voices and the sound of footsteps. Someone at the nearest window, raising the sash. The window opened a crack. She heard a grunt and an expletive.

"Damn thing's stuck," a voice said. "It'd take four men and a boy to raise that sash. No tellin' when it was open last."

Another voice, but Grace couldn't make out the words. "Naw, there's nothin' out there ... probably just some kids that got scared off."

She was stupid ever to have come here. What if one of the fellows inside saw her? What possible excuse could she have for being here? And she was so cold she could barely feel her feet. For a long moment, she stood listening, the cold of the building seeping into her bones. When she was satisfied there was no sound of voices or footsteps, she began moving along the wall again, sliding more than walking, watching her footing every step of the way.

Gaining the end of the alley, Grace looked up and down the street. No sign of the newsboy or anyone else. With the wind at her back, she turned toward home.

By the time she arrived, her hands and feet were numb, and her stomach felt as hollow as a drum. She entered the kitchen through the back door, the aroma of freshly baked bread and rich soup making her mouth water. Removing her boots, she stood before the blazing cookstove, warming her hands and toes, her frozen cheeks tingling.

"Lord, Gracie," Mrs. B said, "whatever were you doing out for so long on a day like this?" Luckily, she didn't wait for an answer, just shook her head and helped Grace off with her coat. "Sit down and I'll get you a bowl of soup. You must be chilled to the bone."

"I am," Grace said, taking her seat. "The wind's awful today."

"And the temperature's no better," the housekeeper said, ladling soup into a bowl. "This will warm you up, and I've made your favorite oatmeal bread, too."

"Thanks, Mrs. B, I'm absolutely starved." The soup was rich with vegetables and chicken, the bread still warm from the oven. Grace ate hungrily, grateful for the food and warmth. And for making it out of that alley without being discovered.

Mrs. B served herself and joined Grace at the table. They ate in companionable silence for a while, then the housekeeper asked, "What are you up to this afternoon, Grace? I hope you're not planning to go back out in that awful cold."

Grace tore a corner from the thick slab of bread on her plate and did her best to look contrite. "I've arranged to meet Alma and Christine at the Savoy for the matinee, so I'm afraid I'll be heading back out soon after I finish lunch. I know it's crazy, but ... .Anyway, I feel a lot better now; the soup really warmed me up."

"You'd better put on another pair of stockings then, and wear your heavy toque and warm mittens. Those leather gloves aren't much good in this weather."

Following Mrs. B's advice, Grace bundled up for her walk to the Savoy. On the short trek down High and onto Main Street, fortified with a bellyful of hot soup and warm bread, she barely felt the cold. Her friends were waiting in the lobby, Christine almost beside herself at the prospect of watching her idol, Rudolph Valentino, in *Beyond the Rocks*.

After the film, they walked up the street to Vincent's Pharmacy. The young woman behind the long marble counter was busy assembling a root beer float. Removing their hats and mittens and unbuttoning their coats, Grace and her friends climbed onto the red upholstered stools as the waitress placed the frothy drink in front of the soda fountain's one other customer. Her hair was a perfect imitation of Gloria Swanson's tightly waved platinum style, but clearly wasted on the fellow with the root beer float.

"Don't you think Rudolph Valentino is the most elegant man in the world?" Christine said. "And he behaved so honorably toward Miss Swanson, even though he was madly in love with her right from the start."

Grace and Alma laughed. "Oh, Chris," Alma said. "You'd think Valentino was a hero no matter what he did. He's probably a cad in real life."

Grace agreed. She and Alma couldn't help but poke fun at their friend's devotion to film stars. Nodding at the waitress, Grace whispered, "Maybe if you had a hairstyle like that, you might attract your very own Valentino. What do you think?"

"I think you're a tease, Grace Montel." Christine raised her chin and patted her dark bob. "And how do you know I haven't already got a Valentino of my very own?"

The girls placed their order and soon the waitress returned with three steaming mugs of hot chocolate. Grace wrapped her hands around her cup and took a tentative sip. She told her friends about her visit to the milliner's that morning. Chris and Alma didn't know Mary, but they were interested to hear what life was like for working girls their age. Grace said she thought Mary liked her work with Miss Andrews as much because it got her out of the house as for the work itself.

"I think Miss Andrews is a bit of a task master, but the money Mary earns helps support her family. Mr. Devlin saddles his wife with a new baby every year or so ... and he drinks, too.

Mary says he spends most evenings at Clancy's," Grace said, watching for her friends' reactions.

"My mother and father sometimes go dancing at Clancy's," Christine said. "A few of my father's friends play in a jazz combo on Saturday nights. They say half the town's there sometimes."

Alma giggled. "Not my parents. They're strict Lutherans. Their idea of excitement is sitting in the parlor listening to the clock tick."

That evening during dinner Grace and her father were exchanging news of their day. Daddy said business had been slow, but February was often a slow month. The holidays were well past and the spring inventory wasn't in yet. Grace related her conversation with Mary at the milliner's and told him about attending the matinee with Christine and Alma.

Trying to sound off-hand, she said, "Christine says there's a jazz combo at Clancy's on Saturday nights, Daddy. Have you heard them play?" She busied herself buttering a dinner roll and waited to see what he'd say.

Setting his wine glass on the table, he patted his mouth with his napkin and nodded. "I have. A few local fellows playing dance music for the crowd. What they lack in skill they make up for in volume." He tipped his head and frowned. "Why do you ask?"

"Oh, just curious." She shrugged. "You're often out on Saturday evenings lately and I wondered if that's where you went."

"Keeping tabs on me, Grace?" His voice was teasing, but there was an edge to it, too.

"I guess a little." She held his gaze. "It's just that you seem to go out a lot more than you used to, and I worry when I don't know where you are."

"Don't worry about me, Gracie. I can take care of myself." He pushed his chair away from the table and sighed. "But since you ask, most nights I do head over to Clancy's. I like the company. There's no harm in that, is there?"

"But there could be, Daddy. Isn't what Mr. Clancy's doing against the law?"

"It is, but it's a ridiculous law. Has been right from the start." He grinned. "We're just practicing a little civil disobedience,

Grace. That's what men do when they're faced with unjust laws. What do you think the Boston Tea Party was all about?"

Her father went out again that night. Maybe to Clancy's Saturday dance or maybe to some other hidden den of drink dotting the town's dark streets. As she sat on the edge of her bed brushing her hair, Grace thought about the events of the past few months, seemingly unrelated, but somehow linked in her mind. The locked drawer. Grandpa's Christmas Eve toast to Daddy. The new blue Pontiac. The string of pearls.

Grace lowered the hair brush and cradled it in her hands. Idly, she pulled the long, tawny strands from the bristles, then stood and deposited the tangle of loose hair in the wastebasket. Maybe Daddy was right. Maybe there was no harm in his going to Clancy's. She couldn't blame him for wanting company. It had been six years since Mama died and he must get lonely. She did.

Jerome was due home in March. Unfortunately, their vacations didn't coincide, and Grace would be in school all week, so they wouldn't have much time together. He'd written to say that his parents were driving to Exeter the following Friday and he'd be back in Chester by Saturday afternoon. The Davisons had invited Grace to have dinner with them on Sunday and to join them after for a ride out to the local sugar house.

The ensuing week dragged by. Grace found it almost impossible to concentrate on her school work and even her painting felt forced and uninspired. No doubt Mr. Standish would be as disappointed with her week's work as she was. In the weeks she'd been studying with him, he'd praised her drawing skills and diligence, but was much less enthusiastic about her attempts at watercolor.

Her assignment had been to capture an aspect of the changing season and aim for spontaneity. Mr. Standish had waved his long arm in an extravagant gesture and told her to paint the quickening pulse of spring. Climbing the dusty stairs to his flat, Grace smiled and shook her head. She wasn't even sure what he'd meant, but was certain the study in her portfolio didn't come close.

The cat lay curled in his usual place on the windowsill, the sun lighting his orange fur. At Grace's approach, he stretched luxuriously and tumbled from his perch, making a perfect four-point landing at her feet. Grace knocked and she and the cat entered the drab kitchen together. Mrs. Standish scooped up the cat, told Grace to go right on into the studio, and tossed the orange bundle unceremoniously out the door.

Mr. Standish was at his easel, dabbing a wet paintbrush onto a section of bright blue sky. He waved her over and Grace watched him transform the sparkling day of the painting into one of muted sunlight.

"Watercolor is a forgiving medium, Grace," he said, swishing his brush in a small dish. "It's marvelous, really, the way you can add layers of color and just as easily take them away." He stepped back and studied his work. "That's better. Looks more like a New England sky now. The colors of nature don't necessarily translate onto the page, Grace. That's why painting fall foliage is so tricky. Always looks fake." He put down his brush and smiled. "Now, let's see what you've got there."

"Not much, I'm afraid," she said. "I don't think I'm particularly spontaneous, Mr. Standish." Resisting the impulse to apologize further, Grace placed the painting on the table. Long blue shadows lay across an expanse of snowy field, unbroken except for a tall elm to the right of the page and random patches of dried weeds poking out of the snow. For a long moment Mr. Standish was silent, leaning over the painting, his brows drawn together.

"It doesn't look much like spring," Grace said, unable to stand the silence any longer.

Mr. Standish straightened and turned to her. "That's where you're mistaken, Grace. That light is spring light. You've captured the lengthening shadows of late afternoon. In winter, it'd be dark at that hour." He crossed his arms and leaned against the table. Grace's face burned under his inscrutable gaze, unsure of whether he was trying to read her mind or waiting for her to read his.

Finally, he pushed himself upright and rubbed his hands together. "Well, let's get started, shall we?"

Seated in the parlor that evening, waiting to be called to dinner, Grace told her father that Jerome would be home on Saturday and that she'd been invited to dine with the Davisons on Sunday.

"That won't work, Grace. It's our week to have dinner with your grandmother and grandfather, you know that." He splashed another dram of whiskey into his glass and returned to his chair.

"But, Daddy, Jerome will only be home for a week and I'll be in school every day. The weekends will be the only chance we'll have to spend time together. I'm sure Grandma and Grandpa will understand. I'll give them a call after dinner."

"No, you won't, Grace. You'll have dinner with us on Sunday. There'll be time enough to see that boy after school." He frowned into his empty glass. "You two spend enough time together as it is. I won't have you disappointing your family in order to spend more time with his."

Grace didn't argue. Daddy wasn't worried about disappointing Grandma and Grandpa. He just didn't want her to see Jerome. There was no point in trying to talk to him now; that third drink had put him beyond reasoning with. But she wasn't ready to give up yet.

Leaving school the following afternoon, Grace headed straight to Pleasant Street. The March sun rode high in a cloudless blue sky, but the wind whipping down from the north stung her face and threatened to dislodge her hat. She hurried up the porch steps and, rapping lightly on the door, stepped inside.

The parlor was empty, so she climbed the stairs to her grandmother's sitting room. At the open door she said, "Hello, Grandma. Am I disturbing you?"

"Of course not, Gracie. Come in, darling." She set her book aside and patted the seat next to her. "What brings you here on a Friday afternoon? I'd have thought you'd be with Alma and Christine."

"I wanted to talk to you, Grandma." Grace smoothed her skirt and looked at the fire. "I've got a bit of a problem I'm hoping you can help me with."

"What kind of problem? Let's hear it and we'll see what we can do."

"Jerome is due home tomorrow for a week's vacation and he and his parents have invited me to have dinner with them on Sunday, but, well, this is our Sunday to have dinner with you and Grandpa."

Her grandmother smiled and patted Grace's hand. "Well, if that's the problem, dear, consider it solved. You can have dinner with us any time. You go ahead and keep your engagement with the Davisons."

Grace wished it was that simple. She shook her head. "Daddy says Jerome and I spend too much time together and that I can't disappoint my family to be with his."

"Ah, that's the real problem, then, isn't it? Your father's worried about your friendship with Jerome." Grandma leaned back against the settee and looked at Grace.

"I think your father's having a hard time accepting that you're growing up, Grace. He's afraid of losing you, and he sees Jerome as the person who will take you away from him. Your grandfather treated Arthur the same way when he began courting your aunt. Fathers can be very protective of their daughters." Grandma fingered the beads around her neck and stared into the fire. Her lips were pressed into a thin line and there was a slight pucker over one eyebrow.

"I can't very well overrule your father's decision, Grace," she said slowly, "but I may be able to make the case for your spending the day with your friend."

14

WORDS AND DEEDS

Grace had been home about an hour when her father called to say that Grandma had asked him to stop by on his way back from the shop. He told her to let Mrs. Blanchard know that dinner would be delayed, then rang off. Slowly she lowered the receiver and stood in the dim foyer. Grandma's summons wouldn't go down well with Daddy and she dreaded facing his anger. Maybe she shouldn't have asked for Grandma's help, should have argued her own case instead. Not that he'd have listened. He'd have just gotten mad and now he was mad anyway.

After Grace delivered her father's message to Mrs. B, she went to her room to collect herself for the scene she knew would come. Daddy would accuse her of disloyalty, of enlisting Grandma's help to override his decision. That's just what she'd done and maybe she'd been wrong, but was it any less wrong for Daddy to refuse to let her accept Jerome's invitation? It would be different if he had a valid reason, but the only really important thing that was happening on Sunday was the very thing he wouldn't let her do. She groaned with frustration. How could she reason with him when he was so unreasonable?

Hearing the front door close, she let out a long, slow breath and straightening her back, went downstairs. Her father was in the foyer and, gesturing for Grace to enter the parlor, followed her in and closed the door. He went to the sideboard and she sat on the edge of the sofa watching him fill his glass, her hands clasped tightly in her lap.

"What did you think you were doing, Grace, going to your grandmother behind my back? I made it clear I expected you to have dinner with us on Sunday and, instead of respecting my wishes, you try to undermine my authority by going to your grandmother. I don't appreciate getting called on the carpet just so you can have your own way." He glared at Grace and emptied his glass.

An icy shiver ran down her back, but she held his gaze and said nothing.

"Well?"

"You're right, Daddy. I did go to Grandma hoping she'd convince you to let me have dinner with the Davisons on Sunday. Maybe I should have tried to convince you myself ... " She slid her cold hands under her thighs and lowered her voice. "But I knew you wouldn't listen. I knew you'd just get mad."

"And why wouldn't I when you deliberately disobey me?" He slammed his empty glass onto the sideboard.

"I didn't disobey you, Daddy, I just went to talk to Grandma. She didn't see any reason why I shouldn't spend the afternoon with Jerome and his family, especially since I won't see him again until June. If Grandma doesn't mind that I miss Sunday dinner, why do you?"

He turned his back to her and refilled his glass. Reflected in the mirror above the sideboard, his face was as drawn and crumpled as an old balloon.

"It's got nothing to do with Sunday dinner, Grace. I don't give a damn about Sunday dinner. It's got to do with you and that boy."

He was right. It had everything to do with Jerome. After an absence of three months, Grace wanted nothing so much as to be with him. She was willing to risk her father's anger, even his humiliation, to spend those few precious hours with Jerome.

Right now, nothing and no one mattered more to her. She cleared her throat and addressed her father's back.

"I'm sorry for the way I went about this, Daddy. I didn't mean to cause a problem between you and Grandma. It's just that ... this is the only time between now and the end of school that I'll get to see Jerome and I don't understand why you're so set against it."

He turned to face her. "No, you don't understand, Grace." He looked at her for a long moment, then sighed and set his glass on the sideboard. "I'm going up to change. Tell Mrs. Blanchard I won't be in for dinner."

Grace stared at the empty doorway unable to make sense of what had just passed between her and Daddy. How could he walk away without explaining himself? She shrugged and shook her head. Could Grandma have been right? Did Daddy see Jerome as a rival for her affections? That was nonsense. She loved her father in spite of his drinking and his volatile temper, because he was her father. She didn't even know what to call the feelings she had for Jerome, but she knew she was her best self when she was with him.

When Grace went down to breakfast the following morning, her father was mopping up the last of his egg with a piece of toast. He was dressed for work and, glancing at the clock, she saw that it was almost time for him to leave. Taking her seat, she wished him good morning and he returned the greeting, though he didn't look at her. Grace busied herself with toast and jam while her father poured himself another cup of coffee.

"I've been thinking about our conversation yesterday, Grace," he said, fingering the handle of his cup. "And while I think you were wrong to enlist your grandmother's support, I probably should have been more straightforward with you." He sipped his coffee, looking at her over the rim of his cup.

"As my mother was quick to remind me, you're not a little girl anymore and that's exactly why I'm concerned about your connection with Jerome." He held up a warning hand.

"I know you're going to tell me that you and Jerome are friends, but I'm no fool, Grace. I can see there's more to it than that." He looked fixedly at her. "Don't pretend you don't know what I'm talking about. We both know you're smarter than that."

Grace nodded and fiddled with the napkin in her lap. She was supremely uncomfortable and dreaded what he'd say next.

His cup clattered as he set it in the saucer. "Whatever you might think you feel for this boy, Grace, seventeen is too young to be courting. There'll be time enough for that after you finish high school. Until then, you'll respect my wishes on this. Is that understood?"

Grace didn't think of spending time with Jerome as courting. Courting led to marriage, a prospect so distant as to be inconceivable. "I think I understand, but ... is dinner with the Davisons or seeing Jerome when he's home from school what you mean by courting?"

Her father heaved a sigh and tossed his napkin on the table. "I mean be careful, Grace. Remember who you are and don't do anything to sully your reputation or the reputation of the family. Don't give the tongues any reason to wag."

He stood and checked his watch. "And call your grandmother to say you won't be at dinner tomorrow."

———————◆◆◆———————

Late Sunday morning, Grace stood at her bureau, struggling to pin her long hair into place. She'd perfected the style since her first attempts during the holidays, but today her skills had deserted her. Her fingers felt like so many sausages flapping away at the back of her head. Uttering a low growl of frustration, she placed her hands flat on the bureau and took a deep breath. She relaxed her shoulders, gathered up her hair again, and this time managed to slide the pins into place. Removing the string of pearls from their velvet box, she fastened the clasp, and settled the necklace into the open neck of her silk blouse.

Grace rang the Davisons' front doorbell, shortly after noon, her stomach full of butterflies. Jerome opened the door, and the light in his eyes made her catch her breath. He stepped aside and beckoned her in. They studied each other in the dim hallway.

"You look lovely, Monty. I've missed you," he whispered, helping her off with her coat.

Mrs. Davison appeared then, wiping her hands on her apron and greeting Grace with her usual warmth. "Dinner's nearly ready," she said. "Jerome, take Grace into the parlor. I'm sure you two have a lot of catching up to do."

Settling onto the sofa, they turned toward one another, their knees inches apart. Jerome's gaze sent the blood rushing to her cheeks, and she marveled again at the perfect symmetry of his face. Shifting slightly away from him, Grace smoothed the front of her skirt and tried to think of something to say. Something that wouldn't sound banal or stupid, something that would break the magnetic force of their attraction.

She asked about his studies and he asked after their school friends. They were relaxing into their conversation when Mr. Davison appeared in the doorway to say dinner was ready. During the meal, the talk continued: inquiries about Grace's studies, Jerome's participation on the debating team, and the spring concert scheduled for the end of May. Mrs. Davison said she and her husband planned to drive down on the morning of the concert and stay the night at the Exeter Inn. They'd spend the afternoon with Jerome, take in the concert in the evening, and head home the following day.

"We thought you'd like to come with us, Grace. I'm sure Jerome would enjoy showing you the Academy and it would be a chance for you to meet some of his friends, too."

Grace looked around the table. Jerome was grinning broadly and his parents were watching her, waiting for her reaction. Had Jerome prevailed upon his parents to invite her or had the suggestion come from his mother? He certainly looked like he wanted her to come, and she wanted to go. Daddy wouldn't like the idea, but she'd cross that bridge when she came to it.

"Thank you, Mrs. Davison. I'd like that very much," she said, "but I'll have to ask my father's permission before I can accept."

"Why, of course, dear. You can assure him that you'll be well looked after. Mr. Davison and I will see to that."

The Davisons dropped Grace off at home after their visit to Mr. Bissonnette's sugar house. She was slightly queasy from the ride along the twisting country roads and the quantity of sugar on snow that she and Jerome had shared in the sugar shack's rough dining room. There had been raised doughnuts and pickles, too, and samples of maple sugar so sweet it made her teeth ache. As she thanked her hosts, Jerome came around to open the car door for her. He walked her to the front porch where they made hurried plans to meet the following afternoon after she finished school.

In the kitchen Grace gave Mrs. B a tiny box of maple candy, the pieces molded into leaf shapes. Her father was out on one of his errands, the housekeeper told her, but he hadn't said where to. He'd left his automobile behind, so he'd probably just gone to the shop or over to visit Mr. and Mrs. Montel.

Grace headed up to her room, thinking about her father's so-called errands. He was often away on Sunday afternoons and had twice left on Saturday afternoon and not returned until the following day. The touring car no longer looked new, its luster dimmed by winter weather and spring's muddy roads.

A short while later, Grace was at her desk finishing her homework when she heard a car door slam. Standing for a better view of the street, she saw her father leaning into the open passenger window of what she was sure was the same car she'd seen behind Clancy's. The same one Raymond had mentioned that January afternoon she'd stopped by the shop looking for Daddy.

She couldn't see the driver, but she could picture him perfectly. A big man expensively dressed. A fellow who exuded wealth and the power that went with it. As the Lincoln pulled smoothly away from the curb, Grace dropped into her chair. Who was he and what was his connection to Daddy?

During dinner that evening, Grace was surprised by her father's ebullient spirits. He acted like their altercation on Friday and his subsequent ultimatum regarding courtship had never happened. Instead, he asked about her visit with the Davisons and their afternoon at the sugarhouse. He told the story of how his father had taken him to Bissonnette's when he was a little boy and how much he'd liked the heat of the great fire and the sweet smell of boiling sap.

"I remember I was so small your grandfather had to lift me onto his shoulders so I could see into the evaporator."

Grace smiled. "I can't imagine Grandpa lifting you onto his shoulders. Was Aunt Louise there, too?"

"No, it was just the two of us. Your grandmother must have been home with Louise. She couldn't have been more than a few months old." He sipped his wine and shook his head.

"I hadn't thought of that day for years. Probably the first and last time my father ever took me anywhere without the rest of the family." He shrugged and emptied the dregs of the wine carafe into his glass.

Grace saw the shadow pass over his face and heard the longing in his voice. While she finished her dinner, he drank the last of the wine, staring silently at something only he could see. Finally, he pushed his chair away from the table saying he had paperwork to catch up on. She nodded and watched him leave the room. Hearing the study door close, she stood and carried their plates to the kitchen.

At sight of the nearly full plate, Mrs. B said, "Who's finding fault with my cooking now? Did you spoil your dinner with too much sweet stuff this afternoon, Grace?" She frowned, but the twinkle in her eye gave her away.

"No, ma'am," Grace said, crossing her heart and holding up her right hand. "I ate every bite and it was delicious, too. The roast beef was perfect." She raised her brows and shrugged. "My father doesn't seem to have much of an appetite this evening."

"Not for food, anyway," she thought, as Mrs. B scraped the uneaten food into the trash.

Seated in a booth at the Corner Cafe the following afternoon, Grace told Jerome about the way her father had objected to her spending Sunday with him and his family. As she related the story, she couldn't explain her father's reasoning or chart the course that took him from the Davisons' dinner invitation to his courting lecture the next morning. Jerome listened, his forearms crossed on the table, a deep vertical crease between his brows. He was so caring, so good, and Daddy had called him *that boy* as though he were some worthless ne'er-do-well. Grace was stung anew by the insult.

When she'd finished her story, Jerome leaned back and studied her, the corner of his mouth twitching. "Your dad didn't say anything very different from what my parents said when they told me Headquarters was off limits. They're just doing what they think is right. They're keeping an eye on us." He curved his fingers like claws and flashed a devilish grin. "And I bear watching, little girl, make no mistake about that."

Grace laughed. The tensions of the last few days melted away and in their place was joy, joy and the thrill of knowing that she, too, bore watching.

Growing serious, Jerome said, "I'm sorry your dad gave you a hard time about Sunday, Monty. Who would have thought a dinner invitation would set him off like that?"

Grace nodded. "That's just it, Jerome. I never know from one minute to the next how he'll react or what he'll say. Like last night at dinner. He was telling about the time my grandfather took him to Bissonnette's when he was a very little boy. Then all of a sudden he got this faraway look on his face and the next thing I knew, he was leaving the table. He hardly touched his dinner. Other times, he's fine. Even on Saturday morning when he was giving me his courtship lecture, he wasn't mean or angry ... he was just telling me what he expected." She toyed with the handle of her cup. "But in the evenings especially ... I feel like I'm walking on eggshells."

Jerome was quiet, his gaze thoughtful. "Do you think your dad will let you come down to Exeter in May? I mean, I want you to come and my folks do, too, but I don't want to cause trouble between you and your father." He grinned. "Anymore than I already have, that is."

"I know you're looking out for me, Jerome, and I appreciate it, but I have every intention of accepting your parents' invitation to Exeter. I'm not sure how I'm going to manage it, but I'm certainly going to try."

Later, passing Montel's on their way up Main Street, Jerome said, "How are things going at the shop, Monty?"

"Pretty well, I guess. My grandfather seems pleased. He says they're operating in the black again. I kind of wonder, though — "

"About what?"

"About where the money's coming from. I mean, there's the new car and those pearls my father gave me for my birthday. You should have seen the look on my grandmother's face when I opened the box. It's almost like there's too much money."

"I'm not sure I follow you," Jerome said.

"Ever since I was a little girl, I've listened to my grandfather and my father talk about the shop. Argue about it, too. Grandpa always worried that my father took too many risks. Daddy said Grandpa was too conservative. Either way, though, I think the business stayed pretty steady, doing well at certain times of the year and not so well at others. So, why is my father able to drive a fancy car and buy expensive presents now, when he never could before? There are only so many customers in Chester, so it makes me wonder what's changed."

On Friday afternoon Jerome was waiting for Grace in front of the school when classes ended. The day was mild. A benevolent sun shone out of a china blue sky and the busy March wind seemed to be taking the afternoon off. Stuffing her gloves in the pockets of her unbuttoned coat, Grace breathed in the scent of rushing water and softening earth. This is what Mr. Standish meant by the quickening pulse of the changing seasons.

"Let's go sit on the green for a bit, Jerome. This is the first warm weather we've had in ages."

They settled on a bench near the monument to fallen soldiers and watched the comings and goings on Main Street. Mr. Scapillini had his crates of vegetables out on the sidewalk and several of the merchants had propped their shop doors open.

Women pushed baby carriages on sidewalks clear of ice and snow, and a gang of young boys raced in and out of the pedestrians, their high-pitched clamor echoing off the brick storefronts.

Cars, trucks, and carts circled the green in both directions. Mr. Hood went by in his white milk wagon, followed closely by Dr. Halvorson, his Model T belching and backfiring like an aged dyspeptic. After a break in the traffic, Grace sat up, shielding her eyes from the sun reflecting off the gleaming paintwork of a sleek, black automobile. She leaned forward, her hand on Jerome's sleeve.

"Do you see that car, the one that just pulled up to the curb in front of the bank?"

"What about it?"

"I want to know who's driving it. Keep your eye on it and tell me what you see." They watched as the door opened and the driver stepped out.

"Tall fellow in a suit wearing a grey homburg is all I can make out from here. Why? Do you know him?"

"Not exactly, but I've got a hunch my father does. Let's go up the street and see if we can get a better look at him." She rose and, gesturing for Jerome to follow, hurried across the green.

"Hold on, Monty, you can't just accost the fellow in the street."

"I don't plan to. Now, please, let's go."

On the sidewalk in front of the bank, she said, "I'm going in to have a look around. Why don't you stand under Scapillini's awning and keep your eye on that car. I'll be right back."

Without waiting for an answer, Grace mounted the granite steps and pushed open the heavy door. Inside she stopped, scanning the lobby for a glimpse of the driver. Several customers waited in line at the teller cages, but the man she was looking for was not one of them. Glancing to the right, she spied him sitting on a visitor's chair in front of Mr. Evans' gleaming mahogany desk, his homburg, gloves, and stick on the chair next to him.

Grace crossed to the counter in the center of the lobby and pulled a deposit ticket from one of the pigeon-holes. Taking up a pen, she shifted her position until she could make out the man's profile. While she pretended to fill out the ticket, Grace studied the fellow's features. His hair, wavy and light brown, was brushed back from his wide forehead. She couldn't make out the color of his eyes, but his face was full and ruddy. Grace knew a thing or two about men's clothing and judged his pin-striped suit to be custom-made. There was a heavy watch chain attached to his vest pocket and a gold signet ring on his right hand. His bearing was relaxed and confident as though he were used to the deferential way the banker nodded and smiled at him.

Replacing the pen in its holder, Grace took up her bag and turned to leave. At the door, she glanced once more in the man's direction. He was definitely the same fellow she'd seen when she'd been snooping around Clancy's, and most likely the same one who'd dropped Daddy off that Sunday afternoon. There was nothing inconspicuous about the man or his automobile.

Surely, she'd be able to find out who he was.

15

Men of Business

Out on the sidewalk, Jerome was talking to the greengrocer. Mr. Scapillini, wearing his white apron, was leaning against the doorjamb, blinking into the afternoon sun. He nodded to Grace as she approached, but continued talking in low tones to Jerome.

"Oh, yes, they call that one The Ramshead," he said, chuckling. "Always push, push, push, that fellow. Anything get in his way he ram right through it." He shook his head. "The man that come up against Rafe Ramsey's gonna get knocked down to size, make no mistake 'bout that."

"I've never seen him before," Jerome said. "He's not from around here, is he?"

"Used to be a big-time Boston lawyer. Anyway that's what I heard. Built himself a fancy place up north of here." Mr. Scapillini lowered his voice to a whisper. "Talk is, he does a lot of business over the border, if you know what I mean."

"I'm not sure I do," Jerome said. Before he could continue, the greengrocer took a step back into his shop, shaking his head and placing a finger against his lips.

Grace turned toward the bank to see the man in question hurry down the steps and slip behind the wheel of the black Lincoln. The automobile pulled away, heading north on Main Street. She entered the delicatessen and Jerome followed.

"Mr. Scapillini, you said something about that fellow doing business across the border," Grace said. "He's not working as an attorney up there, is he?"

The shopkeeper brushed bread crumbs off the counter and wiped his hands on his apron. "I got nothing more to say 'bout it. Back in the Old Country, we learn to mind our own business. You don't wanna get in the way of that fella, that's all I'm gonna say."

Grace woke the next morning to the sound of freezing rain pinging against the window. She moaned and rolled onto her side. This was Jerome's last day at home and they had plans to walk the loop between the Main Street and Brookfield bridges. She'd been looking forward to a few hours alone with Jerome, picturing them walking hand in hand beside the river, maybe sharing a kiss under the shelter of the pines.

Tossing back the covers, she padded to the window. It was even worse than she'd thought. Wet snow sagged off the tree branches, water dripped from the eaves, and passing cars splashed through inches of grey slush. Sleet pelted out of a gunmetal sky, blown sideways on gusty winds. She turned from the window and sat on the edge of her bed. Why couldn't this awful weather have waited until after Jerome was gone? She'd feel sad and lonely then anyway, and might even have welcomed a cold blustery day. She sighed and looked at the clock.

Her father would be leaving for work soon. It was time to dress and go down to breakfast. When she arrived in the dining room, his empty plate was pushed aside and he was scowling at the morning paper folded lengthwise at his place. She wished him good morning and he mumbled a greeting, but did not look up from his reading. When he did, his countenance was as stormy as the weather. He dabbed his mouth with his napkin and pushed his chair back from the table.

"I've got to get going, Grace. Looks like we both got a late start this morning."

"Sorry I didn't get down sooner, Daddy." She glanced at the window as another gust of wind rattled the panes. "It's miserable out there, and I'm not sure an umbrella will do you much good."

He approached her chair and placed a hand on her shoulder. "I'm going to drive today anyway. I've got a couple of things I need to see to after closing." He headed for the door, then turned. "Tell Mrs. B not to wait dinner. I don't know what time I'll be back."

In the kitchen, Mrs. Blanchard shook her head, but said nothing about another missed dinner. "Go ahead and fix yourself a cup of tea, Grace. There are biscuits on the table and I'll bring your eggs in as soon as they're ready."

Back at the dining room, Grace picked up the newspaper, curious to see what her father had been reading. A bold headline caught her eye: *Rumrunner Crushed in Fatal Collision.* The previous evening, Customs patrollers had pursued Wesley Titus, aged 20, whom they suspected of transporting whiskey and beer over the international border. The Customs men fired on the car, puncturing a rear tire and causing the vehicle to swerve out of control. The car collided with a tree, killing the driver instantly. The officers discovered a cache of Canadian whiskey and beer hidden under the back seat of the vehicle. One of the patrollers reported seeing a second man escape on foot, but no one else on the scene could substantiate his claim.

Grace lowered the paper and shook her head. Twenty years old. What a shame for this young man's family, losing a loved one over a few bottles of whiskey. She sipped her tea, thinking about the whiskey stored in the parlor sideboard. She frowned and set her cup in the saucer. Someone smuggled those bottles across the border. Might it have been this Titus fellow? Is that why Daddy'd looked so upset? Grace refolded the paper and rose from the table. She was about to carry her plate to the kitchen when Jerome called.

Bowing to the weather gods, Grace and Jerome settled for the matinee at the Savoy that afternoon. It wasn't a stroll along the river, but it was warm and dry and dark. They sat in the balcony, their knees touching, as Sherlock Holmes defeated his nemesis, Moriarty, and saved the woman he'd eventually marry. By the time they left the theater, the wind had died down and the rain had stopped. There was even a patch of blue breaking through on the horizon.

"Are you game for a walk in the park, Monty? Then we could stop at my house for a snack." Jerome grinned. "My mother promised to bake some treats for me to take back to school and I have a hunch she's done some of those molasses cookies you like so much."

"Sounds lovely," Grace said, taking his arm. As they walked, she said, "Have you ever heard of a fellow named Wesley Titus? He was killed last night bringing alcohol across the border. The patrollers shot at his car and he crashed into a tree. I saw it in the paper this morning."

Jerome frowned. "One of the drivers at Sterling Printers, where my father works, is a Titus. I think he delivers the northern route. My dad's mentioned him a few times ... big, friendly guy ... the kind of fellow everyone likes. I'm not sure if it's the same family, but my dad will know."

Mrs. Davison was busy at the sink when Grace and Jerome came in from their walk. The kitchen was as welcoming as ever, warm and sweet-smelling and unchanged in the months since she'd last been here. The tea things were set out on the table. Jerome put the kettle on to boil, and his mother filled a plate with freshly baked cookies.

As though reading Grace's thoughts, Mrs. Davison said, "It's so good to have you both in my kitchen again. I miss those afternoons when you'd come by for a snack after school."

"I miss them, too, Mrs. Davison," Grace said, moved by the older woman's words. "You were kind to me at a time when I was awfully sad and lonely."

She smiled and reached for a cookie. "And no one makes better molasses squares than you do."

Jerome looked inquiringly at his mother. "Where's Dad?"

Mrs. Davison's face clouded. "He's had to go to the office to reschedule Monday's delivery run." Grace and Jerome looked at each other. "One of the drivers has had a death in his family."

It was nearly 5:00 by the time Grace and Jerome set off for her house. The first two blocks, neither spoke. Jerome's imminent departure and their upcoming separation left Grace tongue-tied. Even if she'd been able to think of something appropriate to say, she didn't trust herself to speak. As they cut through the backyard of the empty Sims place, Jerome led her behind the decrepit garden shed and pulled her close. She wrapped her arms around his neck and raised her face to his.

Their kisses were tender and slow. Grace closed her eyes, shutting out everything but the touch of Jerome's lips and her galloping heart. When she pulled away, he held her at arm's length and smiled into her upturned face. Laughing, he swung her off her feet and spun her around. She was dizzy when he set her down, but whether from the spinning or the kisses, she wasn't sure. Her eyes were moist and he wiped a tear away with his thumb, then kissed her forehead and reached for her hand.

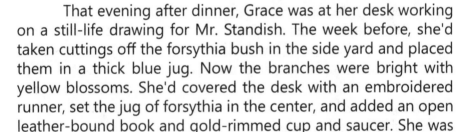

That evening after dinner, Grace was at her desk working on a still-life drawing for Mr. Standish. The week before, she'd taken cuttings off the forsythia bush in the side yard and placed them in a thick blue jug. Now the branches were bright with yellow blossoms. She'd covered the desk with an embroidered runner, set the jug of forsythia in the center, and added an open leather-bound book and gold-rimmed cup and saucer. She was pleased with the arrangement, but her desk had been tied up for most of a week now, and she was anxious to finish her drawing.

Grace sighed and erased a section of the open book. The flowers had come out well, but the proportions of the book were all wrong. She was distracted, too, wondering where her father had gone after work and when he'd be home. She hated to think of him driving after dark when he'd been drinking. Tossing her pencil down, she rubbed the bridge of her nose. She might as well go to bed; she couldn't work anymore tonight. At the wardrobe, she retrieved her dressing gown, and was about to head to the bathroom when she heard the front door slam. Daddy was home.

Grace hurried downstairs, but at the door of the parlor, she stopped. Her father was slumped in his easy chair, his chin resting on his chest, his hair hanging limply over his forehead. His shoes and trousers were covered with mud, his white shirt was rumpled and unbuttoned at the neck, and his tie was missing. What had he been up to? Grace pressed her hand against her queasy stomach and approached his chair.

"Daddy?" she said. "Are you all right?" His hands hung limply on his lap and his eyes were closed.

"Daddy? Can I get you something? Are you ill?" He didn't move, didn't seem to hear or see her. Was he even breathing? Grace leaned over him, watching for the rise and fall of his chest, hardly breathing herself. She started when his head lolled to one side and his mouth fell open and he began to snore. She took a deep breath and headed to the kitchen on the off chance Mrs. B was still up.

Finding the room empty, Grace climbed the two flights of stairs to the housekeeper's room, knocked lightly and waited. A minute later, Mrs. Blanchard, still dressed, but wearing bedroom slippers, opened the door.

"Gracie, what is it? Is something wrong?"

"Something seems to be the matter with my father. He's ... kind of ... well, he seems to be sleeping, but ... " She exhaled. "I think he's had too much to drink."

"Go back to your room, Grace. I'll see to your father."

"No, I'll come with you."

In the parlor, Mrs. Blanchard had no better luck rousing Grace's father than she'd had. "We'll just let him sleep, dear. I think it best not to disturb him now. You cover him with an afghan and I'll put another log on the fire."

"But, do you think he'll be all right? What if — "

"He'll be fine," Mrs. Blanchard said. "Now, turn off that overhead light and go up to bed. A good night's sleep will set him right."

Grace did as Mrs. B said, but it was a long while before she slept. She lay awake trying to figure out what her father's connection was to Wesley Titus, for surely there must be one. It was sad to think of the young man's death, but that alone wouldn't have sent Daddy off in a huff only to return late that night in such a state. She rolled onto her side and pulled her knees to her chest. Somehow, her father must have known this Titus fellow, this person who was involved in the illegal liquor trade. And how else would he know him, unless her father, too, was mixed up in the same sordid business?

When Grace went down to breakfast the next morning, the parlor door was open, the afghan neatly folded on the back of the sofa. Going through to the kitchen, she found Mrs. Blanchard sitting at the table with her coffee.

"Your father's not down yet, Grace," she said. "I expect he'll sleep in this morning. Given it's Sunday, I don't see any reason to wake him."

"But we're supposed to have dinner with my grandparents this afternoon. I wonder if I should call them and ... "

"No need to do anything right now, dear," Mrs. B said. "Have your breakfast and try not to worry. It's early yet."

Later, Grace worked on her drawing, an ear cocked for any sound coming from her father's room. Her grandparents always went to the 11:00 mass and Mrs. Henderson served dinner around 1:00. She'd wait until 10:30 and if Daddy wasn't up by then, she'd check on him.

She'd been scared last night, seeing him all disheveled and barely conscious. She'd read of the dangers of homemade whiskey, poisonous concoctions that blinded and even killed people. If Daddy had gotten hold of something like that, he might be seriously ill ... or even dead. Getting to her feet, she hurried to the door, but stopped with her hand on the knob.

She was being ridiculous. If Daddy'd been that sick, he'd never have made it to bed on his own. Berating herself, Grace went back to her desk. For the next half hour, she did little but stare out the window and wonder what to make of her father's latest misadventure.

By 10:30 there still had been no sound from her father's room, no footfalls, not even the familiar creak of his bedsprings. Grace stood outside his door listening before knocking gently.

"Daddy, may I come in?" He didn't answer, so she opened the door a crack and peeked in. Her father lay on his back, his eyes wide open, staring at the ceiling. His face was ashen, his jaw clamped tight.

She stepped further into the room. "Daddy, are you all right? Is there anything I can do?"

"You can leave me alone, Grace," he said, turning his back to her. "Just go away and leave me alone."

Stunned, she stood for a moment staring at his still form, then backed out of the room. She closed the door quietly and paused in the dim hallway. She'd seen Daddy much the worse for drink plenty of times. She knew all about the headaches and upset stomach, the trembling hands that were the aftereffects of heavy drinking. But she'd never seen him like this. Something had happened to her father. Something that had angered and saddened him and brought him low.

Grace couldn't remember the last time she'd dined alone with her grandparents, not on a Sunday anyway. Daddy was always there and before Mama died, she'd been there, too. Today, though, it had just been the three of them and the meal had been quiet and somehow more formal than when her father was around. Of course, Grandpa and Daddy usually got into some kind of disagreement about politics or the shop or any number of topics. If one said black the other was guaranteed to say white. It was predictable and oddly reassuring.

After dinner, Grandpa retreated to the parlor where he disappeared behind the Sunday paper. Grandma gave Grace a conspiratorial smile and gestured toward the parlor door.

"Come upstairs with me, Gracie. We'll leave your grandfather to sort out the sorry state of the country, while we chat about more mundane matters." Grandpa grunted from behind his newspaper and Grace followed her grandmother upstairs.

She'd always loved Grandma's sitting room. The afternoon light slanted through the sheer pink curtains and cast a rosy glow over the delicate furnishings. In the hearth the small fire was reflected in the shiny, brass andirons. The room was elegant and cozy at the same time, rather like Grandma herself.

When they'd taken their places on the settee, her grandmother said, "So, what exactly is wrong with your father, Gracie? You said he was ill, but that could mean a lot of things. Just how ill is he?"

Grace stared into the fire. "I don't know, Grandma. I don't think he has an illness, exactly, but he ... he came home last night and he was ... "

He was so drunk he passed out and this morning he wouldn't get out of bed. That was the truth, but she couldn't say that to her grandmother.

"Ah, he'd been drinking and drinking so much it made him sick." Grandma shook her head and sighed. "That's what I was afraid of."

For a moment, she was quiet, her hands clasped tightly in her lap. Then she reached over and took Grace's hand in hers. "We failed your father somehow, your grandfather and I. He was such a handsome, intelligent boy, but instead of using his talents to shine in school or in sports, he used them to outwit anyone in authority. Particularly, your grandfather and his teachers and coaches. I never understood what made him waste his gifts that way. He had ... has ... so much to offer."

"I'm worried about Daddy, Grandma. He's out till all hours ... " She leaned forward and lowered her voice. "He mustn't know I've told you this. He'd be so angry at me. He's always accusing me of keeping tabs on him. Please promise you won't say a word to Daddy about this."

"I can't make that promise until you tell me what's worrying you, Grace. You see that, don't you?" She patted Grace's hand. "Now, what's your father been up to besides a few late nights?"

"I think he's keeping company with a fellow who ... at least, I've seen him with this man ... very prosperous looking ... who may be involved in the alcohol trade. I don't know for sure, but I'm afraid for Daddy."

"You saw your father with this fellow? What do you know about him?"

"Not much, Grandma. I've heard he's a lawyer from Boston and that he built himself a big house up north of here. I've seen him drop Daddy off in front of the house a few times. His name's Rafe Ramsey. Have you ever heard of him?"

"No, I can't say as I have, but in a town this size, someone's bound to know him. I'll make a few inquiries and see what I can find out about this Mr. Ramsey."

She smiled. "And for the time being, we'll keep this little investigation to ourselves, shall we?"

As soon as her father left the breakfast table on Monday morning, Grace reached for his abandoned newspaper and searched for mention of Wesley Titus. His obituary stated that the young man had died in an automobile accident and had been employed at the Bond Paper Company. He was survived by his mother and father and two younger sisters. The funeral was scheduled for Wednesday morning at 10:00 at the Bryant Funeral Home.

That afternoon, instead of waiting to meet up with Alma and Christine, Grace left school as soon as the bell rang. She hurried through a cold mist down the long hill from school and turned onto the shortcut that led to Main Street. In the alley behind Montel's, she peeked into the small, dusty window of the milliner's back room. Just as she'd hoped, Mary Devlin was seated alone at a long table sewing under the glare of a bare light bulb. Grace rapped lightly on the window and, when she had Mary's attention, gestured for her to come outside.

Mary stepped out, wrapping her sweater tightly around her. "Gracie, what are you doing here?" She glanced nervously back at the shop. "If Miss Andrews finds me here, she'll have my head."

"I'm sorry to bother you, Mary, but there's something I want to talk to you about and I wondered what time you got off work."

"Not until 6:00 and then I've got to get home to help Ma. Two of the little ones are down with colds and she needs me to watch them while she fixes Da's supper." She shivered and stepped toward the shop door.

"What about another time, then? Please, Mary. I need your help."

"All right then. Come by on your way to school Wednesday, sometime after 7:15. My da'll be gone by then and I've arranged to take the morning off. Now, I've really got to go."

Grace thanked her, but the door was already closed.

Early Wednesday morning, Mary ushered Grace into the Devlins' steamy kitchen. The room was close, filled with the odors of burned toast, sour milk, and wet wool. Mrs. Devlin, a baby on her hip, smiled and said it had been donkey's years since Grace had been by to visit. Grace had always liked Mary's mother, always enjoyed her stories, the way she had of telling them. And in spite of all the work it took to keep her large family afloat, she never seemed nettled or bad- tempered.

"School keeps me awfully busy, Mrs. Devlin," Grace said. "Not as busy as Mary, of course. If I want to see her, I have to bother her at work and I know Miss Andrews takes a dim view of that."

"She's a hard one, that Miss Andrews," the older woman said, jiggling the baby on her hip. "She drives our Mary like a pack horse, and her as hard a worker as you could find." She looked fondly at her daughter. "'Course, I'm guilty of that myself, aren't I, darlin'?"

"Oh, Ma, you know I'd do anything for you." Mary kissed her mother's cheek. "Now, Gracie and I are going to have a word in the parlor and then she'll be off to school."

Mary led Grace across a narrow passage to a cold, tidy room of stiff furniture and even stiffer lace doilies. A picture of the bleeding heart of Jesus and a large, gilded crucifix hung between two lace-curtained windows. Mary shut the door and, gesturing for Grace to sit down, joined her on the horsehair sofa.

"All right, Gracie. You said you needed my help, so what can I do?"

"Well, I was wondering if you knew anything about that fellow, Wesley Titus, the one who was killed bringing liquor across the border."

"What's Wesley Titus got to do with you?" Mary said, her voice hard. "And what makes you think I'd know anything about him?"

"Well, I thought maybe Paddy knew him. The paper said he was twenty, so he'd have been about your brother's age, wouldn't he?" She lowered her voice. "When my father saw that article he was awfully upset and I ... well, I wondered why. I mean, aside from how sad the whole thing is."

She wished Mary would say something, but she just stared at her hands like she didn't recognize them.

"So, did you know Wesley Titus, Mary? His funeral's today. Is that why you took the morning off?"

Mary looked at her then, her eyes glistening with tears. "Wesley and my brother were friends. You're right, they went to school together and then both ended up working at the mill. Wesley used to come by in the evenings when my da was out and the kids were in bed."

She dabbed her eyes with a hanky and managed a watery smile. "He was a great one for listening to Ma's stories. Said she must have kissed the Blarney Stone, blessed as she was with the gift of gab. Wes was always respectful to Ma and me." She shook her head and stuffed her hanky in her apron pocket.

"I'm worried about my father, Mary. I keep thinking he's mixed up in this somehow, but how would he even know Wesley Titus? Maybe he knew the passenger ... according to the paper, one witness saw a passenger get away on foot."

"I don't know anything about a passenger. I do know lots of fellows run whiskey and beer over the border. It pays better than the mill." She shrugged. "Who knows, maybe they like the thrill of it, too, out running the Patrollers in those big cars. But I don't know anything about your father, Grace. Don't know if he's involved in the trade, and if he is, what he's up to." She stood up. "Now, I've got to get busy and you'd better hurry or you'll be late."

Grace followed Mary to the front door. She called good-bye to Mrs. Devlin and thanked Mary for talking to her. She could tell from Mary's stiff nod that her friend was less than pleased with their conversation.

As she passed through the open door, Mary said, "And Gracie, it'd be better if you didn't bother me at the shop again."

16

An Excursion

When Grace got home from school the following after-noon, Mrs. B told her that her grandmother had called and left a message. If Grace arrived before 5:00, she was to call her back, otherwise she should wait until Mrs. Montel called again.

"Did she say what she wanted?" Grace asked.

"No, just that you should call before five." Mrs. Blanchard checked the watch pinned to her shirtwaist. "It's only twenty till, so I'll leave you to it."

Grace frowned, puzzled by Grandma's 5:00 deadline. Lifting the earpiece, she gave the exchange and waited for the call to be put through. Her grandmother answered on the first ring.

"Ah, it's you, dear. Good. I've done a bit of investigating, and wanted to talk to you before your grandfather got home from the shop."

"What did you find out, Grandma?"

"Not as much as I would have liked. I cornered Mr. Evans at the bank and asked him what he could tell me about your Mr. Ramsey, but he wasn't much help. Said confidentiality prevented him from talking about his clients." Grace smiled at her grand-mother's exasperated tone. "I did get him to confirm that this fellow does business with the bank, though."

"I already knew that much, Grandma. I saw him in the bank one day talking to Mr. Evans."

"That's not the end of it, Gracie. As I was coming out of the bank, I ran into Ward Standish. We chatted for a few minutes and he invited me to the hotel for a cup of tea. We talked about you for a while, of course, then I happened to ask Ward if he was still taking commissions. It turns out he's working on a triptych or some such thing for you-know-who."

"Really? What else did he say?"

"He said he'd visited the man's home to see the view he wanted reproduced on canvas. Ward gushed about the size and grandeur of the place. Apparently Mr. Ramsey is a collector of sorts, mostly Chinese porcelain, but also several fine paintings by American artists."

"What was Mr. Standish's impression of the man, did he say?"

"I asked him that. He said the fellow was obviously well educated, probably from one of those old, established Boston families. Mr. Ramsey traced his interest in art to the months he spent in Europe after college."

"Does he have a family?"

"If he has a family, I gather they weren't in evidence. Ward expects to meet with Mr. Ramsey several times as plans for the painting, or paintings, move forward, so I may be able to learn more."

"Goodness, Grandma, you missed your calling. You would have made an ace private investigator." Grace laughed. "It's amazing what you managed to learn over a cup of tea."

"Oh, once you get Ward talking, he's a wealth of information. If you get the chance, you might mention the commission to him during your next lesson, see if anything comes of it. Now, I think I'd better ring off. Your grandfather will be home any minute. Oh, and Grace, let's keep this conversation to ourselves, at least for the time being."

Grace said good-bye, feeling better than she had for days. Grandma had found out more talking to Mr. Standish than Grace had been able to discover in all her weeks of snooping and spying. She could just picture Grandma smiling at Mr. Standish across the table, encouraging him to share all he knew about the mysterious Rafe Ramsey. She grinned and headed upstairs to put the finishing touches on her still life.

The next day, Grace walked to school under low clouds, but by the time she was on her way to her art lesson, the sky had cleared. The afternoon sun rode high in an azure sky and the snow had receded in all but the shadiest places. Red-wings perched on fence posts and tree branches announcing their return from the south. In Mr. Moffett's front yard, Grace spied a group of yellow and purple crocuses pushing up through the leaf litter and stopped to study the delicate veins of color on their petals.

After the brilliance of the spring afternoon, the stairwell at the Standish's was particularly gloomy. Grace climbed the dirty steps to the first floor landing where the orange cat basked in a square of sunlight. He stretched and rolled onto his back, showing the soft fur of his belly. She reached down to pet him and he grabbed her hand with his paws and licked her skin with his rough tongue. Gingerly pulling her hand from his clutches, she made her way to the third floor. With any luck, she'd be able to get Mr. Standish to talk about his latest commission.

When she entered the studio, he was seated on a high stool at his drafting table, sketching. He gave her his broad smile and, slipping his pencil behind his ear, pulled a second stool from under the table. Grace took the drawing from her portfolio and set it in front of the artist. By now, she was used to the teacher's habit of studying her work in silence before beginning his critique, but the wait still unnerved her.

Finally, he cleared his throat. "Why don't you tell me what went well for you in the drawing and what you had trouble with. Let's see if we're in agreement about the good and the not-so-good."

He folded his hands together on his crossed legs and watched her from under his bushy brows.

"Well, I had an awful time with the open book. I just couldn't seem to get the perspective right ... the book's too short. I tried it over and over, but it's still not right." He prompted her to tell him what was right with the drawing. "I like the forsythia ... the way the curve of the stems matches the curve of the jug."

For most of the next hour, Mr. Standish talked about the principles of perspective. He showed her pictures of Renaissance art, told her about visual angles and vanishing points, and helped her see the lines of the book before she tried to draw them. His own enthusiasm for the topic carried Grace along and his good-humored patience put her at ease. By the end of the lesson, she'd managed to correct the troublesome open book and was eager to tackle the painting for which the drawing was a study.

Grace was putting her tools and sketches away when Mr. Standish said, "I had tea with your grandmother yesterday, Grace. We bumped into each other in front of the bank and she graciously agreed to take tea with me at the hotel." He shook his head. "She's a lovely woman, your grandmother."

"She mentioned that she'd spoken to you. She said you've been commissioned to do a triptych. I wasn't sure what that meant until I looked it up." She gave him a sidelong smile. "Is your client decorating an altar?"

Mr. Standish laughed. "I hardly think so. My client's interests are more down to earth, no angels floating on clouds or saints ascending to heavenly realms. No, for whatever reason, this fellow has his heart set on three panels of landscape based on the view of river and mountains seen from the back of his house."

"My grandmother said your customer lives just north of here and is a collector."

"He has an impressive collection of antique porcelains, vases and urns, that sort of thing. He also has a small gallery of American art, some of it quite good. Collecting is a hobby, I guess you'd say. He's a businessman and a successful one from what I've seen. They're the only people who can afford commissions these days."

He lifted his bony shoulders and grinned. "Commissions can be problematic, but they pay the bills."

As she slipped on her coat, he added. "If you're interested, I could ask this fellow if you could come along sometime to see his collection. Providing, of course, your father has no objection."

"I'd like that very much, Mr. Standish." Grace finished buttoning her coat and said, "And if my grandmother were to accompany us, I'm sure my father would have no reason to object."

Skipping down the stairs a moment later, Grace congratulated herself on her quick thinking. Suggesting Grandma go with them had been nothing short of inspired. Mr. Standish had grinned like a schoolboy at the prospect. As for Grandma, she was a match for Daddy any day.

On the first Sunday of her spring vacation, Grace stood at the open door of her wardrobe, taking stock. There was nothing here she wanted to wear, nothing she hadn't worn again and again over the interminable winter, nothing she wasn't sick to death of. Here it was, a lovely April day, perfect weather for something flowery and bright, and she was faced with a row of dark wools, neutral corduroys, and ghastly plaids. She sighed, pulled out a navy skirt and lavender blouse and began to dress.

It was their Sunday to dine with Grandma and Grandpa. Much as she loved her grandparents, Grace had begun to find these dinners tedious. There was the usual shop talk, complaints about the rising cost of gasoline and electricity, mention of people she didn't know. Most of the time she barely listened, but she expected to be fully engaged in today's conversation. Opening her jewelry box, she removed the enameled brooch that had belonged to Mama and pinned the points of her collar together. She smiled at her reflection and hurried downstairs.

Dinner began as it always did. Grandpa delivered the blessing and Grandma passed the potatoes and vegetables around while he carved the chicken. Once the plates were full, they concentrated on the food, the only sound the scrape of cutlery and murmurs of approval, until Grandma cleared her throat.

"I had a call from Ward Standish yesterday," she said.

Grace's grandfather looked up from his plate, but before he could say anything, she continued. "He's invited Grace and me to accompany him to see several fine paintings at the home of one of his patrons." Grace caught the gleam in her grandmother's eye. "Ward's arranged to borrow an automobile for the trip, so we'll travel in style."

"Who is this so-called patron and where does he live?"

"He lives north of here, up on the county road above Brookfield. Apparently, he's built a huge place on the river, and he's commissioned Ward to paint three contiguous canvases of the view."

Grace's father raised his eyebrows, swallowed, and reached for his water glass. "Seems to me your Mr. Standish is going to a lot of trouble to show you a few paintings. I didn't know you had any particular interest in art, Mother."

"He wants Grace to see them, Francis. Ward thinks your daughter shows artistic promise and, since there's a dearth of museums in our area, he'd like to take this opportunity to expose his student to a number of fine pieces."

She smiled at Grace. "I think it speaks well of Grace's skills and is very considerate of Ward."

"I'm very much looking forward to the visit, Grandma. Mr. Standish mentioned two small paintings by Robert Henri and one by John Singer Sergeant." She widened her eyes and shook her head. "Imagine having famous works of art hanging in your own home."

Grandpa stabbed a piece of chicken with his fork. "So, who is this fellow with the big house on the river and the fancy art collection?" He glowered at Grandma.

Slowly, she dabbed her lips with a napkin. "I believe his name is Ramsey. Rafe Ramsey."

Grandma was enjoying herself. It was all Grace could do to keep a straight face.

"Never heard of him." Grandpa frowned, and shoved a Brussels sprout into his mouth.

"He's from Boston, a lawyer and businessman according to Ward. And obviously a man of means."

Grandma put down her fork and looked pointedly at Grace's father. "We'll be able to tell you more after we've met him."

"Grace is not going to meet him," he said. "I'm not having my daughter visiting some stranger's home just to look at a couple of pictures. You can tell that artist friend of yours we're not interested."

"I'll do no such thing, Francis Montel. And I'll thank you to remember who you're talking to. You are perfectly within your rights to refuse to let your daughter make this trip, but if you think for one minute that you can tell me what I can and cannot do, you are sadly mistaken."

Grandma's voice was frosty as a January morning. She lifted her chin and Daddy seemed to shrink under her gaze.

Taking a deep breath, Grace said, "It's more than just seeing a few pictures, Daddy. I'll be able to see how an artist goes from looking at the actual scene to making his studies, to the finished painting. In this case, three paintings." She kept her voice neutral. "It's really a wonderful chance and one I might not have again."

For a long, tense moment no one spoke. Then the corners of Grandpa's mouth twitched and he said, "Sometimes, it's best to let them have their way, Son. Be the hero and let her go. Save your energy for the next battle."

He looked at his wife. "And, believe me, there's always a next battle."

The drive to Mr. Ramsey's home took them from the wide, paved main road out of Chester, to secondary roads bordered by dense forest where dirty patches of snow still lay thick in the shade of the pines. In the front seat, Grandma and Mr. Standish chatted in low voices, but Grace couldn't hear much over the rumble of the engine. There was little sign of civilization up here, just the occasional white farmhouse and stolid red barn tucked into the folds of the landscape. Finally, they turned onto a long drive lined with young maples, and stopped in front of an imposing three-story brick house.

They climbed the shallow granite steps to a portico flanked by white columns. Mr. Standish rang the bell and, almost immediately, the door was opened by a woman in a well-cut black dress. Miss Armstrong was neither young nor old, attractive, but aloof. Her sandy hair was pulled into a tight bun, and her pale face wore an expression that said it would take a lot to make her smile.

She showed them into a sitting room furnished with sofas and chairs covered in pearl grey silk. Over the mantel, a portrait of a gentleman with a pointed beard and lace ruff gazed out of a gilded frame, looking every bit as serious as the housekeeper. She led them to a corner of the room where several small upholstered chairs were placed around a low table. Before Grace had a chance to take in more of her surroundings, Mr. Ramsey entered the room. Unlike Miss Armstrong or the fellow over the mantel, a broad smile was fixed on his ruddy face.

"Good to see you, Standish." His voice was bluff and cordial, his handshake coupled with a pat on the artist's shoulder. "Please, introduce me to your guests." He bowed slightly in the direction of Grace and her grandmother. "Ah, Mrs. Montel, so nice to meet you, and you, too, Miss Montel. Welcome to Riverview. I hope you enjoyed the drive. The countryside around here is lovely, and we couldn't have asked for a finer day." He motioned for Mr. Standish to sit down and seated himself next to Grace.

Miss Armstrong returned and placed a tray on the table. The cups and saucers, napkins, even the sandwiches and cakes were elegant. The whole room had a kind of understated beauty, no garish colors, no tables covered with framed photographs, nothing to break the restrained dignity of the place. Mr. Ramsey nodded to the housekeeper who left the room as quietly as she'd come in.

Grandma offered to pour the tea, filling and passing around the cups in the practiced way she managed all the niceties of social situations. While they had tea, they made small talk, everything from the harshness of the past winter to the difficulty of finding competent contractors and landscape architects to carry out Mr. Ramsey's plans for Riverview. Grace listened and watched their host.

He was polite, but not stuffy, friendly, but not too familiar. He exuded confidence and sophistication, as though he'd been raised with all the benefits of money, class, and education. What was he doing, then, on this rural property so far away from the cultural and social connections of his Boston upbringing? The scenery here was beautiful, but what manner of business did he conduct in this remote part of New Hampshire?

When the housekeeper returned for the tray, Mr. Ramsey said, "Miss Armstrong, I'd like you to conduct these two ladies on a tour of the house. Miss Montel is interested in the picture gallery and you can finish up in the conservatory."

He smiled at Grace's grandmother. "The orchids are particularly beautiful right now. When Standish and I are finished, we'll all go outside to see the work we've done on the riverside property."

After the two men left, Miss Armstrong began their tour with the Dutch master over the fireplace. From there, they moved to the gallery in the east wing of the house. The long room had tall windows on its two outside walls and gleaming parquet floors. Mr. Ramsey's extensive collection of Chinese porcelain was displayed on pedestals throughout the room and the walls were hung with paintings, almost all by American artists.

The housekeeper talked about every painting and several of the most valuable ceramic pieces in a surprisingly disinterested monotone. Grace spent a long time studying a painting by Mary Cassatt of a young woman reading in a garden. She asked Miss Armstrong several questions about the piece, but aside from her memorized script the woman had nothing to add. She was like an automaton in housekeeper's clothing. Grace could almost hear the hum of her apparatus as she delivered a brief description of each item.

On their way to the conservatory, Grace's grandmother asked, "How did you come to work for Mr. Ramsey, Miss Armstrong?"

The housekeeper did not slacken her pace. Her hands were clasped tightly at her waist and when she spoke she looked straight ahead. "I was hired on the recommendation of my former employer. I had been working at a large house in the Berkshires when the owner ... that is, the owner's wife took ill and they had to relocate."

"This seems a remote place to live for a woman alone," Grace's grandmother said. "My family goes back three generations in Chester and I still feel the isolation of the place at times. It must be doubly difficult to make friends this far from town."

Miss Armstrong did not respond, but paused at an open doorway and pointed to a large cityscape. "This painting was commissioned by Mr. Ramsey's father and given to Mr. Ramsey when he joined the family law firm."

"Does he still practice law?" Grace asked.

"Mr. Ramsey is primarily involved in real estate, now," the housekeeper said, in her tour-guide voice.

"I'm sure a knowledge of the law comes in handy in his real estate dealings and his other business ventures as well," Grace's grandmother said. Miss Armstrong nodded and moved on.

At the end of the hall, she opened a set of glass-paneled doors and gestured Grace and her grandmother into the conservatory. The room was flooded with sunlight, the windows damp with condensation. Large potted plants and lush ferns were banked in front of the long row of windows. Grace had seen paintings and photographs of orchids, but she'd never imagined how varied they could be in color and shape. Most were lovely, but others reminded her of large spotted insects.

Miss Armstrong led them to a sitting area between potted palms and said, "I'm sure Mr. Ramsey will join you shortly. Now, if you'll excuse me, I should get back to my duties."

"Thank you for your time, Miss Armstrong," Grandma said. "You must have your hands full looking after a house of this size. I imagine a man in Mr. Ramsey's position does a fair amount of entertaining."

"A fair amount, yes ... " She backed out of the room and hurried away.

Grace and her grandmother exchanged glances. "That's a woman with something to hide. Did you notice how our questions unnerved her?"

Grace nodded. "Something doesn't feel right about this place, Grandma. I mean, aside from the housekeeper. How could dealing in local real estate bring in the kind of money it takes to put a place like this together?"

Her grandmother flashed a wry smile. "Perhaps our host is independently wealthy and has a penchant for rural living. Although he doesn't strike me as a recluse."

She placed a finger on her lips and assumed a bland expression. At the sound of approaching footsteps, she said, "My, those orchids are lovely, aren't they dear? So many colors and varieties."

17

WEEKENDS

On the way home, Grace asked, "Mr. Standish, doesn't it seem strange to you that Mr. Ramsey wants a painting of the exact same view he can see from his terrace? I mean, it's beautiful the way he's reforested the opposite river bank, but—"

The painter laughed. "A man in my position cannot afford to look a gift horse in the mouth, Grace. The fact is, if Mr. Ramsey likes my work, it likely won't hang in his house at all, but in a more public place."

"What do you mean, Ward?" Grandma asked.

"Ramsey's got plans to build a resort that will more or less straddle the Canadian border. There'll be a golf course, a man-made lake, and a grand hotel. So, if my paintings please him they, and maybe others, will grace the lobby and public rooms of what will be the biggest resort of its kind on the northern border."

"That sounds like quite an undertaking. It would seem that Mr. Ramsey is not a man to do things by halves. How far has he gotten with his plans?"

"Well, I'm not sure exactly, but I know he has a few backers lined up and has begun negotiating with several farmers to buy property on either side of the border." He chuckled and shook his head. "This will be a line-house second to none."

Leaning forward Grace asked, "What's a line-house?"

"A line-house," her grandmother said, "is a building that sits right on the border. And since alcohol is legal in Canada, Mr. Ramsey will be able to sell spirits, as well as beer and wine, to his guests ... at least in one half of the establishment."

Grace sat back in her seat. Did Daddy know of Mr. Ramsey's plans for the resort? Surely, he didn't have the kind of capital it would take to invest in such a venture ... but maybe he could be useful to Mr. Ramsey in other ways. Grace shivered. The idea was unsettling.

Returning from school the following Friday, Grace was happy to find a letter from Jerome waiting for her on the hall table. She dropped her satchel, picked up the letter and hurried upstairs to her room. It had been more than two weeks since she'd heard from him, enough time for Grace to imagine all sorts of slights. Almost enough time for her to convince herself that he'd found another girl at one of the neighboring schools or taken a shine to one of his friend's sisters.

Kicking off her shoes, she settled onto the chaise lounge and tore off the end of the envelope. The thick cream stationery bearing the Academy crest was covered in Jerome's neat hand. Grace read through the three pages of tightly packed script, expecting at any moment to be ambushed by bad news. From the time they'd met in seventh grade, her connection to Jerome had made her feel less lonely and more sure of herself in social situations. Their first kiss had changed all that. Now, when they were together she was a bundle of nerves, happy and excited, but off-kilter, too, like a bicycle with one wobbly wheel. And when they were apart, the loneliness came back, stronger and blacker than ever.

There was the usual school news. Jerome was busy with mid-term exams and papers. The debating team had been to

Deerfield Academy. They hadn't won, but the dance that evening with a nearby girls' school had been fun. Grace stopped and reread that line. There was no mention of a particular girl, of course, but surely there had been plenty of attractive girls at the dance who noticed the handsome Exeter boy with the deep brown eyes and beautiful smile.

Jerome wanted to know if she'd managed to get permission to come to Exeter with his parents the following month. He was looking forward to showing her the campus and introducing her to some of his friends. There was also a watercolor exhibit at the Hall Museum that he was sure she'd want to see. In closing he said, *I framed the drawing of the tree house you sent me, Monty, and I keep it on my desk. Remember the time you threw the tomato at me? I miss you, J.*

Grace smiled. "You were the one who threw the tomato," she said aloud. She folded the letter and slipped it into the envelope, thinking of that summer afternoon. She'd been awful to Jerome, angry that he was leaving for the Academy and afraid of facing high school without him. Now, a different fear gnawed at her. If Daddy was involved in the liquor trade, and she was pretty sure he was, what would happen if he were caught? The family would be disgraced. Daddy might even end up in jail. How would Jerome feel about her then? She didn't think she'd be able to face him if that happened.

Since their row over Sunday dinner with Jerome and his parents, Grace had done her best to keep relations with her father on an even keel. She tried not to ask too many questions about his frequent absences, including those that took him away from home overnight, and she hadn't yet broached the subject of the Davisons' invitation to Exeter.

She'd planned to ask him last weekend, but he'd left the house early Saturday morning and hadn't returned until late Sunday afternoon. At dinner that evening, he'd been in fine spirits, describing a house party he'd attended on the outskirts of Boston. The host was in shipping, he'd told her, importing and exporting goods all over North America and Europe. He didn't say how he'd come to be a guest in the home of a shipping tycoon, but she suspected Mr. Ramsey had something to do with it.

Now, the date of the Academy spring concert was only a few weeks away and she couldn't put off asking her father's permission any longer. Daddy was at his best in the morning, so she'd set her alarm this evening and be at the table when he got down to breakfast. As soon as he had his first cup of coffee, she'd put the question to him.

Well before it was time for her father to leave for the shop, Grace was at the breakfast table alternately sipping tea and taking deep breaths to steady her fluttery stomach. Daddy bustled in, pulling at the cuffs of his white shirt, and raised his brows at the sight of her.

"Look who's up! I didn't expect to see you at this hour, Gracie. I'm usually long gone by the time you make it down on Saturday." He sat down and reached for the coffee pot.

"You're looking very smart this morning, Daddy. Is that a new suit?"

"You've got a good eye, sweetie. Just got it back from old Mr. Klein. He hemmed the trousers and took the sleeves up an inch or so." He reached for a piece of toast and tipped his head. "You off somewhere this morning?"

Grace shook her head. "There's something I've been meaning to ask you, so I came down early so we'd have a few minutes to talk." Her father took a bite of toast and checked his watch.

"I don't have much time this morning. I've got to get on the road by nine. Can it wait?"

She took a steadying breath. "Not really, Daddy. The Davisons have invited me to go to Exeter with them in a couple of weeks to see Jerome perform in the Academy's spring concert." She kept her voice neutral and tried to sound matter-of-fact. "We'd go down on Saturday and come back on Sunday. Mrs. Davison said she'd be happy to talk to you about it. She said to tell you I'd be well looked after."

The clock in the foyer bonged the three-quarter hour and her father checked his watch again. "Where would you stay?"

"At the Exeter Inn with Mr. and Mrs. Davison. Well, not Jerome, of course, he'll be staying in his dormitory." Grace steeled herself for the barrage of objections sure to follow.

Instead, her father drained his cup and pushed his chair back from the table. "I've got to get going, Grace. Have Mrs. Davison call me and we'll talk about it. I'll be back by dinnertime tomorrow."

Wide-eyed, Grace watched him exit the room. After all the fuss he'd made about that Sunday dinner back in March, and today he hadn't said a single thing about her going away with the Davisons overnight. And what about all that hoopla about courting and family honor and reputation? She shrugged. Obviously, Daddy had something more pressing on his mind today than protecting his daughter's good name. She didn't know where he was off to, but she was going straight to the Davisons'.

Stepping out into the May morning, Grace headed down High Street. Clouds moved across the hillsides driven by the stiff north wind, but the sun was bright and the fresh greens of the grass and leaves put her in mind of the Emerald City. After the dull palette of winter, it was hard to believe the world could contain so much color. She couldn't wait to give Daddy's message to Mrs. Davison. Once she had, she'd be on her way to Exeter.

Grace knocked on the back door and peeked into the kitchen, expecting to see Jerome's mother busy at the stove. The room appeared empty, though, the counters clear, the table free of dishes. She knocked again, her spirits sinking with each passing minute. At last, Mrs. Davison bustled into the kitchen, waving and hurrying to open the door. She welcomed Grace with her usual warmth, taking her coat and leading her to the table with an offer of tea or hot chocolate.

"Oh, I've just finished breakfast, Mrs. Davison, but thank you. I've come by about the Exeter visit."

"You've spoken to your father, then? Please, sit down and tell me what he said."

"Well, he asked that you call or stop by the shop to talk about it when you get a chance. I've told him about the concert and about staying at the inn. I think he wants to talk to you to make sure ... well, that I've got all the details right, I guess."

"And who can blame him? I'm going out later to run some errands, so I'll stop by and chat with him if he's not too busy." She reached across the table and squeezed Grace's hand. "I'm so glad you'll be coming with us, and I know Jerome will be, too. In his last letter, he said how much he's looking forward to seeing all of us."

"I'm afraid you won't find my father at the shop today, Mrs. Davison. He'll be away all weekend, but he'll be back at work on Monday."

Jerome's mother shook her head. "That's fine, dear. Would it be better if I telephoned him tomorrow evening?"

Grace said no, as she wasn't sure what time her father would be getting home. She smiled. "Besides, Daddy's much more likely to agree to my going, once he's talked to you in person. You're sure to win him over and set his mind at ease."

They chatted a few more minutes about the trip. Then Mrs. Davison said, "I miss Jerome, but at least at the Academy, he's out of harm's way."

Puzzled, Grace said, "I'm not sure I know what you mean."

Mrs. Davison sighed and leaned forward. "Well, look what happened to that poor fellow, Wesley Titus. His father works for my husband, you know, and the family is devastated by the young man's death. By all accounts, Wesley was a good boy." She shook her head. "I can't imagine what made him get involved in smuggling liquor over the border."

"Maybe he needed the money, Mrs. Davison. It's hard to get ahead working at the mill."

"The family isn't well off, I know. Still, it's a terrible thing for a fellow to get mixed up in." She brightened. "That's why I'm glad Jerome is safely tucked away in the halls of academia."

"Oh, Jerome's much too sensible to get himself in that kind of trouble — "

"Even sensible people succumb to temptation, Grace. Prohibition has made criminals out of more than one honest man."

Grace left the Davisons' and turned onto Main Street. It was silly to think Jerome would be tempted to take up illegal activities for money or thrills. For one thing, he didn't really need money and he was more likely to get excited by a good book or theater performance than by high speed chases across the northern border. But Daddy was a different story. He'd raved about the shipping tycoon's luxurious home and extravagant hospitality and was keeping company with rich men like Mr. Ramsey. Had the promise of such wealth tempted her father to break the law? And if he had, would he be able to stop?

Raymond was lowering the striped awning over the big display window as Grace approached the shop. She waved and called, "Hello, Raymond. Beautiful morning, isn't it?"

He brushed his hands together and tugged his vest into place. "Sure is, Miss. Wind's a little chilly, but I think I'll keep the door open for a while, freshen things up inside. Gets pretty stuffy in there." He shoved his hands in his trouser pockets and looked around. "Plenty of people out this morning, so I guess I better get inside. Could be a busy one."

Following him in, Grace said, "You're all alone today. My father headed out early this morning."

Raymond busied himself behind the counter and didn't comment.

"Is there anything I can do to help? I could unpack those boxes for you, if you'd like." She smiled. "I've had lots of practice with that sort of thing."

Raymond shook his head. "No need, Miss. I'll get to them before the day's out. Things get kind of slow the last hour or so."

He looked so uncomfortable that Grace took pity on him and left the store. She'd stopped by hoping to find out if Raymond knew where Daddy'd gone, but if he knew anything about her father's whereabouts or activities, he was keeping it to himself. She sighed and turned toward home.

The door to Miss Andrews' millinery was propped open, and Grace caught sight of Mary arranging hats on a series of display shelves to the right of the door. She hadn't talked to Mary since the morning she'd asked her about Wesley Titus. That had been an unsatisfying conversation, and she'd come away feeling that Mary was put out with her. She'd even asked Grace not to come by the shop anymore, yet here she was.

Stepping up to the open door, Grace peeked inside. "Hi Mary, is Miss Andrews around?"

Mary shook her head. "She's over at the library collecting another pile of books for her mother. That woman must read a book a day." She straightened the veil on a pink hat. "Is there anything I can help you with?"

"Not really," Grace scanned the shop, "it's just that I feel badly about coming to your house and asking all those questions."

She looked up and down the street, but saw no sign of Miss Andrews. "I didn't mean to be such a nosy parker and I'm sorry if I said anything to insult Paddy or your friend, Wesley." She sighed. "I'm just so worried about my father."

Mary waved a dismissive hand. "I was a bit put out with you, I admit, but ma said who else did you have to talk to. Sometimes I forget you're all alone, no mother or sisters or brothers ..." She shook her head. "And no one knows better than me what troublesome creatures dads can be."

Grace laughed. "Well, I won't keep you. I know I shouldn't bother you when you're working."

"Never mind what I said about the shop, Grace. I was just ... well, it was the day of Wes's funeral and I ... "

Hearing the tremor in Mary's voice, Grace realized that Wesley was more than just a family friend. "Oh, Mary, I didn't realize you and Wesley were ... I'm so sorry."

Mary bit her lip and looked away. "He was a good man, Gracie. He didn't deserve to die." She took a deep breath and smoothed the front of her dress. "It's no wonder you're worried about your father. I'm scared for Paddy, too. If anything happened to him, it would kill my mum. He's her pride and joy."

Grace had just turned off the bedside lamp when she heard the Pontiac pull up in front of the house. Daddy hadn't made it home for dinner, even though she'd waited a full hour before giving up and eating in the kitchen with Mrs. Blanchard. All evening she'd alternated between worry and annoyance, wondering where he'd been from Saturday morning until late into the evening on Sunday. Rolling onto her side, Grace gave her pillow a savage punch. She knew next to nothing about Daddy's life away from home, and that was just the way he wanted it.

The following morning, Grace was finishing the last of her toast when her father came into the dining room. In spite of a close shave and starched white shirt, he looked worn out. Deep pouches sagged under his eyes and the web of tiny red capillaries across his nose and cheeks stood out in the light from the tall windows. When he spoke, his voice was raspy as an old hinge.

"Morning, Grace," he said, reaching for his napkin. "Sorry I was late getting home last night. Something came up." He lifted the cup to his lips and didn't meet her eyes.

"We waited dinner for you. By the time we ate, the roast was pretty dried out. I felt bad for Mrs. B."

"It couldn't be helped, but don't worry, I'll make my apologies. Don't want to upset the worthy Mrs. Blanchard."

Grace frowned. She was fed up with his evasions and sick to death of that jokey way he had of putting her off. "So, where did you go, Daddy? It must have been pretty important to miss a whole Saturday at the shop."

His cup clattered into the saucer. "I've spent more Saturdays than I can count at that infernal shop, Grace, and I don't have to justify missing one to you or anyone else."

He took a breath. "A fellow invited me to a weekend party and I went, that's all."

Waiting for the banging in her chest to subside, Grace folded her napkin carefully and placed it next to her empty plate. Then she clasped her hands in her lap and said, "Mrs. Davison will stop by the shop today or tomorrow to talk to you about my going to Exeter with them."

Her father busied himself with his breakfast, but she kept her gaze focused on him. "School's going to be a grind from now until the end of the year. I'm looking forward to getting away for a weekend myself."

He looked at her then. "A little quid pro quo, eh, Grace?"

"Something like that," she said.

18

DECISIONS AND REVELATIONS

When Mr. Davison pulled up in front of the Exeter Inn, Jerome was sitting in one of the wicker rockers on the wide porch. He looked spruce in his school blazer and white shirt, but his hair was as tousled and unruly as ever, just the way Grace liked it. He jumped up and, hurrying down the steps, rounded the car and opened the door for his mother. He helped her out and leaned down to kiss her cheek. Grace climbed out of the back seat and stood on the sidewalk, waiting. Finally, Jerome was at her side, smiling into her face, and welcoming her to the Academy. He took her hand, and with a deep bow, lifted it to his lips. She laughed and pulled her hand away.

Mr. Davison cleared his throat and said, "How about some help with these bags, son?"

After lunch at the Inn, they headed to the museum. Huge trees shaded the gravel paths and ivy, shiny with new growth, clung to the walls of the brick and stone buildings. There were mullioned windows and Latin inscriptions over the great oak doors and Roman numerals carved into the cornerstones. Jerome waved at passing boys and pointed out his English teacher, a grey-haired man in worn tweeds carrying a bulging leather satchel in one hand and a pipe in the other.

Compared to Chester High, the Academy was like Olympus, a beautiful place inhabited by gods. That was overstating it, but something about these boys was special. Assured of promising futures, they carried themselves with confidence and poise. No wonder Jerome was happy here. He'd always been different from the other boys in school, but here he fit right in. He belonged with these boys of privilege and good breeding more than he'd ever belonged with the sons of mill workers and lumbermen.

At the arched entrance of the Hall Museum, Jerome held the door and Grace followed Mr. and Mrs. Davison inside. As she passed, Jerome's hand lingered on the small of her back, warm and reassuring.

They moved into a series of rooms which housed the watercolor exhibit. The walls were hung with paintings of New England: seascapes of the rugged Maine coast, views from the tops of Mount Washington and Mansfield, pastoral scenes of grazing cows in languid summer fields. Enthralled, Grace studied each piece, noting the composition, colors and application of paint, the rendering of bark and water and cloud. In two dimensions the artists evoked the smell of fresh cut hay, the roar of breaking waves, the stifling humidity of a threatening July afternoon. Would she ever learn to make paint come alive like this?

Well before she'd had her fill, Mrs. Davison said it was time they got back to the inn to rest and prepare for dinner and the evening's festivities. Jerome checked his watch and agreed, saying he had to change and head to his final rehearsal. Making their way back along the gravel paths, Grace and Jerome walked behind his parents. Falling into step beside him, she took his proffered arm and felt her pulse quicken.

A few hours later, Grace sat next to Mrs. Davison, watching as the auditorium filled with members of the faculty, students, their families, and friends. Jerome's mother pointed out the trustees seated together in the front row and several distinguished alumni who had attended the Academy in her father's day.

The program opened with the band, after which the Glee Club sang. Jerome was at the end of the second row next to a blond fellow Mrs. Davison said was his good friend, Myles. A quartet of senior students wearing false handlebar mustaches sang *When You and I Were Young, Maggie* and *Smile and the World Smiles with You.* Three boys read original poems and one recited the Band of Brothers speech from Henry V. Finally, the Headmaster invited everyone to stand for the national anthem, bringing the program to a close.

As the applause died, the audience began collecting wraps, hats, and gloves and filing out of the auditorium. Grace followed Mrs. Davison along the row, up the incline, and into the lobby. The great chandeliers glowed brightly, lighting up the ladies' elaborate up-do's and feathered headdresses. Family members milled about waiting for their sons to join them. Women gushed over their boys' performances, while their husbands shook one another's hands and talked about politics and the state of the economy. Standing beside Jerome's parents, Grace took in the well-dressed crowd gathered under the vaulted ceiling and looked around for a ladies' room. Spotting a sign down an adjoining corridor, she excused herself and hurried away.

Glancing in the mirror as she washed her hands, she noticed a young woman standing off to one side looking at her. Their eyes met in the mirror and Grace smiled. Instead of returning her smile, the girl lifted her chin and looked away. Grace tidied her hair, smoothed the front of her dress, and turned to leave. The girl hadn't moved, neither had she taken her eyes off Grace. What possible interest could this girl have in her? Was it so obvious that she didn't belong here?

In the lobby, Grace caught sight of Jerome standing with his parents. He waved her over with a smile so warm and eager, she felt her face flush. Just as she reached the Davisons, the tall blond boy who'd stood next to Jerome during the concert approached, greeting the family with an easy familiarity and favoring Grace with a bright smile and formal little bow.

"Grace, this is my great friend and suitemate, Myles. Myles, Miss Grace Montel, great friend, budding artist, and—"

Before he could finish, he was interrupted by the approach of Myles' parents, Mr. and Mrs. Caruthers, and his sister, Adelaide.

The girl from the ladies room.

Introductions were made. Mrs. Caruthers told Grace how much they enjoyed Jerome's frequent visits to their home in Massachusetts. Her husband welcomed Grace to the Academy. Adelaide smiled coolly and said hello. She was a year or so younger than Grace, but a great deal more assured of her place among these affluent and sophisticated people. She was lovely, blond and graceful, her silk frock the exact blue of her eyes. Grace disliked her immediately. Not only had Adelaide snubbed her, but now she completely monopolized Jerome's attention, standing too close, her voice low and intimate.

Standing alone amid the buzz of conversation, the familiar sense of invisibility settled over Grace. Crowds did that to her and it was no help that Jerome had obviously forgotten her very existence. She shouldn't have come this weekend. She didn't belong here with these well-to-do people and their handsome children. Though she was no more than a few feet from Jerome, she'd never felt more distant from him. Finally, Myles interrupted his sister's tête-à-tête and the Caruthers took their leave. Jerome and his friend headed back to their dormitory, Grace followed the Davisons to the inn, and retreated to her room.

The following morning when Grace went down to breakfast, she found Mr. and Mrs. Davison seated at a window table, and joined them just as the waiter returned with their coffee. As he handed her the menu, Jerome arrived, stopping in the doorway to scan the room. Mrs. Davison waved and he approached the table, smiling and flushed from his walk across campus. Ordinarily, Grace would have been thrilled by his warm greeting and confidential smile, but not this morning. Not after he'd ignored her and practically thrown himself at Adelaide the evening before. She managed a half smile and busied herself with the menu.

After breakfast, Jerome said he wanted to show Grace the river walk. His father said they were leaving around 11:00 and to be back by then. The May morning was mild and smelled of new grass and lilacs. Grace followed Jerome along a side street and down a gravel path bordered by elms. All around the earth was opening, blooming and swelling with spring, but Grace's insides were glacial, her icy hands balled into fists in the pockets of her coat.

The path opened onto the river, fast moving and swollen with snow melt and spring rains. When they'd first set off, Jerome had made several attempts to engage Grace in conversation, but her one-word answers had silenced him and they walked without speaking. They came to a well-worn spot on the bank where a huge old cottonwood grew almost horizontally over the water.

"Let's stop here for a while, Monty. It's a good place to sit and watch the river."

Grace settled on the tree's broad trunk and he sat beside her. She watched the rippling surface of the water as the current rolled toward them, and listened to the breeze rustling in the trees, but couldn't bring herself to speak.

Jerome shifted on the log, turning toward her and cleared his throat. "What's wrong, Monty? You haven't said two words to me all morning. I've wanted to show you this place for so long. I thought you'd love it here, but ... "

Grace couldn't tell him what was wrong. If he didn't understand how she'd felt watching him with Adelaide, she didn't know how to explain it. She'd just sound jealous and petty, which she supposed she was.

Without taking her eyes off the moving water, she said, "This is a beautiful place, Jerome. It's just that this weekend has made me realize some things. Seeing you here with your friends ... I mean, the kind of people you know here, I feel as though I don't know the person you are when you're at the Academy ... or the person you're becoming." She shook her head. "Last night after the concert, I — "

"So that's it, isn't it?" Jerome said, standing up and looking down at her. "You're upset because I talked to Adelaide." He frowned and shook his head. "She's my friend's sister. I often spend the weekend at their home. What was I supposed to do, ignore her?"

Grace looked down at her clasped hands. "You ignored me."

"Oh, Monty ... " He ran his hand through his hair and sat down heavily beside her. "I didn't ignore you. I was just being ... What could I do? Adelaide is one of those girls who's used to ... She has a way of getting attention. It's nothing ... she's nothing to me. I was just being sociable."

His voice softened and he took her hand. "When you live in a place like this you have to be. It's expected."

"I'm not very good at being sociable," Grace said. "I felt so foolish standing there with no one to talk to. I don't know what to do in those situations. I want to disappear."

"Well, you can't disappear in a place like this. There's no privacy, no place to be alone. At first that really bothered me, but I've had to get used to it, just like I've had to get used to not seeing my parents every day and doing without my mother's cooking."

He shrugged and stood up. "Truth is, Monty, I can't be the same person here as I am at home. I've had to find a way to be at home here and so, I've had to make some changes."

He checked his watch and held out his hand. "We'd better get back, but before we go ... " Jerome leaned forward and kissed her gently on the lips, then once more on the forehead. "And I've had to get used to being without you, too."

"I hope you don't get too used to it," Grace said, managing a smile.

As they walked back along the river path, she said, "Until this weekend, I didn't understand that this is more than school for you. This place is fitting you for a certain kind of life with a certain kind of people ... and eventually you'll be one of those people."

"I guess you're right." Jerome smiled, a little sadly Grace thought. "The question is, will you still like me when I'm one of those people?"

Grace searched his face. "The real question is, will you still want me to?"

———————◆◆◆———————

The last weeks of school were every bit the grind Grace had told her father they would be. Along with Alma and Christine, she worked doggedly through the lengthening afternoons studying for exams, finishing final papers, and rehearsing with the chorus for the closing assembly.

One lowering Wednesday afternoon, gathered with the other students in the stifling music room, Grace was near her breaking point. Her head throbbed and she was so congested she could hardly breathe. To make matters worse, they were going over the same songs they'd practiced for weeks, songs she hadn't particularly liked when they started learning them and which she hated now. Added to the usual patriotic and spiritual numbers that made up most of the program, Miss Mathews had chosen two so-called popular tunes. No doubt they were popular with someone, but most everyone in the chorus thought they were awful. *Danny Boy* was impossible to sing and *I'm Always Chasing Rainbows* was just plain morbid.

After they'd tried and failed for the hundredth time to hit and hold a particular high note, Miss Mathews rapped her baton against the music stand and called for quiet. She stared at the rows of sweating singers and sighed, obviously as fed up with them as they were with *Danny Boy*. She closed her sheet music, put down her baton, and said they'd try again on Thursday. Grace and her friends gathered their belongings and filed out of the room, making their way down the wide oak stairs and out into the afternoon heat.

On the sidewalk, Alma shook her blond bob and said, "That was torture. Whatever was Miss Mathews thinking?" She cleared her throat, threw back her head, and screeched her way through the passage they'd just been practicing. "*Danny Boy*," she said. "Really."

Christine laughed. "Well, it's no worse than her other choice. Here we are finishing the school year and she picks a song about a hopeless failure ... Poor Miss Mathews."

Grace was only half listening. She was thinking about the letter she'd received from Aunt Louise the day before. Her aunt and uncle were taking the cottage for the entire month of July this year and wanted her to spend as much of that time with them as she could. She thought with longing of the cool mountain air and quiet lake and especially of the easy sanity of life with her aunt and uncle. She'd get a break from Daddy's moods and her constant worry about his late nights and questionable activities. She'd also miss the few weeks of summer that Jerome would be in Chester.

"Gracie, are you there?" Alma teased. "Chris just asked you a question."

"Oh, sorry, I guess I'm kind of distracted ... and my head's killing me. What'd you say?"

"I asked if you wanted to stop at Vincent's for a soda. Wet your whistle as my grandpa would say."

Grace shook her head. "Thanks Chris, but I think I'll head home. It's so muggy and all this pollen ..." She rubbed her forehead.

"You two go on and I'll see you tomorrow. I'm going home to lie down."

At the corner the girls parted. Alma and Christine turned down Main Street toward the pharmacy. Grace trudged up the hill toward home.

The dim foyer felt cool after the heat of the afternoon. Grace lowered her book bag onto the floor and massaged the space between her brows, pressing her thumbs against flesh that was as tender as a bruise. Upstairs, she took two aspirin and got into bed. The cold compress over her eyes blotted out everything but the pain in her head.

She was awakened some time later by the insistent ringing of the telephone. The cloth had slipped off and she stared at the ceiling willing someone to answer it. Finally, she heard her father's voice, harsh and impatient, and sat up. Tiptoeing to the door, she opened it a crack and listened. She couldn't make out much of what he was saying, but he was definitely angry. She crept down the hall, avoiding the creaking floorboard in front of her mother's room, and stopped just before the stair landing.

"I don't give a damn what we agreed to," she heard him say. "I'm willing to do plenty myself, but I'm not going to risk involving anyone else. Not after what's already happened."

He paused, obviously listening to whoever was on the other end of the line, then said, "No, I'm telling you. Count me out. Find someone else to do your recruiting. I'm finished."

With an oath, he slammed the ear piece onto its hook. Grace heard his footsteps on the foyer tiles and the bang of his study door. She shivered in spite of the heat and hurried back to her room.

Her grandmother called shortly after her father left for the shop on Saturday morning. "I have something I'd like to talk to you about, Gracie," she said. "Two things, actually, one being your summer plans."

"And the other, Grandma?"

"That can wait until you get here. Come up to my sitting room. Your grandfather's going out for the paper, but he won't be gone long."

Returning to the dining room, Grace refilled her tea cup and spread jam on her last piece of toast. Grandma wanted to talk about Aunt Louise's offer, but Grace hadn't decided what to do yet. If she went to the lake for a month, she wouldn't see Jerome during the few weeks he'd be in Chester before leaving for the Cape. On the other hand, if she stayed home until he left, every day together would be clouded by their looming separation. She'd been through it all before; just thinking about it made her miserable.

The sidewalks were dry by the time Grace headed down High toward Pleasant Street. Overnight the rain had swept away the humidity and the sun shone clear and bright. People were out tending flower beds and mowing lawns. Grace waved to a woman she recognized on her way to the shops and old Mr. Carlisle, still in his bedroom slippers, shuffled down his front steps to retrieve his newspaper from the shrubbery.

Turning onto Pleasant Street, Grace met her grandfather. "Off to get the paper, Grandpa?"

"Yep, headed to Smitty's to pick up the bad news." He grinned. "I understand you've been summoned. What's your grandmother up to this time?"

"She wants to talk to me about going to the lake this summer." She lowered her voice conspiratorially. "I think she's going to help me make up my mind."

"Don't know why that's any of her business," he chuckled, "but don't tell her I said so."

Grace let herself in the front door and climbed the stairs to her grandmother's sitting room. In the doorway she paused, struck by the scene before her. Grandma was seated at her writing desk, the light from a nearby window adding a halo effect to her perfectly styled white hair. She was wearing a pale green frock that flattered her still slender figure and made her seem one with the foliage outside.

"Hello, Grandma. You look lovely this morning," Grace said, kissing her cheek. "If Mr. Standish could see now, he'd want to paint your portrait."

Screwing the cap on her fountain pen, her grandmother arched her brows and said, "I'm sure Mr. Standish is not so desperate for subjects that he'd stoop to painting old ladies at their correspondence."

Grace laughed. "You look anything but an old lady this morning, Grandma. I'm sure Mr. Standish would be delighted to have you sit for him. I happen to know he admires you a great deal." She sat down on the Queen Ann chair next to the desk. "Almost as much as I do."

"On to business, dear. When do you plan to let your aunt and uncle know how long you'll be staying with them this summer? I understand they've taken the cottage for the whole month and, personally, I think being away that long would do you good."

Grace sighed and shifted on the uncomfortable chair. "I don't know, Grandma. I love being at the lake with Aunt Louise and Uncle Arthur, but I don't want to wear out my welcome. They might like some time alone during their vacation."

"If they'd wanted time alone, they wouldn't have made the invitation." Her grandmother searched her face. "The real question is, do you want to be away from home that long?"

"I do and I don't," Grace said, slowly. "I don't like to leave Daddy for a whole month. He wouldn't like me to say so, but I worry about him."

"I know you do, Gracie, which is precisely why I think you should take advantage of this chance to get away. The change of scene will do you good, give you a chance to rest and put those worries aside for a while."

She leaned back in her chair. "And this year you'll be able to set your easel up and paint outdoors."

Grace pictured herself standing at her easel, studying the play of light on the lake and the dark mountains behind. What might she accomplish with a month to focus on her art?

"That sounds lovely, but there's something else — "

"Something else or someone else?"

Grace flushed. "You see right through me, don't you, Grandma? The problem is, if I go to the lake in early July, I'll be away during the only time Jerome will be home this summer."

"Ah, I see. Well, it's your decision, of course, but I'm not sure it's wise for you to give up the pleasures of the lake just to accommodate Jerome's schedule."

She paused. "Men are interesting creatures, Grace. It may not be a bad thing for Jerome to be in Chester without you ... give him a little taste of what you experience when he's away at school. You know what they say about absence making the heart grow fonder."

She patted Grace's hand. "As for your father, no one knows better than I, how trying he can be at times. He'll do what he likes whether you're here or not."

Grandma was right. Grace had never been able to influence Daddy, no matter what she said or did, and she rather liked the idea of Jerome in Chester without her company.

Grace nodded. "Thanks, Grandma. You've given me a lot to think about. I'll make a decision soon and write to Aunt Louise this week."

She clasped her hands in her lap. "Now, what was the other thing you wanted to talk to me about?"

Her grandmother glanced at the open door and lowered her voice. "I've done a bit more detective work, dear. I was curious about our Mr. Ramsey and wanted to see what else I could learn about him. Specifically, I wanted to know why he left his practice in Boston. So I wrote to my friend Margaret Peyton."

"Who?" Grace said, frowning.

"You wouldn't remember Margaret; she was well before your time. We went to school together and still keep in touch occasionally. Anyway, her husband is an attorney in Massachusetts, so I asked him if he knew anything about this fellow Ramsey. When Mr. Peyton checked the state's registry, he discovered something interesting." She paused and Grace leaned forward.

"What, Grandma? What did he find out?"

"Well, the records indicate that Mr. Ramsey comes from a long line of attorneys going back to his great-grandfather."

"We knew that already, didn't we?"

"Perhaps, but now it's been confirmed. We also now know that the Ramsey family law firm is one of the most prestigious in the state. Think about this, Gracie. A long-standing law practice has a long-standing clientele, generations of well-to-do, influential people with connections to business, government ... So, what would induce Mr. Ramsey to leave a lucrative position working in the highest echelons of Boston society and move to the North Woods?"

Grace shrugged. "I don't know, Grandma." She grinned. "Maybe he was tired of the law and wanted to live a quieter life."

"Or perhaps it was because he'd been disbarred from practicing law in Massachusetts." Her grandmother sat back in her chair and looked at Grace.

"Did Mr. Peyton say why?"

"He looked into it, but all he could find was a short article in the *Globe* announcing that Mr. Ramsey was leaving the firm for personal reasons." She smirked. "Personal reasons, indeed.

It's a measure of his family's influence that Mr. Peyton searched the court records but could find nothing more."

Grace was quiet for a long moment. "What do you suppose he did, Grandma? I mean, if he lost his license in spite of his family's connections, it must have been pretty bad, but, apparently, not bad enough to land him in jail." She frowned. "What do you think — "

Grandma shrugged. "Something to do with money would be my guess ... fraud or embezzlement. Something his family had the wherewithal to settle out of the public eye."

19

LEAVE TAKING

Grace and Jerome sat on the wicker settee, not looking at each other. This corner of the porch, shaded by a lattice covered with a thick growth of Virginia creeper, had become a favorite spot for conversation, but today neither of them had much to say. The late June day was sultry. The still air settled on them like fog, moistening their skin and further dampening their spirits. Up in her room, Grace's trunk was packed, her easel and paint box strapped together, her train case open on her dresser, ready for any last minute items she might need for a month at the lake.

Grace lifted the sweating glass of lemonade to her lips, but finding the lump in her throat made swallowing difficult, set it back on the table. Since she'd visited Exeter in May, she and Jerome had seen little of each other. He'd come back to Chester when the Academy term ended, but left shortly after for the Caruthers' cottage in Maine.

Learning of his planned visit to Myles, and by extension his sister Adelaide, had cinched Grace's decision to make herself scarce during the two weeks he'd be in Chester before heading to the Cape. At the time, this tit for tat arrangement had seemed inevitable, but now the thought of leaving, and the long separation that would follow, was unbearable. So was sitting here beside him. She wanted this visit to be over and she wanted it never to end. Jerome shifted position, turning slightly towards her and placing his arm across the back of the settee. She lifted her gaze to meet his. Under his furrowed brow, his dark eyes were flat and lusterless.

"Monty," he said, his voice barely a whisper. "Talk to me, please. I know you're upset with me for going to Myles's place ... for spending time with him when I could have been with you, but I didn't know you'd be away these next two weeks. I thought we'd have some time — "

"That's the trouble, Jerome. When you go off to visit friends or spend time at the Cape, you just expect me to be here when you get back. Good old Monty, she's a fixture in Chester. Anytime I get home, she'll be there waiting. Well, not this time." There was a lot more she wanted to say, harsh words she'd said countless times to an imaginary Jerome, but she held back.

Jerome pulled away as if he'd been stung. "That's not fair and you know it. When I'm away it's because I have to be."

"Like you had to go to Maine? Come on, Jerome, school's one thing, but surely you aren't telling me staying a week with Myles and his family is something you had to do. You went because you wanted to, because you were going to have fun ... more fun than you'd have at home."

"More fun than I'd have with you? Is that what you're trying to say, Grace? Or maybe you'd like to take this further, maybe we should talk about Adelaide and all the fun she and I had together. Should we do that, too?"

Leaning forward, he held his head in his hands. "Why do you have to make everything I do into some kind of betrayal? Why can't you just trust me ... trust my feelings for you?" He looked at her then and the pain in his eyes made her heart contract.

"Oh, Jerome, I'm sorry. I know I've been awful to you. I don't mean to be, but ... " She swallowed and blinked back tears. "I'm just afraid, I guess. We spend so much time apart, so much of our lives doing different things with different people. I feel like we hardly know each other anymore."

Jerome's face softened. "I know it feels like that sometimes, but it's up to us isn't it? I mean, we can let the time apart, the time doing different things with different people, come between us ... or we can do our best to stay in touch no matter what's happening to us when we're apart."

He took her hand. "Our lives are changing, Monty. We're changing, but that doesn't mean our feelings for each other have to change. Does it?"

Weaving her fingers through his, Grace studied their clasped hands. "I don't know," she said slowly. "And if everything else changes, will it really matter if our feelings don't?"

That evening Grace and her father went to her grandparents' for a farewell dinner. As they took their places around the candlelit table, she watched her father warily, hoping that being with his parents would prevent a repeat of the liquor-sodden diatribe of the evening before. Ever since she'd decided to spend a month with her aunt and uncle, Daddy hadn't missed a chance to criticize or insult them. Last night, he had railed against Uncle Arthur, calling him an ill-paid pedagogue who spent his working life teaching girls to paint flowers.

Usually, Grace put on a bland face and neither agreed nor disagreed when her father became argumentative. She'd learned to wait for the tempest to pass, knowing the flame of his outrage would quickly flare and die. But yesterday, she couldn't contain her anger and disgust any longer.

She'd covered her ears with her hands and demanded that he stop. She wasn't going to listen to another word. She defended her uncle as a decent, kind, sober man who treated people, all people, with respect. Instead of criticizing Uncle Arthur, her father should thank him for being such a good husband to his sister and showing Grace just how responsible and upstanding a man could be.

At that Daddy had slammed his fist on the table and staggered to his feet, upsetting his chair and sending it crashing to the floor. He glared at her, red-faced, shouted that she was ungrateful, that she cared more for her uncle than she did for her own father, that her mother would be ashamed of her impudence and disrespect.

Grace had shot back, "I wonder what Mama would think of the kind of father you've turned out to be?"

Then she'd fled, running up the stairs and locking the door to her room. For a long time, she'd stood with her back against the door, bathed in a cold sweat, hating her father and wishing he'd died instead of her mother.

Now, her grandmother was quizzing her about her preparations for the trip and asking about the train schedule.

"Oh, I've been packed for a week, Grandma. I've packed and repacked that trunk so many times I've lost count," she said. "I take the 10:15 to Concord and Aunt Louise will pick me up. We're going to stop by the school before we head to the lake. Uncle Arthur's interviewing candidates for one of the teaching positions and Auntie's going to give me a tour of the college."

She'd said too much. Her father lowered his wine glass and looked at her. She hadn't mentioned the college visit lest she give him more reason to criticize her aunt and uncle, but now the cat was out of the bag.

Before he could register a reaction, Grandma said, "Louise is so proud of what Arthur has done at the college. Be sure to act suitably impressed, Gracie, or you'll hurt her feelings." She smiled and turned the conversation to the church's fund-raising efforts.

After dinner, Grace's father and grandfather stayed at the table with snifters of brandy, while she and her grandmother went upstairs to the sitting room. As they took their usual places on the settee, Grandma gave Grace a box of pale blue monogrammed stationery and a sheet of postage stamps.

"I'm going to miss you, dear, so I'm making it as easy as possible for you to keep in touch."

Grace thanked her grandmother and promised to write regularly. Then she lowered her voice and asked if Grandma had heard any more from Mr. Peyton.

"That's really why I brought you up here, dear. Margaret wrote to say her husband discovered that our neighbor to the north was implicated in the death of a fellow who worked in one of his warehouses."

"Warehouses? What kind of warehouse? I thought he had a law practice."

"Had a law practice, yes, but after prohibition went into effect and the whiskey distilleries closed, it seems our Mr. Ramsey bought several warehouses ... conveniently stocked with barrels of whiskey which he then bottled and sold. Illegally, of course. As far as Margaret's husband could tell, one of Ramsey's employees tried to blackmail him ... threatened to reveal his operations to the revenuers." She leaned forward. "Within a week the would-be blackmailer was the victim of an accident at work."

Grace frowned. "Did Mr. Peyton think the man's death was accidental?"

"Apparently, the man's family didn't. They tried to press charges, but there wasn't enough evidence to back up their wrongful death claim, so the matter was dropped. And we still don't know why Ramsey lost his license to practice law. Mr. Peyton said he found no connection between the two events."

Grace stared into the empty grate. The more she knew about Mr. Ramsey, the more afraid she was for her father. "This Ramsey is a bad character, Grandma. Even if that man's death was an accident, this fellow's still a bootlegger and maybe worse." She shuddered. "I'm afraid for Daddy, Grandma. What are we going to do?"

"You are going to the lake tomorrow, Gracie, and I'm going to keep an eye on things here. There's a fellow I know of who might be able to help us."

She stood up. "Try not to worry, dear, and do your best to enjoy your time away." She held out her hand. "Now, let's get down to the parlor before your father and grandfather get into one of their tiffs."

The train pulled into Concord station shortly after noon the following day. Watching out the window, Grace saw Aunt Louise on the platform. With one hand shading her eyes, she peered at the slowing train and Grace waved, not sure she could be seen through the smudged and dusty window.

Grabbing her purse and case, she hurried out to join her aunt. They embraced, talked briefly about the trip and the folks back home, then located a porter to see to the trunk. Once it was stowed in the Hudson, they headed through town and up a steep hill past a sign for Mansfield College, Normal School.

Grace wasn't sure what she'd expected, but it wasn't this plain, clapboard building surrounded by patchy lawn and shaded on one side by a straggling cluster of birch and poplar. As her aunt pulled up in front, Grace thought of the Academy's impressive brick and stone buildings, towering trees and lush green spaces. Parched and bleached by the July sun, this place looked abandoned, the silence broken only by a trio of crows protesting their arrival. Grace tried not to show her disappointment. Mansfield College looked more like a neglected public house than an institution of higher learning.

Aunt Louise, though, seemed not to notice the shabby yard or humble structure. She took Grace's hand and led her in the front door, eager to begin their tour. Immediately inside the door, a steep staircase led to the floor above. To the right of the stairs, several rooms opened onto a long hallway that led to the back of the building. Grace followed her aunt, their shoes reporting sharply on the polished wooden floors, to an open door at the end of the passage. Directly inside, a middle-aged woman sat at a desk shuffling through a sheaf of papers. She glanced up at their approach, studied them over the rim of her half-moon glasses, and worked her thin lips into a peevish smile.

"Hello, Miss Fraser," Aunt Louise said. "Is Professor Eastman in?"

"He's in, but he's not available," the woman answered, looking down at the papers on her desk.

"Do you know when he might be available?" Her aunt's tone was so saccharine, her smile so bright, Grace had to bite her lip to keep from grinning.

"I really couldn't say, Mrs. Eastman," the woman answered, emphasizing the Mrs. "He's conducting interviews for the position of History and Civics teacher. I expect he'll be busy for the next hour or two."

"In that case, I'm going to take my niece on a tour of the building and then we'll stop in town for lunch. Please let Mr. Eastman know we'll meet him back here around 3:00."

"I'll see he gets the message." Without looking at either of them, Miss Fraser gathered her papers into a pile and aligned the edges with a sharp rap against the desk top.

Making their way back down the hall, Grace whispered, "Is she always that friendly, Auntie?" Her aunt put an arm around her waist and said no, she was usually a real harpy, and the two of them broke into stifled giggles.

The promised tour didn't take long. Except for the science laboratory and the art and music rooms, the rest of the classrooms were identical. They had the same chalkboards, scarred desks, and tall windows, the same limp American flag hanging in the corner as did those of Grace's secondary school.

"Not much to look at, I know," her aunt said, "but I've saved the best for last. Come with me."

They climbed a short flight of stairs to the space under the eaves. "The library and the theater," she said, opening doors on either side of a landing. "Not the best arrangement in terms of noise, but until your uncle took over as Headmaster, neither of these facilities existed. He raised most of the money himself, designed the spaces with the help of one of the trustees, and did a lot of the actual work, too."

Grandma was right. Aunt Louise was proud of what her husband had done here and Grace was suitably impressed. The wood-paneled library, lit by skylights and a small stained-glass window on the far end, was furnished with oak tables and chairs, study carrels, and shelves and shelves of books. In the theater, a painted curtain hung over the stage at one end of the long room and folding chairs were piled against the wall, leaving the floor open.

"In the winter, the students have physical education classes here and, of course, there are plays and musical performances as well the Christmas and spring dances."

Aunt Louise smiled. "So, you see, it's not all as shabby as it looks from the outside. Arthur has plans for the school, Grace, and he's working hard to recruit good people for the faculty. If you pursued your art studies here, you'd be prepared to teach when you graduated or you could even transfer to an arts program at a university."

Listening to her aunt, Grace thought how like Daddy she was. Her voice vibrated with the same breathless excitement, her eyes burned with the same warmth, but they were different, too. Her father's enthusiasms carried him away and clouded his judgment, whereas Aunt Louise's made you feel anything was possible.

Even launching an artistic career at dumpy, little Mansfield College.

Grace settled quickly into her vacation routine: breakfast in the bright kitchen, morning paddles on the quiet lake, campfires in the evenings, and in between, time to read or sketch or just watch the water. Aunt Louise filled the cottage with the aroma of baked bread, wrote letters, and worked her way through a pile of Agatha Christie novels. When her uncle wasn't paddling the lake with Grace or sketching birds and plants, he wrote fund-raising appeals or planned for the upcoming school year. Life with her aunt and uncle was as placid as the lake at dawn.

One sparkling afternoon Grace and her aunt packed a lunch and set off on foot for the far end of the lake. From there, they climbed a steep path under the shadow of the mountain until they reached a boulder high above the lake. The huge rock easily accommodated both of them and the lunch Aunt Louise spread on a napkin between them. Grace was sticky with sweat and grateful for the breeze that stirred the boughs of the pines shading them from the afternoon sun. For a while they ate in silence, watching the play of light on the rippling water and a lone canoe drifting lazily in the shallows far below.

Rummaging in the knapsack, Aunt Louise pulled out a mason jar of water, filled two tin cups, and handed one to Grace.

The water was warm, but refreshing after the long walk. Grace drained her cup, her gaze fixed on the vista of lake and forest below.

"I just love it here, don't you?" her aunt said.

"It's beautiful ... and so peaceful. It's awfully good of you and Uncle Arthur to put up with me for a whole month. And you're both so easy to be with ... " Not like Daddy or Jerome. Somehow nothing with either of them was simple any more.

"Well, you're not exactly a handful yourself." Her aunt smiled, but the smile soon faded. "I know things have been rough at home. We're happy to give you a chance to get away from all that for a while."

"I had this idea I should stay home and keep an eye on things ... that I shouldn't leave Daddy alone for a whole month, but Grandma was pretty insistent." Grace's smile was rueful. "She was right, of course, I really needed to get away."

"In case you hadn't noticed, your grandmother is always right, Grace. At least as far as she's concerned."

Aunt Louise packed up the remains of their lunch, and they headed back down the trail toward the cottage. Picking their way along the mountain path, they were quiet, watching for loose rocks and tree roots that might threaten their footing. The descent was quicker than the climb, and soon they reached the lake walk, well-trodden and wide enough for them to walk side by side.

They talked about their plans for the rest of the day. Grace said she was going to sit in one of the chairs down on the dock and read for a while. Aunt Louise planned to prepare the chops she'd bought yesterday when she'd gone to town for her weekly shopping and errands.

"I found a recipe in *The Ladies' Home Journal* that sounds delicious, but it has to marinate for an hour, so I'll get that going as soon as we get back." She described her trip to the library and the post office. "I saw that Jerome wrote you again, Grace. Has he left for the Cape yet?"

"Not till next week," Grace said. "They'll be back around the middle of August."

"How are things going between the two of you? I'm sure it's hard to spend so much time apart."

"It is hard, Auntie, and it seems to be getting harder. Jerome's got a whole new group of friends now. Most of the boys at the Academy are from wealthy families. Their fathers and grandfathers went to the school. Until I went there in May I didn't realize how exclusive the place is. It's as though they all belong to the same club. They have summer houses and sailboats ... " she wrinkled her nose, "and pretty sisters. Everyone I met was polite and perfectly nice, but I felt like an outsider."

"And do you think Jerome's interested in any of those pretty sisters?"

"I think it's that the pretty sisters, one in particular, are interested in Jerome. It's really more that I don't feel like I've got a place in his life anymore."

Grace stopped walking and faced her aunt. "To be honest, one reason I came for the whole month was so I'd be away while he was in Chester. I wanted him to see what it's like to be at home without good old reliable Grace for company."

"And I've no doubt he's missing you, too. You may not go to a fancy private school or have a rich family, but I'm sure you're every bit as smart and pretty as any of his friends' sisters."

Her aunt squeezed her shoulder and smiled. "And I bet Jerome knows that as well as I do."

Grace hoped so, but would he be able to resist the allure of his school friends' privileged lives? Or would their exclusive social circle close around him and put him beyond her reach?

That evening she reread Jerome's latest letter. He missed her, he said, and since he'd lost touch with most of his other Chester friends, he'd been at loose ends. Then his dad asked if he'd work a few days a week at the printer's. One of the drivers had thrown his back out, so Jerome rode with him and carried the boxes of brochures and flyers and posters into the shops and businesses who'd ordered them.

Other than that, he'd been working his way through his summer reading list and helping his mother clean the cellar. The letter was newsy with only a hint of affection in the closing. *"I hope you're having a good time with your aunt and uncle. I do miss you, Monty, maybe even as much as you hoped I would."*

Grace smiled. Maybe, but she wasn't sure that was possible.

It was raining when she woke the following morning. Not hard, but hard enough to keep them all indoors. After breakfast, she retreated to her room to write letters.

On the lovely blue stationery, she thanked her grandmother for convincing her to extend her stay at the lake for the entire month. She and Uncle Arthur had been out sketching both on foot and in the canoe and she was working *en plein air* on a painting of the lake. With her easel set up on the front porch, she was trying to capture the play of morning sun on the water. Grace asked if Grandma had learned anything more about Mr. Ramsey's activities and if her father had been by lately. He wasn't much for writing letters and she wondered how he was getting along.

In her letter to Jerome, Grace was careful not to express any of the misgivings she'd talked to her aunt about. They'd covered all that ground before. Instead, she told him about the book of paintings and haiku her uncle was helping her make for her grandmother's upcoming 70th birthday. He'd suggested she might like to collect some of her small watercolor studies into a book and add a short poem for each one. In the evenings, she and her aunt and uncle worked on the poems together. She'd show them a study of an aster or fern or hermit thrush and they'd each come up with a haiku and read them aloud.

Some of the poems are really awful, but the worse they are the harder we laugh. I'm having a wonderful time here with my aunt and uncle, Jerome. We all get along so well and they are both very kind to me. Now that I'm away from home, I realize just how tense and anxious I've been. I know I've been testy with you, too, and I'm sorry for that ... I'm not sorry you miss me, though. I miss you, too.

Grace and her uncle went into town several days later, stopping first at the college to collect the heavy tag board, bookbinding twine, and awl they'd need to bind her paintings and poems into a book. Next, they went into the village and Uncle Arthur parked the Hudson in front of Potter's Stationery.

The shop was small, but well stocked and Grace perused the shelves while her uncle chatted with the owner. There were shelves of bound journals and boxed stationery, a display of envelopes and writing papers in pastel shades, boxes of colored pencils, fountain pens and inkwells, calendars, and racks of greeting cards.

Toward the back of the narrow shop, textbooks required by Mansfield College filled several bookcases. Grace studied the course names: Reading and Orthography, Modern Geography, Botany, Drawing and Handwork, Methods of Mathematics, General Literature. If these texts were any indication, Grace would be equipped to teach a lot more than painting and drawing when she finished at Mansfield. And she'd be living with her aunt and uncle, away from the stress and worry of home. The more she knew about Mansfield Normal School, the more appealing it became.

Grace returned to the front of the shop where Mr. Potter pointed out the display of bookbinding paper. On a wall rack, row upon row of marbled sheets curled over wooden dowels. The colors were beautiful, rich and varied, with no two pieces exactly alike. Grandma was fond of blue. Grace flipped through a dozen or so sheets in shades from palest pastel to deep indigo, finally settling on one called azure. She'd like to buy one of every color, they were so lovely, but her pocket money would allow only one.

At the counter, her uncle complimented Grace on her choice.

"It was hard to pick just one. They're all so beautiful, but somehow this one reminds me of Grandma."

Mr. Potter rolled the sheet in brown paper and wrote out a receipt. Grace opened her change purse, but her uncle gestured for her to put it away.

"It's my treat, Grace," he said, grinning. "I'm almost as excited as you are to see this book come together. Your grandmother will love it."

On their last day at the lake, Grace collected kindling for the fire just as she'd done on her first visit four years before. After dinner, Uncle Arthur built up the fire and the three of them sat on the make-shift bench watching the flames and eating the last of the blueberry pie. The evening was still and mild, quiet except for the hum of crickets and the occasional burst of laughter from a neighboring camp.

Grace was quiet, too, only half listening to her aunt and uncle's murmured conversation. They were talking about packing and train schedules and the new school year. She was thinking of home and what awaited her there. It would be good to see Daddy and her grandparents and settle into her own room again, good to see Jerome once or twice before he left for Exeter. And it would be hard, too. Hard to trade the calm and safety of this place for the upheaval and uncertainty of life with her father. She sighed.

"Are you all right, Gracie?"

She looked up from the fire to find her aunt and uncle watching her.

"Oh, I'm all right. Just feeling a little blue, I guess." She smiled, not wanting to worry them. "It's just that I've had such a wonderful time here, it's hard to leave."

"Is it more than not wanting your vacation to end?" her aunt said. She paused. "You're not afraid to go home, are you, Grace?"

Grace shook her head. "Oh, no, it's not that. But you and Uncle Arthur are so easy to be with, and Daddy ... well, I'm always on pins and needles waiting to see what he'll do next."

20

GONE

Grace stood at the table in the hot kitchen arranging flowers, while Mrs. B formed dough into dinner rolls and fretted over the timing of the pork roast. Earlier, she'd set the dining room table with Grace's mother's best china and silver. Tonight Grace and her father were hosting Grandma Montel's 70th birthday party. It was the first dinner party Grace had ever planned and she wanted everything to be perfect.

Carrying the vase into the dining room, she placed the flowers between the tall silver candlesticks that had also belonged to her grandmother Seymour. As she was admiring the table, Mrs. Blanchard came in wiping her hands on her apron.

"What do you think?"

"It looks beautiful, Mrs. B. You must have spent hours polishing all that silver."

"Well, it wouldn't be the first time, but I admit it's been a while since that silverware has seen a polishing cloth." She smiled and shook her head. "Your grandmother Seymour was a stickler for a well-set table. They always entertained in style, your grandparents."

She adjusted the position of a water glass and moved a fork a fraction of an inch. "I didn't know the first thing about setting a proper table when I came to work for your grandparents all those years ago. Your grandmother was very patient with me."

"I wish I'd known them." Her mother's parents had been killed in a railway accident just two years before Grace was born. They'd been on their way home from a trip to Philadelphia when their train hit a load of timber on the tracks.

"It must have been awful for Mama to lose both her parents at once."

"It was a terrible thing." Mrs. Blanchard shuddered. "More than sixty people died in that accident and as many were badly injured. It was a tragedy, no doubt about it. Thank goodness your parents were married by then. Your father was a tower of strength, saw to everything and took such good care of your mother. I don't know how she would have gotten through it without him."

She shook her head. "Now that's enough of that. This is a happy occasion and it's going to be a lovely party. Go ahead and get yourself ready, Grace, while I finish up in the kitchen."

Upstairs, Grace ran her bath and laid her clothes out on her bed. It was hard to imagine Daddy being strong and clear-headed enough to help Mama through that awful time. She could hardly remember her father before drink had muddled his thinking and soured his temper, could hardly remember the man he used to be.

Grace was ready and downstairs by the time the big clock in the foyer struck six. Her father had promised to be home in time to freshen up before her grandparents arrived around 6:30. Already fidgety with anticipation, she moved through the parlor and into the dining room, checking to see that everything was ready. In the kitchen, Mrs. Blanchard said she had things well in hand and to stop fussing and relax. But Grace couldn't relax. What was keeping Daddy? Grandma and Grandpa would be here in fifteen minutes.

Back in the parlor, Grace checked her hair in the sideboard mirror and smoothed the lace collar of her dress. Should she call the shop? Surely, he hadn't forgotten. He wouldn't miss his own mother's birthday party, would he? Hearing footsteps on the front porch, she hurried into the foyer.

Her grandparents were at the door. They exchanged greetings and Grace led them into the parlor.

"Where the deuce is your father?" Grandpa asked, looking around the room. "You'd think he'd have the courtesy to be on time for his mother's birthday dinner."

"Now, Henry, there's no need for that. No doubt Francis has been held up at the shop. I'm sure he'll be here any minute."

"The shop's been closed for an hour. Besides, I was over there earlier and Francis wasn't there. Raymond didn't know where he was."

Grace felt her stomach drop, but Grandma's smile was reassuring.

"Well, let's not jump to conclusions just yet. I'm sure we can manage to carry on until he gets here."

Mrs. Blanchard came through from the dining room with a tray of hors d'oeuvres which she set on the table in front of the sofa. She greeted the Montels and offered Grace's grandmother a glass of sherry before asking Grace to join her in the kitchen.

Closing the dining room door, Mrs. B said, "I think I can move dinner back a half hour without ruining the roast, and hopefully your father will be home by then." She frowned. "Any longer though, and I'm afraid it won't be worth eating."

"But what if — "

"Now, Grace, try not to worry. Pass around the hors d'oeuvres and give your grandmother her present. Then you'll be ready to sit down to dinner as soon as your father arrives." She placed a hand on Grace's shoulder. "I'm sure everything will be fine."

Grace didn't believe everything would be fine and, by the look on her face, Mrs. B didn't believe it either. Taking a deep breath, she squared her shoulders and headed back through the dining room door.

"Dinner's been set back a bit, so we'll eat at 7:30. Daddy should be home by then."

He should be home now, celebrating his mother's special day and keeping his promise to Grace. But he wasn't.

"Seven-thirty will be fine, won't it, Henry? Mrs. Blanchard's put together these lovely canapés, so you won't go hungry." Grandma filled a small plate with a sampling of hors d'oeuvres and held it out to him. Frowning, he took the plate and sat heavily in Grace's father's chair.

While Grandma and Grandpa ate the canapés and sipped their drinks, Grace listened for the sound of Daddy's arrival. No matter how hard she listened or how many times she checked the clock, she was unable to conjure up her missing father. As the minutes ticked by, the canapés disappeared, the roast cooled, and a great weight settled in the pit of her stomach.

By 7:00 Grace couldn't sit still any longer. She took up the wrapped package from the sideboard and sat on the sofa next to her grandmother.

"Well, Grandma, I wanted to wait until Daddy got home to give you your present, but Mrs. Blanchard said she'd have to serve dinner by 7:30 or it wouldn't be worth eating. So, Happy Birthday, Grandma. I hope you like it."

Setting the gift on her lap, her grandmother pulled the card out of its envelope and read the inscription. She smiled, set the card aside, and untied the lavender ribbon. It seemed to take Grandma forever to open the wrappings, and when she finally did, she turned the book over in her hands, studying its blue marbled cover and running her finger along the stitched binding.

Grace's palms were damp and she took a deep breath to calm her nerves. If only Aunt Louise and Uncle Arthur had been here to share this moment. The book would never have happened without their help; it was as much their gift as it was hers.

Grandma turned the pages slowly, studying each painting and deliberating over each poem. Grace wished she'd say something, but Grandma went through the entire book before she closed it. When she turned to look at Grace, her eyes were moist.

Reaching into her sleeve, she pulled out a hanky and dabbed her eyes. She shook her head and smiled. "It's beautiful, Gracie. It's the loveliest book I've ever seen. To think you did all this yourself. How did you manage it?"

"Truthfully, it was Uncle Arthur's idea. He and Auntie helped me write the poems and he showed me how to bind everything into a book. All the time we worked on the pages, I wondered how they'd ever come together in a book, but, really, Uncle Arthur made it seem easy."

She kissed her grandmother's cheek. "I'm glad you like it, Grandma. I wanted to give you something special, something no one else could give you."

"And you have, dear. It's perfect. Thank you."

Grandpa joined them on the sofa and the three of them looked through the book together. Grandma asked about the paintings, where she'd found the Indian pipes or how she'd managed to capture the chickadee, and she wanted to hear Grace read each poem aloud. For a few minutes, Grace forgot about her missing father and basked in her grandparents' praise and delight.

The respite was short-lived, and dinner was a somber meal. Grace could barely swallow her food for the lump in her throat. Grandma worked hard to keep a conversation going, praising the roast, asking Grace about the lake, talking about her volunteer work at the hospital.

Grandpa concentrated on eating. He emptied his plate, bite by bite, and said nothing more about Daddy's unexpected absence. Grace cleared the plates and Mrs. Blanchard came in with the cake. They sang "Happy Birthday," Grandma blew out the seven candles, and served each of them a piece. When the meal was over, Grandma went into the kitchen to thank the housekeeper.

While she was out of the room, Grandpa said, "I think I should stay here tonight, Gracie. If something's happened to your father, and I don't say anything has, then I'd be here to see to whatever needs seeing to." He frowned and hooked his thumbs into his vest pockets. "I don't like to think of you here all by yourself."

Grandpa was furious with Daddy. Grace could tell by the sound of his voice that he was keeping a tight rein on his temper. He'd never been slow to criticize her father, but he was restraining himself for her sake. He was worried, too, or he'd never have offered to stay over.

"Thank you, Grandpa, but I'll be fine. Mrs. Blanchard will be here and she'll know what to do if there's a problem." She hoped she sounded more confident than she felt. "And if something should happen ... if there's been an accident or something, we'll let you know right away. I promise."

"Well, if you think you'll be all right. Be sure to telephone if you hear anything, no matter what time it is." He cleared his throat and patted her shoulder. Grandma came in then. "I've offered to stay the night, but Gracie says she'll be all right."

"Mrs. Blanchard's promised to be in touch if anything happens, Henry." She turned to Grace. "Of course, you're welcome to come home with us, dear. Would you like to do that?"

"No, thank you, Grandma. Daddy might get back any minute and I want to be here when he does."

The night seemed endless. For a long time Grace lay listening for any sound that would signal her father's return. She imagined him stumbling in after a long night of drinking, and once even convinced herself she'd heard him in the foyer. When she did finally sleep, she searched for him among the scattered bodies and derailed train cars of her dreams.

Sitting alone at the breakfast table, Grace sipped her second cup of tea. She'd pushed away the plate of eggs as soon as Mrs. B returned to the kitchen. The smell made her nauseous. Maybe Daddy had gone to one of those parties he talked about and had had too much to drink. If that was the case, he'd behaved very badly, but he'd come home, full of remorse and apologies, as soon as he sobered up. But if he hadn't been out drinking all night, if he'd had an accident ... She got to her feet and carried her dishes into the kitchen.

Mrs. Blanchard stood at the sink, her face drawn and pasty in the morning light. She didn't look as though she'd slept any better than Grace had. Grace was struck by just how much Mrs. B did for her every day, how reliable and steadfast a presence in her life she'd always been.

Approaching the sink, she set her untouched plate on the counter. "I can't seem to get my breakfast down this morning, Mrs. B. I'm sorry to have put you to all that trouble for nothing." Resting her hand on the housekeeper's arm, she said, "I know I don't always show it, but I am grateful for all you do. I don't know how I'd manage without you."

Mrs. Blanchard covered Grace's hand with hers. "That's kind of you to say, dear, and as long as I'm needed I'll be here." She smiled. "You're as much family — "

She stopped at the sound of loud, insistent rapping at the front door. Grace bolted from the room with Mrs. B close behind.

Two men stood on the doorstep. The taller one wore a dark blue uniform, the other a business suit. Both removed their hats and the fellow in the suit handed his identification to Mrs. Blanchard. "Mrs. Montel? I'm U.S. Deputy Marshal Michaud and this is Patrolman Jenkins. We'd like to have a word with you. May we come in?"

"I'm Mrs. Blanchard, the housekeeper. I'm afraid my employer is not at home."

"That's what I want to talk to Mrs. Montel about, so if you'll just let her know we're here ... "

Grace stepped forward. "My mother died several years ago, Mr. Michaud. I'm Grace Montel. Do you have news of my father? Is he all right? He didn't—"

The officer held up his hand. "May we come in?"

"Excuse me, of course." She motioned the men into the parlor. Mrs. Blanchard went to the telephone.

"Please, come in and sit down. My grandparents ... my father's parents ... will be here soon. This is about my father, isn't it?" She sat on the edge of the sofa, her hands clasped tightly in her lap, shivering in spite of the heat.

The marshal nodded, but remained standing. "I'm afraid your father was involved in an automobile accident, Miss Montel. He was injured, but fortunately not seriously." His face softened. "I'm sure you're worried, but I think we'd better hold off on the details until your grandparents arrive. Meanwhile, I'd like to ask you a few questions."

Mrs. Blanchard came in to say that Mr. and Mrs. Montel would arrive shortly. She glanced at Grace, then back at the officer.

"Please, take a seat, Mrs. Blanchard." He gestured to the sofa next to Grace. Mrs. B sat down and immediately took Grace's hand in hers.

"When was the last time you saw your father, Miss Montel?"

"Yesterday morning. We had breakfast together and talked about the dinner party ... My grandmother's birthday was yesterday and we had a party and Daddy was supposed to be home by six, but ... " Grace shook her head. "He didn't come home."

"Has anything like this ever happened before? I mean, has your father been away overnight without letting you know in advance?"

"No, never. He's been away overnight before, of course, but I've always known beforehand. He wouldn't have wanted me to worry."

"So, you were expecting him at six, and you didn't hear from him? Didn't get a call saying he'd been held up or couldn't make it? No notification of any kind?"

"Nothing. We were worried, but ... " But Daddy drank and couldn't be counted on. He missed work and spent weekends away and kept company with the likes of Rafe Ramsey. And now there was a US Marshal in their parlor and he wanted answers. Answers that Grace didn't have.

She exhaled slowly and glanced at Mrs. Blanchard who said, "Mr. and Mrs. Montel will be here any minute, Mr. Michaud. Might it be better to wait until they arrive before proceeding with your questions?"

The officer checked his watch. "When do you — "

Before he could continue, the front door opened, and Grandpa hurried into the room. Holding out his hand, he said, "Henry Montel, Francis's father. My wife, Mrs. Montel. What's all this about, officer, has something happened to Francis?"

"There's been an accident, sir, but your son was not badly hurt." He paused. "We don't have the whole story, but the car Francis Montel was driving was carrying a load of whiskey and champagne. He was apparently on his way to Worcester, Massachusetts, though we don't know the exact location of the planned delivery."

"There must be some mistake," Grandpa said, reddening. "My son's a lot of things, but he's no criminal."

"Oh, there's no mistake, Mr. Montel. Agents identified him as the driver of the vehicle in which the contraband was found. We were acting on an anonymous tip; a female caller saying she had the information on good authority. Told us the make of the car, the route it would take ... even knew about what time he'd be passing through our area."

He cleared his throat. "All turned out to be quite accurate. We dispatched a couple of patrol cars along the route and wait-ed. Sure enough, a vehicle matching the informant's description passed through just about the time she said it would. We tailed the car, but we couldn't keep up ... These bootleggers rig their cars up with faster engines and heavy duty shocks. Our patrol cars are no match for them."

"Where is my son, now, Mr. Michaud? Has he been taken into custody?" Grandma asked.

"Yes, Ma'am, he has. He was arrested by the agents on duty and taken to the hospital immediately after." The marshal pulled a handkerchief from his pocket and wiped his brow.

"You said the injury was not serious. What exactly happened?"

Mr. Michaud straightened. "Your son was shot resisting arrest."

Grace gasped and put her hand over her mouth. Shot. Resisting arrest. This was even worse than she'd imagined. Why hadn't she done something to stop him? Why hadn't Grandma confronted him? How had they let this happen when they knew he was in trouble?

"Shot!" She heard Grandpa shout. "Are you people mad?"

"The agents shot at the vehicle, Mr. Montel, not at your son. They hailed the car and when the driver didn't stop, they fired on the vehicle to disable it. One agent shot out a rear tire, but the driver cut the wheel and drove straight at the agent on the opposite side of the road. Fellow said he was sure the driver meant to mow him down. That's how your son was injured. Shot in the arm ... just grazed him, really."

"Oh, Francis," Grandma murmured, clutching the back of the sofa. Collecting herself, she fixed her gaze on the officer.

"Why weren't we notified before this? My son is shot and arrested and you wait until this morning to tell his family?" She frowned and shook her head. "I don't understand."

"By the time we'd booked your son and gotten him to a hospital, it was nearly 8:00. When we asked him who we should notify, he told us to wait until morning. Said he didn't want you folks heading down country at that hour."

Mr. Michaud looked at Grace. "He said we should wait until we could tell you in person."

"Huh. Didn't want to worry us, I suppose," Grandpa grumbled. "Mighty thoughtful of him." He glanced at Grandma. "I guess we'd better get down there to see him. Where is he, exactly?"

"We were hoping you could tell us that, Mr. Montel." The Marshall closed his notebook and put it in his breast pocket.

"Your son apparently slipped out of the hospital sometime in the night. When we arrived this morning to question him, he was gone."

PART 3

1927-1928

21

A Lot to Learn

Grace rolled onto her back, suspended in that grey space between waking and sleeping, the space where her father's voice drifted up from the breakfast table and his face was more than a memory. If she kept her eyes closed, she could almost believe she'd find him downstairs dressed in a dark suit and crisp white shirt, his hair brushed and tamed with Brilliantine. But she knew no more where her father was today than she had on the morning of the U.S. Marshal's visit two years before.

Grace couldn't remember much about those first few days after her father disappeared. She'd stayed in her room, curled on her side in bed, sleeping and eating little. Her father had run away and abandoned her. The thought ran through her mind like a needle stuck on a phonograph record, carving a groove in her heart. Then one rain-swept afternoon, Aunt Louise came to Chester and carried her away to Concord. She'd been grateful to escape the curiosity of her neighbors and the shame of her fugitive father, grateful to settle into a place where she wasn't known as Francis Montel's daughter.

She'd drifted through her last two years of high school in Concord, focused on her studies and did her best to be useful to her aunt and uncle. Lily Pearl was born the spring of her junior year, turning the household upside down with her angelic smile and insistent demands. Grace could hear her now, mumbling softly to herself in the next room. Tossing back the covers, she grabbed her dressing gown and made her way quietly to the baby's room. Tarry too long, she knew, and those soft mumblings would be anything but.

The baby was standing in her crib, gripping the rail and bouncing on her chubby legs. Grace picked her up and nuzzled the warm neck, as the baby's arms tightened around hers.

"Lily Pearl, what are you doing up so early? The sun isn't even up yet, you little minx." Grace lowered herself into the rocker with the baby on her knee.

"Shh, Pearl. Listen." She held her finger to her lips. "Who's coming?"

"Mama!"

"Well, if it isn't my little Early Bird." Aunt Louise came in, still buttoning the front of her dress. "Did she wake you again?"

"Not exactly. I was dozing when I heard Miss Pearl humming her wake-up tune. She's a regular little songbird, aren't you?" Grace tickled the baby's belly and they both giggled.

"I've got to get going anyway. I need to finish the reading for my Philosophy of Ed class." She rolled her eyes. "I just couldn't make it through the whole chapter last night." She handed the baby to her aunt. "I'll dress and be right down."

Back in her room, Grace gathered her clothes and went to the bathroom to wash and dress. She loosened the single braid and brushed her hair. For the hundredth time, she considered getting it cut, but knew she wouldn't. It was too easy just to pull it into a bun and be done with it. She didn't have much interest in fussing with her appearance these days.

As she pulled her middy blouse over her head and fastened the ties, she was reminded of the first morning of seventh grade. She'd been a bundle of nerves that day and all thumbs. Daddy'd come up behind her and, like a magician pulling a scarf out of his sleeve, turned the tie into a smart knot. She shook her head and turned from the mirror.

Three post cards. That's all the word she'd had of her father in two years. The first one came right after he disappeared. No picture, just a two-penny card with "I'm sorry." scrawled in a shaky hand. The other two marked her birthdays. None of the postmarks was the same.

Collecting her belongings, Grace returned to her room. She made her bed and packed her book bag. The sun was streaming through the window, lighting the peach colored walls, making the whole room glow. She and her aunt had decorated the room together. They bought the desk, bureau and bookshelf in a trash and treasure shop and painted them white. Grace set her easel in front of the south facing window, and on one of their trips to Chester, they'd brought back Mama's chaise lounge. The room was cozy and bright, free of the ghosts of her missing parents.

In the kitchen, Pearl was sitting on her father's lap, fiddling with the buttons of his vest. Aunt Louise was at the stove buttering toast. Grace filled the baby's bowl with oatmeal, cut a piece of toast into tiny pieces, and prepared to feed the baby her breakfast. She loved this time of day, the warm fragrant kitchen, the quiet talk about the day, the baby's delight in her bit of toast and spoonful of oatmeal.

"Well, Grace," Aunt Louise said, "what's on your schedule today? Anything interesting?"

"I've got methods classes in mathematics and reading this morning and a drawing class this afternoon." She made a face. "But first I have to get through Mr. Richardson's History and Philosophy of Education class."

Her aunt laughed. "Is it the material or is it Mr. Richardson?"

Grace glanced at her uncle. Mr. Richardson was his protégé and she didn't want to say anything to offend him. "Oh, it's probably just me. Learning about pedagogical theory ... well ... I find it hard going."

Her uncle grinned. "You and everyone else. Poor Richardson, I hated to saddle him with that course, but someone's got to teach it or we won't be in compliance with the state curriculum."

He poured himself a second cup of coffee. "I'm due to observe one of his classes this week. Maybe I should come in for that one."

"I don't know, Uncle Arthur. It might be better for Mr. Richardson if you sat in on one of his American History classes." She gave her uncle a wry smile. "He seems a lot more interested in the initiation rites of the Plains Indians than he does in Mr. Dewey's educational theories."

Shortly after breakfast, Grace and her uncle left for Mansfield College. Uncle Arthur had a faculty meeting and Grace had to finish that reading assignment before her 10:00 class. The library had become her favorite place in the building, especially in these early hours when she had it to herself. She made her way down a long aisle of stacks to a study carrel lit by one of the two skylights. Though she had that pesky chapter to finish, she'd read Grandma's letter first. She'd forgotten all about it until she'd seen it poking out of her notebook as she was checking her book bag before heading out the door. Somehow the letter had gotten lost in the shuffle between Grace's supper chores, homework, and Pearl's bath time.

Tearing off the end of the pink envelope, Grace pulled out several folded sheets covered with her grandmother's elegant script. Their faint smell of rosewater made her instantly homesick. She missed her grandparents awfully, as much really, as she missed her father. Of course, she knew where they were and when she'd see them again, which she might never know about Daddy.

After his disappearance, Grandma had hired a lawyer to look into the legal aspects of the case and a private investigator to track down anyone who might have information about her father's connection to the alcohol trade. Grace didn't know the lawyer, but she'd met the investigator, Lockwood Sprague, once. He'd come to Concord not long after she moved in with her aunt and uncle. Asked lots of questions about Daddy's friends, how often he was away from home, if she'd noticed any changes in his routine. She hadn't liked Mr. Sprague. There was something about his eyes, hard and black as two stones and just about as warm.

In her letter, Grandma said Mr. Sprague was keeping track of Mr. Ramsey's movements. He'd evidently found backers for his resort and had only to acquire one more piece of property before breaking ground on the project. The man was making himself agreeable in town by engaging local suppliers and contractors to do the work. None of this was news to Grace.

What did capture her attention was Grandma's reference to Kate Armstrong, Mr. Ramsey's former housekeeper. Grace and her grandmother had suspected all along that it had been Miss Armstrong who'd made the call to the U.S. Marshal and that Mr. Ramsey had put her up to it.

Early in his investigation, Mr. Sprague had learned that on the very afternoon the call had been made, Miss Armstrong left Chester on the 5:20 train for Boston. After that she seemed to have vanished. Not a single ticket agent or porter at any of the stops along the route remembered seeing a woman of Miss Armstrong's description. Without a photograph, they'd hit a dead end.

Frustrated, Grandma contacted Mr. Standish and the two of them collaborated on a drawing which Mr. Sprague had printed and sent to employment agencies specializing in domestic staff. But that, too, had led nowhere. Until now.

It seems, Grace, her grandmother wrote, *that Mr. Sprague received a note from a woman who works at an agency in Worcester. Apparently, in the secretary's absence, the letter containing Miss Armstrong's picture had mistakenly found its way into a folder and been filed away. When the secretary pulled the file recently, she found the unopened letter.*

At first, she couldn't place the face in the drawing but was certain she'd seen it before. Eventually, she remembered that both she and our Miss Armstrong had been on the southbound train for Boston the evening of your father's arrest. And both had disembarked at the Worcester station.

Mr. Sprague suspects it was no coincidence that your father and Miss Armstrong were both headed for Worcester on that fateful day.

Grace stared at the blank wall of the study carrel. Kate Armstrong was responsible for her father's arrest. She knew he'd be in Worcester, so why would she go there, too? It made no sense, unless that was part of a plan. But that was ridiculous. Daddy wouldn't go along with a plan that included being arrested. Of course, he hadn't planned to get arrested. He'd planned to deliver his goods and what, rendezvous with Kate Armstrong?

The bell signaling the beginning of classes sounded shrilly, setting Grace's heart racing. Cramming the letter back in the envelope, she collected her books and headed downstairs. She still hadn't finished that chapter.

Grace took her place next to Carrie Laurence in the row of desks near the window. The room smelled of chalk and floor polish. The faint aroma of dried leaves wafted through the breeze coming in the partially open window. There was the usual shuffle of girls moving down the rows, stuffing their belongings in the space under the seats, greeting each other, and settling into their places. They all turned toward the door as Mr. Richardson hustled in like a man hurrying to catch an omnibus.

The teacher set his bulging briefcase on his desk and unloaded an untidy array of books, folders, loose papers, and, finally, a stack of blue test booklets. Carrie glanced nervously at Grace. The class fell silent. Running his hands through his hair, Mr. Richardson squared his shoulders and looked at his students. He wished them good morning, rounded his desk, and perched on its corner. He wore one blue sock and one black sock and his shoes were badly in need of polish. Pointing at the pile of test booklets, he shook his head and favored the class with a rueful smile.

"Well, ladies, I have both good and bad news." He took up the booklets and began circulating the room, passing them out.

"The good news is that I did not grade this exam. The bad news is that, had I done so, very few of you would have achieved a passing mark."

Anxious looks followed this little speech which Mr. Richardson delivered as if he'd rehearsed it. He was too smooth, too disarming for Grace's taste; she liked her teachers straightforward and business-like. Pausing at her desk, the teacher gave her the booklet and turned to the class.

"You'll find your score on the inside cover, written as a fraction. You might remember those." He raised an eyebrow. "The denominator, that would be the bottom number, represents the whole; the top number, the numerator, represents the number correct."

Several of the girls giggled, but Grace didn't think it was at all funny. She didn't like being mocked. Mr. Richardson passed out the last booklet and returned to his desk.

He flashed one of his brilliant smiles and said, "Put those away, ladies. Now that I know what you didn't learn, I'll try to teach it to you."

At noon, Grace and her friends were eating lunch at a picnic table in back of the school. Usually, they ate in the basement lunchroom, but all agreed that today was much too nice a day to be inside. The talk was of Mr. Richardson. The teacher, much younger and more handsome than any of their other instructors, was a favorite topic of conversation among Grace's friends. She was only half listening, when she saw her uncle approach the table.

Carrie didn't see the Headmaster come up behind her and was rhapsodizing about Mr. Richardson's willingness to overlook their poor performance on their recent test, not to mention his gorgeous smile and sparkling eyes. Uncle Arthur was trying hard to keep a straight face, pressing his lips together to avoid a smile, but his eyes gave him away. Finally, he cleared his throat.

"Sorry to interrupt, Miss Laurence, but let me say I'm delighted that you appreciate the merits of your history teacher." Carrie uttered a surprised yelp and everyone, including the Headmaster, laughed.

Turning to Grace he said, "I need to have a word with you," and gestured for her to follow him. "I've been asked to attend an impromptu dinner meeting with some of the board members this evening and I have little choice but to accept. I've arranged for you to ride home with Mr. Richardson this afternoon."

He grinned. "I'm sorry to have to ask this of you, Grace, but there isn't time enough to drive you home and be back for the start of the meeting. Mr. Richardson goes right by our place on his way home, so it's no trouble for him."

The thought of riding home alone with Mr. Richardson made Grace's cheeks burn. She wasn't impressed by his teaching, but she wasn't proof against his charms, either. "Oh, that's fine, Uncle Arthur. How will I know when Mr. Richardson's ready to go?"

"He'll meet you in front of the building at 4:00. I've already called your aunt, so she knows about the change of plans." His eyes twinkled. "I'm afraid your friends will be jealous."

Grace shook her head. "I have no intention of telling them. If I did, I'd never hear the end of it."

She was on the steps of the college promptly at 4:00. Several minutes later, the front door flew open and Mr. Richardson emerged, clutching his crammed briefcase in one hand and buttoning his jacket with the other. He led her to an ancient Ford and held the door open for her. Stuffing spilled from several tears in the upholstery and the interior smelled of stale tobacco and something like mouse droppings. Wrinkling her nose, Grace set her book bag on the floor beside her and arranged her skirt over her knees. The teacher slid into the driver's seat and they began the steep descent to the main road.

"It was kind of you to give me a ride home, Mr. Richardson," Grace said. "I hope this doesn't take you too far out of your way."

"No trouble at all, Miss Montel. I'm happy to do whatever I can for Mr. Eastman ... and giving you a ride home is not a particularly onerous task." Slowing at an intersection, he glanced at her. "Besides, it gives me a chance to ask your advice."

Grace shot him an inquisitive look.

"I'd like to know how you managed to pass that exam, when so many others didn't. You can't be the only person who studied for it."

Studying wasn't the reason she'd passed the exam. She'd pored over her notes, read and reread the textbook, but until she'd talked to her uncle none of it made much sense. Grace chose her words carefully.

"Actually, Mr. Richardson, I couldn't quite figure out what Dewey was talking about until I asked my uncle for help." She shrugged. "My notes were ... well ... I had a few phrases down, but they didn't make sense when I went back to them. And frankly, that textbook is so dense I can't find my way through it."

The teacher uttered a sound halfway between a laugh and a choke. "It's pretty bad, isn't it?" he said.

"Anyway, I showed my uncle my notes and he explained what Dewey meant by children using objects to increase knowledge. He reminded me of the things I learned about plants and animals by observing and sketching them. He asked me if drawing and painting deepened my understanding ... I knew I'd learned a lot about birds from watching them, but I'd learned different things from drawing them. We talked about my niece, too, and how she uses her toys to practice certain skills."

They'd come to a stop in front of the Eastmans' home. Mr. Richardson turned off the engine and was studying her, his face a curious mix of concentration and amusement. Was he laughing at her?

"So, the reason you did so well on the exam is that you had a better teacher than the rest of the class. Is that it, Miss Montel?"

Reaching for the door handle, Grace considered the question. "I'm not sure I'd put it that way, Mr. Richardson. I think it's more a case of two teachers being better than one."

Later that evening, after the dishes were done and the baby put to bed, Grace and her aunt settled in the parlor to wait for Uncle Arthur. Aunt Louise was knitting something lacy and yellow, another baby sweater probably to add to the several Pearl already had. Grace was struggling to follow a troublesome algebra equation through several steps, but kept getting sidetracked by Grandma's letter. Speculating on Miss Armstrong's appearance in Worcester was a lot more compelling than solving for x, y, or z. She slammed her book shut.

"What is it, Gracie?" Aunt Louise looked up from her knitting. "Anything the exhausted mother of a toddler can do to help?"

Grace smiled and shook her head. "I can't stop thinking about my father and Miss Armstrong both being in Worcester on the day of the accident. What do you think it means, Auntie?"

"Oh, it could mean a lot things or ... it could just be coincidence." She set her knitting in her lap and sighed. "I suppose it's possible they'd arranged to meet in Worcester. Who knows? Maybe this Armstrong woman had something to do with your father's escape from the hospital." She shrugged. "It's all speculation at this point."

"But, if Daddy and Miss Armstrong were involved romantically, she wouldn't have tipped off the police, would she?"

"She might, if she'd been forced to."

"But how could she have been forced to? Why wouldn't she just refuse? She'd probably have lost her job, but ... "

Aunt Louise unraveled a bit of yellow wool and went back to her knitting.

"Supposing your Mr. Ramsey knew something about Miss Armstrong ... a secret, maybe, and he threatened to use it against her." The corner of her mouth twitched and she lowered her voice. "It's all very cloak and dagger, isn't it?"

Grace pursed her lips. "In a way, I hope Miss Armstrong and Daddy did rendezvous in Worcester. At least that way, he wouldn't be alone. Wherever he is and whatever he's doing, I'd like to think he's with someone who cares about him."

She dropped her head onto the back of the chair and closed her eyes. It was awful not to know where Daddy was, not to be able to picture the place he lived or know how he was getting along. Over the past two years, she'd cursed his selfishness and worried about his health and ached with missing him. Every day, she'd hoped for word of him and dreaded what that word might be.

And every day, he'd managed not to be found.

22

TANGLED WEBS

As the days shortened and the leaves fell, Grace settled into life at Mansfield College. The work was more varied and challenging than the boring routine of read, memorize, write, and test she'd known in high school. At Mansfield, she was learning what she needed to know to become a teacher, to take her place in the working world. She especially liked her art and children's literature classes; pictures and stories had always fired her imagination.

The student body was small, but there were girls from all over New England and upstate New York. Most came from small towns and boarded with family members as she did; others lived right in Concord. There were a half dozen or so male students in attendance, only one of whom could be considered even remotely handsome. Unlike many of her classmates, Grace did not lament the shortage of boys on campus. She wasn't looking for a beau. Jerome remained firmly planted in her heart, though she was less sure of her place in his.

Grace had seen little of Jerome since she'd left Chester, an afternoon here or there when both were home for the holidays. By the time he'd returned from the Cape the summer of Daddy's disappearance, she was living with her aunt and uncle in Concord. Jerome's letters were sympathetic and kind, but Grace couldn't shake her shame and humiliation, couldn't believe he'd want to have anything to do with a girl whose father was in trouble with the law. She missed Jerome, but when they were together, she felt so unworthy, so degraded, that it was almost easier to be apart.

On a bright Saturday morning in October, Grace was tidying the art room. Classes were over for the week and the other students had already left for the weekend. Uncle Arthur was meeting with the art and drama teachers and Grace had volunteered to clean the paint pots and brushes. She'd stacked the chairs on top of the long, paint-spattered tables and was standing at the sink elbow deep in soapy water when Mr. Richardson stuck his head in the door.

"Ah, Miss Montel, there you are," he said, crossing the room. "I've been looking for you."

She set a clean jar on the drain board and reached for a towel. "Looking for me? Why would ... Is it my uncle? Is he ready to go?"

The teacher grinned and shook his head. "No, nothing like that. I have some friends coming up for the weekend. We're going to take a hike up Balsam Hill tomorrow and I wondered if you'd like to come. If this weather holds, the view from the top will be spectacular."

"I don't understand. You want me to — "

"To take a walk, Miss Montel. An autumnal walk to enjoy the prospect and admire the foliage. Nothing untoward, I assure you."

There was that mocking tone again, and that particular way he had of raising one eyebrow she supposed was meant to charm, but which came off as patronizing. Did he seriously think her uncle, the Headmaster, would approve of her walking out on a Sunday with her history teacher? She was insulted by Mr. Richardson's attention. Even worse, she was flattered by it.

"I'm sorry, Mr. Richardson. I can't accept your invitation." She heard the tremor in her voice, but lifted her chin and kept her gaze fixed on his face.

He was leaning against the counter, his arms crossed over his chest watching her, clearly enjoying her discomfort. "You don't enjoy hiking or you don't think the Headmaster would approve?"

"I'm sure he wouldn't approve and I'm not sure I do either."He was about to speak, but she continued. "It wouldn't be proper."

The teacher tipped his head and in a wheedling tone said, "Proper? It's just a walk, Miss Montel. I don't see — "

Grace turned and plunged her hands into the soapy water. "I'm sorry, Mr. Richardson. Even if I was comfortable with the idea, I'd never risk my uncle's good opinion of either of us by doing something I know he'd find objectionable."

Pushing himself upright, the teacher bowed slightly. "I beg your pardon, Miss Montel. I certainly wouldn't want to jeopardize Mr. Eastman's good opinion." He took a step back. "Please excuse my lapse in judgment."

Grace nodded. "Done. And I actually do enjoy hiking." She flashed him what she hoped was a cheeky smile. "Maybe we could arrange a school trip to Balsam Hill sometime before winter, and you could teach us all about the hunting and gathering habits of the Indians who lived there."

"Touché, Miss Montel." Mr. Richardson laughed "I hope you have an enjoyable weekend."

Later that afternoon, Grace walked up to Main Street to visit the shops. She'd kept her conversation with Mr. Richardson to herself. Uncle Arthur was fond of the history teacher and would be upset if he knew about his breach of etiquette. It could be that she was over-reacting, but she didn't think so. Surely, teachers and their students should keep a respectful distance from each other, not be strolling the woods together on a Sunday afternoon. Why had Mr. Richardson chosen to invite her on the hike anyway? Had she given him any reason to believe she was one of his admirers?

The bell above the door tinkled as she entered the stationer's, but Mr. Potter wasn't at his usual post behind the counter. Looking around, she saw him in the back of the shop where the textbooks were shelved. Curious, she crossed to where he stood to see what he was up to.

"Ah, Miss Montel," he said, pushing his glasses into place. "Please excuse the mess. Some wag rearranged all the class labels on the textbooks while I was busy with a customer and now I've got to sort them out."

He shook his head and tut-tutted. "No doubt one of those unruly Turner boys. One or another of them is always making mischief." He slid a label into a holder above several hefty texts called *Physiology and Hygiene in the Elementary Classroom*.

"Would you like some help, Mr. Potter?" Grace picked a stray label off the floor and returned it to its rightful place.

"No, no, Miss Montel, please don't trouble yourself." He clasped his hands over his vest. "Is there anything I can do for you?"

"I'm here mostly for inspiration, really. I have to come up with a project for my Children's Literature class and hoped something in your shop would spark an idea. If you don't mind, I'll have a look around and see what jumps out at me."

Grace left the shop a half hour later with a roll of white paper, a package of colored paper, and a headful of plans. She'd make a mural based on *The Story of Doctor Dolittle* with a painted background and paper cut-out details. Her other purchase, tucked carefully in her purse, had nothing to do with the good doctor.

As soon as she got home, Grace went to her room to start work on the mural. She painted the background first, a vast waterfall against a sunset sky. On the colored paper, she drew and cut out the characters: Dr. Dolittle and his dog, Jip, then a pig, crocodile, duck and, finally, Polynesia, the parrot. Before long she was fully immersed in her work, adding details with colored pencils and bits of felt and yarn. She'd lost all track of time until a persistent knock at the bedroom door brought her back to the present.

Aunt Louise poked her head in. "My goodness, Grace, what are you up to?"

Grace fit a tiny cut-out hat on the doctor's head with a bit of glue. "I'm making a mural for my Children's Literature class."

Aunt Louise smiled wryly. "Really? If this is what you're doing in college, perhaps I'd better have a word with the Headmaster." She leaned over the mural for a closer look. "It's lovely, Grace, and you're obviously enjoying yourself. I've called you twice to come down and keep an eye on Pearl while I get dinner."

Grace looked at the mess of paper scraps, pencils and crayons, the cut-outs of palm trees and ferns littering the floor. "I'm sorry, Auntie. I didn't even hear you. Too busy adventuring with Dr. Dolittle, I guess. I'll tidy up and be right down."

Just before bed, Grace pulled the flat brown bag from her purse and sat down at her desk. She'd dithered too long over the greeting cards in Mr. Potter's shop, and was none too pleased with her final selection. She'd looked through no end of flowery sentiments, but none seemed right for Jerome. Choosing a birthday card should be a simple thing, but nothing about their friendship was simple any more.

Jerome had been her best friend almost from the moment they'd met. He made her laugh, helped with homework, challenged her to pursue drawing and painting. He could read her, too. More than once, he'd known what was troubling her before she knew herself. But as they'd grown, their friendship had changed, complicated by their mutual attraction, the differences in their schooling and social lives. Then the U.S. Marshal arrived with news of her father's arrest. She'd moved to Concord. He'd finished at the Academy and gone on to Dartmouth.

Grace studied the card it had taken so long to select, a drawing of a tall pine with mountains in the background, framing the message, "Birthday Greetings." Inside, she wished him a happy birthday, wrote that she hoped his school year was off to a good start, that she'd be in Chester for Thanksgiving.

There was so much she wanted to say to Jerome, so much she wanted to hear him say, but cards and letters, the rare holiday visit, were the only tangible evidence of their friendship now. She rested her chin in her hand and sighed. She hadn't seen Jerome in months, but she thought about him every day. Pictured him crossing the quad to class, imagined telling him about Mr. Richardson and the girls in her classes. Remembered the feel of her hand in his, the light in his eyes when he looked at her.

Grace stood and turned off the desk lamp. So much had happened to keep them apart, she wondered if they'd ever be able to come back together.

One Sunday afternoon several weeks later, she was working in her room when her aunt called from the bottom of the stairs to say she was wanted on the telephone. She received few calls, but each one kindled a tiny spark of hope that the voice on the other end would be Jerome's...or her father's. Most likely, though, one of her school friends was ringing up to ask about an assignment.

In the parlor, Aunt Louise was listening to whoever was on the other end of the line. She held her hand over the receiver and whispered, "It's your grandmother."

Grandma wrote regularly, but she wasn't one for long-distance calls. "Hello, Grandma. Is anything wrong? Are you all right?"

"I'm fine, dear. I have some news that I wanted to talk to you about."

"What news, Grandma?"

"Well, I thought you'd want to know that Paddy Devlin, Mary's brother, was arrested, caught by the Border Patrol late Monday night."

"Oh, no, that's terrible. Where is he now?"

"According to what that old gossip, Smitty, told your grandfather, they've got him down at the courthouse. They're holding him on five hundred dollars bail, so he'll likely be there until his case comes to trial. His family won't be able to raise that kind of money."

"Poor Paddy. Mrs. Devlin must be worried sick. What else have you heard?"

"I talked to Mr. Sprague as soon as I learned of the arrest. He didn't speak directly to Paddy, but he knows a fellow on the Force who told him the boy can't, or won't, say whose car he was driving or who he was working for."

"But isn't there a way for the police to find out who the car belongs to?"

"That's what I asked Mr. Sprague. He checked the records at City Hall, but the plate numbers didn't match the vehicle Paddy was driving. They were for some other automobile altogether."

"So, they can't trace the car and Paddy won't say who he's working for," Grace said. "You know, Grandma, Paddy was friends with that fellow, Wesley Titus, the one who died in the car crash. The Patrollers shot out his tire, just like they did when they were trying to stop Daddy, but Wesley ran into a tree." Poor Mary, first Wesley and now Paddy, Grace thought. "I wonder if Daddy was working for the same man as those boys."

"I think it's highly likely, Grace. I'd say Mr. Ramsey has a lot to answer for."

At dinner that evening, Grace talked to her aunt and uncle about Paddy Devlin's arrest. She wondered why Paddy didn't just tell the police who he was working for.

"Paddy may not actually know who's behind the operation, Grace," her uncle said. "The fellows who drive the liquor over the border are probably hired by someone local, someone who knows them and can vouch for them. And that individual most likely answers to a higher-up, who might answer to someone even further up the chain of command." He shook his head and picked up his fork.

"A man in charge of an extensive illegal operation like this fellow Ramsey can't afford to be known to every cog in the wheel of his enterprise. The fewer people who know his identity, the better, I should think."

But Daddy knew Mr. Ramsey's identity. He'd ridden in his big automobile and probably visited his home. He'd also spent weekends at the houses of other wealthy men, men who were most likely friends or business acquaintances of Mr. Ramsey. And when her father had been arrested, he'd been on his way to Worcester with a carload of whiskey and Champagne. Had he been making similar deliveries to those weekend parties he'd talked about? Parties to which the likes of Paddy or Wesley would not be welcome?

Grace stared blankly at the empty chair on the other side of the table. Finally, she said, "I've asked myself a thousand times why my father ran away, why he didn't just go to court, pay the fine, and be done with it." She looked from her aunt to her uncle.

"Do you think he ran off because he didn't want to tell the judge who he worked for?"

"That's one possible explanation, I suppose," her aunt said.

Grace sighed heavily. "I still don't understand. If my father had told the judge what he knew about Mr. Ramsey's operation, wouldn't the police have arrested him? And once he'd been tried, wouldn't he go to prison?"

"Maybe," her uncle said, "but men like Ramsey have friends in high places, people who are indebted to them for some reason or about whom they know too much. Even if Ramsey was arrested, he probably wouldn't go to trial."

No, he'd get off like he did after the death of his former employee, the would-be blackmailer. Here was a fellow who'd been disbarred from practicing law, and yet Grandma's friend, Mr. Peyton, said there'd been no mention of it in the court documents or the press. When Daddy'd been arrested, his story had been splashed all over the local paper. Poor Paddy Devlin was being held on five hundred dollars bail, while Rafe Ramsey was free to build his fancy resort and leave the dirty work to his underlings.

Grace went to her room after dinner, but not back to her studies. For the next several days, she moved through a fog of distraction, unable to concentrate on her lessons or comprehend what she read. More than once, she'd been called upon to answer a question she didn't even know had been asked. She tried to focus on her school work, but her mind kept coming back to her father and Paddy and who knew how many others trapped like so many flies in Ramsey's hateful web.

On Thursday evening Grace was in the kitchen finishing up the dinner dishes while Aunt Louise and Uncle Arthur were upstairs putting Pearl to bed. She was wiping the table, scooping crumbs into her free hand, when her uncle came into the room. He leaned against the doorjamb, hands in his trouser pockets, watching her.

"How's the term shaping up for you, Grace? Classes going all right?"

"Pretty well, I guess." She didn't sound too convincing, even to herself.

"I wondered, because a couple of your teachers seem concerned about you. One said you'd been unusually quiet all week. The other mentioned you were late turning in an assignment."

Grace sighed and tossed the dishcloth in the sink. "Oh, that would have been Mr. Richardson. I'd written only part of the essay on Sunday and ... well, after Grandma's telephone call, I didn't have time to finish it." Really, she was developing a positive dislike for her history teacher.

"Did he tell you I turned it in the next day?"

Uncle Arthur grinned. "He did. And I told him from now on, should he have any concerns about your academic performance, he should direct them to Louise." He pulled a chair out from the table and gestured for Grace to sit down, just as her aunt returned to the kitchen.

"We're not worried about your schoolwork," Aunt Louise told her, pulling her chair close to Grace's. "We just want to make sure you're all right. You haven't been yourself since you heard of Paddy's arrest." She tipped her head. "Is there anything we can do to help?"

"I keep thinking about how unfair this whole thing is. I mean, Daddy being arrested, now Paddy, and before that, that poor fellow Wesley Titus. It makes me so mad!" She let out a long, slow breath.

"I can't believe my father got mixed up in all this. That he ruined everything for ... for I don't know what. So he could drive a flashy car or go to fancy parties? Didn't he care what happened to the rest of us? Didn't he care that he was ruining my life, making it impossible for me to face my friends, bringing shame on the whole family?"

Her voice broke and she was crying. Crying like she hadn't cried through all the heartbreak and worry since her father went missing, eyes and nose streaming, chest aching, gasping for breath. Her aunt passed her a hanky. Uncle Arthur set a glass of water in front of her. Neither of them spoke. The handkerchief was soaked through by the time Grace was calm enough to pick up the glass. She drank deeply, the cool water washing away the phlegm that had collected in the back of her throat. She dabbed at her eyes and exhaled.

"I'm sorry, I ... " Grace looked from her aunt to her uncle and shook her head.

"Don't be sorry," Aunt Louise said. "You have every reason to be upset, Grace. I'm just glad you're finally letting your feelings out. You've kept a pretty tight rein on them for too long."

Her aunt looked at Uncle Arthur. "Your uncle knows the tears I've shed since Francis disappeared." She shook her head. "I don't know what made him do what he did. He might not even know himself. But I've come to believe however much he's hurt us, he's hurt himself more."

She managed a half smile. "That doesn't mean I'm not mad as hell at him, though."

"I am, too," Grace said, "but that's nothing new."

23

DEAD END

Through the train window, Grace watched the November countryside slide by. Drizzle seeped from an unbroken mass of cloud, and the landscape lay exposed, every branch and twig etched darkly against the grey sky. The flattened grasses and corn stubble in the empty fields added to Grace's melancholy. She leaned her head against the seat. Here she was on her way to Chester for Thanksgiving and feeling anything but festive.

Maybe it was the holiday itself. Too many memories of ruined dinners and sad, lonely afternoons wondering where her father had stormed off to. The first year she'd lived with Aunt Louise and Uncle Arthur, they'd stayed in Concord, the holiday marked only by a dressed turkey and two kinds of pie. Last year, they'd returned to Chester. Dinner had been an almost solemn affair, with none of the strife and little of the liveliness and humor Daddy had brought to the table. She didn't miss the scenes, but she did miss the family stories, the banter, the good-humored teasing.

Following that awful evening she'd broken down in the kitchen, her aunt and uncle had agreed to let Grace take a few days off from classes so she could spend the entire holiday week in Chester. It was time, she decided, to take a more active role in finding Daddy. For the past two years, she'd concentrated on making a new life for herself, one that her father wasn't a part of. She thought if she could get used to life without Mama, then she could get used to life without her father. She knew now, it didn't work that way. Death was final, absolute, but Daddy had disappeared and might, at any moment, reappear. Mama existed in Grace's memory, in her heart and mind, but where was her father? He might be near or far, sick or well, drunk or sober. Alive or dead.

Rain was falling heavily now, lashing against the windows like sea spray. The wind lifted fallen leaves, swirling them into eddies and dropping them back down. Grace shivered and pulled her sweater closer. Every time she thought about her father, where he was, what he was doing, she came to the same dead end. How could he have abandoned her to wonder and worry all these months? She needed to know, and that meant she had to find him.

That's why she was on this train rattling toward Chester, instead of at Mansfield listening to Mr. Richardson lecture on progressive education. She wanted to talk to Mr. Sprague and visit Mary and her mother, too. In the back of her mind, she hoped to talk to Paddy. And then there was Jerome. In his last letter, he'd asked her to set time aside on Friday for them to get together. They hadn't seen each other for several months, not since they'd started college. Her heart raced at the thought of being with him again.

As the train pulled into the station, Grace caught sight of Grandma waiting under the building's overhang, poised and perfectly turned out in a fur-collared maroon coat and matching hat. She hadn't been able to escape the shame of Daddy's disappearance as Grace had, but she hadn't bowed under it, either. Grace felt a rush of gratitude and love for her grandmother. Slipping on her coat, she grabbed her bag and hurried off the train, all but knocking Grandma's hat off in the eagerness of her embrace.

"Oh, Grandma, it's so good to see you." Stepping back she took in the familiar face, the grooves between her grand-mother's brows and around her mouth deeper than Grace re-membered them. "I've missed you and there's so much I want to talk to you about."

"We have a lot of catching up to do, dear. I want to hear all about your studies and the latest news of Lily Pearl, but first, a nice cup of tea. Mrs. Henderson has made some of your favorite treats."

The rain had let up by the time they passed through the station and onto the street. On the pavement, Grace halted in her tracks. Her father's Pontiac, its blue paintwork spangled with raindrops, was parked at the curb. She was even more surprised when her grandmother opened the driver's door.

"Put your bag in the back seat, dear, and let's go."

Dumbfounded, Grace did as she was told and slid into the passenger seat. Grandma pulled the Pontiac into the traffic with all the confidence of a seasoned driver and headed toward Pleasant Street.

"Grandma, when did you ... I mean ... who taught you — "

"I've been very busy since your father's disappearance. There have been financial issues to see to, appointments with the lawyer and Mr. Sprague. And with your grandfather working full-time at the shop, these things fell to me to take care of." She glanced at Grace.

"Your father's car had been sitting in the driveway for the better part of two years and I thought, why not put it to use? So I had Mr. Panetta tow it to his garage and make the necessary repairs." She checked the rear-view mirror. "I signed up for driv-ing lessons and now I can come and go as I please. It's so much easier than bothering with cabs and buses."

Grace laughed for the first time that day. "You're a won-der, Grandma. What else do you have up your sleeve?"

Grandma's sitting room had never looked more inviting. There was a fire in the grate and the glow of the lamps were a welcome contrast to the dull light of the November afternoon. Grace stood with her back to the fire and chatted with Mrs.

Henderson who set the tea tray on a low table in front of the fire. Grandma took her customary place on the settee and Grace joined her. Mrs. Henderson had made Grace's favorite ginger cookies, but the best part was the fresh popovers and homemade strawberry jam. Grace stuffed herself with both and drank enough tea to float a small boat, before dabbing her lips with a napkin and sighing contentedly.

"Oh, Grandma, that was lovely. No one makes popovers as light and tender as Mrs. Henderson." She set her cup in its saucer. "I didn't realize how hungry I was."

"You certainly did justice to Mrs. Henderson's offerings, dear. She'll be pleased." Her grandmother refilled their cups and looked at Grace.

"You're pale. Have you been feeling all right?"

Grace shifted position and met her grandmother's eyes. "I'm all right. That is, I'm not sick or anything, but ... " She paused, trying to put into words what she was feeling.

"Even though I've finished high school and started college, I feel adrift...like I'm treading water, instead of moving forward. I've tried so hard to put Daddy's disappearance behind me, to get on with my life, but it's no good. I can't stop wondering what's happened to him. If I just knew where he was, that he was all right, maybe then I could..." She sighed and shook her head.

Grandma squeezed Grace's hand. "The uncertainty is the worst part. You know as well as anyone that losing a loved one is terrible, but you also understand that one passes into a kind of acceptance, a sense that the person is now within you rather than separate from you. It's a lot harder to come to terms with ambiguity. We all want to know where and how he is, but without answers, we're as lost as poor Francis." She looked into the fire. When she spoke her voice was barely above a whisper.

"Without answers, we fear the worst."

Releasing Grace's hand, she pulled a handkerchief from her sleeve and wiped her eyes. Grace had never seen her grandmother cry. All through the first weeks of her father's disappearance, through the shutting of the High Street house and finding employment for Mrs. Blanchard, through Grandpa's tirades and

Grace's grief, the police questioning, the bail issues, Grandma had never shed a tear. She'd been dignified and stalwart and determined to clean up the mess her son had left behind.

Grace stared at her clasped hands, at a loss what to say. She'd been selfish, too wrapped up in her own sorrow to think how awful her father's disappearance had been for her grandparents. At a time when they should be taking life easy, Grandpa was working full-time at the shop and Grandma was dealing with lawyers and bankers and private investigators. Instead of being a comfort to his parents in their later years, her father had become a burden.

Clearing her throat, Grace turned to face her grandmother. "You've done so much for me, Grandma, you and the rest of the family. I don't know how I would have made it through this trouble without your help. And all this time, I was too caught up in my own sorrow to see what Daddy's disappearance meant for you and Grandpa." She leaned forward and placed a hand on her grandmother's arm.

"I know you've never given up trying to find Daddy, Grandma. There must be something I can do to help."

Entering the Stimson Building at the end of Main Street, Grace studied the directory. The office of Mr. Lockwood Sprague, Private Investigator, was on the third floor. At the bottom of the long, steep staircase, she wrinkled her nose at the musty smell and peeling, dun-colored walls, and began the long climb to the top. She stood in front of the opaque glass door and took a steadying breath. Grace entered the outer office and waited at the reception desk, but if Mr. Sprague had a secretary she was not in evidence. After a few minutes, Grace crossed the room and knocked on the inner door.

Once inside, Grace introduced herself. Mr. Sprague's reception was cool. She hadn't made an appointment, hadn't until the last moment worked up the courage to go to his office, and he seemed none too pleased by the interruption. He motioned her to sit in the visitor's chair and they faced each other across a jumble of books, loose papers, and files on his battered wooden desk. Now that she was here, Grace wasn't sure what to say and, clearly, Mr. Sprague wasn't going to help her. He peered at her stonily from under his brows, his curiously delicate hands busily loosening and tightening the cap of his fountain pen.

Grace shrugged out of her coat, straightened her back, and clasped her hands in her lap. "Thank you for seeing me, Mr. Sprague. I wanted to talk to you about my father's case."

"I gathered as much." His voice was deep, the voice of a much larger man. "I'm surprised Mrs. Montel hasn't kept you informed of our progress thus far."

"Oh, I believe she has, but I'd like to hear your views first-hand and follow up with a few questions." She smiled, but his face remained blank.

"I may be able to add to what my grandmother has already told you about my father's activities prior to his disappearance." She paused. "I was in rather a bad way the one other time we met."

"Yes, well, no doubt that's true." Shifting his chair closer to the desk, he pulled a folder from the stack and opened it.

Grace leaned forward for a better look, but couldn't make out what was written in the file. Sprague read off a yellow sheet clipped to the inside cover, outlining his visits with police departments, his attempts to trace the car her father had driven, and more recently, his conversation with the woman who remembered Miss Armstrong from the Worcester-bound train.

"I was surprised to hear that both Miss Armstrong and my father were in Worcester on the evening of his arrest," Grace said. "But then, they were both associated with Mr. Ramsey and I suppose that might account for it ... "

Mr. Sprague looked up from the file. "I know Miss Armstrong was Ramsey's housekeeper, and your grandmother mentioned you'd seen Ramsey drop your father off at the house once or twice, but that's no reason to assume their connection was anything more than social. Ramsey told me as much during one of our interviews. He indicated that he and your father were both Rotarians and that Mr. Montel had attended social gatherings at his home on more than one occasion."

He sat back in his chair. "He assured me that was the extent of their association and I have no reason to doubt him."

"Well, I do, Mr. Sprague. I think my father worked for Ramsey."

Sprague raised his brows. "I think there was some kind of falling out between the two of them. I heard my father on the telephone one evening. He was very angry and I'm pretty sure he was talking to Ramsey."

"Your father might have been talking to any number of people, Miss Montel. And from what I've learned about him, he had a tendency to be somewhat combative when he was drinking."

He leaned forward. "Did you actually hear your father refer to the caller by name?"

"No, but I — "

"Miss Montel, I have interviewed Mr. Ramsey, and he has assured me his contact with your father was of a purely social nature." He spoke slowly and with exaggerated clarity, as though Grace were hard of hearing or lacking in wits.

"Mr. Ramsey is a wealthy and influential man. He's building a large resort on the border for which he's purchased materials locally, to say nothing of the men he's hired to work on the construction. Once that resort is in operation, its proximity will put Chester on the map. I'm not going to risk alienating a man of Mr. Ramsey's caliber because you suspect him of having words with your father on the telephone."

He rose from his chair, and walking to the door, opened it for her. "What I am going to do is conduct this investigation as I see fit. And continue to report my findings to your grandmother."

Grace thanked Sprague for his time and made her way down the corridor. At the top of the stairs she stopped to collect herself. What an odious little man, ready to take Ramsey at his word simply because he was rich and influential. Had Sprague even looked into Ramsey's various business dealings? Or was he content to write his monthly report, collect his fee from Grandma, and leave the Great Man to put Chester on the map?

Out on the sidewalk, Grace turned up the collar of her coat, tugged on her gloves and headed down Main Street. When she arrived at the millinery shop, Miss Andrews was busy with a customer, but nodded a greeting which Grace returned. Mary was at the counter, rearranging the ribbons, feathers, beads, and artificial flowers displayed in the glass case.

"Gracie, what are you doing here? Don't you have school this week?"

"I do, but I've taken a few days leave." She glanced in Miss Andrews' direction and lowered her voice. "I've just met with the private investigator Grandma hired to find my father, and I wanted to come by and say how sorry I was to hear about Paddy."

Mary shook her head and looked nervously at her employer who was approaching the counter with her customer.

"Hello, Grace," Miss Andrews said. "Home for the holiday?"

"Yes, and I've come by to take Mary out to lunch, that is, if you can spare her for an hour." She wrinkled her brow. "This will probably be the only chance we get to see each other while I'm here and ... well, Mary's one of my oldest friends."

Miss Andrews placed a comforting hand on Grace's shoulder. "I understand, dear. I think I can get by without Mary for an extra half-hour."

She added, "Just finish up what you're doing, Miss Devlin, and then you may go."

As the girls walked toward Alfred's Diner, Mary said, "I don't know how you managed that, Gracie. I only ever get a half hour for lunch and most of the time she's got me working part of that. The woman's a regular slave driver. And cheap ... I haven't had a raise in almost three years. I told Ma, I'm thinking of going to work at the shoe factory. They pay half again as much as Miss Andrews does."

Grace shuddered. "Oh, Mary, you don't want to work in a noisy old factory. At least at Miss Andrews you're learning a trade. Someday you might be able to open your own shop or even take over this one when Miss Andrews retires."

"God forbid I should live that long, Gracie. Besides, business has been falling off for the past couple of years. Only old ladies wear hats now. Modern girls can't be bothered."

Mary grinned, hiked up her skirt, and performed a quick Charleston step. A passerby frowned and both girls giggled.

At Alfred's they slipped into a booth and ordered lunch. Grace leaned across the table. "I'm so sorry about Paddy. How's he doing? How's your mother?"

"Oh, Paddy's all right, at least that's what he'd like us to think. Ma's in a bad way, though. It's a struggle every day to make ends meet now that Paddy's not bringing in a wage. To say nothing of the bail. For the love of God, Grace, where would a family like ours come by five hundred dollars?" She shook her head.

"It's an awful lot of money," Grace said, "but at least Paddy can't run away like my father did. The bank's got a lien on our house for Daddy's bail ... and it wasn't even his house. It was left to my mother. And my poor grandparents, it's terrible what they've gone through."

Mary frowned. "I'm sure it's been bad for all of you. And you're right. At least we know where Paddy is. Have you heard anything from your father? Do you know where he's living?"

"Barely a word. A postcard on my birthday, that's it. We don't know where he is and we don't seem to be any closer to finding out." She blinked and rubbed her nose.

"That's partly why I'm here. I got nowhere with the private investigator, but.. I'd like to talk to Paddy. Can you help me do that? Can you get me in to see him?"

Mary sat back, eyes wide. "How could our Paddy help, Gracie? What are you thinking he'll be able to tell you?"

"I want to ask him about a fellow called Rafe Ramsey."

"You mean the one who's putting up that big resort on the border? Why would Paddy know a fellow like that?"

"Because I'm pretty sure building that resort is not the only business Mr. Ramsey does across the border."

The following afternoon, Grace stepped onto the portico of the County Courthouse. She'd passed the building hundreds of times, but had never before had reason to enter the big double doors. She straightened her spine, a move that always seemed to fortify Grandma, but did nothing to calm the jittery feeling in her stomach. In the foyer, she approached the window where a fellow in a blue uniform sat at a narrow counter. She smiled and he slid aside a small panel at the bottom of the window and asked what he could do for her.

"I'm here to visit Patrick Devlin," she said. "I was told his attorney would let you know I was coming."

The fellow pulled a clipboard off a hook and ran a stubby finger down a handwritten list. "Your name, Miss?" Grace told him and he pointed to a stairway on the opposite side of the hall.

"Down those stairs and to the left. Just tell the fellow at the desk what you want."

In the basement, Grace waited at a scarred table in the center of the dingy room. Two high windows at street level and a row of frosted-globe lamps barely penetrated the gloom. The ceiling and walls were water-stained and the whole place reeked of damp and mildew. Grace sneezed just as the door opened and Paddy came in, accompanied by a fellow in uniform.

"Bless you." Paddy grinned, slid the chair out from the table, and sat down. "This here's Roddy Boyd, my old school chum. He'll keep an eye on me so you've nothing to worry about." He waggled his brows and Grace chuckled.

"How are you, Paddy? I hope they're treating you all right in here."

Paddy shrugged. "It's not so bad, Gracie. Half the fellows workin' here are ones I've known since I was a kid. Roddy and I used to play in the band together. He's a regular King Oliver on the cornet, aren't you Roddy?"

"You've got fifteen minutes, Paddy. I'll be right outside the door so no funny business."

"Right you are, Officer Boyd." Paddy gave Officer Boyd a smart salute and he and Grace were left alone.

"He seems like an accommodating fellow," Grace said. "I'm glad you've got a friend here."

She placed her forearms on the table and lowered her voice. "I was hoping you'd answer a few questions for me. There's been no sign of my father for over two years. It's such a long time and I ... well, I can't stand not knowing what's happened to him." She shifted in her seat. "It's awful not knowing."

Paddy frowned. "I don't think I can help you there, Gracie. I never had no dealings with your father. Fellows like me never had nothing to do with the guys in charge. All's we did was pick up the goods, drive the loaded cars into the warehouse, and collect our pay packets."

"But someone must have hired you ... someone must have approached you. Otherwise how would you have gotten involved in the first place?"

Paddy leaned back in his chair. He didn't look at her.

"Who was that person, Paddy? Who told you where to go and what to do?" Paddy crossed his arms over his chest, his mouth set in a thin line.

"Gracie, you got to stay out of this. These guys, they ... if I give anything away, they'll know who spilled the beans and they'll ... " He glanced toward the door. "I can't help you, Gracie."

"Then, please, just tell me one thing. Was the person who approached you the same one who got poor Wesley Titus involved in all this?"

Paddy shook his head. "No, that was somebody else." He held up his hand. "And that's all I'm going to say."

Grace lowered her voice. "What do you know about a fellow called Rafe Ramsey?"

"You mean the guy who's building the big place up on the line? Everyone in town's heard of Ramsey. The lucky ones are workin' for him." Paddy motioned toward the door and stood up.

"What's going to happen now, Paddy? Will they send you to jail?"

"I'm already in jail." Paddy laughed. "They'll probably let me off with time served ... least that's what the lawyer says."

He nodded at Officer Boyd. "Roddy and his lads will see that I keep my nose clean from now on, won't ya?"

The policeman rolled his eyes. "Come on, Paddy. Time's up."

Outside, Grace paused and adjusted her hat, squinting though the cold drizzle that all but obscured the buildings across the street. A miserable day and all of her questions still unanswered. She jammed her hands into her pockets and turned up Main Street towards the shop. She'd been a fool to think she was going to find out anything that she didn't already know. If

Sprague and the police hadn't been able to find her father, what made her think she'd be able to? It was hopeless.

"Damn!" she muttered. "Damn, damn, damn."

Grace crossed the street to the shop and took shelter under its dripping awning. In contrast to the darkening afternoon, the shop's interior was bright, its light spilling invitingly onto the damp sidewalk. Grace had always loved this place, the neat stacks of shirts and sweaters, the mellow oak cabinets and shining glass cases, the colors and textures of wool, cotton, and silk.

Through the plate glass window, she could see her grandfather talking to a customer. He seemed heavier than the last time she'd seen him and she didn't remember him as stooped, either. Poor Grandpa. He was doing his best to keep the business afloat, but at what cost to his health?

The haberdashery was Grandpa's link to his father and grandfather, his way of keeping faith with past generations of Montels. And he'd groomed Daddy to carry on the work they'd begun. All those Saturdays and hours after school Grandpa had spent teaching Daddy the business and her father had resented every minute of it.

The Montels had built their reputation on fair dealing and community service. For decades, they'd been civic leaders and trusted merchants, but Daddy had broken that trust. He'd run out on his responsibilities, abandoned his daughter, and left the rest of his family to pick up the pieces.

24

PERSONAL MATTERS

Carrying her sketchbook and a small portfolio of water-colors, Grace climbed the three flights of stairs to the Standish apartment. Maybe it was just her imagination, but the hallway seemed even dirtier and more cluttered than she remembered it. Tattered spider webs hung from the ceiling and every stair creaked. There was no sign of the ginger cat. Mrs. Standish was unchanged, though. She even wore the same faded housedress and the same dour expression. Without a word of welcome, she motioned Grace through to the studio. Pausing on the threshold, Grace breathed in the mingled odors of oil paint and gesso, and the stale smell of cabbage and onions.

At her greeting, Mr. Standish turned from his study of the canvas propped on his easel, and crossed the room in his long-legged stride. He held out his hand and taking hers, said, "Hello, Grace. How's my favorite student?"

They settled into the chairs in the corner of the room and Mr. Standish, his lanky frame bent at the waist, leaned toward Grace, his blue eyes fixed on her face. He asked all about her art classes at Mansfield and lingered over the sampling of water-colors she shared before opening her sketch book. After a few moments, he looked up, a wide smile on his wrinkled face. He was pleased with her drawings and complimented her on the progress she'd made.

Watching Mr. Standish peruse her work, Grace thought of the days just after her father's disappearance. She'd refused to leave the house and had missed her weekly art lesson, but Mr. Standish had paid her a visit. She'd dragged herself down to the parlor and found him dressed in an ancient black suit, perched on the sofa like a lively old crow. He'd stood and greeted her, then pulled an envelope out of his breast pocket. Opening it, Grace found a pen and ink cartoon of a cringing Mr. Standish huddled with the orange cat on the sill of the porch window, and towering over them, his wife, brandishing a rolling pin and scowling fiercely. Grace had laughed in spite of herself.

"What have you been working on lately, Mr. Standish? Still busy with commissions for Mr. Ramsey?"

He rose and led her to the end of the room where several canvases leaned against the wall. One by one, he stood them on the easel, scenes of the mountains, meadows, and river around Ramsey's home and a drawing of what would be the grand hotel planned for construction on the line between New Hampshire and Quebec. As she studied the paintings, Grace couldn't help but resent the man who'd commissioned them. His influence and wealth put him beyond the reach of the law, while her father and Paddy were arrested for doing his bidding. And then there was poor Wesley Titus. He'd paid the biggest price of all.

"These are beautiful pieces, Mr. Standish. Mr. Ramsey must be very pleased." She gave her teacher a sly look. "Does he come here to view the work or do you have to bring it to his home?"

Mr. Standish grinned. "Neither. My patron has opened an office in town. I meet with him there."

"Ah, and where is this office?"

Mr. Standish lowered his voice to a dramatic whisper. "Third floor of the bank building, take the hall to the right of the stairs. The office is on the left. Riverview Enterprises. You can't miss it." His smile faded.

"Watch your step, Grace. Mr. Ramsey is not a man to be trifled with."

Riverview Enterprises was easy to find; getting access to the great man was not. Grace was stymied by a lean, sallow-faced clerk obviously tasked with guarding Mr. Ramsey's privacy. Halting her right at the door, he asked no end of questions. Did Miss Montel have an appointment? Was Miss Montel known to Mr. Ramsey? What was the nature of Miss Montel's visit? Grace wasn't surprised, and did her best to remain friendly and calm.

"Mr. Ramsey is acquainted with my father and I've had the pleasure of visiting him at his home." She tipped her head and spoke confidentially. "I'd like to speak to him on a personal matter. I know he has a great many demands on his time, but a few minutes is all I need."

She lifted her brows appealingly and leaned toward him until their faces were inches apart. "You see, I attend school in Vermont and am only in town for a few days. You would be doing me and my family a great favor if you could convince Mr. Ramsey to spare me a few minutes of his time."

She was gratified to see a scarlet blush rise in the clerk's pallid cheeks. He stammered, "Yes ... well, Miss, I'll see what I can do. Please wait here." He gestured to a chair near his desk, then knocked softly and entered the inner chamber.

Most likely, Ramsey would refuse to see her, but at least she'd have tried. She clasped her hands tightly in her lap and tried to steady her breathing. The door opened and Ramsey himself, trailed by his clerk, stepped into the outer office. His greeting was surprisingly cordial, and Grace followed him into the inner room wondering what that might mean.

She hadn't given much thought to what Mr. Ramsey's office would look like, but once she was sitting in the visitor's chair, she gazed around the large room. The furniture was dark and shiny, the huge desk placed in front of the bank of windows facing the street. On the wall hung a framed photograph of his riverside home, and on the credenza below there were two smaller pictures in silver frames. In one, Mr. Ramsey shook hands with a middle-aged fellow in a tailored suit whom Grace recognized from newspaper photos as a state senator. The other was of a young woman, a girl really, in a demure white gown and elbow-length gloves, surrounded by several others similarly dressed.

Grace was staring at the photograph when Mr. Ramsey said, "Now, Miss Montel. What's this personal matter you'd like to talk to me about?" No longer cordial, his tone was sharp, and she had to force herself to meet his gaze. His almost colorless grey eyes had all the warmth of a winter sky.

Clearing her throat, Grace said, "I want to talk about my father, Mr. Ramsey. That is, I want to find my father and I'm hoping you can help me."

Ramsey frowned and sat back in his chair. "What makes you think I know anything about your father's whereabouts, Miss Montel?"

Grace clutched her purse tightly and tried to keep her voice level. "I think you know a great deal, Mr. Ramsey, and while you may not know where my father is, I believe you could find him if you wanted to."

She inhaled and sat up straighter. "I saw you and my father together more than once, and I'm pretty sure you telephoned him at home on at least one occasion. I know my father made several trips to the Boston area during the months before his disappearance. It was on one of those trips that he was ambushed by the police, shot at, and arrested."

Grace's heart was racing and she paused for breath. Ramsey remained silent, leaning back in his chair, fingering his watch chain. Unnerved, Grace leaned forward, her voice pleading.

"Please, Mr. Ramsey, I need your help. I've got to find my father before it's too late."

Ramsey pushed himself out of his chair and stood staring down at her. "It's already too late, Miss Montel. Your father was lost long before he went missing. The man's a hopeless drunk and there's nothing you or anyone else can do about it."

He drummed his fingers on the desktop. "You'd do well to let him go and get on with your life."

Grace got to her feet. "I've tried. For the past two years, I've tried to get over my father's disappearance. I tell myself he's gone, that I'll never see him again, but somehow I can't make myself believe it." She stared out the window at the gun-metal sky. "Until I know for sure what's happened to him, until I see him again or find out he's ... no longer alive, I'll be left wondering. Picturing him in all sorts of awful situations ... " She shook her head.

Glancing at Ramsey, Grace followed his gaze to the photograph on the credenza. His expression was impenetrable. She couldn't make out what he was thinking or feeling.

"I'm sure my father's drinking caused problems for you in your dealings with him, but he must have been useful to you, too. In a way, that's how it's always been for me. It's true my father was difficult and irresponsible at times, but when he was sober, he was a good father. He was kind and caring and generous. That's what I miss about him and that's why I want to find him."

When Ramsey failed to respond, Grace picked up her purse. At the door, she turned, "Good-bye, Mr. Ramsey. Thank you for your time."

She passed through the outer chamber and into the hall. As she stopped outside the door to button her coat, she heard Ramsey call his clerk into the office.

Grace made her way along the hall and down the stairs. She'd actually spoken to the infamous Rafe Ramsey and, except for a churning stomach and shaky knees, she'd come to no harm. He had called her father a hopeless drunk. Was Daddy's drinking hopeless? Mama hadn't been able to do anything about it and neither had Grace. Maybe Daddy couldn't either. Nothing in his life had more of a hold on him than alcohol. He'd abandoned his daughter, his family, his work, and his home. But Grace was sure that if he was still alive, he was still drinking.

The following afternoon, Aunt Louise and Uncle Arthur arrived with Lily Pearl, a large suitcase, several bags, and a pie basket. Grace helped her uncle unload the Hudson and stow their belongings in the guest room, while her aunt and grandmother took Pearl into the parlor. When Grace and her uncle joined them, Mrs. Henderson served coffee and tea and laughed good-naturedly as Pearl spread cookie crumbs from one end of the sofa to the other.

As dusk was falling, Uncle Arthur asked Grace if she'd like to walk over to the shop and help him pick out a couple of new shirts. He said they wouldn't be gone long and would return with both his purchases and his father-in-law. On their way up Pleasant Street, Grace told her uncle about her disappointing meetings with Mr. Sprague and Paddy Devlin and passed on Mr. Standish's compliments on the art program at Mansfield College.

"Grandma and Grandpa don't know this yet, but I also paid a visit to Rafe Ramsey."

Her uncle halted mid-stride. "You did what?"

Grace laughed. "Mr. Ramsey has an office practically across the street from the shop. I stopped in never thinking he'd agree to see me, but he did, so I asked him to help me find my father."

"What'd he say?"

"He called my father a hopeless drunk. He made it sound like Daddy would never be able to give up drinking. Do you think that's true?"

They were at the corner now, about to turn onto Main Street. Her uncle didn't answer right away, and when he did, he chose his words carefully.

"If your father made up his mind to give up drinking, he could do it, but it would be very, very difficult. His body craves alcohol now, so it wouldn't just be a matter of stopping. He'd have to pass through a period of extreme physical and mental discomfort. Your father's need for alcohol is a sickness. If he were to give it up, he'd have to do so under a doctor's care, at the very least. Most likely, it would mean a lengthy stay in a hospital or sanatorium where they know how to manage these things."

"So, if my father's drinking is a sickness, will he die of it?"

"It's likely he will, eventually. There are no end of complications associated with excessive alcohol consumption." He shook his head. "The folks who supported Prohibition thought they could legislate people's drinking habits. That if alcohol was illegal, people would give it up. Some have, of course. The rest rely, directly or indirectly, on men like Ramsey to keep them supplied."

They were quiet the rest of the way. Just before they arrived at the shop, her uncle said, "So, did Ramsey agree to help you find your father?"

"Far from it. He told me to let him go and get on with my life."

———————◀◆▶———————

This was Lily Pearl's first real Thanksgiving and her wonder and delight were infectious. She'd been too little last year to sit with them at the table, but this year she was the center of attention. She clapped her hands as the candles were lit, squealed as the huge turkey was brought in, and had them all laughing at her failed attempts to keep the jellied cranberry sauce on her tiny spoon.

Everything the baby did made Grandpa laugh. When he made the fork and spoon talk to each other in silly voices, Pearl's giggles brought everyone else to a pitch of hilarity. Grace couldn't remember the last time she'd laughed so hard or felt so happy.

After dinner, Grace went upstairs to work on her assignments, and keep an ear out for Pearl who was napping in the next room. Her aunt and uncle went for a walk, Grandma retired to her sitting room to rest, and Grandpa slept in his chair by the fire. The house was quiet, but Grace couldn't keep her mind on her studies. All she could think about was seeing Jerome the next day.

He called for her shortly before noon. Grace was brushing her hair when the doorbell rang, and stood with the brush in her hand, staring at herself in the mirror. Her heart fluttered behind her ribs like a trapped bird and she felt the heat rise in her cheeks. Pinning up her hair, she straightened the collar of her dress and made her way to the top of the stairs. As she descended, she caught her first glimpse of Jerome in more than four months.

He stood at the bottom of the stairs, wearing a dark grey overcoat she hadn't seen before and holding a tweed cap. He smiled up at her, his dark eyes aglow and she reached for the banister to steady herself. In the foyer, he took her hand and she looked into his once familiar face, struck by how changed he seemed. Was he thinking the same about her? They went into the parlor and chatted briefly with the family before Jerome helped her on with her coat and watched as she adjusted her hat in the hall mirror. Out on the sidewalk, he offered his arm and they headed toward Main Street and lunch at the hotel.

Seated in a corner of the dining room, Grace and Jerome faced each other across the small table. The lines of his jaw were more pronounced than she remembered, his cheeks less full. The lock of dark hair that usually fell over his forehead had been tamed and swept back smoothly, making him look more like a man than a boy.

As if reading her thoughts, he said, "You've changed, Monty. You're even prettier than you were last summer."

She dipped her head shyly. "And you look very grown-up, Jerome. Do all the men at Dartmouth look so sophisticated?"

He grinned. "It's just a little hair tonic. It won't last."

"Good," she said, smiling back at him.

The waiter arrived, took their orders, and hustled off. Jerome leaned forward and asked quietly, "How are you, Monty? Have there been any changes in your father's situation?"

She shook her head. "Not really. We've still had no word of him." She told him about visiting Paddy at the Courthouse and meeting with the private investigator.

"I even went to see Mr. Ramsey."

Jerome stared at her, wide-eyed. "You didn't."

"I did." She frowned and lowered her voice.

"I'm desperate, Jerome. It's been over two years and I'm almost out of my mind wondering where my father is ... how he is. At first, I was just glad to be away from Chester. I thought I'd put all the ugliness behind me and start fresh with my aunt and uncle, but as happy as I am with them, there's this shadow hanging over me." She sighed. "Anyway, I didn't get any further with Ramsey than I did with Mr. Sprague or Paddy."

The waiter arrived with their food and the talk turned to college. Jerome said he'd had a devil of a time finding his way around campus during his first weeks of school. He told her about his tutorial with an eccentric history professor whose office was three flights up in a turret room, decorated with ancient weapons and faded French tapestries.

Grace told him her problem wasn't finding her way around campus; it was more that there wasn't a campus, just a shabby three-story building perched on the side of a mountain. She described her drawing and painting classes and her growing interest in children's literature, surprising herself by saying she'd like to illustrate children's books.

Jerome's eyes shone. "That sounds like the perfect job for you, Monty. You've always loved reading and drawing."

He waved his fork in the air. "You'd use the story to create the illustrations and the reader would use the illustrations to understand the story. It's brilliant."

Grace laughed. "You're brilliant, Jerome. I hadn't known until that moment that I wanted to illustrate books ... and somehow you helped me figure it out." She affected a mystified look. "How'd you do that?"

"I have made an exhaustive study of your psyche, my dear," Jerome said, frowning and stroking an imaginary beard. "And beside, I know what you like and what you're good at and what makes you happy. " He grinned at her. "Now, eat up and let's get out of here."

The day was overcast, but mild, and they crossed the lower bridge to the other side of town and followed the path that led to the upper bridge. The river was low and sluggish, grey water reflecting the grey sky, but Grace's mood sparkled like a summer day. They walked arm in arm, their bodies tucked close together. Even through their thick coats, Grace could feel Jerome's warmth radiating through her.

For several minutes they were quiet, but finally she said, "In your letter, you said you had something you wanted to talk to me about. What was it?"

Jerome stopped to face her. He put his hands on her shoulders and looked into her eyes. At first his lips felt cool and slightly chapped, but soon they softened, melting against hers. She wrapped her arms around him and they stood locked together, their kisses eager and searching. At the sound of approaching voices, they both stepped back and continued walking.

As they crossed the bridge that led back to Main Street, Grace asked again, "So, what did you want to talk to me about?"

Jerome slowed his pace and tightened his hold on her arm. "I want to talk about us, Monty," he said, not looking at her. "I know the past two years have been hell for you and the ones before that weren't much better. But since you left Chester I've felt, well, like I don't know what you want from me anymore. It's weeks before you answer my letters and even then they're ... It's like you're writing to your pen pal or distant cousin, someone you don't really ... "

He stopped walking and turned toward the river. "Ever since you visited me in Exeter, you've been different. Like you're not sure about me anymore."

"How can you say that after what just happened back there?"

Jerome jammed his hands in his coat pockets and hung his head. "What happened back there makes it even harder to understand what you want from me. What am I supposed to think when we have a moment like that and then I don't hear from you for weeks on end?"

He glanced at her, then looked away. "And all the time you've been in Concord, you've never invited me to visit. Never let me in on that part of your life."

Grace stared out over the grey river to the bare, frozen meadow beyond. She'd never even considered inviting Jerome to Concord. In her daydreams, she'd imagined him showing up there countless times. She wasn't sure what made her avoid answering his letters, but something held her back.

Jerome cleared his throat. "My mother told me to be patient, and I've tried, but now, well, there's someone who's made it pretty clear — "

Something bitter rose in Grace's throat. "So that's it. All this talk about letters and visits is really just a way of saying you're interested in someone else."

"No, that's not it."

She waved away his protest. "You say I'm not sure about you and all the time you've got another girl — "

"Monty, stop." His voice was hard. "I don't have another girl and you aren't sure about me. Not the way I am about you. If you were, nothing else would matter."

"What do you mean nothing else? What else?"

"Well, your father for one thing. His drinking has always embarrassed you. And then what happened, his arrest, his disappearance ... " He looked at her. "You ran away, Monty, without even telling me."

Grace sighed. "We've been through all that, Jerome. I've told you, I was upset. I wasn't myself. My aunt practically kidnapped me."

"And all those weeks after? You never even wrote. I had to get my mother to find out where you were, to get the address so I could write to you."

He frowned. "And you're jealous of my friends. You think they're spoiled rich kids. You don't even know them, but you don't like them." The words tumbled out, sounding loud in the still air.

"That's what I'm talking about, Monty. I don't care what your father did. I don't care that your friends are different from my friends, but you do. And you've let that come between us."

"I don't dislike your friends. I just don't feel comfortable with them. And what happened with my father ... I'm so ashamed, Jerome, so humiliated by what he did."

"So you take it out on me. You hide away in Concord and ignore my letters and keep me dangling. Well, I'm tired of it, Monty. I don't want to play that game anymore."

Game? She wasn't the one playing a game. She'd looked forward to seeing him for weeks, and all he could do was accuse her of not caring for him. How could he be that blind?

"You're blaming me for ruining things between us," she said, "but it's as much your fault as mine. You're the one who went away first. You left and went off to your fancy school and made new friends and I was stuck here with my drunken father and — "

"I couldn't help that and you know it."

"And I couldn't help what happened to me, either. It's hard to answer your letters, Jerome, hard to be cheerful and friendly and talk about ordinary things when I'm so crushed by what my father did. I feel tainted by what happened, Jerome, and you're like this shining, perfect person with this shining, perfect life."

"That's nonsense, Monty, and you know it. Look, I know what your father did has been hard on you, but I've never held it against you. And I think you know that. Instead, you hold it against me. It's true, Monty. Why else would you run away to Concord without a word or leave my letters unanswered? It's like you're trying to punish me for caring about you."

He shook his head. "It's no use, Monty. I want a girl who'll meet me on equal terms. Someone who trusts my feelings and who won't hold back."

A girl like Adelaide. Beautiful, confident, and worthy of the attention of her brother's handsome friend. A girl who knows what she wants and goes after it.

Before Grace could frame a response, Jerome had turned and hurried down the path, leaving her alone under the leaden sky.

25

WINTRY MIX

The winter term was well underway at Mansfield College. One morning, snow was falling thick and fast as Uncle Arthur navigated the Hudson along the slippery streets of Concord. Grace gripped the strap over the door and pressed her feet against the floorboards as the big car turned onto the dirt road leading to the college. How would they ever make it up the steep hill through all this snow? Grace swallowed and braced her free hand against the dashboard.

At the bottom of the hill, Uncle Arthur pulled the car into a byway and turned off the engine. "Feel up to a constitutional, Grace? I don't think we can make it up that incline, and I don't fancy trying to back down if we don't."

He grinned at her. "There are worse things than getting a little snow in our boots."

Grace exhaled. "I'd much rather be on my feet than skating all over the road in the car."

She fastened the top button of her coat, grabbed her book bag, and stepped out into several inches of new snow. After the tense drive in the overheated car, the air outside felt wonderfully fresh. The snow softened the contours of the landscape, settled onto the branches of the bare trees, and covered the dark winter fields in a blanket of white.

By the time they reached the top of the hill, Grace's boots were soaked through and her stockings clung wetly to her legs. She was winded and flushed and warmed from the inside out. At the front door, Uncle Arthur shook the snow off his wool cap, grinning like a schoolboy.

"We should do this more often," he said. Grace agreed.

It was nearly dark by the time Grace and her uncle, along with Mr. Richardson, headed down the hill that afternoon to where the Hudson was parked. They passed the teacher's old Ford about half-way down, off the road and mired up to the wheel wells in deep snow. It was plain to see why he had asked for a lift into town. Without a tow from Mr. Savage's tractor, it would be spring before that car was back on the road.

At home, Grace shed her wet boots and hung her coat to dry by the cook stove. She was chilled and tired and whatever Auntie was fixing for supper made her mouth water. Aunt Louise brewed a hot toddy for Uncle Arthur and a cup of tea for Grace, who'd no sooner wrapped her cold hands around the warm mug when there was a knock at the front door. Aunt Louise asked who that could be and got up to answer it.

"I'll bet that's Mr. Richardson," Grace said, shaking her head. "Probably Mr. Savage is out straight and won't be able to pull that car out tonight."

Just then, they heard the history teacher's familiar voice, as he and Aunt Louise made their way back to the kitchen.

"What's up?" Uncle Arthur sounded annoyed, but Grace saw the corners of his mouth twitch.

"I'm sorry to bother you, Mr. Eastman, but Savage says he won't be able to get up to the college and pull me out much before noon tomorrow." He shrugged. "I, well, I guess I'm kind of stuck."

"In more ways than one, it would appear," her uncle said dryly.

The teacher stayed for dinner, but when Aunt Louise offered dessert, Uncle Arthur pushed his chair back.

"I'll take you home now, Andy," he said. "I'm afraid there'll be no pie for you tonight."

As they were cleaning up, Grace said she couldn't remember seeing her uncle as put out as he'd been this evening. Her aunt lifted a dripping plate onto the drain board and chuckled.

"Oh, he was just giving that young man a what-for, Gracie. Trying to teach him a lesson. He's pretty fond of Andy Richardson, but he's not blind to his faults either. He thinks the fellow has the potential to be a fine teacher, but he has some growing up to do first."

She glanced at Grace. "I get the feeling you don't share your uncle's good opinion of Mr. Richardson."

"Not so far. It's not so much his teaching as it is his ... Well, he's awfully full of himself. Of course, the other girls practically swoon every time he looks at them, so I suppose it's no surprise."

She told her aunt about the teacher's invitation to hike Balsam Hill earlier in the year. "Don't you think that was out of line, Auntie? I mean, one of his students and the headmaster's niece at that."

"I admit it doesn't show very good judgment," her aunt said, laughing. "Did you tell your uncle about it?"

"No, I figured it wouldn't be long before Mr. Richardson got in Dutch with the headmaster." She rolled her eyes. "I knew he wouldn't need my help."

Late the following afternoon, Grace was alone in the library studying and waiting for her uncle to finish for the day. The winter dark pressed against the skylights, and the lamps cast pools of light on the polished table tops. Beyond the door, she heard footsteps on the stairs and turned, expecting to see her uncle, but finding Mr. Richardson instead. He approached the table and stood over her, his hands stuffed in his trouser pockets, his face in shadow.

"Mr. Richardson, hello. I was just getting ready to go. My uncle — "

"Your uncle sent me up here, Miss Montel. He asked me to tell you he's going to be a few minutes late." He stepped back, giving Grace room to haul her book bag onto the table.

Gathering her books and papers, she said, "Was Mr. Savage able to get your car out for you?"

"Not only did he get it out, he drove it up the hill and parked it in front of the building. I'll have to add a hefty tip when I stop over to pay my bill."

He frowned and cleared his throat. "Look Grace, Miss Montel, I know you don't particularly like me ... " He waved away her protests. "You don't have to deny it, I've felt it right from the beginning."

"Mr. Richardson, I — "

"No, please, let me get this out. I'd consider it a favor if you'd keep this business to yourself. It's bad enough I almost buried my old jalopy in a snow bank, but I'd be pretty embarrassed if it got around that I was dressed down by the Headmaster."

The teacher's face was hard to read. Was he teasing or was he really concerned about his standing with the students?

"You weren't the only fellow to get his car stuck yesterday. Mr. Savage was pretty clear about that. And as for telling my friends what happened, I've too much respect for my uncle to tell stories in or out of school. Besides, you weren't dressed down so much as sent home without your pie." Picking up a pile of notes, she slid them into her bag. "Which, by the way, was delicious."

On the way home, Grace thought about her conversation with Mr. Richardson. He was right. She didn't particularly like him and she wasn't sure why. He was awfully conceited and that was part of it, and he could be patronizing, too. Maybe if he tried to be the kind of teacher Uncle Arthur believed he could be, she'd feel differently. But he seemed more interested in entertaining his students than in teaching them.

Something her grandmother said came back to her. They'd been talking about Daddy, and Grandma said he'd spent more time trying to buck authority than trying to succeed in school or on the playing field. Maybe that's why Grace was put off by Mr. Richardson: he was too much like her father. Both clever and good looking and smart, but wrong-headed, too. Tossing off a sarcastic remark in place of a thoughtful response, cutting corners in their work, more charming than sincere.

Her heart contracted. Jerome was clever, good-looking, and smart, too, but he was also hard-working and loyal. It had taken a long time for him to give up on her, but eventually she'd driven him to it. They hadn't exchanged a single word since he'd walked away that day by the river, no visit at Christmas, no letters. She missed him something awful, and she had no one to blame but herself.

In March, just before the end of the winter term, Grace arrived home to find a letter waiting for her on the hall table. She frowned as she picked up the long, official-looking envelope. Her name was typed in crisp black letters and the return address listed a post office box in Boston. Puzzled, she lowered herself into a nearby chair, slit the envelope open, and pulled out a single sheet of paper.

She unfolded the heavy stationery and scanned the typed page. There was no letterhead, only the date and two short paragraphs. She didn't recognize the signature, had never heard of George Blake. She read the letter through. Mr. Blake, whoever he was, had made inquiries on her behalf and learned that Francis Montel was currently in residence at a sanatorium in western New York state.

Grace slumped against the back of the chair and exhaled. If what the letter said was true, her father was no longer missing, but was literally in the next state. She could go to him, bring him home, and end the long months of wondering and worry. But what then? She could never go back to the life she'd known with her father. She was a different person now. Her home was with her aunt and uncle and Pearl, and she had plans for her future. Plans that did not include playing dutiful daughter to the father who'd abandoned her after years of neglect.

She reread the letter slowly, word by word, the way she did her French homework. Finishing the two paragraphs, she looked again at the closing. Typed under the tidy signature were the words, George Blake, Secretary. If Mr. Blake was a secretary, he worked for someone, someone who'd charged him with locating her father. Grace shot to her feet. Who else but Rafe Ramsey had the influence and the means to find a man who didn't want to be found? She swallowed hard and headed up the stairs.

Aunt Louise was in the sewing room, not more than a closet really, next to the baby's room where Pearl was napping. Stepping inside, Grace waited while her aunt fed the seam of flowered material through the machine and broke off the thread.

Keeping her voice low, she said, "Auntie, you'll never guess .... Did you see this letter that came for me today?"

"I wondered about that letter. Who's it from?"

Grace held out the envelope. "Here, read it and tell me what you think."

She watched her aunt check the return address and scan the short text, watched her brows lift and her eyes widen. She stared up at Grace, then turned back to the letter.

"Who's George Blake, and why is he looking for my brother?"

"Remember my telling you about going to see Mr. Ramsey when I was in Chester at Thanksgiving? He said he didn't know where my father was, but I guess he decided to find out ... unless he'd really known all along." She shook her head.

"George Blake must be Ramsey's secretary." She picked up the envelope. "The curious thing is, the return address says Boston, but it was obviously mailed from Chester. Unless Mr. Ramsey thinks I'm awfully stupid, he must have known I'd figure out it was from him." She pursed her lips. "Maybe he wanted me to."

"Frankly, I don't know what to think," her aunt said. "All these months without a word of Francis and now, out of the blue, this letter?"

She folded her sewing and stood. "It's hard to believe."

In the kitchen, Grace put the kettle on and pulled two mugs from the cupboard. All these months of asking herself the same questions: was Daddy still alive and, if so, where was he? Now, the answers had arrived with the afternoon post. The mail had come and the long months of wondering had ended. The kettle whistled just as Aunt Louise came in, a sleepy Pearl in her arms.

Turning off the burner, Grace said, "You know, Auntie. None of this feels real. I mean, Ramsey was barely civil when I asked him to help me find my father."

Her aunt sat at the table with Pearl on her lap. She fondled the wispy hair at the child's neck and stared absently across the room.

"I don't think we should get our hopes up, just yet, Grace. Supposing the letter's a hoax? Supposing it's not from your Mr. Ramsey at all?"

Uncle Arthur came in the back door before Grace could reply. He slipped out of his overcoat, but didn't have a chance to shed his galoshes before Aunt Louise handed him the letter. He gave his wife a quizzical look, pulled the single page from the envelope, and scanned it.

Pulling off his wool cap, he said, "Well, what do you know?"

He looked at Grace. "Apparently, your visit to Mr. Ramsey bore fruit after all. And if your father really is in a sanatorium, that's probably the best news we could get."

"Do you think that's on the level?" Aunt Louise said, pointing to the letter.

"Probably. Anyway it won't be hard to find out. I'll have Mrs. Fraser get the number for me tomorrow morning and I'll put in a call as soon as classes begin. Once we know for sure, we'll arrange a visit."

He kicked off his boots and took a seat at the table. Grace poured her uncle a cup of tea and they talked about making the trip to upstate New York during the upcoming spring break.

Staring into the bottom of her empty cup, she said. "What if my father's in the sanatorium because he's really sick? What if he's — "

"He is sick, Grace, and has been for a long while. His only hope was to find his way into a place where he could dry out and begin his recovery. However he ended up there, it's the best thing that could have happened."

"Does this mean he'll get better Uncle Arthur?"

Her uncle shrugged. "That will depend on him."

Grace lay awake a long while that night. Over the many months her father had been gone, she'd wished for news of him, had pictured him returning to her chastened and sober. What she hadn't imagined was how confused and resentful she'd feel at the thought of seeing him again. How could she face him after what he'd done? How could she forgive him for deserting her, leaving her behind with the rest of his cast-off belongings?

Rolling over on her side, she drew her cold feet under her long nightgown and squeezed her eyes shut. Mr. Ramsey'd said her father was lost way before he'd gone missing and it was true. The father she'd known as a child had been gone a long time, almost as long as Mama.

At lunchtime the next day, Grace headed to her uncle's office where Mrs. Fraser was at her post near the door. Grace thought of the secretary as the Dragon at the Gate and always approached her warily. With exaggerated courtesy, she asked to see the Headmaster.

"He's busy right now, Miss Montel. I suggest you come back later."

Grace smiled and said Mr. Eastman had asked her to come by at the end of morning classes and he was expecting her.

Mrs. Fraser sniffed. "Well, he didn't say anything to me about it." She waved Grace through to the inner office. "Go ahead in."

Uncle Arthur told Grace he'd confirmed that her father was a patient at the sanatorium, and had arranged for the family to visit the facility during the week of their school break.

Walking her to the door, he said, "If all goes well, you'll be reunited with your father before the month is out."

Grace nodded and forced a smile. She wasn't sure that was possible.

End-of-term exams, reports, and projects kept Grace busy for the next two weeks. She welcomed the distraction. Plowing through pages of text, reviewing for tests, finishing reports, left her less time to think about seeing her father after their long separation.

Now, when she climbed the steps to the library at the end of the school day, every chair was occupied. Books and papers littered the table tops, and the tension in the room crackled like summer lightening. Then it was exam week and a hush descended on the college. Proctors paced the aisles between widely spaced desks, while she and the other students filled blue test booklets to the nerve-wracking ticking of the big wall clock.

On the last day of term, Grace jostled with the crowd gathered in front of the hall bulletin board, anxiously scanning the lists for her grades and test scores, checking off her classes one by one. Moving to the back of the crush, she took a deep breath. She'd studied hard to prepare for her exams and had achieved a successful third term.

But Grace had no idea how to prepare for her next challenge: facing her father at Hycliffe Manor.

26

HYCLIFFE MANOR

Grace, along with her aunt and uncle, left for western New York by train the following day. The weather was mild for March, the air moist and filled with the promise of running sap and melting snow. The train took them around the Northern end of Lake Champlain and then across untold miles of desolate landscape. As the hours ticked by, they passed shabby Indian villages, lonely farms, towns that were no more than a few houses clustered around a general store, all backed by an unbroken grey-green blur of forested hills and mountains. Compared to the craggy majesty of the White Mountains or the pastoral beauty of Vermont, northern New York looked forlorn, like a poor relation down on its luck.

After a grueling overnight ride, they arrived in Rochester mid-morning, tired and gritty. Uncle Arthur bundled them into a cab and gave the driver the name of the guest house, saying it was adjacent to Hycliffe Manor. Grace sat in the back seat with Aunt Louise and stared out the window at the unfamiliar town. They drove along the main thoroughfare past the shops and office buildings of the business district. Down the side streets,

Grace caught glimpses of the busy harbor and dingy warehouses along the waterfront. They passed through neighborhoods of attached brick buildings and along streets of spacious houses set on generous lawns, finally stopping in front of a faded three-story Victorian home surrounded by a wrought iron fence.

"This here's Sully's and down there," the cabbie said, pointing, "is the Manor. See those brick gateposts? You'll just pass through there and up the drive."

After they were settled in their rooms and had a chance to freshen up, Grace and her aunt and uncle went downstairs to the dining room. The landlady, Miss Sullivan, served them tea and pastries and told them about opening the guest house after inheriting the place from her parents. She said most of the residents of the Manor were there for respiratory ailments. Then she dropped her voice to a whisper to add that others came to be cured of their dipsomania.

Across the table, Aunt Louise raised her brows over the rim of her cup, threatening Grace's fragile composure. She sipped her tea, but her roiling stomach made eating impossible. Finally, her uncle said it was time they got over to the Manor for their appointment with the Director.

All three were quiet as they made their way down the street, through the gateposts, and up the gravel drive to Hycliffe Manor. The March sun glinted through the bare trees and the wind tugged at their hats and coats. Grace shivered, as much from nerves as from the cold, and realized she'd been holding her breath. Even as they approached the large, brick building and stepped onto the columned portico, she found it impossible to believe that in a matter of minutes she'd see her father again.

They were greeted by a young woman in a striped uniform who led them down a carpeted hallway to the Director's office. Dr. Myers rose from his desk and shook Uncle Arthur's hand before inviting them to sit down. After a few pleasantries, Aunt Louise asked how her brother was doing and how long he'd been at the Manor.

Dr. Myers opened the folder placed squarely in the middle of a spotless green blotter. Flipping through the pages, he said Mr. Montel had been there about a month.

"Prior to his arrival here, he'd spent a fortnight in the hospital where he'd been treated for a variety of complaints resulting from prolonged and heavy drinking." He glanced at Grace, then back to her uncle before continuing. "Apparently, Mr. Montel had passed out and when he did not immediately come to, an ambulance was called. He's anemic which might account for the fainting and shortness of breath and his blood pressure is elevated."

The doctor straightened, folded his hands on his desk, and looked at Aunt Louise. "We're treating the high blood pressure with a low sodium diet and administering a sedative to manage the anxiety and agitation, symptoms brought on by the body's craving for alcohol."

"How is my brother doing overall? Is his health improving? Will he recover?"

The Director cleared his throat and shuffled through the folder again. "Well, his blood pressure is down somewhat, still high, but manageable. The anemia is proving to be more difficult to bring under control. Mr. Montel is still exhibiting symptoms of fatigue and lightheadedness."

Grace leaned forward in her chair. "Excuse me, Dr. Myers. Would you explain what you mean by the body's craving for alcohol?"

The Director picked up a fountain pen and ran his thumb and forefinger along its smooth shaft. He didn't look at Grace, glancing instead at Aunt Louise.

"Please, Doctor, answer my niece's question." She smiled at Grace. "She's witnessed the effects of my brother's drinking first hand and deserves to know as much as you can tell her."

The Director nodded and returned the fountain pen to its place near the ink well. "When a person has a prolonged history of alcohol consumption, changes take place in the body, that is, the body adjusts to the effects of the alcohol, comes to rely on it, so to speak. Once that person stops drinking, the body reacts by displaying certain symptoms."

"What kind of symptoms?" Grace said.

"It varies. Anything from nausea and headaches to seizures." He rested his forearms on the desk and leaned towards her. "Frankly, these symptoms are often severe, in some cases even fatal. Fortunately, your father found his way to us, and we've been able to see him safely through that stage of his recovery."

"What happens now?" Uncle Arthur asked.

"Abstinence is the only solution to your brother-in-law's problem, Mr. Eastman. While he's here, that is a given as is the on-going treatment of the high blood pressure and anemia. Once he's released ... " He shrugged. "We recommend a complete change of scene, new interests, new friends, to guard against resumption of old habits."

Grace listened, her eyes on the sprinkling of dark hair on the back of the Director's hands. Obviously, a change of scene wasn't the answer to her father's drinking problem. How long before he'd resume his old habits?

Lifting her gaze, she said, "How did my father find his way here? Do you know who called the ambulance that brought him to the hospital?"

The Director looked surprised. "Why, I suppose his wife did. She's the one I met with prior to your father's admittance."

Grace looked at Aunt Louise. "Are you familiar with my brother's wife, Dr. Myers?"

"Well, of course, we've consulted about her husband's treatment and I believe she visits most days. I'm sure Matron could tell you when she usually arrives."

Uncle Arthur stood up then, signaling an end to the interview. He glanced at Grace and her aunt. "I know my wife and niece are anxious to see Francis, so we won't take up anymore of your time. Thank you for meeting with us, Dr. Myers. You've been very helpful."

Grace, her aunt, and uncle made their way to the reception desk, where a nurse directed them down a series of corridors to the east wing of the Manor. Grace had the curious sensation of watching herself from above, as though all this were happening to some other Grace Montel. The hallways were silent except for the occasional cough or groan seeping from under the closed doors they passed. The gleaming linoleum reflected the overhead lights and the air smelled of floor wax and disinfectant.

There was something else in the air, too, not so much an aroma as a brownish undertone of melancholy and despair.

At the entrance to the ward, they were stopped by a brisk nurse who led them down the central aisle to the last bed in the row. Admonishing them to keep their visit short, she flicked the curtain closed and padded away on thick rubber soles. Grace's father blinked at them from his pillow and for a moment no one spoke.

"Daddy?" Grace said, the word catching in her throat. "Daddy, it's me."

Her father lifted his hand off the blanket and Grace took it, holding it in both of hers. His face was ashen except for the red capillaries over his nose and cheeks. Surrounded by dark, pouched flesh, his blue eyes were dull, with none of the spark and luster she remembered.

"Gracie, how did you ... what are you doing here?"

"I got a letter. It said you were here, so we came to find you."

Aunt Louise bent over the bed. "Hello, Francis. It's good to see you. How are you feeling?" She kissed his cheek.

"I've felt worse," he said, a tiny smile playing on his lips.

While Aunt Louise talked to him, Grace lowered herself into a chair by the bed and stared at her father. He looked awful. Sick and wasted and old, as though the past two years had been twenty. She should feel sorry for him, and she would have, if he'd had a real illness like Mama, but he'd brought this on himself. His drinking had ruined everything, and the hollowed-out place behind her chest was empty of sympathy.

As if reading her thoughts, her father turned to her. His searched her face as though seeking reassurance, some measure of forgiveness or understanding. Grace looked away, chilled by the depth of her bitterness. Even in the face of his suffering, she wanted to punish him, wanted to hurt him the way he'd hurt her.

He spoke then, his voice barely above a whisper. "You look more like your mother than ever, Grace." When she didn't answer, he cleared his throat. "Gracie, I'm sorry. I know I should have written, but — "

"You should have done a lot of things, Daddy," she said, her throat tight. "Instead, you ran away and left the rest of us to pick up the pieces. You deserted me and just about broke Grandma's heart."

She shot to her feet and stood looking down at him. "Do you know what the past two years have been like for us? Do you even care?"

"Gracie!" her aunt hissed. "Stop!"

Grace dropped into the chair and covered her face with her hands. Her father said, "Leave her alone, Louise. She's right. I should have gotten in touch, but I wasn't — "

The curtain was whisked aside before he could finish, and the nurse bustled in. She refilled the glass from a carafe on the bedside table and offered Grace's father a sip of water. He waved her away and held his hand out to Grace.

She approached the bed. He curled his fingers around hers and looked up at her. Resisting the urge to look away, Grace met his gaze and her eyes filled with tears. She bent and kissed his cheek.

Shortly after 2:00, Grace and her aunt and uncle returned to Hycliffe Manor. At the desk, the receptionist checked her notes and said Mr. Montel could not receive visitors that afternoon. He'd been agitated and short of breath during lunch, and the doctor had ordered an oxygen tent and prescribed a sedative to help him sleep.

As they were absorbing this news, a woman in her mid-thirties, slender and neatly dressed, approached the desk. Grace recognized her at once. The receptionist did too, and was obviously taken aback when Mrs. Montel appeared to ignore the three family members standing next to her. Instead, she asked the receptionist if she knew what had caused her husband's attack and when she might be able to see him.

"I'm afraid our unexpected visit was a bit too much for Francis," Aunt Louise said. "We just arrived this morning and apparently he didn't know we were coming." She held out her hand.

"I'm his sister, Louise, this is his daughter, Grace, and my husband, Arthur Eastman. Do you have a few minutes to fill us in on how Francis ended up here and how he's doing?"

The woman gave no hint of having met Grace before. Maybe she didn't recognize her or maybe she'd forgotten their meeting. Or maybe she was accustomed to lies and deception. Whatever it was, she received their introductions without any hint of embarrassment or confusion and suggested they sit in the solarium.

Grace and her uncle followed the two women along another corridor to a sunlit room filled with wicker furniture cushioned in bright yellows and greens. They settled under a bank of windows on the far side of the large room. Grace sat opposite the woman. Her aunt and uncle shared a settee in front of a low table. Smoothing her skirt across her lap, the woman took a deep breath.

"I suppose you're all wondering who I am and how I came to be here with Francis." Aunt Louise nodded and she continued. "My name is Kate. Francis and I met at the home of my former employer. I was the housekeeper and he visited there on several occasions."

"I had no idea my brother was married," Aunt Louise said. "None of us did, but then, we've had no word of him since his disappearance, so I suppose that's not too surprising. How long — "

"Actually, we're not married," Kate said, lowering her voice and looking around. "When Francis was hospitalized, I told the admissions nurse that I was his wife. It seemed the simplest explanation."

"Miss Armstrong," Grace interrupted, "I don't suppose you remember me, but we met several years ago at Riverview. You gave my grandmother and me a tour of Mr. Ramsey's art collection." Aunt Louise and Uncle Arthur looked surprised, but Kate Armstrong just nodded.

"I know you left Chester for Worcester the afternoon of my father's arrest."

"Francis and I had made arrangements to rendezvous in Worcester that evening. We planned to meet after he'd made his delivery."

"But weren't you the anonymous caller the police told us about, the one who set my father up to get caught? Why would you do that? Why would you put my father in danger, especially if you and he were ... ?" Grace lifted her hands in a helpless gesture and stared at Kate.

"I made the call because Ramsey said to. He told me exactly what to say and stood right by my side to make sure I did as he instructed."

"Why didn't you refuse?"

Kate shook her head. "You don't know Ramsey."

Uncle Arthur spoke for the first time. Leaning forward, he asked quietly, "Had Ramsey threatened you, Miss Armstrong?"

"In a way, yes, he threatened both of us." Kate dropped her gaze and absently fingered the pleats of her skirt. A long moment passed before she spoke again.

"Francis and I needed to get away from Ramsey. Because of what we knew, he had a kind of hold on us and could pretty much make us do whatever he wanted."

"What kinds of things?" Aunt Louise said.

"Whatever he wanted done. Whiskey deliveries, recruiting runners ... " She shrugged. "Anonymous calls."

Grace sat back in her chair, looked at her aunt and uncle, then back to Kate. It wasn't just what Kate and Daddy knew, it was what they'd done, too. Her father had delivered whiskey and gotten arrested. What had Kate done?

Aunt Louise's voice broke through Grace's thoughts. "How did you and my brother meet up that evening, Kate? Did you know he was in the hospital?"

Kate shook her head. "No, I didn't learn that until later, but I wasn't surprised when he didn't show up at our appointed meeting place. Ramsey had practically assured that with his tip off to the police."

"So, what happened?" Grace asked.

Kate shrugged. "I went on to the station and bought a ticket to Lake George on the overnight train. I was afraid for Francis, but we'd agreed that if something went wrong, I was to go on ahead. I waited in the station as long as I dared, waited until the last call for Lake George before I boarded the train. Soon after we were underway, Francis walked in from the dining car, arm in a sling and a big grin on his face."

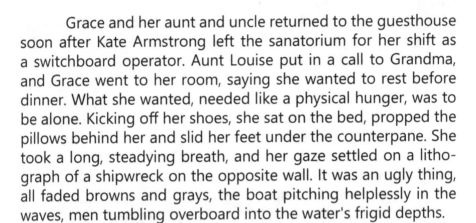

Grace and her aunt and uncle returned to the guesthouse soon after Kate Armstrong left the sanatorium for her shift as a switchboard operator. Aunt Louise put in a call to Grandma, and Grace went to her room, saying she wanted to rest before dinner. What she wanted, needed like a physical hunger, was to be alone. Kicking off her shoes, she sat on the bed, propped the pillows behind her and slid her feet under the counterpane. She took a long, steadying breath, and her gaze settled on a lithograph of a shipwreck on the opposite wall. It was an ugly thing, all faded browns and grays, the boat pitching helplessly in the waves, men tumbling overboard into the water's frigid depths.

Daddy's hold on life seemed almost as tenuous as that of those drowning men. He was sick and, though he'd made it through the worst stages of his recovery, was in danger of falling back into his old habits once he was discharged. If that happened, she'd never get her father back. For her own sake, she'd have to let him go.

The next morning, Grace walked alone through the brick gateposts and up the gravel drive to the Manor. Sullen grey clouds hung low and the air was heavy and damp. Grace's steps were heavy, too. She hadn't slept well, her mind roiling all night with snatches of conversation and visions of her father in that hospital bed. Hearing that he'd decided to run off with Kate and leave her behind, even before he'd been arrested, had cut her to the quick. It was one thing to think he was running away from the law and quite another to think he was running away from her. She felt as worthless and cast out as an old shoe.

In the brightly lit reception area, Grace asked after her father and was directed to the solarium. As she entered she saw him sitting by the fire slumped in a wheelchair, a plaid blanket draped across his lap. Several other men were in the room, too. At a table, one fellow played solitaire and another read the newspaper. The rest sat staring out the dripping windows.

Grace crossed the room and stood by her father's chair. He looked up at her and for a moment neither spoke. There were deep lines around his mouth and the hair at his temples had turned grey. His eyes were moist and Grace was afraid he might cry. She turned away, pulled up a chair, and sat down facing him.

"Hi Daddy. Are you feeling any better this morning?"

He nodded and reached his hand out. She held it and he said, "You took me by surprise yesterday, Gracie. I wasn't expecting ... They didn't tell me you were coming." He grinned. "The shock kind of set me back, I guess."

"I didn't mean to be so ... I'm sorry I got mad."

He shook his head. "Don't be. You have plenty of reason to be angry. I'd made your life pretty miserable even before I walked out on you. On you and everyone else." He shifted in his chair and gazed at the fire.

Grace, too, stared into the flames. "We talked to Kate yesterday," she said, her voice low. "She told us about your plans to meet in Worcester and run away together. All this time I thought you'd run off because you'd been arrested, but you were going to leave anyway."

She frowned. "I can't believe you'd do that ... walk out on your daughter, your parents, everything." She cleared her throat. "Of all the things you've done, that hurts the most."

Without taking his eyes off the fire, he said, "I was desperate, Grace. Kate and I wanted to make a life together, but we knew we had no future in Chester. Once Ramsey started building his resort and established himself as a mover and shaker in town, we were just a liability. Besides, I was sick to death of my life in Chester. Going to that infernal store every day, your grandfather criticizing my every move. And your grandmother, I've always been a disappointment to her."

"But what about me?"

He exhaled. "I needed to get away from you most of all."

Grace stared at him, dumbstruck. "What did I do?"

"You made me see what a heel I was." He ran a trembling hand through his hair. "I told myself you'd be better off without me, that Louise and Arthur could give you a proper home and, anyway, you cared more for them than you did for me."

Grace was about to speak, but he held up his hand to silence her. "Of course, that was just another lie I told myself, a way to justify deserting you and turning your life upside down. When you're deep in the drink, the lies come easy."

"When Mama died, I thought nothing else could ever be that awful, but then you left. We didn't know where you were, if you were dead or alive."

She looked at her fallible and broken father, and understood that whatever she'd wanted from him had been beyond his capacity to deliver.

"For a long time, I hoped you'd change, Daddy, that you'd give up drinking and be the father I wanted you to be. Now you've stopped, but it's too late. My home is with Auntie and Uncle Arthur and Pearl. And I guess yours will be with Kate."

Her father turned to face her. "I hope so. If I have any chance of pulling my life together once I get out of here, I'll need Kate's help. She's made it clear that if I go back to the drink, she'll write me off." He gave her a rueful grin. "Says she loves me enough to do that."

"Maybe that's just what you need, Daddy, someone strong who'll make you toe the line." Grace arched her brows. "According to Grandma, no one's been able to do that yet."

For the first time since she'd arrived, her father laughed.

27

THE END OF AMBIGUITY

Grace waved to her aunt and uncle standing in the solarium doorway and felt an upsurge of affection for them. Earlier, she'd told them she wanted some time alone with her father, and they'd agreed to linger for a while at the guesthouse before joining her at the Manor. It was the kind of thing she could count on them to understand.

Her aunt greeted Daddy with a kiss on the cheek and asked how he was feeling. Grace was surprised to see her father grasp Uncle Arthur's hand and shake it warmly. The three chatted for a few minutes, talking about the weather and the sanatorium food and the tyranny of the ward nurse. Then Grace's father asked her uncle to wheel him back to his room. He was tired and wanted to lie down. When they arrived at the ward, the nurse informed them that Mr. Montel could only have two visitors at a time, so one of their party would have to wait in the hallway or visitor's lounge.

As it turned out, Grace was the one chosen to sit out this visit; Daddy wanted to talk to her aunt and uncle. Once he was in bed, she kissed her father and set off for the visitor's lounge.

It was a small room at the end of the hall, a cozy space furnished with an uncomfortable-looking horsehair sofa and a couple of wing chairs. Near the window, an oval table held an urn of hot water, a box of tea bags, and a plate of cookies under a domed glass lid. Grace made a cup of tea and was thumbing through an issue of *Collier's Weekly* when Kate Armstrong came in. She helped herself to a cup of tea and settled into the chair across from Grace.

"I'm surprised to see you here at this hour," Grace said. "We were told you usually visit in the afternoon."

Kate nodded. "Yes, I usually drop by on my way to work." She sipped her tea and rested the saucer on the arm of the chair.

"I came by this morning hoping for the chance to talk to you, Grace. I think it's about time you knew what happened between your father and Rafe Ramsey. And what my part in the whole thing was."

Grace watched Kate fiddle with the handle of her cup. "I told you I didn't want to notify the authorities, and that's true, but what you probably don't know is just how deep our involvement with Ramsey was."

"My father had been acting strangely for quite a while, going out at night, spending weekends away, leaving the shop early or not going in at all," Grace said. "Then I saw him with Ramsey. The more I learned about him, the more I worried about my father."

Kate got up, set her cup on the oval table, and closed the lounge door. She sat down and leaned toward Grace. "As you know, Francis and I met when he visited Riverview. At first, we hardly spoke, but as his visits became more frequent, we got better acquainted." She smiled, remembering.

"He got so he'd come in the back way. I had a small office off the kitchen and we'd have coffee and talk for a while before he walked around to the front entrance and rang the bell. I looked forward to those visits. Ramsey doesn't mistreat his staff, but I was lonely and your father was, well, he made me feel special."

She went on to say that Ramsey liked Francis, too, and found him useful. He could mix with working men as well as with

Ramsey's wealthy customers, and he knew everyone in town. He introduced Ramsey to local businessmen and other professionals who provided him with financial and legal services for his enterprises. Through Francis's contacts, Ramsey procured the necessary permits for his resort from local officials, connected with builders and suppliers, and hired laborers to work on the project.

"Francis also helped Ramsey find runners, mostly young men from the mill, who'd make the runs over the border. That's where the real trouble between your father and Ramsey began." Kate sighed. "I'm sure you heard about Wesley Titus, the fellow who died in the crash trying to outrun the revenuers?"

Grace nodded. She remembered that day like it was yesterday. Her father absorbed in the newspaper, his abrupt departure, and the shape he was in when he finally got home. He'd been morose for days after, cranky and withdrawn, and drinking even more than usual.

Kate cleared her throat. "Your father arrived at Riverview the afternoon he saw the article in the paper. He was a mess and much the worse for drink. He stormed into Ramsey's study, saying he was through. Done. He wouldn't recruit another runner, wouldn't make another delivery. He was going to the police, going to tell them everything."

She shook her head. "Ramsey just laughed. Said he had half the state judiciary on his payroll, and enough on Francis to put him away for a long time. Then he told him to get out or he'd be the one to call the police."

"How do you know all this, Kate?"

"I let your father in. He pushed past me before I could stop him. From where I stood in the foyer, I could hear every word. I knew Francis was no match for Ramsey, and I was afraid for him." She shook her head. "We were both taken in by the man. He's all polish and good-humor, generous even, as long as you don't cross him." She frowned. "I knew it was just a matter of time before Ramsey found a way to retaliate."

The word echoed in Grace's mind. All her life, she'd felt the lash of her father's drunken tirades, made excuses for his mistakes, been buffeted by his erratic behavior. The whole family had, but Mr. Ramsey gave no quarter. Daddy had stepped out of line and gotten his comeuppance.

"But Titus died months before my father's arrest," Grace said. "Wasn't he working for Ramsey during that time?"

"Yes, he made deliveries to some of Ramsey's best customers in and around Boston. That's probably where your father was on those weekends he was away from home." Kate's smile was ironic. "Ramsey was biding his time, letting your father think all was forgiven. He gave Francis the best runs and found someone else to recruit runners. Then Ramsey discovered your father was skimming off his deliveries. Keeping some of the whiskey for himself. That's when he decided Francis had to go."

Grace rubbed a tender spot above her left brow. Did Daddy really think he could steal from Ramsey and get away with it, or was he just too addled by drink to think at all? And what about Kate? Neatly dressed, attractive, and obviously well-bred, she'd taken up with a man she knew to be a problem drinker. People did the most unaccountable things.

"So, what will happen next, Kate? For you and my father, I mean."

"For the time being we'll stay here," Kate said. "My job pays the bills and I'll need to hang onto it until Francis is back on his feet. After that, I'm not sure what we'll do."

She was interrupted by a knock on the lounge door and Aunt Louise poked her head in.

"Ah, there you are, Gracie. Hello, Kate, I didn't know you were here. Francis is ready to rest, but he's asked to see Grace first. I'm sure it'd be all right if you wanted to go in, too."

Kate declined, saying she'd stop by on her way to work. Grace made arrangements to meet her aunt and uncle back at the guesthouse, then set off to see her father. She was met by the ward nurse, her winged cap stiff with authority, who admonished her to limit her visit to ten minutes and no longer. She reminded Grace of Mrs. Fraser, the Dragon at Uncle Arthur's gate. She smiled, wondering how the two women would get along should they ever meet.

Her father, propped against pillows, was clean shaven and there was color in his smooth cheeks. She kissed him and he smiled and took her hand. He looked better today; spending time with Aunt Louise must have done him good.

"I'm sorry you had to wait out there, Gracie." He grinned. "Nurse Battleaxe follows doctor's orders to a T."

Grace smiled. "It's all right. Kate came by and we had a chance to talk."

"I wondered why my ears were burning." He winked at her. "But I'm glad you two had some time to get acquainted. Kate's, well ... Kate saved my life. If she hadn't called the ambulance, I might never have come to. I was pretty far gone."

He sat up straighter. "I know I don't look like much, but I'm feeling better than I have in a long time."

"Kate told me all about what happened with you and Mr. Ramsey. How you threatened him and how, eventually, he found a way to get rid of you." Grace studied his face. "What made you do it, Daddy? What made you take up with a man like Ramsey and risk everything you had?"

Her father exhaled. "I did it for the money, Grace. The shop renovations had set me back and I was having trouble keeping up with the loan payments. The new inventory wasn't selling fast enough to keep the creditors off my back and I was damned if I was going to give your grandfather the satisfaction of saying I told you so. So when a fellow approached me about working for Ramsey ... " He shrugged.

"The money was good, better than I'd expected and it wasn't just the money." His voice took on a tone of urgency. "It was a chance at a different kind of life, Gracie. Ramsey lived well. He had connections, people who'd been places, seen things. I wanted to be part of that."

Grace knew her father had always chafed at his responsibilities at the shop, always wanted more than his small-town life. Now it struck her that she'd never really understood his restlessness, the sense that what he had was never enough. Instead, she'd tried to temper his restive dissatisfaction, as if she could make the leopard change his spots.

"Kate said you were stealing from Ramsey. Skimming, she called it. Why do that? You must have known Ramsey'd find out."

He sighed. "By that time, I just wanted out. Once that boy died I soured on the whole business. I couldn't just walk away, I was in too deep for that, but I knew it wouldn't be long before Ramsey found a way to get rid of me." He shrugged. "I figured I'd hurry the thing along and maybe turn a little profit, too."

Grace stared at her father. Even with a powerful and possibly dangerous man like Ramsey, he couldn't resist putting something over on the man in charge.

He sat up taller against the pillows and gave her a crooked smile. "'Course, I hadn't planned to get shot, but when I finally got on the train that night and found Kate in the passenger car, I felt freer than I'd felt in a long time."

He looked at Grace and his smile faded. "Couldn't get free of the drink, though. Not sure I'll ever be able to do that."

Aunt Louise and Uncle Arthur were in the parlor when Grace returned to the guesthouse. They were seated by the hearth where a small fire did little to warm the large, high-ceilinged room. She could hear the window panes rattle in their casements and sidled up to the fire to warm her hands. She was cold, as though what she'd learned from Kate and her father had chilled her very bones.

Grace told her aunt and uncle about her father visiting Kate's office off the kitchen at Riverview and described the scene there the day after Wesley Titus's death. Aunt Louise and Uncle Arthur were stunned to learn that Grace's father had recruited Titus for that fateful run. Of all the things they'd heard, this upset Aunt Louise the most. It wasn't until Miss Sullivan called them to the dining room for lunch that she was able to pull herself together.

By the time they finished eating, sun was shining through the lace curtains and the sky had turned from grey to a bright china blue. Uncle Arthur suggested they take a walk before their final visit with Francis at the Manor. Miss Sullivan told them about the Cliff Walk that led to Hycliffe along a circuitous route overlooking the lake. It was a favorite walking path for local residents, she said, and frequented by tourists in the summer season, too.

It would be windy, she warned, but the views were well worth bundling up for.

Armed with a hand-drawn map, Grace and her aunt and uncle headed out the back door of the guesthouse and followed a footpath across a wide expanse of open land. The path forked as it reached the high cliffs for which the Manor was named, one fork leading to a shale beach and the water, the other climbing steeply along the cliffs to the grounds of the sanatorium.

They walked single-file up the narrow path. The wind snatched their words away as quickly as they uttered them, so they walked in silence, concentrating on their footing, and blinking at the sun glinting off the wind-tossed waves. As they progressed up the sharp incline, warmth spread through Grace's limbs and the clamor of her mind cooled. At a widening in the trail, they stopped to scan the lake, restless and blue under a cloudless sky. The rocks on the shore below were surrounded by pools of melting ice. They watched as a crow landed on a driftwood log. No sooner had it settled it ruffled feathers than it sprang from its roost with a peevish croak and rose into the air.

Arriving at the sanatorium, Grace and her aunt and uncle checked in with the receptionist then made their way to the ward. At the entrance, they were stopped by the nurse.

"Mr. Montel has a visitor, so only one of you can go in right now." She held her hands clasped at her waist and her shoulders squared with military precision. Grace was tempted to salute.

"You go on in, Gracie," her aunt said. "Your uncle and I want to meet with the Director anyway. We'll visit Francis when we're finished."

Grace was not surprised to see Kate sitting close to her father's bedside, her hand resting protectively on his shoulder. They seemed comfortable with each other, happy to be together in spite of Daddy's poor health and fugitive status. She wondered at their optimism.

The three exchanged greeting and Grace said, "You're looking better, Daddy. How are you feeling?"

"Can't complain, given the company. You've got some color, Grace. Did you walk over?"

"We did. There's a lovely path accessible from the inn that runs right along the cliffs overlooking the lake. The water was beautiful, all frothy from the wind."

Her father told her about the commercial traffic on the lake and how he and Kate often walked along the harbor in mild weather. Grace wanted to know where they were living. Kate said they'd rented a small house on a quiet street.

"Its sparsely furnished, but we've replaced the wallpaper in the living room and painted the kitchen. I've even put in a few perennials along the front porch."

Grace turned to her father. "How'd you end up at the Manor, Daddy? It seems like a pretty fancy place."

"The doctors at the hospital arranged for your father to come here," Kate said. "It's one of the few rehabilitation centers in the area that handle ... that offer the kind of treatment Francis needs." Kate's face clouded. "Of course, they don't keep people indefinitely. We expect your father will be discharged in the next couple of weeks."

"Can't say as I'll miss the place," her father said, "but I'm kind of worried about what happens once I leave."

"You're going to be all right, Francis," Kate said, stroking his cheek with the back of her hand. "You're stronger than you think you are, and I'll be right by your side."

Grace's father took Kate's slim fingers in his, and brushing them lightly with his lips, smiled into her face. Witnessing this tender interchange, Grace thought of Jerome. She remembered the way his eyes warmed when he looked at her, the touch of his lips on hers. Overwhelmed by the force of her longing, she struggled to compose herself.

As if he'd read her mind, her father said, "What about Jerome? Are the two of you still friends?"

Grace shook her head. "It's been a while since we've been in touch. We had a falling out."

"That's too bad, sweetie," her father said. "I hope you two can make it up. Jerome's a good fellow." He frowned. "I know I gave you a hard time about him. I guess I was a little jealous, and you were growing up so fast."

Grace interrupted. "That's in the past, Daddy. Whatever's wrong between Jerome and me is my doing, not yours." She managed a half smile.

"You made a lot of messes, but this one's mine."

Kate rose to leave, saying it was time she went to work. Grace said she'd head out, too, and let Aunt Louise and Uncle Arthur come in before the sergeant-at-arms sent everyone home. She made her father promise to keep in touch and let her know how he was doing. Kate smiled and said she'd see that he kept that promise. Grace kissed her father good-bye and he squeezed her hand. They studied each other for a long moment, before she turned away.

Back in the visitors lounge, Grace made a cup of tea and pulled one of the winged chairs closer to the window. Beyond the wide brown lawn, a row of evergreens marked the eastern edge of the property. Yesterday the view had been dolorous under the grey sky, but today the winter-burned grass and dark conifers shimmered in the sun.

Sipping her tea, Grace considered the revelations of the past few days. Finding out that her father had planned to run away with Kate was something Grace hadn't yet come to terms with. On the other hand, she was grateful to Kate for standing by her father. She had literally saved Daddy's life, and not just because she'd called the ambulance in time.

Setting her cup on the table, Grace shook her head. She'd spent her childhood waiting for her father to be the reliable, sober person she wanted him to be. And, if she were honest, blaming herself for not being able to curb his restlessness and dissatisfaction. But, Daddy was more than his drinking problem and restless nature, he was kind and funny and he loved her. She knew that as surely as she knew that she loved him.

Grace stood up and walked to the window. The wind had died and the sun sat low on the horizon. She thought of her father in that hospital bed, how he'd looked when they'd first arrived, like a man near death. Today, though, with Kate and his daughter by his side, he seemed glad to be alive.

28

$\diamond$

Out of the Shadows

Grace was relieved to board the train early the following morning. The long ride back to Concord would give her a chance to make sense of all that had happened in the past two days. For the first hour or so, she and her aunt and uncle talked generally about her father: how he looked, his surprising connection to Kate Armstrong, what might happen once he was discharged from the sanatorium. It was ground they'd gone over before leaving Rochester, but they covered it all again. Maybe they were just trying to convince themselves they'd really seen Daddy after the long months of his absence. It was like passing through one of those long tunnels blasted through the mountains; it seemed like the dark would never end, and then you were almost blinded by the light.

After lunch in the dining car, Uncle Arthur opened his briefcase, spread his papers on the folding table, and went to work. Aunt Louise pulled a magazine out of her bag and Grace took up the novel she'd started on the way over. She wasn't sure what she thought of *Mrs. Dalloway* or Virginia Wolfe, for that

matter, but reading was a welcome escape from the all the hub-
bub of the past few days.

They had tea in the late afternoon and that's when Aunt
Louise told her about their meeting with the Director on the last
day of their visit.

"When I talked to your grandmother after our first visit
with Francis, she asked me how he was paying for his rehabilitation. I told her I didn't know, I just assumed he and Kate had the
money for it." Aunt Louise raised her brows. "But you know your
grandmother. She said she very much doubted it and made me
promise to find out."

"I hope she's not planning to foot the bill," Grace said,
frowning. "It's Daddy's responsibility to take care of that. After
all, he's already forfeited the bail money Grandma and Grandpa
put up — "

Her aunt raised a hand to quiet her and Grace sat back in
her chair. "Sorry, Auntie. I guess I'm still not over being mad at
Daddy."

"Anyway," Aunt Louise said impatiently, "we did as your
grandmother asked, and talked to Dr. Myers about it."

"Actually, he didn't really know," her uncle said. "He had
to have his secretary check with the bookkeeper."

Her aunt and uncle looked at each other, the way they did
when they were sharing a joke. Or a secret.

"Well?" Grace said.

"Well, according to the good doctor, Kate's made weekly
payments, not in full, but enough to demonstrate good faith,"
her uncle said.

Aunt Louise leaned forward, her eyes bright. "But here's
the really interesting thing, Gracie. Last week the bookkeeper received a telephone call directing all outstanding and subsequent
expenses be billed to a post office box in Boston."

"George Blake?" Grace asked, wide-eyed.

"None other," her uncle said.

"Why didn't you tell me all this before? Why'd you keep it
a secret until now?"

Her uncle laughed. "Louise's been bursting to tell you for
24 hours, but I wanted to wait. I thought you'd need some time

to mull over the events of the visit. I sensed you were already overwhelmed. Seeing your father, meeting Kate, it's a lot to take in." He grinned like a naughty schoolboy. "Besides, it's a long ride. This way I knew we wouldn't want for conversation."

And he was right. All through dinner and into the evening, they talked of nothing else. Ramsey'd been so cold and unrelenting during Grace's short visit with him back in November. And now he'd not only located her father, but was paying his expenses at the Manor. She and her aunt and uncle came up with theories for Ramsey's change of heart: remorse, manipulation, control, religious conversion? All possible, but Grace had her own theory, one she kept to herself. Not so much a theory, as a feeling about the photograph in Mr. Ramsey's office of the young woman in a white gown and elbow-length gloves.

Later, Grace climbed into the narrow berth, pulled the covers up to her chin, and closed her eyes. She hoped the sway of the car and the sound of the wheels would lull her to sleep, but it was no good. Her mind chugged and clattered, busy as the train's locomotive, her head filled with snatches of conversation, images of starched caps and gleaming linoleum, the sound of her father's voice. And of all the things he'd said, one of the most surprising was when he'd asked about Jerome.

She'd told Daddy they'd had a falling out. She didn't tell him how filled with remorse she was for the way she'd treated Jerome, didn't tell him she hadn't seen or heard from him since Thanksgiving. Grace had written Jerome that same evening to apologize. The following morning, she'd left her grandparents' house before anyone else was up. No one was awake at the Davisons' either, when she pushed the note through the letter slot and hurried away.

While they were eating breakfast that morning, all during her packing and the loading of the car for the return trip to Concord, Grace had waited for Jerome to come. For surely he would come and when he did, she would tell him she was through holding back; she was ready to return his affection, ready to meet him halfway. But Jerome had not come and Grace had climbed into the back seat of the Hudson with a broken heart.

As the holidays approached, she was sure she'd hear from Jerome. But the only word from any of the Davisons had been a card from his mother. Grace knew Jerome was punishing her and she knew she deserved it. What she didn't know was what had made her so hateful to him. What had prevented her from understanding his point of view or sympathizing with his feelings? What had made her accuse him of transgressions she didn't even believe he'd committed? Why had she distanced herself from the person she most wanted to be close to?

Shifting onto her back, Grace stared at the ceiling of the train just above her head. She thought of Kate, casting her lot with a man like Daddy, a man she knew to be in trouble with the authorities and whose drinking could lead them both to ruin. Yet she had rejected Jerome whose only sin had been to travel in a different social circle from hers and be the kind of fellow other girls admired. Jerome had always been patient with her moods and jealousies, her social discomfort, her reticence, but he'd finally had enough. He'd walked away and hadn't looked back.

Uncle Arthur left for Mansfield College the morning after their return to Concord. The remainder of the week he'd spend in meetings: planning for next term, finalizing the budget, making arrangements for graduation. Grace and her aunt unpacked, ran piles of laundry through the ringer washer, and put away the heaviest of their winter clothes.

Of course, there was Lily Pearl to see to as well. They'd all remarked on how much she'd changed in just the few days they'd been gone. She'd grown and she was talking more, too. Pearl had become a little parrot, repeating every word or phrase she could get her tongue around. At the babysitter's she'd added bad dog, radio, and Sally, the name of the family cat, to her growing vocabulary.

After supper on that first evening home, Aunt Louise telephoned Grace's grandparents. Grandpa answered and wanted to know all about this Armstrong woman who was living with Francis without benefit of marriage. Aunt Louise held the receiver away from her ear and rolled her eyes as she and Grace listened to him carry on.

"That's just like Francis," he sputtered."Getting mixed up with someone who worked for a big-time bootlegger. He's already in Dutch with the law, and then he takes up with someone who's likely some kind of criminal herself."

Grandpa could never give Daddy the benefit of the doubt. Grace knew he loved his son, but wondered how many of Daddy's problems stemmed from her grandfather's constant criticism of him. If she'd been subjected to that kind of censure, would she have become as reckless, as rebellious as her father? Daddy and Grandpa were both kind, affectionate men and both were guilty of hiding their better natures; her grandfather with testiness and bluster, her father with drink.

Then Grandma got on the line. After a brief conversation, Aunt Louise handed the telephone to Grace. "Your grandmother wants to talk to you. I'm going up to check on Pearl."

"Hello, Grandma. How are you?"

"I'm fine, dear. I wanted to let you know, I'm going to meet with our lawyer next week to talk to him about how best to proceed now that we know your father's whereabouts. I'm also thinking about asking Mr. Sprague to delve a little further into Miss Armstrong's past. If she's to be a member of our family, I think we have a right to know what, if any, skeletons are lurking in her closet. What do you think?"

"I'm not sure, Grandma. I mean, Daddy's not fully recovered yet. He told me himself, he doesn't know how he'll manage once he's out of the sanatorium. I'd hate to do anything to upset him at this stage. I agree we need to hear what the lawyer thinks we should do, but as far as Kate is concerned, I think we should leave that alone. She loves Daddy, Grandma, and I don't think he'll get better without her help."

For a moment the line was quiet, then Grandma said, "Perhaps you're right, dear. We need to do all we can to safeguard your father's recuperation, but I won't feel right until Francis is either cleared of the charges against him or makes amends for his wrongdoing." She sighed and when she spoke again she sounded weary and dispirited.

"I'd like to hold my head up again, Gracie. I'm tired of living under this cloud of suspicion and guilt."

Poor Grandma. Finding Daddy meant Grace could get on with her life, but her grandparents' ordeal wasn't over. There were legal issues, maybe fines or even a jail sentence, lawyer's fees ...

"I'm sorry, Grandma, I was so relieved to find Daddy, I hadn't thought much beyond that, but I see there are still a lot of things to work out. I don't know what I can do to help, but — "

"Oh, don't worry about us, Grace," Grandma said with her usual fortitude. "We'll get everything cleared up. Your father's going to have to pay for what he's done one way or another. I won't accept anything less from my son."

Grace thought he'd already paid dearly, but she didn't say so.

The final term at Mansfield College began on a sparkling March day. The morning was bright with frost as Grace and Uncle Arthur drove to the school, but by lunch time the temperature was well above freezing. Grace and Carrie ate their sandwiches in the basement lunchroom, then put on coats and boots and headed out to sit on the wide steps of the front entrance. The breeze was sharp, but in the lee of the building the sun was lovely and warm. Grace could almost hear the sap running in the trees.

All through the first week of the new term, Grace put off the promise she'd made to herself during the long sleepless night on the train. It was easier to concentrate on her new classes and her chores at home than it was to write to Jerome. Every day she told herself she'd sit down that evening and get a letter off to him, and every evening she found another excuse not to.

The only correspondence she'd received from Jerome since that disastrous walk by the river had been a card on her birthday. Her spirits had lifted when she'd seen the envelope addressed in his familiar hand; finally, he'd relented and forgiven her. But when she'd pulled out the card, there'd been no greeting, no best wishes, no words of reconciliation — just his signature scrawled at the bottom.

On Friday evening after Pearl had been put to bed, Aunt Louise and Uncle Arthur settled in the parlor to listen to the radio. Grace excused herself and went up to her room determined to compose a letter to Jerome if she had to stay up all night to do it. Sitting at her desk, she pulled several sheets of paper off a sketch pad. Grandma's dainty stationery wouldn't hold the story of her visit to Hycliffe Manor or the apologies and assurances of affection that filled her heart almost to bursting.

For a long while she sat, pen in hand, staring at the blank sheet, trying to bring her thoughts and feelings into some kind of order. Two failed attempts had found their way to the waste basket by the time Grace settled on an opening line.

Dear Jerome, I have begun this letter to you a hundred times in my head, but have never gotten further than saying how sorry I am for the way I've treated you.

She went on to describe the mysterious letter with the Boston return address and the Chester postmark that had led her and her aunt and uncle to Hycliffe Manor. She struggled to express how it felt to see her father again, the confusing mix of anger and relief, resentment and love. Above all, she said, she had realized it was time to step out of the shadow of her father's choices and make her own.

And one of those choices, Jerome, has been to contact you in the hope that we can salvage some part of the closeness and under-standing we once shared. It's difficult to describe how castoff, how rejected I felt after my father left. Whatever belief I had in my own worth was stripped from me. I felt cheapened and unworthy of your regard. I know that's no excuse for treating you badly, but somehow I couldn't accept you didn't feel the same way about me.

Sitting back in her chair, she reread the last few lines. She sighed and, frowning, took up the pen again.

Over the years we've been friends, there have been other times when I've hurt and angered you, Jerome, and you've always set me straight. Each time, you've been able to help me see where I've gone wrong and we've put the problem behind us. Until now.

After receiving your birthday card in January, I wrote hoping to explain myself and repair the damage I'd done, but you did not respond. Now, I am writing again to ask you to give me, give us, one more chance.

I have not, for one moment, stopped caring for you, and no matter what the future holds for us, you will always have a place in my heart.

Grace read through the letter, cringing at its tone. It sounded so pathetic, but if she had to grovel to get Jerome's attention, that's what she'd do. She stuffed the pages into an envelope, addressed, sealed, and stamped it before she could change her mind. The letter was not perfect, but it was written. She'd send it out like Noah's dove and hope for a sign.

———— ❖ ————

In the middle of April, Grace's father was discharged from the sanatorium. Kate wrote to say he was eating well and, at the recommendation of his doctor, they walked along the lake most afternoons before she left for work. He still had the tremor in his hands and his spirits weren't very good, but so far he'd avoided the speakeasies where he used to spend most of his evenings.

Grandma called one Sunday afternoon to report on her efforts to settle Daddy's case. Her father could avoid a jury trial if he pleaded guilty and agreed to the punishment negotiated between his defense attorney and the U.S. Attorney. Similar cases had resulted in a fine and a suspended sentence. The family's lawyer would travel to Rochester with the forms necessary to secure the guilty plea. The case against Daddy could be settled by summer.

"That's great news, Grandma. It's a relief to know Daddy won't have to go to court."

Or worse, to jail, she thought. And what about Grandma and Grandpa's thousand dollars? Neither one had ever talked to her about the money, and she'd never asked.

"Grandma, what about the thousand dollars ... and the house? I don't even know if the house still belongs to us."

"It does, Grace. Your mother's parents left her the house unencumbered. There was no mortgage, but your father had taken out a loan when he was renovating the shop and used the house as collateral. He'd paid some of it back, no doubt with some of his ill-gotten gains, but then he disappeared. The payments stopped and the bank has a lien on the house for the balance." She paused. Grace heard Grandpa's voice in the background, but she couldn't make out what he was saying.

"Your grandfather objects to this conversation, dear. He says I shouldn't burden you with money issues."

"But Grandma, I want to know. I'm ashamed it's taken me this long to even think to ask. Please, go on."

"Well, to make a long story short, your grandfather and I borrowed enough money to cover the balance of the loan and the bail. We've done business with Mr. Evans's bank for years, so he agreed to loan us the money using the house as collateral. It's all a bit irregular, because we don't own the house, you do, but your father as your legal guardian held the house in trust. Once he disappeared, we claimed guardianship and secured the loan."

"So, you and Grandpa have been paying off the balance of the shop loan and the bail money all this time?"

"Yes. By the time you reach your majority, the loan should be repaid and the house will be yours. We couldn't let our son rob his daughter of her inheritance. Your mother wanted you to have that house. We want you to have it, too. And you will."

"But Grandma, Daddy has to pay you back. Those are his debts, not yours. Or I could pay you back, we could sell the house and then — "

"No, Grace," Grandma broke in, her voice sharp. "If Francis is ever in a position to pay us back, we'll expect him to do so, but we wouldn't take a penny from the sale of your house. And I don't want to hear another word about it. Is that clear?"

Grace understood. Money was not a topic of polite conversation as far as her grandparents were concerned, even with other family members. Grandma had answered Grace's questions, but would not tolerate her interference.

"I'm sorry, Grandma, I didn't mean any disrespect. And thank you for taking care of everything the way you've done and for taking care of me. I don't know how I would have managed without your help."

"We did what we had to do, dear. Your father made an awful mess of things, but we probably didn't do enough to help him."

"There wasn't much any of us could do about his drinking, Grandma. And that was the very thing that kept him from being the person we all felt he could be. "

"Maybe so, but I still feel we failed him in some way." She cleared her throat. "Well, it's water under the bridge now, dear. All we can do is look ahead."

Grace said her good-byes and set the receiver in its cradle. She slumped into a nearby chair and crossed her arms over her chest. She'd told Grandma there was nothing anyone but Daddy could do about his drinking, but what made him start in the first place? Was there something in her father's upbringing that caused him to drink? What made some people slaves to alcohol and not others? She didn't know and probably never would.

In the kitchen Pearl was busy with the pots and pans, lining up the lids by size, talking to herself as she worked. Aunt Louise was standing at the counter cutting vegetables and keeping an eye on the ham bone simmering on the stove. Grace sat at the table, watching Pearl, but thinking about her conversation with Grandma.

"Auntie, did you know Grandma and Grandpa were paying off Daddy's bail and the rest of the loan he took out for the shop renovations?"

"Of course, I did. Someone had to take on those debts, and you know your grandmother." Still holding the peeler, she turned toward Grace, and leaning against the counter, looked at her fixedly.

"Grace," she said, sounding exasperated, "sometimes I wonder if you know how awful this whole thing with your father has been for your grandparents. Paying off loans is the least of it. Raising a son who runs afoul of the law and abandons his family has been a bitter disappointment to your grandmother and grandfather."

She glanced at Pearl. "It would be to any parent, but it's worse for them because they have some standing in Chester. Both their families go back generations. So, of course, they paid your father's debts. Can you imagine how mortified your grandmother would have been to see a foreclosure sign on the front lawn of your house?"

At the sound of her mother's sharp tone, Pearl's lower lip trembled and she said, "Mama?"

Aunt Louise picked her up and held her close, murmuring reassurances. She kissed the top of Pearl's head and looked at Grace. "I'm, sorry, Gracie. I guess seeing Francis has stirred up a lot of feelings I thought I'd come to terms with. I didn't mean to make it sound like you've done anything wrong."

"Don't be sorry, Auntie. I need to be reminded I'm not the only one he's hurt." She leaned an elbow on the table and rested her chin in her hand. "I don't know if I'll ever be able to forgive him for what he's done. Sometimes I hate him for all the trouble he's caused."

"If you hate him sometimes, imagine how he feels about himself."

Aunt Louise set Pearl back on the floor and joined Grace at the table. "Alcohol changes people, Grace. It takes away their reason, makes them behave in unaccountable ways. Your father didn't set out to hurt you or your grandparents or any of us. He's not a bad person. He's sick."

"I know that's what they say, but my mother was sick. She got sick and she died. It wasn't her fault, but wasn't Daddy's drinking his fault?' She shook her head. "He knew we all wanted him to stop, but he wouldn't."

"He couldn't, Grace. Remember what Dr. Myers said about the body's craving for alcohol? How the body becomes dependent on it? So even when Francis made up his mind to stop, his body wouldn't let him."

Aunt Louise went back to the stove to stir the soup, one eye on Pearl busy dropping building blocks into a large pot.

Grace remembered exactly what Dr. Myers had said, but a part of her didn't believe it. Didn't believe that her father couldn't have stopped drinking if he'd really wanted to. Maybe she was just too angry to muster any sympathy for him. Or maybe she wasn't any better at being a daughter than he was at being a father.

"But I didn't leave him, he left me," she said under her breath.

"What's that, Grace?" her aunt said, looking puzzled.

"Just thinking out loud, Auntie. Thinking about that time at Thanksgiving when you invited me to live with you and Uncle Arthur. I was tempted, but I couldn't bring myself to leave Daddy. Instead, he left me."

Grace leaned back in her chair. "How could he do that? I mean, I had plenty of reason to want to get away from Daddy. His tirades, worrying about where he was and what he was up to. But what reason did he have for wanting to get away from me? Didn't he care what happened to me?"

Her aunt turned from the stove and brushed a loose strand of hair off her forehead. "Of course, he cared. He wasn't throwing you out on the street, Grace. He knew the family would look after you. I'd already talked to him about it."

Grace looked at her aunt. "You had? When?"

"The day before I invited you to live with us. I went to the shop to see Francis, to tell him what your uncle and I were thinking and ask if it was all right to approach you about it."

Aunt Louise frowned. "I knew his drinking was getting the better of him. When you don't see a person often, you notice the changes that much more and he looked bad. I asked him if he thought he was doing right by you and he said no; he wasn't half the father you needed him to be. That's when I told him we'd be happy for you to come and live with us, finish school, and maybe go on to Mansfield College."

She smiled at Grace. "We'd both grown awfully fond of you after all those weeks at the lake. Anyway, he said you'd never leave. He said, go ahead and ask her, but she won't go."

"And I didn't," Grace said. The thought was oddly comforting.

29

SECOND CHANCES

While the April days lengthened and the snow melted in all but the deepest part of the woods, Grace waited for a letter from Jerome. Every day when she returned from school, she checked the hall table hoping to find her name written in his familiar hand. But, the days turned to weeks and still no letter came.

She'd been clear about her undiminished affection for Jerome, admitted her wrongdoing, begged his forgiveness. She'd opened her heart to him and he'd remained resolutely silent. Grace hadn't believed him capable of such out and out cruelty. She was stunned by it. When she'd first written to him, she'd been filled with anticipation, but as the days passed with no word from him, her spirits flagged.

One evening after putting Pearl to bed, Aunt Louise knocked on Grace's bedroom door. She'd been staring at the same page of her geography book for she didn't know how long, but couldn't have said what it was about to save her life. Her aunt came in, perched on the edge of the chaise lounge, and gazed at Grace for a long moment.

"I came to see what's wrong, Gracie." She raised a warning hand. "And don't tell me nothing's wrong. Something's been bothering you for a couple of weeks now and I want you to tell me about it."

Grace closed her book and took a deep breath. Auntie knew things hadn't been right with Jerome for a long time, but she didn't know about the argument at Thanksgiving or the long months without word from him. Nor did she know about Grace's decision to make amends or the letter she'd written seeking to repair the damage she'd done to their friendship. By the time she finished her story, Grace was teary and feeling enormously sorry for herself.

Aunt Louise sat up straight and fixed Grace with a look that reminded her very much of Grandma. "Well, Grace, you've written the letter and you've waited for an answer. Obviously, you're going to have to try something else. That is, if you're serious about getting Jerome back."

Grace sat with bowed head, studying her clasped hands. "I'm not sure what you mean, Auntie. Of course I want Jerome back. That's why I wrote the letter. That's why I've been so miserable these past weeks." She looked to her aunt for sympathy, but Louise's expression remained severe.

"Well then, maybe it's time to stop waiting and do something."

Grace felt her face flush. "What do you suggest?"

Her aunt leaned forward. "Stop feeling unworthy of his affections, and start believing you're the very best girl for him. My hunch is, deep down, that's what Jerome believes, and he's waiting for you to declare that you know it, too." She stood and placed her hands on Grace's shoulders. "If you know, without reservation, that your feelings for Jerome are real and true, and if you're willing to stand by those feelings, well then, he'd be a fool not to take you back." Stroking Grace's cheek, she arched her brows and smiled.

"And we both know Jerome's no fool."

For a long while after Auntie left the room, Grace huddled on the chaise lounge, replaying their conversation. She'd written letters and waited in vain for them to be answered. She'd spent countless hours imagining scenes of their reconciliation: Jerome appearing at the door in Concord or showing up at Mansfield all tousled hair and brilliant smile, Grace falling into his arms. Aunt Louise was right. It would take more than letters and daydreams to win Jerome back. She knew what she had to do. Now all she needed was a plan.

Grace woke early. Slipping on her dressing gown, she crossed to the window and drew back the curtains letting in the bare oyster light of the April morning. The house was quiet, no sing-song sounds from Pearl's room, no cooking noises from the kitchen, no gurgling pipes from the bathroom. She tiptoed down the stairs, rummaged in the drawer of the hall table, removed a dog-eared pamphlet, and returned to her room.

That afternoon at the end of her final class, Grace collected her books and said good-bye to her friends. Mid way down the long corridor, she stopped and peeked through the window of a closed classroom door. Squaring her shoulders, she knocked, tentatively at first, then harder. The teacher, working at his desk, looked up at the sound of the knock, and gestured for Grace to come in.

Setting her satchel just inside the door, she apologized for interrupting his work and asked if she could have a word with him. Mr. Richardson came from around his desk, grinning and rolling down the sleeves of his wrinkled white shirt. He pointed to one of the student desks in the front row. Grace sat down and he took the seat beside her.

"Well, Miss Montel," he said, the familiar half-smile lifting a corner of his mouth, "to what do I owe this honor?"

Too nervous to muster the kind of cool remark she usually affected during their exchanges, Grace said, "I have a friend attending Dartmouth College and I'm planning to visit him. I hoped you might be able to tell me a few things about Hanover that would help me with my arrangements."

Mr. Richardson raised his eyebrows and asked what she wanted to know.

"Well, I'll need lodgings while I'm there. Somewhere suitable for a girl traveling alone and managing on a limited budget. Hopefully not too far from the station."

The history teacher folded his hands on the narrow desk-top and leaned forward. "As a matter of fact, I know of just the place. A guesthouse frequented by female visitors to the school. You know, mothers, sisters, the occasional sweetheart."

Grace felt the heat rise in her cheeks. Mr. Richardson shifted in his seat, resting one arm on the chair back.

"The guesthouse is a few blocks from the station, right in the center of town. It's run by a highly respectable middle-aged lady. I know she's respectable and middle-aged because she's my father's older sister, my Aunt Agatha. When I attended Dartmouth, my mother always stayed with Aunt Aggie during her solo visits to Hanover."

He pulled a small pad of paper out of his shirt pocket and took a pencil from behind his ear. He scrawled his aunt's name and the address of the guesthouse on one of the pages, added the telephone number, ripped off the sheet with a flourish, and held it out to Grace.

"Anything else, Miss Montel?"

For a moment, Grace stared at the history teacher. She'd made the question of lodgings such a monumental problem, to have it solved so quickly and easily left her breathless.

"Well, Mr. Richardson, it looks like I came to right place," she said, taking the proffered sheet. "I'm very grateful for your help. I'll get in touch with Miss Richardson right away and make arrangements." She paused. "May I say that you recommended I stay there?"

"Of course. And it's Miss Agatha, unless you want to start off on the wrong foot." He smiled. "Any other questions?"

Grace folded and tucked the small sheet in her pocket. Getting to her feet, she said, "There is one more thing. What is the protocol for visiting a student at his residence? I mean, shall I ... " Her cheeks flamed and she trailed off.

Mr. Richardson moved back to his desk and busied himself straightening a pile of papers. "Simply inquire at the reception desk and your friend will be summoned."

As he glanced at her from under his brows, Grace detected the hint of a smile. "I hope you have an enjoyable visit, Miss Montel."

Grace boarded the train for Hanover on a Saturday morning in early May. She carried a small case, a note from Miss Agatha directing her to the guesthouse, and what she hoped was the courage necessary to see her through whatever the weekend might hold.

She wasn't at all sure what kind of reception she'd get from Jerome. She could still picture him walking away from her that day by the river, head thrust forward, coat flapping in the wind. He'd been angry then and, if his silence was any indication, still was. That's why she hadn't told him she was coming. She was determined to see him and couldn't take the chance he'd deliberately avoid her. Of course, there was the very real possibility he'd left campus for the weekend, maybe even gone with his friend Myles to visit his family, including the dreaded Adelaide. She wouldn't think about that now. At the very least, he'd return to his residence to find that she'd paid a visit and left him a note.

The train steamed into the Hanover station shortly after noon. Several young men wearing dark green blazers milled about on the platform. Grace watched them through the dusty window of the car, calling greetings, jostling one another, making sport of some poor fellow's cap. Then two more young men emerged from the station deep in conversation. Both carried bags, but one was obviously reluctant to board the train. He shook his head and raised his hand as if to fend off his friend's appeal.

Grace watched Jerome come to an abrupt stop and begin to turn away from his companion. Myles, though, placed a restraining hand on his arm and continued his entreaties. Finally, Jerome nodded, Myles clapped him on the back, and they crossed the platform toward the train.

As Grace pressed close to the window to follow the boys' progress, the train lurched into motion, tossing her back in her seat. Her gut twisted in a rush of panic and for a frantic moment she eyed the emergency cord. As the train picked up speed, her heartbeat slowed and she was able to assess her situation. It wasn't so terrible, really. She'd simply get off at the next stop and take the train back to Hanover.

But no, Jerome was on this train. She just needed to find him and surely that wouldn't be difficult. He was in one of these cars and once she figured out which one, she'd ... She didn't know what she'd do, but she was about to find out.

Getting unsteadily to her feet, Grace brushed the loose wisps of hair off her forehead, straightened her back, and stepped into the aisle. As the train rattled and swayed, she moved through first one, then another of the cars. There were middle-aged couples, fellows traveling alone, and Dartmouth boys, but it wasn't until she peeked into the third car that she spotted Jerome.

In spite of her wrecked nerves, her heart leaped at the sight of him. He and Myles sat on opposite sides of a small table facing one another. The seat next to Jerome held the boys' satchels and cast-off jackets. The one next to Myles was empty. Grace pushed through the door.

Afterward, she wouldn't remember crossing the short distance to their table, but she'd never forget the look on Jerome's face when he saw her.

"Monty?" The incredulity in his voice was almost comical, the look on his face a mixture of wonder and disbelief. "What? I mean how ... "

Myles jumped to his feet. "Miss Montel, isn't it? Myles Caruthers," he said, extending his hand. "We met at the Academy. Please join us."

With a gentleman's aplomb, he gestured to the seat next to him and Grace, unable to speak, smiled dumbly and sat down. She met Jerome's eyes across the small table. He held her gaze and everything else fell away. Myles prattled on, something about his father's new Mercer Raceabout and a history test, while Grace's cheeks blazed under Jerome's fixed stare.

Rousing himself, Jerome reached into his pocket for his billfold and said shakily, "Myles, be a good fellow and find us something to drink."

His friend saluted and took himself off, assuring them he wouldn't hurry back. Grace slid her hands across the table and Jerome grasped them in his. At his touch, her eyes grew moist and she spoke for the first time.

"I took the train to Hanover, but I didn't get off, that is, I was so busy watching you and Myles ... and then the train started." She took a deep breath and tried again.

"I had to see you, Jerome. To see if there's any chance that you still ... There's so much I need to say, to explain." She shook her head. "I'm sorry. That's what I came to say. I'm sorry. Sorry that I was jealous of your friends, that I didn't trust your feelings for me. I thought if my own father could leave me, why wouldn't you? When you don't believe in yourself, it's hard to believe in anyone else." She frowned. "I'm not making sense. I thought I had this all figured out, but — "

Jerome lifted her hands and kissed first one, then the other. Looking at her from under his brows, his dark eyes shining, he said, "You're making perfect sense, Monty. There's a lot I want to say to you, too, but this isn't the place. We'll be hitting the next stop soon, so we should go and collect your bag. There'll be plenty of time to talk once we get off."

At the door, Jerome leaned close and whispered, "When you stepped into the car, I thought I was dreaming. I'm awfully glad I wasn't."

Just as they returned to their seats with Grace's belongings, Myles entered from the other end of the car toting three bottles of ginger beer. Jerome told him they were getting off at the next stop and to please let Mrs. Caruthers know something important had come up.

Myles smiled broadly. "Perfectly understandable under the circumstances, old man. It's not every day a fellow has a surprise visit from a special friend."

All during the wait for the northbound train and all through the return trip to Hanover, Jerome held Grace's hand and told her about courting Myles's sister, Adelaide. He described visiting her on Sunday afternoons at her boarding school and seeing her on weekends when he and Myles were at the Caruthers' home in Massachusetts.

"Almost from the first time I met Adelaide, I sensed she was interested in me. At first, she was just Myles's little sister, but we saw a lot of each other and ..."

"And she's awfully pretty," Grace teased.

"True, but more than that she was, well, let's say she made no bones about her interest in me and I just fell into it."

"You didn't fall into it, Jerome. I pushed you into your courtship with Adelaide. If I'd been reasonable that day by the river, if I'd listened and opened my heart to you, would you have taken up with her?"

Jerome held fast to her hand, but didn't look at her. "I asked myself that question almost every time Adelaide and I were together. I never really knew if I was with her because of her or because of you."

They were quiet for a moment, then he said, "When your letter came. The one you wrote after you'd seen your father, I didn't know what to do. I wanted to answer it, but first I had to sort out my feelings ... about you and about Adelaide."

Grace's stomach tightened. She forced herself to breathe, to listen and hear him out. She pressed her lips together and waited for what he'd say next.

In her letter she'd asked him to give her, give them, a second chance. Jerome told her he'd thought long and hard about what that might mean. Would he be giving her another chance to twist his words around and accuse him of things he hadn't done or blame him for things her father had done? Was Grace really ready to leave her shame behind and meet him on equal terms?

"I didn't know if I could risk giving us another chance, Monty. I mean, things haven't been easy between us for a long time." He'd been staring out the train window, but turned to look at her. Grace saw the hurt in his eyes and her heart contracted.

"Is that why you haven't written, because you haven't decided? Or is it because you've decided I'm not worth the risk?" She smiled weakly unable to keep the tremor from her voice.

Jerome looked out at the passing countryside. "I didn't write because I had to talk to Adelaide first. To explain myself and to break it off. It was hard. Myles is my best friend and the Caruthers have been good to me." He shrugged. "What else could I do? You've been part of my life for so long."

"But what about Adelaide?"

"I went to see her this past weekend. Did my best to explain myself. She was awfully upset; mostly I think her pride was hurt. But I'd never made her any promises. We enjoyed each other's company, but it didn't go much deeper than that."

Grace was quiet, thinking about the scene on the platform earlier. "Was Adelaide going to be at the Caruthers' this weekend, Jerome? Is that what you and Myles were talking about this morning before you got on the train?"

He nodded. "Just as we were leaving the station, he told me his mother had telephoned to say Adelaide would be there, too." He frowned. "I knew it wasn't a good idea to see her so soon after breaking it off with her."

"But you got on the train anyway?"

"I did. Myles convinced me. He said no matter what went on between his sister and me, it didn't change our friendship or what his parents thought about me. He said he knew his sister. She'd probably give me the cold shoulder, but she'd have a new beau before long." He smiled. "So I got on the train and, the next thing I knew, you appeared out of nowhere."

Arriving in Hanover, they went directly to the guesthouse. Miss Agatha told them her nephew, Andrew, had given Miss Montel a fine reference and asked his aunt to show her guest every consideration. To that end, Grace and Jerome were treated to tea and sandwiches coupled with tales of her nephew's academic triumphs at the college.

Later, Jerome took Grace to a small Italian restaurant up an alley off the shopping district. They talked about their classes and Jerome told her he was having second thoughts about majoring in accounting. He didn't mind his mathematics courses, but he couldn't see himself totting up numbers and keeping ledgers for the next thirty years.

"You can do whatever you set your mind to, Jerome, and you've got time to decide. You're only just finishing your first year." Grace studied his face in the candlelight, remembering the first time she'd seen him back in seventh grade. With his thick, curly hair and fine features, she'd thought him almost beautiful. She still did.

Grace boarded the train for Concord early Sunday afternoon. Settling into her seat, she could still feel the pressure of Jerome's lips on hers, and the shiver of joy as he'd pulled her close and kissed her in full view of everyone on the platform. She'd been right to come, right to believe in her feelings for Jerome and in his for her. She'd been right to stand up for her love.

Waking early on a June morning, Grace watched the summer sunlight play on the papered walls of Aunt Louise's childhood room on Pleasant Street. The room where Grace had spent those first weeks after Mama died, bereft and numb with grief. She'd huddled on the window seat gazing out at the dense foliage of the huge maple or buried in one of Auntie's books, weighed down by a crushing sadness. Since then, she'd woken in this room lots of times, but she'd never felt as buoyant and pleased to be here as she was today.

The month she'd spend with her grandparents stretched out before her: days helping Grandma in the garden and Grandpa at the shop, evenings with Jerome, and outings with her old school friends, Alma and Christine. She'd see Mary, too, even if it meant helping her look after her gaggle of younger siblings.

There were voices in the hallway and birdsong outside the window and the aroma of something lovely coming from the kitchen. Grace threw back the covers and swung out of bed. She had lots of plans for the coming weeks and one in particular she would execute this morning.

She dressed slowly, taking time with her hair and savoring the feel of the new summer frock Grandma had bought for her. It was linen, light and airy as a cloud, and just about the same color. Actually, it was blue, but so pale as to look almost white, with a row of embroidered flowers along the scoop neck. Standing at the mirror, Grace turned to admire the simple lines of the dress which, she admitted to herself, suited her perfectly.

Leaving the house shortly before ten, she arrived at the hotel just as the church clock struck the hour. In the lobby, she settled into an armchair and fixed her gaze on a closed door to the right of the reception desk. Soon the door opened and several men in suits emerged. Shaking hands and donning their hats, the Rotarians headed off to their offices and shops. At last, she saw Mr. Evans, the banker, come through the door followed by Mr. Ramsey.

As soon as Mr. Evans crossed the lobby to the exit, Grace stood, and walking quickly, stepped up to her quarry before he had a chance to escape.

"Hello, Mr. Ramsey," she said, offering her hand. "Grace Montel. We've met before."

"We have, indeed. What can I do for you this time, Miss Montel?"

"I hoped you'd take a few minutes to speak with me. I promise I won't keep you. It's just that I — "

Ramsey checked his watch. "I can give you five minutes, then I have to get back to my office."

She followed him into the meeting room. He closed the door and raised an eyebrow as her turned to face her.

"Well?"

"I came to thank you for finding my father, Mr. Ramsey and for helping to cover his expenses at the sanatorium."

Ramsey slipped his hands in his trouser pockets and frowned. "I've been accused of a lot of things in my time, but paying the bills of no-accounts like your father is not one of them."

Grace tipped her head and smiled. "Then maybe you should have done a better job of covering your tracks. That letter signed by your personal secretary was a dead give-away."

"All right, Miss Montel. You've found me out." Dropping his bantering tone, he said, "I know something about fathers who disappoint their daughters. I also know just how unforgiving those daughters can be."

Grace heard the regret in the big man's voice and thought of the girl in the photograph.

"But not all daughters, as it turns out," he continued. "Personally, I'd written Francis off as a lost cause, but when you showed up at my office I could see that you weren't ready to give up on him. Blake made a few inquiries and when I found out Francis was drying out at the sanatorium, I thought maybe it wasn't too late for the two of you to ... reconcile." His brow clouded and he looked away.

"That's why I came to thank you, Mr. Ramsey. You gave my father and me a second chance. Now it's up to us to see what we can do with it."

Her smile was rueful. "Life with my father has never been easy. I don't have to tell you how impulsive and head-strong and unreliable he can be." She shook her head. "But, he's still my father."

Ramsey looked at her then. She touched the sleeve of his jacket and his cool grey eyes warmed slightly.

"I hope you won't think me too forward Mr. Ramsey if I offer a bit of advice?"

"You? Forward, Miss Montel? How could I think that?" He raised an ironic brow, "Please, I await your counsel."

Grace drew a long breath. "If there's one thing I've learned in the last two years, it's that as difficult as life with my father was, life without him was worse. He's disappointed me more times than I can count, but nothing he's done has severed our essential connection. He's a part of me, just as your daughter is a part of you, a part we can't cast out or deny." Grace lifted her eyes to Ramsey, but his gaze was fixed on something only he could see.

"I'm not sure I have the wherewithal to win back my daughter's affections. At our last encounter she made it clear she wanted nothing to do with me. And she did so publicly. She walked away and left me standing there like a rejected suitor." He shook his head. "She never said a word, but her meaning was clear."

"I'm sorry, Mr. Ramsey," Grace said. "I know what it is to be rejected by someone you love. I'm trying to see beyond my hurt to what my father was going through, trying to understand why he did what he did."

"Oh, I know why my daughter turned her back on me. Let's just say, she didn't approve of my activities."

Grace nodded. "I can appreciate how she feels. I suffered a great deal of shame over my father's drinking and his arrest."

Ramsey leaned against the table and crossed his arms. "So you know what I'm up against."

"I do, but don't give up on your daughter. It's because she cares for you that your actions have the power to anger and disappoint her." Grace sighed. "Believe me, I know."

For a moment neither spoke. Then Ramsey said, "I believe you do, Miss Montel, and I'll consider your advice." He pulled himself upright and checked his watch again. "Now, it's time I got back to my office." Bowing slightly, he opened the door and gestured for Grace to precede him.

He followed her out onto the sidewalk and said good-bye. As she watched his retreating figure, a movement across the street caught her eye. Turning, she saw Jerome waving to her, his smile as bright as the June morning. Returning his greeting, Grace crossed the street to join him.

ACKNOWLEDGEMENTS

This book began with a writing prompt and grew organically over the course of several years. During that time, my Writers Group dutifully read every chapter of every draft. Through their thoughtful critiques, probing questions, and abiding faith in her, Grace became the person she was meant to be. I also thank the readers of the completed manuscript whose encouragement sustained me through the final revisions.

I am grateful for the many enjoyable hours spent at the Vermont Historical Society in the company of the men and women who recounted their adventures and misadventures during the turbulent years of Prohibition. Their stories of rum-running, high speed chases, and run-ins with revenuers inspired the characters and shaped the narrative of this novel.

Lastly, I thank the readers who embraced my first novel, *Scattered Pages*. Through the long years of writing *State of Grace*, they kept abreast of its progress and cheered me on to its completion. The waiting, dear readers, is over. Grace has finally arrived.

CPSIA information can be obtained
at www.ICGtesting.com
Printed in the USA
BVHW031302271020
591927BV00012B/58